L. Carswell

This is Not a Test

Liv Wigen Carswell

FriesenPress

Suite 300 - 990 Fort St
Victoria, BC, V8V 3K2
Canada

www.friesenpress.com

Copyright © 2016 by Liv Wigen Carswell
First Edition — 2016

All rights reserved.

No part of this publication may be reproduced in any form, or by any means, electronic or mechanical, including photocopying, recording, or any information browsing, storage, or retrieval system, without permission in writing from FriesenPress.

ISBN
978-1-4602-9008-8 (Hardcover)
978-1-4602-9009-5 (Paperback)
978-1-4602-9010-1 (eBook)

1. YOUNG ADULT FICTION

Distributed to the trade by The Ingram Book Company

This book is dedicated to:

My husband, Benjamin, who saved me.
My sister, Boo, who helped me.
And my son, Harry, who peed on me.

"Maybe there's something you're afraid to say, or someone you're afraid to love, or somewhere you're afraid to go. It's gonna hurt. It's gonna hurt because it matters."

— John Green & David Levithan, *Will Grayson, Will Grayson*

Author's note

Although this book was inspired by true events from my life, a majority of it is fictionalized—either to make the mistakes I made look better or make more sense, or just because I had the power to give this story the outcome I always wanted. Please remember that, if you are in a situation similar to the protagonist you are going to read about, *there are ways out!* There is no shame in asking for help.

Yours truly,
Liv Wigen Carswell

CHAPTER 1
SCHOOL'S OUT

In high school I wasn't popular. That's not to say that I was *un*popular, though. I had a small group of friends and a steady, albeit surprisingly out-of-his-league-but-I-could-not-see-it boyfriend. My nose was always in a book, even ones I had read plenty of times in the past. I did not really care, though. I was perfectly fine with blending into the olive-coloured walls of Vancouver Island's Fairview High School. I would have preferred being a wallflower to having either of the two nicknames I received in my four years of schooling there.

By tenth grade most people knew who I was, if not by name than by one of two titles:

1. Seizure-girl. (I was an epileptic—nothing to be ashamed about, I know, but still embarrassing.)

2. The-girl-who-got-caught-with-a-boy's-hand-up-her-shirt-in-the-make-out-closet. (I was not the only girl with this title. I was eventually narrowed down to 'the one with long hair'.)

(Unfortunately, just after spring break of grade eleven, I would get a new nickname that stuck until graduation: That-girl-whose-mom-offed-herself. Real nice.)

Andbutso, as my entire drama class waited for the last bell to ring to signal the start of a two-week freedom, I found myself being pulled into a conversation about my mom and stepdad's pending divorce.

"So, is the separation between your mom and dad final yet, Beth?" Candice asked, leaning toward me. I tore my stare away from the clock above our drama teacher's head and turned to face her. Spring break started in ten minutes.

"Will is *not* my dad. I live with my dad," I corrected her. "And yeah, it is. My mom just bought a new place up island, and Will lives down here now... with his girlfriend."

"Did she keep the cat and dog?" Candice asked.

I looked back up at the clock. It amazed me that *that* is what she was concerned about. Not the fact that my ex-stepdad was living with his new girlfriend so soon after the separation.

Fuzzy groaned behind us. "Candice, come *on*, have a little tact." Even as a teenage guy, he knew that this was not cool. Fuzzy and I had known each other since sixth grade, but had really gotten close in the ninth. Now, in grade eleven, we were best friends. He had been branded with the nickname 'Fuzzy' when he gave himself a poorly done buzz cut. The adjective had described his hair perfectly.

Candice and I turned to look at him. I gave him a thank-you smile and Candice scowled. She hated it when people spoke to her in any negative tone, no matter how much she deserved it.

"My mom gave the dog away, but thankfully she kept the cat," I said eventually, not looking at her.

"I really am sorry for all this crap." Fuzzy put his hand on my arm gently. I smiled grimly and patted his fingers.

I was about to thank him when the last bell of the term rang. Everyone in the class cheered and stood up. We gathered our things, ignoring Mr. Thomas' request that we head out the door in single file. Even a teacher the entire class respected and loved could not be paid attention to when there were two weeks of freedom at our fingertips.

When we got into the hallway, the three of us spotted my boyfriend, Connor, leaning on a wall down the next corridor. I headed in his direction, dodging a couple of over-excited students. I guess I was kind of the leader of our group. Wherever I headed, Fuzzy and Candice seemed to follow. That's actually how Candice and I became friends; she seemed to take to Fuzzy very quickly and wherever I went Fuzzy went. We were a package deal. It didn't surprise me that the two of them were right behind me when I reached Connor.

"Hey you," we said to each other, kissing quickly.

"Why do you always wear your hair in this stupid bun, Bethy?" Connor asked, reaching behind me and pulling out the elastic. "You look like a stressed-out librarian. A hot one, but still…"

"Really man?" I heard Fuzzy grunt behind me. I glanced over my shoulder at him and saw him scowling at Connor.

I ran my fingers through my long brown hair and messed it up a bit. "There. Better?" I flipped it over my shoulder. I felt the end of my hair brush along the waistline of my low-cut jeans.

"Totally." He reached into his pocket. "Besides, you won't want to look like a stressed-out librarian when you're on stage," he continued, as he pulled out a folded piece of paper from his jeans.

"What are you talking about?" Candice asked slowly, as I took the paper from Connor.

I opened it and gasped. It was the casting list for the school play, *RENT*, and I was one of the lead characters.

"Holy fuck!" I yelled. I threw my arms around Connor and kissed him. "I got in! I play Mimi!" I let go and turned to Candice and Fuzzy. Candice grabbed the paper and Fuzzy hugged me. "I got in! I got in!" I squealed, jumping up and down and clapping my hands.

"Well, was there a doubt in your mind?" Fuzzy laughed, holding my shoulders. "We helped you with that audition song for weeks."

"And of course she *would* get the part as the stripper," Candice added, giving her points on the bitchiness scale. "She'd make a great one." She gave me a hug and I stiffly wrapped my arms around her. I saw Fuzzy roll his eyes. She had a talent when it came to veiled insults.

When I pulled away, all smiles, Connor swooped in and kissed me. "Feel like celebrating?" He winked, putting his hand in my back pocket and pulling me closer to him. When we first started sleeping together, the year before, I had done the stupid thing of telling Candice. She had called me promiscuous and ranted about how she was disgusted that we had only been fifteen and were 'totally not ready'. It is not like it was a big deal. We'd had sex; so what? It was not a life-changing experience. There was nothing on TV so... we did it. It had not been any good either. It was clumsy and a little painful—not to mention that, at fifteen, neither of us knew what we were doing. I was hoping to have a girlfriend to talk about that with, but I guess that was too much to ask from her. She needed to have the stick removed from her ass.

"Sure, I'd love to," I agreed, more to annoy Candice than to actually have sex. I turned to Candice and Fuzzy. "Have a great spring break, you guys." I grinned, as Connor put his fingers in the loopholes of my jeans. "I have to head home."

"Why so soon? So you can get all 'hot and bothered'?" Candice snapped, putting her hands on her hips.

"Actually Candice," Fuzzy said, smiling at me and putting his hand on her head, which was a good foot lower than his, "they're going to get ice cream."

As Candice whipped around to scold Fuzzy for making a joke, Connor grabbed my hand and we ran down the corridor to the main entrance.

"Where are you two off to in such a hurry?" someone asked as we passed the front office. We automatically recognized Connor's mom's voice. Stopping in our tracks, we turned to face her.

I absolutely *adored* Lynn. She was just a fantastic person in general. She was somehow raising three teenagers, and Connor was an extra handful due to his ADHD and OCD. For some time now, whenever I needed motherly advice, I would go to her. Lynn somehow knew all the right things to say and would give honest feedback to problems I found myself in, without making me feel bad about myself.

"We, uh… we're just excited to get out of school," Connor said, shrugging. "Spring break has been a long time coming."

"I agree." Lynn sighed. She was the art teacher at our school and had to put up with some serious hell raisers for ten hours a day. She needed this break just as badly as we did. "Oh, Beth, I heard that you got into the school play. Congrats!"

"Thanks!" I beamed as she hugged me. "I was actually pretty nervous about the outcome. A lot of people auditioned for the part of Mimi. This isn't just some drama class production; over thirty girls tried to get the part I ended up landing."

"There wasn't a doubt in my mind," Lynn said. She glanced at Connor, who was looking longingly at the front doors. "I suppose I should let you go. Be good."

Connor starting jogging toward the exit, holding onto my hand. "And home by seven, please!" she called after him.

It was time for spring break, and little did I know, it was going to *suck*.

CHAPTER 2

1, 2, 3... BYE

It was seven o'clock. Connor had just left to catch a bus home and I was settling down to watch a movie that my dad had rented: *Fiddler on the Roof.*

I put the DVD into the player and sat myself down on the couch, grabbing the remote and a box of Mr. Maples Cookies. Seconds into the opening credits, my cell phone started to ring. I paused the movie and looked at the caller ID.

"Hey, Marmee!" I greeted happily.

"Hey, sweetie! How are you?" my mom chirped into my ear.

"I'm great. I got into the school play" I informed her. "Connor, just left, and now I'm watching a movie."

"That's amazing!" she yelled into the phone, sounding more excited than I did when I found out. "I'm so happy for you!"

"What did you get up to today, Marmee?"

"I went to an AA meeting, got a refill on my prescriptions, and cleaned the house. You know, the usual. What movie are you watching?"

"*Fiddler on the Roof,*" I said, popping a whole Mr. Maples cookie into my mouth.

"It's so great! I've wanted you to watch it for the longest time!" Marmee exclaimed, and then began to sing poorly into my ear, something about being a rich man. I did not get it, so I laughed.

Finally she stopped singing. "So, what did you and Connor do?"

"Oh, you know, nothing much," I lied.

"Did you have sex?"

"What? How did you—"

"A mother knows, sweetie," she said. "You told me you would wait until you got onto the pill."

"I told you, Marmee, the pill won't work because of the medications for my epilepsy," I groaned. "It would be about as effective as having an Advil before knocking boots."

"Elizabeth!" Marmee scolded. "Don't say that!"

"Okay, before making love or whatever," I corrected myself. "I'll wait. Okay?"

"No, you won't." Marmee sighed. "Oh well." There was brief pause and I ate another cookie. "Is your sister home?"

"I actually don't know where the stinky 12 year old is," I told her. "Haven't seen her since this morning. I was kinda busy when I got home though…" I kidded inappropriately.

"Eliza*beth*!" Marmee laughed/scolded. "Will you check?"

"Hang on." I put the phone down and yelled, "AMY!" No answer. "Sorry Marmee, she's not here."

"Oh," she said, clearly disappointed. "I guess I'll try again later."

"For sure." I nodded, even though she couldn't see me.

"You know I can't see you when you nod, right?" she said.

I laughed at how well my mom knew me. "Can I watch my movie now?"

"Sure thing, sweetie," she said. "I love you."

"I love you, too."

"1, 2, 3, bye!" we said together and hung up.

My mom was a huge fan of Louisa May Alcott, and while pregnant, had insisted that my sister and I be named after characters from *Little Women*. It just worked out that she ended up having two girls.

About ten minutes or so into the movie, the land line rang. I paused *Fiddler* and grabbed the cordless from the table in front of me.

"Hello?"

"Hi, sweetie!" my mom greeted on the other line.

"Hey, Marmee. Haven't talked to you in a while."

"Are you liking the movie?"

"Yeah, I am," I answered. "What's up?"

"Is Amy home yet?"

"No, not yet," I replied, looking at the clock above the TV set. Seven thirty.

"Do you know when she will be?"

"Not a single clue at all."

"Oh. Okay," my mom said, sounding very disappointed. "Well, I'll try again later."

We said goodbye and hung up.

By 'later' she meant every ten minutes. It was so weird. Usually, when my sister did not get home until later, or spent the night at a friend's, my mom would ask me to tell her sweet dreams or something. Tonight she was determined to talk to my baby sister.

Eventually I found out that Amy was spending the night at her best friend's house. The last time my mom called, around ten (which was late for her), I told her this.

"Well," she sighed, "tell her I say nighty-night."

"I will," I promised.

"I love you, Beth."

"I love you too, Marmee."

"1, 2, 3… bye!"

And we hung up for the last time.

CHAPTER 3
BAD NEWS

I woke up the next morning to the phone ringing. I realized I had fallen asleep on the couch. My dad must have turned the TV off. I looked at the clock. It was eleven. I groggily reached for the phone at my feet and answered it on the last ring.

"Hey," I grumbled into it.

"Bethy?"

"Morning, Marmee," I said, rubbing my eyes with one hand, and holding the phone to my ear with the other.

"No, it's Aunt Melanie." My mom's identical twin sister.

"Oh, hey," I said. I was surprised to hear from her. I had not talked to her in a couple months.

"Is your sister home?" she asked. She sounded strange. Nervous.

"No. She spent the night at Claire's," I told her. "Probably won't be home for a few hours."

"Okay," she sighed. "I guess I'll tell you first. I'm coming over."

"Wait, tell me what?" I asked, sitting bolt upright, suddenly wide awake.

"I'll see you in a few minutes," Aunt Melanie told me.

"Wait, tell me what?" I demanded, but she had already gone.

I put the phone down and unwrapped myself from the blanket my dad must have put on me before he left for work. My heart was pounding. What was going on? What was wrong? Why did my aunt's voice sound so shaky?

I stood up and the empty box of Mr. Maples fell to the floor. I suddenly felt very, very sick. I hurried to the bathroom, fell in front of the toilet, and retched into it until there were nothing but dry heaves left. I waited a couple more seconds but nothing else was coming up. I shakily got to my feet and stood in front of the bathroom mirror. I turned on the tap and watched the water flow from the faucet, then rinsed my mouth. I saw my medicine box beside the sink and quickly swallowed all my anti-seizure medication. Closing my eyes, I splashed cold water on my face.

Something must have happened to my cousin, I thought. *That would explain why Aunt Melanie sounded so... unusual on the phone. Yes, something happened to Ellie.*

I brushed my teeth quickly. Then I pulled my mane of brown hair out of the ponytail I had fallen asleep in, and quickly brushed it out. I knew it didn't matter how I looked when my aunt arrived, but I didn't want to appear as if I had poorly done dreadlocks... or have my breath smell like bucked-up maple cookies.

I didn't realize how long I had been in the bathroom until I heard my aunt burst in the front door and call my name.

"Beth?"

"I'm here!" I called back, coming out of the bathroom. I walked down the hall and watched my very pale aunt (who looked so much like my mom that my sister, cousin, and I sometimes got them mixed up at first glance) walk up the stairs toward me. Her pixie-cut hair was messy, as if she had been attempting to tear it out.

"Why don't we sit in the living room?" she suggested, taking my shoulder in a shaking hand and leading me into the other room.

She sat me down on the couch and sat on the edge of it beside me.

Without looking at me, she started to talk. "This is the hardest thing I've ever had to say," she began.

Then don't say it! I thought. I was cold all over, and my aunt was shaking so badly beside me that the whole couch seemed to be moving. I stared at her, concentrating so hard that my eyes started to water, as if I had forgotten how to blink.

"Last night, your mom died," she continued.

I'm not sure, but I think I screamed or something. My ears rang as if I had just left a loud concert. I felt every emotion and thought drain from me. Goosebumps covered every inch of my body, even though I wasn't cold. I tore my eyes away from Aunt Melanie and down to a thread that was poking out of the couch.

"What happened? How did she…" I already knew the answer, but I was praying silently to every god that it was a car accident or her appendix broke.

"She… she took a bunch of pills. All her anti-depressants are gone," she told me, wrapping her arms around me.

We both sat there, in complete silence. I have no idea for how long. I was confused as to why I was not crying. It made no sense. I should be gushing sobs, like any other daughter. I wondered if my aunt had cried yet or if she was still in as much shock as I was. I imagined that my aunt wanted her husband, Uncle Mitch, wrapping his arms around her. I gathered that she would feel safer and might even stop shaking if he was hugging her.

"Where's Uncle?" I mumbled, pulling the couch thread out of the cushion.

"He's in the car. Waiting."

For what? I wanted to ask, but I guessed that I did not really want to know.

Eventually, I realized that I wanted Connor with me.

"Can… can I call Connor?" I asked quietly.

"Oh course, sweetie," my aunt said, not letting go of my shoulders. I picked up the phone in front of me and speed dialled my boyfriend's number.

He answered after a few rings.

"Hey you," he said.

"I need you to come," I said tonelessly.

"Bethy, I just woke up," he complained. "Can't you come over here?"

"My mom just killed herself, so no, you can come over here," I demanded, suddenly pissed off.

"Are you serious?" he hollered. I heard mattress springs creak as he leaped out of his bed. "Yeah, I'm on my way," he promised.

"Please hurry," I asked, and hung up.

"You should call your dad," my aunt suggested. "He needs to know. We have things we need to talk to him about." I knew by 'we' she meant her and my uncle. Feeling sick again, I dialled my dad's number too.

"Hey, sweetheart," my dad said. "I can't really talk right now, I'm on top of a ladder."

"Dad, Marmee's dead. She killed herself."

He did not say anything. I heard traffic in the background. Eventually, he grunted, "I'm coming home," and I turned off the phone.

Aunt Melanie turned to me. "Don't tell your sister like that. You need to be gentler. She's only twelve." I hadn't even thought of that. How the fuck was I going to tell my baby sister that our mom was dead? "Do you want me to tell her?" she offered. I looked over at Aunt Melanie and nodded. She nodded back.

Not a few moments later, I heard the door open and close again, followed by the giggles of two preteen girls. When Amy and Claire reached the top of the stairs and saw our aunt, my sister's smile faded.

"Uh... hi?" Amy waved a bit and headed over to us. I noticed that she had cut her blonde hair short. It looked nice. "Aunt Melanie, what are you doing here?"

"Sweetie, why don't you sit down?" my aunt said, standing and gesturing to the big recliner that was kitty corner to the couch.

"Okay," my sister agreed. She placed herself on the chair and my aunt finally let go of me and sat next to Amy, who exchanged glances with me and then with Claire, who was standing in the doorway. I wasn't sure if I even wanted to look, but I couldn't tear my eyes away from the scene in front of me.

"Sweetie, it's your mom," our aunt said. Amy looked up at her, her already big blue eyes widening. "She took a bunch of pills last night. She passed—"

Before she could finish the sentence, my sister let out a loud wail, jumped up, and ran out the back sliding glass door. Claire ran after her and I finally stood. I saw my sister fall to her knees in the back yard, pulling up chunks of the dark green grass. All I could make out of her screaming was the word "no". That's the word I kept thinking too, but hadn't yet said out loud.

I turned around slowly, feeling like my legs were about to give way. Through the large living room window, I saw Connor jump off a bus across the street and jaywalk into our driveway. Usually he knocked, but he didn't bother this time. He slammed the door behind him, bounded up the stairs two at a time, and threw his arms around me.

As usual, he smelled like pasta sauce, and he was wearing those stupid sandals he wore every day, even if it was snowing. Connor pressed his mouth against mine and I pushed him away. *Not the time.* He helped me lower myself onto the chair my sister had been sitting on. I curled into a ball, hugging my knees to my chest. Connor sat on the couch across from me and watched me try to digest the fact that I would never see Marmee again.

CHAPTER 4
REACTIONS

About twenty minutes later, my dad got home and hurried to my side. I had not moved from the seat I was in and barely moved when he wrapped his strong arms around me. His big beard tickled my neck before he stood himself back up.

"Where's Amy?" he asked me. I could not find my voice and Connor knew this.

"She's outside with Claire," Connor said, not taking his worried eyes off of me.

Without glancing at him, my dad walked away. I listened to his big carpenter boots thump across the hardwood floor. I listened to him quickly say hello to my aunt and uncle, who were now sitting at the dining room table, quietly talking to each other.

I stared at my socks and remembered getting them in a Christmas stocking from my mom a year ago. They had little penguins on them. I closed my eyes and leaned my head back, trying to shut everything out. They snapped back open again when someone threw themselves at me.

I looked down at my sister who had snuggled up next to me on the chair. I wrapped my arms around her, and pulled her into me. I stroked her short hair, and rocked back and forth as she cried into my shoulder. Her legs were folded over mine and she gripped onto one of my knees. I saw bits of dirt stuck under her nails. I closed my eyes slowly, and finally, tears started flowing down my cheeks. The harder Amy shook, the tighter I wrapped my thin arms around her. I silently vowed to myself that I would never let anyone hurt her—never let her feel any kind of pain again.

I glanced up at Connor who was watching me and Amy. He was crying too. I wondered why. It's not like *his* mom just died. I adored his mom. Lynn was such an amazing person, almost a mentor to me. She had three kids, and somehow dealt with Connor's OCD and ADHD without tearing her hair out. I wished I could talk to her.

Eventually, my aunt walked over to my sister and me.

"I have to get going sweeties," she said quietly. She bent down on one knee and wrapped her arms around both of us. "I'll call later, okay?"

Amy and I nodded into her shoulders. She stood and my uncle gave us a hug as well. He quickly stood up again and followed his wife out of the house after exchanging a few more words with my dad.

A few minutes later, my dad walked up to my sister and me and said, "Amy, do some laundry."

My sister's eyes widened with disbelief that he had the nerve to ask something like that when our mom had just died. While she was too shocked to say anything, I was not the tiniest bit hesitant to shout "Fuck you!" Dad did not put up a fight. He walked away. I knew that he was trying to get our minds off the devastating news, but suggesting doing laundry, his youngest daughter's least favourite chore, was not the way to go about it. Years later, I understood that he had been trying to get our minds off of the mental torture we were going through, but still… there is this thing called 'tact'.

No one spoke for a long time. The main noises heard were the sounds of me rocking Amy back and forth, the sniffles of stuffed noses, and my dad pacing in the kitchen. I watched cars drive past the house, wondering what the drivers were thinking about and if they had ever lost someone so close to them.

"Girls?" my dad muttered from the doorway. Amy, Connor, and I all looked over at him. "Would you like me to call anyone?"

I was a lot like my dad that way. I liked to have people around me when I was sad. It made me feel like people really cared about me. My sister and mom were always the other way around. When they were sad, they liked to be left alone. That never made sense to me, because that is how people feel when they are sad, right? Alone? Why not feel alone with lots of people around you? In a way, that's worse. But sometimes bad things feel good.

"Yes, please," I nodded. Amy shrugged. "Will you call Yvonne and Greg, and maybe Madison?"

Yvonne and Greg were distant relatives that we had become close to over the years. They had been married for at least eleven years. I had actually been at their wedding, but I could not have been more than five, so I only remember bits of it. Madison was my dad's ex-girlfriend. We had lived with her and her two kids for three years before their mutual break up. We still saw her often, and Facebooked each other all the time.

As my dad started dialling numbers, my sister stood up and walked down the hall to her room, with Claire close behind her. They closed the door behind them with a quiet *click*, and I was alone in the living room with Connor.

He came closer to me and took my hand. "Do you want to talk to my mom?" he asked, stroking my fingers.

I looked up at him and nodded. "I would like that."

Connor helped me to my room and pulled out his cell phone.

"Damn," he muttered, scrolling through his contacts. "I just remembered my mom is up island with some family. I don't have that number."

"Does your dad?" I questioned, sitting in my computer chair.

"Good idea." Connor nodded as he dialled his home number. "Hey, Dad. I'm at Beth's' place. I meant to leave a note, but I was in a hurry. Anyway, do you have Mom's number? Beth wants to talk to her. Hang on, just a sec." He held the phone to his shoulder and glanced over at me. "My dad wants to know why you want to talk to my mom. Can I tell him?" I nodded. He balanced his phone again. "Because Beth's mom killed herself last night."

There was a sudden uproar on the other line. I can honestly say that I did not even know that Bob liked me all that much until that moment.

"Oh my God! The poor thing! Let me talk to her!" I heard Bob shout. I reached over for the phone and took it out of Connor's outstretched hand.

"Can you ask my dad if you can spend the night?" I requested, before I put the phone to my ear. Connor nodded quickly and left the room.

"H-hello?" I greeted quietly.

"Beth!" Bob shouted. "I am so sorry! You poor thing, is there anything I can do? Anything at all?"

"Well, I was hoping that you would let Connor spend the night? I don't really want to be alone—"

"Of course!" Bob cried. "As long as it's okay with your dad," he added. Connor walked in and nodded, telling me that my dad had agreed.

"It is," I told Bob. "Here's Connor." I handed the phone back to him.

"Hey, Dad. So is it okay if... great thanks. I don't know, maybe drop off some movies? Some funny ones? And my toothbrush. Thanks. And Mom's number?" Connor reached for a pen on my desk and started writing down numbers on his hand. "Thanks Dad. I'll see you soon. Bye."

Connor hung up and looked up at me. "My dad will be here in about half an hour. I thought some movies might take your mind off of... you know."

"Thanks." I nodded. "Can we call your mom now?" I whispered.

"Of course," he said, flipping open his phone and reading the numbers off his hand. "Hey, Mom. Yeah, I'm okay, sort of." He stopped himself and shook his head. "Who am I kidding? I'm not okay. Well actually, I'm calling for Beth. Something's happened. It's her mom. She killed herself."

Again, I started hearing shrieks on the other line. Connor held the phone away from his ear and we both heard, "I need to talk to her! I need to talk to her!" With a shaking hand, I took the phone out of Connor's grasp and put it to my ear.

"Hi, Lynn," I gulped.

"Oh, Beth, my dear Beth. I'm so sorry about your mom." I was surprised to hear that Lynn was sobbing. "I think of you as my own daughter. You're a huge part of my heart and will always be part of this family! If you ever want to talk…"

And that's what did it. That's what made me break. The thought that I did not have a mom anymore, but I still had a woman who thought of me and loved me like a daughter. I freaked out. I could not stop crying. I was howling so loudly I could not hear what Lynn was saying, even though it was right in my ear. If fireworks had started exploding right outside my bedroom window, I would not be able to hear them I was sobbing so loudly. Connor got up and took the phone away from me. I threw myself across the room and onto my bed, and screamed into a pillow while my boyfriend talked to his mom.

I'm not sure how long I lay there, screaming, sobbing, and biting my pillow. When Connor sat down next to me, I finally sat up.

"Baby?" he whispered, reaching over to me. I pushed his hand away from me.

"I don't understand!" I sobbed, loudly. "How can she be dead? How could she do this to me? To my sister? To her sister and brothers? She will never hug me, kiss me, sing to me… brush her hair or order pizza ever again! I will never see my mom again!" I got off my bed and wiped my eyes. I grabbed a tissue from off my desk and blew my nose. I suddenly felt very trapped, claustrophobic even, and had to get out of my room. I pulled open my door and headed down the hall to the kitchen where I was surprised to see Yvonne, Greg, and Madison standing in the doorway to the dining room. I had forgotten my dad had called them.

They were all very pale, and had the same stunned look on their faces.

Yvonne crossed the room and hugged me, her long brown hair falling over my shoulders. "Bethy, I am so sorry," she breathed, squeezing me. She let go and held onto my hands. "It's such a shock."

I said nothing, just nodding.

Greg walked over to me and handed me a plastic bag. "I never know what to say when these things happen, but in the movies chocolate seems to help. So, here." I took the bag from him and glanced inside it. Filled to the brim of it were chocolate bars. Not the corner-store kind, but the real, rich, fatty ones that you get on Valentine's Day.

I mumbled a thank you and put the bag on the counter. "But I don't think I can eat right now."

"I can't blame you," Madison agreed from my dad's side. "I can only imagine what's going on in that head of yours. It must really hurt."

"It hurts everywhere," I whimpered. A loud knock at the door announced another visitor and I started down the stairs to answer it.

I had barely opened the door when Bob's arms were around me, giving me the strongest hug I had ever received. I hugged him back and heard Connor walk down the stairs to talk to his dad. As Bob handed him a plastic bag full of movies, and another with clean clothes and his toothbrush, I thanked him for letting Connor spend the night.

"Of course, whatever will help you get through," Bob said, patting my shoulder. "I'll see you tomorrow." I watched him get into his car and start back down the driveway.

I closed the door behind me and went back up the stairs while Connor rummaged through the bag to see what movies his dad had brought.

We joined everyone in the living room. I sat down next to Amy and wrapped my arms around her again. I saw her fingering the necklace that Marmee had bought her for Christmas a few years back. We all sat in silence for some time before my dad piped up.

"Will is going to come by with your mom's cat and the note tomorrow morning," he told my sister and me. "I'm sure we'll be making a lot of calls tomorrow, and receiving quite a few. If you need to rest, just leave the lines be."

CHAPTER 5

WELCOME TO MY LIFE

I can honestly say that I don't remember any of the late night guests leaving. I do not remember falling asleep. All I remember from that night was pacing the living room floor while Connor watched me, with a movie playing in the background. Claire spent the night in Amy's room, and my dad would not let Connor sleep in mine, so I stayed out in the living room with him. My first act of rebellion.

Somehow I had fallen asleep and ended up squished between the back of the couch and Connor, who was snoring quietly. I wiggled my way out from the uncomfortable position and sat at Connor's feet, closing my eyes again. Sunlight streamed in through the curtains, searing my eyes. I groaned, trying to remember why I felt so empty. Eventually the day before surfaced and I remembered that my life sucked. The land line started to ring, but I ignored it. Whoever the fuck it was could suck it. I didn't need or want to talk to anyone. Then my cell phone started to ring. When I did not answer that, my land line started again.

"Ugh! Fuck!" I whined and grabbed the receiver. "Hello?"

And so began my first day without a mom.

My dad was right; it was full of phone calls: my mom's friends from AA, my aunt calling to see how Amy and I were doing, Yvonne and Greg, Madison, some people I did not know... even Lynn and Bob called.

"Beth," Lynn sighed in my ear and my throat tightened. She had been like a second mom to me for so long and now she was my— "Beth, I wish there was something I could do. I feel so useless."

"You're not." I croaked out, then handed the phone to Connor, because I knew I wouldn't be able to get another word out.

Eventually, Will arrived, holding an envelope and a cat carrier. Mr. Darcy was inside it and I was relieved that he had been found. The poor thing must have been so scared. My sister and I put him in her bedroom and we led Will into the living room. I shooed Connor to my bedroom, because Will wanted to speak to us alone.

"I have your mom's note girls," he said, his eyes welling up. "I'd like to read it to you," he continued, opening the envelope and pulling out a looseleaf piece of paper. I noticed a cigarette burn in it. My mom had been a really heavy smoker. Will cleared his throat and started to read:

"My dearest babies,

I am so sorry, I just can't go another day. Please, forgive me. I will never stop loving you. Will, I hope to always be in your heart. Melanie, you have been the best twin a sister could ask for. I love you. Terrance and Marcus, my brothers, I love you as well and wish I could have spent more time with you over the last few years. Sidney, please take care of our baby girls.

I will love you always,
Margret"

"Jesus," I breathed. "Can I see it?"
"Of course."

I may as well have snatched the note out of his hand. I smoothed it over my leg and read it again. I handed it to Amy, who was crying again.

Will stood up. "I just wanted to see you girls again… give you my condolences."

Amy stood too and hugged him. He wrapped his arms tightly around her. She let go, put the note on the coffee table, and sat down again. I stiffly stood up and gave Will a quick let's-get-this-over-with hug.

"Well, I should get going. Call me anytime," he said quietly, picking the note up. "I'm supposed to drop this off at your aunt's house. I'll see you around," he added, and showed himself out of the house.

"Marmee told me to tell you nighty-night," I mumbled, sitting next to Amy.

"I never got to say goodbye," she sniffled.

"You didn't know there was going to be one," I gulped. "No one did." I looked at the ceiling. I do not think I had any more tears left in me. "I love you, baby sister."

"I love you too, older sister," Amy replied.

We sat on the sofa together for a few minutes. We could hear Dad talking on the phone in his room. We heard Mr. Darcy meowing in Amy's room, desperately wanting out of his kitty carrier. I followed Amy to her room and closed the door behind me. Claire was sitting on Amy's bed, flipping through a magazine, and the cage was in the corner of the room. I opened the carrier and the cat dove under Amy's bed.

"Shit," I grumbled, getting on my knees and looking under the bed-frame after him. "It's okay, buddy. You know us," I cooed. I heard him growling and backed away.

"He's just scared," Amy said. "Leave him be; that's what he wants."

"All right," I agreed, standing up. "I love you," I said again.

"I love you too," Amy echoed as I left the room, closing the door behind me.

I walked down the hall and entered my room, closing the door quickly behind me and wishing I could weld it shut. I needed a break from the stale depression on the other side of that door.

"How are you doing, Bethy?" Connor asked from my computer chair.

I sighed and shook my head, wrapping my arms around myself. "I don't know. Numb, kind of. I can't really feel anything, but I can't seem to stop feeling at the same time. The note was addressed to Amy and me. Mr. Darcy won't come out from under the bed. He's going to be scarred for life." *Just like me.*

He stood up and walked over to me. "I love you, you know that, right?" he said, gently holding my face in his hands.

"I know." His words didn't make me feel any less abandoned.

Suddenly, as if it wasn't even me doing it, my arms were around his shoulders and I was kissing him hard. I didn't even like kissing him all that much. He was really bad at it, and he only brushed his teeth, like… every other day. Connor wrapped his arms around my waist and picked me up, carrying me to my bed. Even though he was able to lift me effortlessly, Connor still insisted I needed to lose weight. He threw me on top of the covers and started to take off my clothes. I had not changed since yesterday morning, so I was happy to get off the tear-stained shirt and the jeans that still had dirt from Amy's fingers on the knee. Wait… I was "happy"? Of all things, I was happy about taking my clothes off.

Well, whatever worked, right?

Connor was naked before I was. When it came to the bedroom, he was always faster at *everything*.

He lay on top of me and struggled with the clasp of my bra. I had an unspoken rule that Connor only sort of respected: I never got completely naked. That made sex way too intimate. If there was still some article of clothing on, there was a barrier between us and not the rubber kind.

"Connor, just"—I swatted his hand away irritably—"stop it. It's not like you've ever been able to get it off anyway."

Connor didn't fuss. He spread my legs and I closed my eyes. Besides our first time (and even then hardly), Connor was never very gentle. He didn't work his way in, he just... pushed. I may have rubbed the fact that I was not a virgin in Candice's face, but that did not mean I enjoyed it. This time, though, something unexpected happened: I was not thinking about anything. My brain had shut up. I felt nothing, instead of sad and alone. I was hearing someone making a noise that was not crying. Connor found a rhythm he liked and attempted to keep his sounds to a minimum—this not being *nearly* the first time we had snuck away with people currently occupying nearby rooms. It was barely five minutes before Connor stilled and muffled a groan into my neck, then rolled off of me. How romantic.

I was never one for snuggling or shit like that. It was sweaty and sticky and awkward. And what were you supposed to say afterwards? Thank you? Did you get there? Was that okay? Are you hungry? I hopped off the bed and grabbed some clean clothes, pulling them on quickly. Then I threw the bag of clothes Bob had brought for Connor at him.

"Get dressed," I said bluntly.

"You sure you don't want to go for another?" Connor smirked, grabbing my wrist and halfheartedly pulling me back to the bed.

"Right now I just want to shower, Connor. Now put some fucking clothes on."

"Fine," he whined, slowly getting dressed.

I squeezed out of my room, closing the door quickly and hurrying to the bathroom.

I turned on the shower and jumped in the tub, letting out a moan of relaxation as my shoulders went limp. I stood in the hot water for a good minute before I washed my hair and shaved my legs.

Although my life was officially a mess, it was nice to be clean.

CHAPTER 6

HOLLY

The next couple of days were full of funeral plans, phone calls of condolences, trying (and failing) to eat, staring blankly at walls, showing Mr. Darcy where the kitty-litter box was, holding my sister while we silently cried in the big blue chair, and constant sex with Connor. Of course, Connor never complained or questioned why our 'sessions' had increased dramatically over the course of no time at all. He was a guy after all.

One morning, about a week after Marmee had died, my Aunt Melanie picked me up to drive me to my mom's house. We would be going through the now-empty place, packing things up, and taking anything that I thought Amy and I might want or need back down island with us at the end of the day.

I did ask if Amy wanted to come, but she just shook her head and continued to read the book she had either been engrossed in or was pretending to be engrossed in—I'm not sure which. I was sure that it was too soon for her to go up to the house.

I still was not very talkative, so when my aunt spoke up after a good twenty minutes of driving in complete silence, I actually jumped.

"Is there anything in particular you would like?" she asked me, glancing over at me.

"Huh?" I replied, stupidly.

"Of your mom's," Melanie explained slowly. "Is there any belonging in particular you would like to keep?"

I nodded, slowly. "Her ring. The diamond one that belonged to your mom at one point," I answered. "Marmee told me that she would give it to me when I turned eighteen. I guess I'll get it a couple years early."

"Okay," my aunt noted. "Anything else?"

"Not that I can think of."

"If you see anything in there you'd like, let me know."

I bit my lip and looked out the window, allowing myself to zone out and watch scenery that I would not be seeing every other weekend anymore.

About twenty minutes later, my aunt pulled into the driveway of my mom's house. The place was old and tiny, with a living room, eat-in kitchen, one big bedroom, one small bedroom, and a little bathroom. That was it.

I had only spent one weekend in the house before my mom ended her life.

Barely a minute after we had pulled into the drive, a bright red jeep pulled in behind my aunt's van.

Confused, I glanced over at Melanie. "Who...?"

"Do you remember Holly? She was a friend of your mom's from AA?" She was watching the jeep in the rear-view mirror. I nodded. "Well, she and Margret became really good friends over the last couple months, so she's offered to help out with the estate. Since we live forty minutes away and she only ten, and because she's very persistent, I couldn't say no."

"Makes sense," I said, opening the door finally and stepping out onto the gravel driveway. I stood awkwardly beside the van. I had only met Holly once, so I was not exactly beaming at the sight of her. I watched as she clambered out of her jeep, a huge leather bag slung over her shoulder and bouncing red curls falling down her back. She bee-lined right to me and embraced me tightly. I patted her on the back a couple times, relaxing as she stepped away. She held my shoulders gently in her warm hands.

"Hey, Beth." She smiled weakly. "How are you holding up?"

"Beats me." I shrugged.

Holly nodded, letting go of my shoulders. "Yeah, I know what you mean."

How? How could she possibly fucking know what I'm going through? I wanted to scream, but I bit my lip hard and focused on my sneakers.

"Well"—my aunt sighed loudly behind me, making me jump and spin around, since I hadn't realized she was there—"let's head inside, shall me?" Holly brushed past me, searching for a key in her gigantic bag.

I followed the two adults to the front door and waited on the porch with Aunt Melanie, while Holly rummaged through her bag grumbling. I glanced around the postage-stamp, uncut front lawn that my mom would have been going OCD over if she saw it. I smiled a little, remembering what a clean freak she had been. Holly finally unlocked the door and we all hurried inside to get out of the chilly, rainy March morning.

As I closed the door behind me, I glanced around the living room nervously. I remembered overhearing my aunt tell my dad that Marmee's body had been found in here.

While Holly and Aunt Melanie discussed where to store things for now, I shuffled over to the couch, staring down at it intently. I probably looked like I was trying to move it using only my mind.

I found myself wondering if the TV was on while the drugs worked their way through my mom's system. If she watched an infomercial to take her mind off the fact that she had just ended her life. Every Friday night she would watch the *CSI* marathon on her favourite channel. We used to watch it together. It never mattered how many times we had seen the episode, we still pointed out foreshadowing or scolded the detectives for missing something 'so very obvious'.

"So... this is where they found her." I gestured at the cushioned seat in front of me. Holly and Melanie stopped talking and looked over at me.

"Oh, no sweetie," Holly said quietly. "Her housekeeper found her on the floor. Where you're standing."

I let out a cry and practically threw myself across the room, tripping over a coffee table and landing on my butt.

"Oh, honey!" my aunt cried, hurrying over to me and helping me to my feet. "Are you okay?" she asked, still holding my arm.

"Yeah," I nodded, my eyes not leaving the part of the floor I had just been standing on. I felt like I had just danced on my mom's grave or something. I shuddered. No one said anything for a few moments. I could feel two pairs of eyes staring at me.

"So, Melanie, shall we?" Holly said quietly, from the other side of the room. I was grateful for the distraction. My aunt rubbed my arm affectionately and walked back over to Holly, leaving me to meander around the house.

I had only spent two nights in it: the weekend before spring break when Marmee and Will had officially separated. I had fallen asleep on the couch, watching another *CSI* marathon, and woken up around four in the morning having one of my monthly epileptic seizures. I had screamed for help, and Marmee had been there in seconds to help me through the forty seconds (that felt like forty years) of undeserved agony.

I closed my eyes and waited for the memory to fade away before entering the room Amy and I had shared for one night. One could tell which side of the room belonged to each of us by the decorations around and above the two twin beds.

Amy's duvet cover was light blue, and Platty (a lime-green stuffed-animal platypus) was seated on one of the pillows. Above the headboard was a poster of two dolphins leaping out of the ocean. I noted that Amy would want the bed (seeing as she'd had the same single bed since she was about six at home), the dolphin poster, and Platty.

My duvet was black with navy blue squares on it, making it look like an Emo quilt. I had exactly four stuffies on my bed: Spencer the teddy bear; two *Wishbone* dogs; and Franklin, another teddy bear about the size of a five year old. Above my headboard was a poster of a soaking wet Orlando Bloom. I decided that I wanted the stuffies and the poster. I already had a queen-sized bed at my dad's place.

I walked over to the vanity my sister and I shared on the other side of the room. Nothing was on the surface of it, and in the two drawers there were only some looseleaf papers with doodles on them and old teen magazines I had absolutely no use for. No ring.

I sighed and glanced in the vanity mirror. I looked as ugly as I felt. Blinking away the oncoming tears, I exited the room into the minuscule hallway.

I heard Holly and Melanie murmuring in the kitchen and quietly made my way to my mom's bedroom. It was amazingly cramped inside. There was a queen-sized bed pushed against the far wall, a small bedside table, and a half bookshelf beside the closet. I sat on her bed and looked down at the bookshelf, seeing if there was anything on it worth taking. Most of the titles were things like *God Loves Me* or *Help Me Pray*. But there was also the AA bible and information on Smokers Anonymous. What caught me by surprise was seeing *Hannibal* between a copy of the Bible and a plain black book with no title on the spine.

Tentatively, I leaned forward and pulled the black book off the shelf. I turned it over and was startled to see the words *My Journal* embossed in a golden ink scrawl. I didn't know my mom kept a diary. Not that she would have told me, but still...

I was about to open it when Holly appeared in the doorway. "Hi, sweetie," she said. "I thought you'd want to know that Melanie ran out to get some boxes to pack up some of the belongings. What have you got there?"

"I found my mom's journal," I told her, showing her the cover.

"You didn't read it, did you?" she frowned.

"No, but she wouldn't care," I answered, like the little shit I felt like.

"You're not actually going to read it, are you?" Holly asked in a warning tone.

"If it gives me any insight as to why she would leave me and Amy, of course I am," I told her, a little more snappily than I had intended. Holly put up with me being a turd and sat herself next to me as I slowly opened the journal to the first entry. She grumbled something, but it was too late. I was already reading my mom's perfect loopy handwriting.

I had to call my lawyer from Perry's house today. I shouldn't do that at a client's house. It was very awkward and embarrassing to have an anxiety attack while doing his housework. Holly says I should write, that it will help.

That was two days before she died. I assumed the lawyer thing was about the separation she was going through. I shakily turned the page and gasped when I saw the date at the top of the page. March fourteenth. The day she died.

It hurts. It hurts that Will found someone so fast. I wish I could pay my brothers back. I miss my beautiful girls. My anxiety is getting worse and—

The letters had started to blur together as my eyes filled with tears. I slammed the book shut more violently than necessary and closed my eyes. I silently digested what I had just read while Holly still lingered beside me.

Will found someone so fast.

"That asshole," I hissed through gritted teeth.

"Beth, language," Holly said quietly.

"He didn't 'find someone else'," I continued, more to myself than to Holly. "He had already *found* her! That ass—uh... *jerk* was cheating on my mom!"

"Beth, you're jumping to conclusions." Holly sighed, taking my shoulders and turning me to face her. "You don't have any proof that—"

I stopped her, holding the journal up in front of her face.

"Yeah, I do. And that was dated the *night she died*. They weren't even divorced yet! The separation had been final for, like... a day. God!" I had always disliked him, but now... I hated that man.

"Beth..."

"Whatever," I mumbled, holding the diary to my chest. "Auntie said that I could keep anything I wanted, so I'm keeping this." There was screaming silence between us for a few minutes before I finally burst. "Why does shit always have to happen to *me*?"

"Oh, sweetie," Holly simpered, shaking her head sympathetically. "This is God's way of testing you."

"There is no God, and this is not a *test*," I nearly spat. "I have been tested all my life and I've gotten through all of that shit! Why did I need another pop quiz? If there was a God, he would show pity on me and Amy and none of the past ten years would have happened! My parents wouldn't have divorced, my mom wouldn't have become a drunk, so we had to go live with our broke dad; I wouldn't have been diagnosed with tumour-related epilepsy, or had to have had *unsuccessful* brain surgery on my sister's tenth birthday three years ago; and my boyfriend wouldn't be such a dick! There *is* no test; there is no *God!* Those who say differently are kidding themselves."

Holly sighed again, stood up, and left.

The rest of the day went by in a daze. I decided that I wanted all of the books, movies, posters, jewelry, and the TV and TV stand. Amy would want her bed, all the clothes in the closets, including

Marmee's, and lastly... the couch. It kind of weirded me out that Marmee had died on it, or at least beside it, nearly a week ago, but it was much better than the ugly leather one currently occupying my dad's living room.

I had stuffed the journal in alongside all the other books, so I would not have to carry it around for the rest of the day, and when I looked closely at the box full of books, I mentally cringed when I saw that I would be taking home two copies of the Bible. Needless to say that my faith had altered considerably over the last couple days.

It was nearly six by the time my aunt's van was packed with boxes of my inherited belongings—the ones that we would not need a U-Haul to retrieve.

I sat down on the couch for a few minutes to collect my thoughts and looked up when I heard my aunt say my name.

"Beth, I couldn't find it," Melanie said grimly.

"Find what?" My brain was so tired that I doubt I could have spelled my own name. *E-L-I-Z... was it an 'I' or an 'A' that came next?*

"The ring," Melanie breathed. "I looked everywhere. I couldn't find it; I'm so, so sorry."

I swallowed a lump in my throat and shook my head.

"Don't be," I whispered, looking down at the promise ring from Connor that I was currently wearing. "It's not your fault."

Auntie crossed the room and sat beside me, putting an arm around my shoulders. My mind flashed to the last time we had been in this position. *"This is the hardest thing I've ever had to say..."*

"Holly is going to take care of the house for us," Aunt Melanie said suddenly, bringing me back to the present. "She's going to rent it out with all the furnishings, other than the things that you and Amy want, and all the rent money is going to be added to the trust fund for you and Amy. You'll inherit it when you're eighteen. It will be quite a bit of money, so be sure to save as much as you can. Maybe invest in..."

I did not mean to, but I zoned out when she told me about what Holly was going to do for us. I knew she was close to my mom, and that she only lived ten minutes away instead of nearly an hour like us, but she didn't have to do that. I suddenly felt the way I had treated her earlier that day: like shit. I did not care about the money, but Holly clearly cared about me and Amy and I owed her an apology.

"Has Holly left yet?" I asked suddenly.

"No," my Aunt said, surprised that I had interrupted her. "She's outside, having a smoke." She gestured to the door.

"I'll be right back," I said, standing up, striding across the living room, and leaving the house.

Holly was leaning against a railing on the tiny porch, taking a drag off a cigarette.

"Hi," we said in unison, although I did not have smoke billowing from my mouth as I said it.

"I'm sorry," I said quickly, Holly watching me intently. "I was a brat to you today. My aunt just told me what you're doing for Amy and me... and Auntie and my mom really. It's really very kind of you... thank you. Thank you so much." I choked back a sob. "I just... I just... I'm... I'm so, so sorry."

Holly dropped the stub of the smoke on the ground and stomped on it to put it out. Without saying a word, she stepped over to me and gently wrapped her arms around my shoulders in a gentle hug. I did not hesitate to hug her back this time. I clutched onto her and let her rock me back and forth. When she finally pulled away, her eyes were brimming with tears, just like mine.

"I'd do anything for your mom," she said, wiping a stray tear from my cheek. "That includes putting up with a teenage brat."

I laughed softly as my aunt joined us on the porch.

"Everything okay out here?" she asked slowly. I nodded. "You want to go home?"

I nodded again.

"I'll need to move my jeep then," Holly said, pulling a key out of her jacket pocket, reaching past my aunt, and locking my mom's door. Aunt Melanie looped her arm through mine and we walked down the few steps to the driveway, with Holly right behind us. "Well, I guess I'll see you at the service next week?" Holly said, now holding her car keys. "I look forward to seeing you both again. Despite the reason." She gave us both a hug and headed over to her jeep.

My aunt and I watched her clamber in, buckle up, and rev the engine before backing out of the drive and heading down the road. I turned to face the house again. It really would have been a cute place to live. I took a deep breath of the clean, country air. I missed it when I was in the city.

I was certain it would be the last time I would be in the area for a long time.

I was right.

CHAPTER 7

BACK TO SCHOOL

The rest of spring break went by slowly, but seemed to end rather quickly as well. Amy and I spent a lot of the week trying to show Mr. Darcy the litter box—he seemed intent on peeing on the bathroom mat. My dad spent a lot of that week trying to get Amy and me to eat something. Anything.

Once and a while I would be able to keep something down, but other than that, the only meal I ate was at a restaurant with my aunt and uncle.

One morning, at about seven, my dad knocked on my door to wake me up.

"It's time for school, sweetie," he said, poking his head in the door.

I turned my head to look over at him and frowned.

"I can't believe you're making Amy and me go back to school," I grumbled. "Like... a week ago our mom died."

"Going to school will get your mind off of it. Besides, you have rehearsals now, don't you?" He looked pointedly at me. "Something to look forward to." He left my room, closing the door behind him, and I listened as he knocked on Amy's door down the hall.

"Ffffuuuuuuccccckkkk," I complained to no one in particular, unless my posters of the Canucks and Robert Downey Jr. had suddenly come to life. I sat up, swinging my legs off my bed.

For the rest of spring break, I had spent most of my time in my room with Connor, having frequent sex. It was the only thing that could make everything in my head shut up. There was only one thing to think about, instead of a million questions I knew I would never have answered. Connor was far more aggressive in bed now, though. He'd started pinning my arms down or biting my shoulders; once he even pulled my hair. If I hadn't been searching for an escape from the constant pain and emptiness where my heart used to be, I'd have objected. Instead, I let him do what he want. Anything to move my focus onto something else.

I pulled off my pj's and put on a pair of ripped jeans and a t-shirt with a teddy bear on it, then covered my torso with my black sweater and brushed my hair. Brushing my teeth and skipping breakfast, I waited for Amy to get her bag, and together we headed out the door with a few minutes to spare.

"So routine it's like nothing happened," I said, as we walked down the road to the bus stop.

"Yeah."

"How are you going to tell your friends?" I asked, looking over my shoulder to see if the bus was coming.

"I don't know," Amy shrugged. "I'll figure something out. What about you?"

"I'll probably just tell them flat out. I don't want to beat around the bush, you know?" We started jogging to the stop as we heard the bus coming up the road.

"That makes sense," Amy told me, pulling her bus-pass out of her pocket as the bus slowed to a stop in front of us.

I copied her, and followed her onto the bus, quickly swiping my card through the scanner.

The bus ride did not take long. My stop was before Amy's. I gave her a hug, wished her luck, stepped off the transport, and headed to my high school. Fairview High was only a couple of blocks from my stop and it usually took me five minutes to get to the front doors. Today my feet felt like they were made of concrete, so it took me twice the time. I was a half hour early for classes, so the foyer was basically empty when I stepped through the front doors. I headed to the main staircase to the fourth floor, where Candice, Fuzzy, and I shared a locker. When I reached the top of the staircase, I saw one of my resource centre teaching assistants, Carol, outside a classroom.

"Beth!" she called brightly, waving me over to her. "How was your time off?"

"If I act strange, or distant, it's because my mom killed herself," I said bluntly, not stopping to answer any questions. I continued down the hall to the locker, dreading every moment of the upcoming day. I reached the locker and held the combination lock in my hand, staring at it. "Fuck," I said. "What is your code?"

"Forty-two, fifteen, twenty-seven, eight," Candice replied behind me. I jumped back, and out of her way. "Did you really forget?" she asked, giving me a hug that I did not return. "It doesn't matter. I had a great week. Got so much done! I even cleaned my room for once... and waited for you to call of course. Why didn't you?" she suddenly snapped, yanking open the locker door and whipping around to glare at me. "I called you all the time, and when I Facebooked Connor to see how you were, he told me that it 'wasn't his place to say'. Are you *mad* at me or something?"

"My mom killed herself. I didn't want to tell you on the phone," I told her, praying that she would shut the fuck up.

"Oh... my... God. I, I, I don't know what to say," she stammered. "Are you... how's your sister? Is everything..." She could not seem to finish a sentence. I was grateful.

"Hey, guys!" Fuzzy called down the hall. We both turned and said nothing back. His long, pacing stride slowed down as he saw the looks on our faces. "What's going on?" he asked, shrugging off his bag and shoving it into our locker.

Candice looked at me, her big blue eyes tearing up.

"My mom killed herself," I announced, crossing my arms across my chest.

Fuzzy took a few steps away from me. His knees seemed to buckle.

"Oh my God!" He leapt at me and threw his arms around me, burying his face in my hair. "If there is anything that I can do for you, anything at all, please let me know." I wrapped my arms around his waist. I turned my head and leaned the side of my face against his chest, my eyes welling up. I saw Candice glaring at me. She thought she owned Fuzzy, because of a crush he was oblivious to.

Jesus.

Eventually Fuzzy stepped back, leaning against the wall behind him.

We all stood in complete silence, staring at the floor, all of us wishing we were talking about parties that we had gone to or homework assignments we had completely forgotten about.

"Hey," I heard Connor say behind me. "So, you guys know?" He put his arms around my shoulders and exchanged nods with Candice and Fuzzy.

"How did she do it?" Candice asked quietly. I knew that she was dying to know.

"She swallowed every pill in her house," I answered, appreciating the look of disdain that Fuzzy was giving her.

"Oh God," Fuzzy said, burying his face in his hands and rubbing his forehead, as if trying to get rid of a headache. "Will you be going to classes and stuff?" he asked, knowing that the bell was going to ring any second.

"Yeah," I told him, as Connor took my backpack from me. "A death in the family is no excuse to miss school," I said. The three of them stared at me. Their jaws dropped. "I just reworded what my dad said."

Fuzzy let out a hollow laugh. "Sounds like him."

The bell rang finally and we all headed silently down the hallway to our first class of the new semester, English 11. I was glad that no homework had been assigned for this class over the break, because there was no way in hell I would have done it.

We took our seats near the back of the class. They were two large desks facing each other. Connor and I sat on one side, with Candice and Fuzzy facing us. We put our notebooks in front of us and flipped to blank pages, getting ready to take notes.

Before the second bell rang, the class started. Mrs. Wing started messily writing notes on 'symbolism in poetry' on the blackboard, her left hand smudging the words she was scribbling. Without really reading the notes, I copied the words onto the paper in front of me. I watched my fellow students scuttle into the room and slip into their desks, pretending they did not see the scowl Wing gave them.

Something touched my knee and I looked over at Connor, who was smiling at me the way he did when he closed my bedroom door behind him. His hand slowly made its way up my thigh. I pushed his hand away quickly and pretended to pay attention to whatever Wing was going on about. Within seconds, Connor was doing it again. This time, his hand did not start at my knee. He placed his palm just below my crotch. I stiffened and gave him a dirty look, which I thought would give him a clue on how I felt about what he was doing. He started moving his pinky closer to my fly and I kicked him under the table. Or tried to.

"Ow!" Fuzzy yelped. "What? I wasn't doing anything!"

"Oh shit, sorry," I apologized. "I thought you were—"

"Beth?" Mrs. Wing called from the front of the class.

I looked up at her. Connor yanked his hand away from my lap.

"Yes?" I asked. I noticed Carol standing beside her, wringing her hands.

"Can I talk to you in the hall for a moment? Bring your things," she added, leaving the room with Carol.

I tossed a stony look at Connor, throwing my things into my bag and following my teachers out of the room.

"Beth, why are you here?" Mrs. Wing said without hesitation. "You should be at home. There is no way that you are ready to be back at school after your loss."

"My dad told me to come. Besides, I don't want to miss first day of rehearsal."

"Well, we're studying odes today, so… why don't you take one of your friends down to the cafeteria and get some coffee? Maybe go to your next block?"

"I'll get Connor," Carol agreed, starting to the door.

"No!" I almost shouted. "Not Connor."

"Candice?"

"No, I want Fuzzy," I mumbled.

"Who?" both of my teachers asked.

"Oh, I mean Daniel," I corrected myself, forgetting that only Candice, Connor, and I called him that.

"Sure," Carol nodded, whipping back into the room.

"Oh Beth," Mrs. Wing said, giving me a gentle hug. "If there is anything I can do, please let me know."

"Thank you."

Over Wing's shoulder, as she pulled away, I saw Fuzzy step into the hall.

"Take it easy, honey," she suggested, entering her classroom again as Carol came back out.

"I'll see you in third block," Carol said, putting her hand on my shoulder before heading upstairs.

"I can understand why you didn't ask for Candice but… why did you ask for me? Why not Connor?" We made our way down the hall and started down the nearest staircase.

"He'd just want to go to the not-so-secret make-out room, and I'm not in the mood for that right now."

"There's a make-out room?" Fuzzy repeated, stopping mid-step.

"Yeah, in the gym beside the PE teacher's office. You'll be out of high school before you've even kiss a girl though, so how would you know about it?"

We both laughed. It felt weird to laugh. Good... but weird. I listened to the chuckles bounce off the walls. I had not heard that in a long time.

"Wait, why would Connor try to get you to make out with him?" Fuzzy questioned, as we passed the third floor and kept going down. "Shouldn't that sort of thing be the last thing on your mind right now?"

"Over the break that's pretty much all I did," I informed him. "It was the only thing I could do to stop thinking about my mom, or what I was going to say at her service. Besides, it's not like he was going to say no."

"Well, he should have," Fuzzy snapped. "You were vulnerable and he took advantage of that."

"You wouldn't have said no either Fuzzy," I pointed out.

"That's not true."

"Lose your virginity and tell me that with a straight face."

We reached the bottom floor and entered the cafeteria. We walked up to the counter and the cashier did a double take when she saw me, then ran around the counter.

"Oh, honey!" she cried, throwing her arms around me. "What are you doing at school? You should be at home, or seeing a counsellor."

"Wait... how do *you* know?" I demanded, stepping away from her.

She straightened up and fixed her apron. "The whole staff knows. When something like this happens, the school has to know."

"What? Why?" Fuzzy said behind me, pouring two cups of coffee.

"We need to know how to act around you, of course," the lunch lady said, crossing the counter again and standing behind the till. She shook her head as I tried to pay for the coffee. "No, no... take it. Enjoy."

"Thanks," Fuzzy called over his shoulder, following me to our regular lunch spot. It was a large windowsill, deep and wide enough for the four of us to sit and still have enough room to eat our lunches in front of us. More than once I'd snuck a nap there when I was supposed to be in PE.

We dropped our bags on the ground and I hopped up onto the ledge, crossing my legs beneath me. Fuzzy handed me my coffee and a fistful of sugar packets and cream. He stepped up beside me. At six foot four, he was easily one of the tallest kids in the school.

"I never met her," he grumbled, pouring some sweetener into his coffee. "Your mom. What did she look like?"

I took a deep breath as I dumped three packets of sugar into my cup.

"You know my aunt Melanie?"

"Yeah."

"Imagine her, but tanner and holding a smoke. That's her."

Fuzzy did not say anything. He just shrugged... then shrugged again and turned away from me. It took me a moment to realize that he was crying. This was the same guy that I had seen get hit in the crotch with a dodge ball in sixth grade, fall off the monkey bars in seventh, break his collarbone wrestling in ninth, and take it all in stride. Just last month his entire left side was trampled by cleats during a rugby game and I had dressed those wounds for twenty minutes, without a single tear from him. Now he was crying at my expense. His tears made me feel guilty.

I turned and wrapped my arms around his huge shoulders and leaned my head against the back of his neck. Tears slowly started falling down my cheeks, landing on his white t-shirt. They left little dots. Gradually his sobs subsided and I pulled away. I rubbed his back as he wiped his nose on his sleeve and rubbed his eyes hard.

"Will you tell anyone?"

"No," I assured him. "What just happened will not leave this room."

Fuzzy put an arm around my shoulders and pulled me into him.

"What the hell?" Candice's shrill, annoying voice shrieked into the room.

We looked up and saw the mousy four-foot-nine girl marching over to us, Connor lazily following behind her.

"Why didn't you take me?" Candice demanded, standing in front of me with her hands on her hips. "Marge's death affects me just as much as it does him." She always did have a way of playing the victim, but usually it was almost amusing. This was just sad.

"Her mom's name was Margret, Candice," Fuzzy corrected her, letting go of me.

"Well, I knew her," Candice defended herself.

"You met her once, for about five minutes," I pointed out, annoyed.

"I'm your best friend!" she cried, stomping her feet. "I should be the one comforting you!"

"Actually, I should be," Connor said behind her, raising his hand above his head. "I'm her boyfriend. I think that rates me highest on emergency contact."

"You have a weird way of comforting her, though, man," Fuzzy growled. "Look, I've known her the longest."

"Oh my God!" I shouted, jumping off the windowsill. "Are you guys seriously fighting over who gets to console me?" I grabbed my bag at Candice's feet and set it on my shoulder, then grabbed my coffee off the sill. The bell for second block rang and we heard classroom doors bang open all over the building. "I have psych," I said, leaving the room, glad to be away from them for a while

CHAPTER 8
RUDY

When I got to psych, not many of the students were there yet. Just as I was about to take a seat, one of my classmates, Annie, bounded over to me. If I was to describe anyone as jolly, it would be her. She was just the cutest thing.

"Beth!" she grinned, giving me a big hug. "How was your break?"

"My mom died." Damn, I was getting really sick of saying that. I waited for her to shout, *'Oh my god, I'm so sorry, if there's anything I can do, just let me know'* like everyone else did. But not Annie.

Her left hand covered her mouth, as if stifling a scream, while her other hand reached out behind her to find a chair to sit in. She landed in the one behind my assigned desk. She stared at me in horror, as if waiting for me to continue.

"Look, Annie, can you please not tell anyone?" I whispered to her, as more students started to pile into the room.

She nodded and shakily headed back to her desk, just as Mrs. Jenkins stopped in front of mine.

The teacher knelt in front of me and looked me right in the eye. "Are you up to being here?"

I nodded.

"If you need to go, just wave and head out, okay?"

I nodded again. Finally, something almost as routine as taking the bus had been earlier.

When the bell rang for lunch, Annie hurried over to me while I was gathering up my homework.

"We need to hang out sometime," she said, giving me a tight hug.

"Yeah, I'd like that," I agreed, patting her on the back with one hand.

Annie let go and left the room, her lower lip trembling.

When I exited the classroom, I was greeted by Connor, Fuzzy, and Candice.

"We're sorry," Fuzzy apologized.

"You didn't have to yell," said Candice.

"I love you," Connor said, raking his fingers through my hair and pulling me into a kiss.

"Are you kidding me, man?" I heard Fuzzy groan.

"Wanna go find a closet?" Connor breathed in my ear, his fingers trailing down my back.

I stepped away from him and shook my head. "Let's just go and eat," I said, as Candice looped her arm through mine. The four of us headed to the cafeteria as I accepted their apologies.

When we entered the cafeteria and headed to our spot, some of the students' eyes seemed to linger on me. Others would see me and start whispering to their neighbours.

"You guys didn't, you know, tell anyone... did you?" I asked, as we reached the sill and clambered up onto it.

"No," Connor and Fuzzy said together.

The three of us slowly turned our heads to Candice, who was pretending to fumble through her bag.

"Candice?" I said quietly. "Did you tell people what happened to me over the break?"

She threw her arms in the air. "I needed someone to talk to!" she cried. "This is really hard for me. For *us!*" She put a hand on her chest as if clenching her heart.

"But there are so many people staring at me!" I hissed. "How many people did you need to talk to?"

"People were asking why I was crying in class. I told them that my best friend's mom died and that we were really close."

"Oh my God, you met her once!" I groaned, putting my face in my hands. "Just... don't tell anyone else, please?"

"Fine, fine," Candice grumbled, as if very offended.

"I don't think you understand, Candice," Fuzzy said, taking a big bite out of his sandwich. "This is Beth's business and her news to share. The entire staff knows already. The entire student body knowing won't help her stress level."

Candice scowled at him and crossed her arms in a huff.

"I said *'fine'*," she snapped.

We ate in silence, watching people walk by me and staring as they did. They would shake their heads or wave a little bit. It started to annoy me that people I didn't even know knew what was going on. I averted my eyes and stared down at my fingers.

"Are you gonna eat that?" Fuzzy asked, pointing to my granola bar. Before he got an answer, he snatched it up and ate it in two bites.

"Pig," I joked, pretending to be annoyed.

I zoned out for a little bit, staring at some crude words scribbled on the wall behind Fuzzy.

"Beth?" Conner said, trying to get my attention. "Beth?" He poked me in the side.

"Hey! What?" I snapped, coming back into reality.

"Your phone," he said, holding up my flashing cell. "It's ringing."

I snatched it out of his hand and swiped across the screen.

"Hello?"

"Hi, sweetie," my mom said.

"Marmee?" I cried, sitting bolt upright, the rest of the group staring at me.

"No, it's Aunt Melanie."

My lip quivered and I let out a jagged breath. "Sorry," I mumbled. "How are you?"

"My first day back at work. It's hard. I'm calling to see how you're doing though."

"Basically, the whole school knows," I said, glancing at Candice, who avoided eye contact. "The staff knew in a couple minutes after I told one teacher. I was more or less kicked out of English, but I was allowed to stay in psych."

"How did your friends take the news?"

"Every person takes it differently, I guess."

"What classes have you got left?"

"I have resource centre next block, then drama to end the day. So it's more or less teachers helping me do my homework or I read for ninety minutes, and then goof around with your friends for ninety minutes before the final bell rings."

"That is a really good way to end the day."

"I agree. Thanks for calling Auntie, but Fuzzy is stealing my food so I should go."

"I'm glad you're eating again."

"I have my days. I'll talk to you later, okay?"

"I love you."

"I love you, too."

I ended the call and grabbed my bag of trail mix out of Fuzzy's hands.

"You thought your aunt was your mom?" he asked, peanuts flying from his mouth.

"You know how I said she looked exactly like my aunt? She sounded exactly like her, too," I explained, wiping a bit of trail mix from my eye.

"You're not supposed to have cell phones in the school, Beth," Candice scolded, as I was putting it back in my bag.

"Speak for yourself, Candice," Fuzzy snapped, grabbing the trail mix back from me. "I saw you texting under the desk in English."

"That was an emergency," she lied.

As Fuzzy and Candice started their daily bicker (which she always thought was a weird kind of flirting), Connor reached behind me and put his hand up my shirt.

"Are you sure you don't want to get some privacy?" he asked, leaning in and slobbering on my neck.

"Yes," I assured him, leaning away. That didn't stop him from putting his hand down the back of my pants and making an annoying whining sound.

"But Bethy..." he pouted, playing with the elastic of my panties.

"Dude, she said no," Fuzzy growled at him. "Now take your hand out of her pants."

"Fine," Connor snapped, sounding like the male version of Candice.

Grateful, I looked up at Fuzzy and sighed.

"I'm going to get to class," I said, gathering my things and putting them in my backpack.

"But Beth, class doesn't start for another ten minutes," Connor said. Moving his legs, I tried to clamber over them and off the windowsill.

"I'll *slowly* make my way to class then," I said, putting my backpack on one shoulder.

"Do you want me to come?" Connor asked, putting his stuff into his bag.

"Dude, she wants to be alone," explained Fuzzy, curtly.

"See you in class," I said, walking quickly out of the room, unable to ignore the looks my fellow students gave me as I walked by them and out the doors. "Fucking gossip," I breathed, heading to the most unused staircase in the building. It was the first time I had wanted to be alone in over a week, and of all the people I wanted to hide from it was my friends.

"Beth?" a male called from down the hall, just as I was reaching the stairs.

"Nope," I shouted back, not looking over my shoulder.

"Hey, Beth!" he shouted again. I didn't recognize the voice, and started up the stairs anyway. "Wait, you *are* Beth, right?"

"What?" I said, confused. I was not popular per say, but people knew who I was. More now than ever. I heard him coming up the steps behind me and curiosity got the better of me. I stopped and turned around. I gasped. "Oh my…"

Two steps below me was the most beautiful boy I had ever seen. He had pale skin, and his strong jaw had a hint of facial hair. He had piercing blue eyes and black hair that was just long enough to show that, if he grew it longer, he would have adorable curls. He had broad shoulders and long, muscled arms. He appeared to be average height, but then he was two steps below me.

"You are Beth, right?"

"Yeah, that's her"—I shook my head quickly—"she, me!" I stammered. "I'm Beth." A.K.A. *idiot.*

"I'm Rudy." He grabbed my hand and shook it.

"So, we haven't met?" I asked, as he let my hand go.

"Not formally. I saw you at the auditions for the school play. You were really good."

I grinned. "I got the part as Mimi."

"I know," he nodded, pulling a folded-up piece of paper out of his back pocket. "I play Roger," he said, unfolding it and handing it to me. It was the casting list. "I'm your boyfriend. On stage, that is." He sat on the stair between us and patted the spot beside him. "So, how was your break?" he asked, as I sat myself down.

"It was… I stayed in most of the time."

"I know, the weather was awful," Rudy complained, pulling a binder out of his bag. "I didn't get to go out rowing once." *He rows.* I swooned in my head. "I got an early copy of the play," he told me, waving the binder in front of me and opening it. "I saw how many scenes we have together and wanted to introduce myself before rehearsal today." He paused for a moment and turned to me. "I transferred here from Crest High in December, so I don't know everyone's back-story yet. I probably won't actually. I tend to keep to myself, but you must be really popular. Everyone seemed to know where to find you."

"I guess," I shrugged.

Unexpectedly, he reached over and curled a lock of my hair around his finger.

"Your hair in the moonlight," he said smoothly. I think I actually got lost in his eyes for a second before he pulled away and took his hand out of my hair. "So, what did you think? How was that?"

"W-what?" I stuttered, confused. *What just happened?*

"It's a lyric from the play," he explained, flipping to a certain page and pointing to a highlighted monologue.

"It was very believable."

"Come on, Beth," Rudy laughed. "I saw the way your boyfriend was looking at you during your audition. There is no way I would come on to you. That guy is huge."

"Connor's not all that tall," I said, pulling my hair into a ponytail.

"Connor?" Rudy said, puzzled. "I thought the rugby star's name was Danny or Daniel or something."

"Danny? Daniel? *Fuzzy?*" I almost laughed. "No, he is not my boyfriend. Connor is. He was there too."

"You mean the shorter guy with brown hair?"

"Yeah, that's him."

"He was flirting with some tiny, weird-looking girl the whole time you were on stage," Rudy said, leaning back on the step behind us.

"What?" I said loudly. "Mousy hair? Bad acne? Permanent frown?"

"That's her," he nodded, frowning.

"Oh my God!"

"I didn't mean to upset you, Beth," he said, putting his hand on my back. "I'm sorry."

"It's not your fault," I grumbled, standing up. "This wouldn't be the first time he's gotten too close to my best friend," I added, referring to the time he had made out with my tenth-grade best friend, Jane.

"What?"

"Never mind," I said, starting back up the stairs. When I reached the top of the flight, I turned around again. "Hey, Rudy?"

"Yeah?" He was still sitting on the steps, flipping through the script.

"What did you mean by 'the way he was looking' at me?"

"I mean that Danny really likes you, like… a lot," he explained, "and that your real 'boyfriend' (he put air quotes around the term) is a total dick."

We stared at each other for a moment.

"See you at rehearsal," I said, going up the next flight of stairs.

CHAPTER 9

THE DICK AND JANE

On my way up to third block, where my friends and boyfriend were probably waiting for me, I thought about March of last year. I had thought that my life was over then. Grade ten. Fifteen years old. Seems like a lifetime ago. In a way, it kind of was.

It was a late March afternoon and Connor was walking me to my bus stop after school. We were walking in the middle of a street that was so quiet we could have laid down on the pavement and not had to worry about being run over. He looked very perplexed.

"Penny for your thoughts?" I asked, shifting my big book bag from one shoulder to the other. It was crazy heavy because I'd been to the library earlier and stocked up on books to help me procrastinate with my homework. "Connor? Tell me what's wrong?"

"You won't like it," he grumbled, putting his hands in his pockets and looking at his feet.

I took a big step in front of him so he couldn't walk any farther.

"Well, now you have to tell me."

"Beth, when you left my place yesterday evening…" He paused and shifted from one foot to the other. "Jane came over."

My heart jumped into my throat. I had seen the way she looked at him and vice versa.

"We were watching a movie," Connor continued, "and next thing I know... we were making out."

My ears started to ring. I could see that Connor's mouth was still moving, but I could not hear a word he was saying. God, I was pissed!

Without thinking, I swiftly grabbed my book bag off my shoulder and swung it up into his gut. He made a shocked, wheezing sound and stumbled back, tripping on his own feet. Rage pumped through my veins as I kicked him in the balls, screaming, "WHY?"

Connor started to crawl to the side of the road, placing himself on the edge of the sidewalk.

"She was looking at me in that way, you know?" he heaved. "And Jane is really pretty."

"What?" I bellowed, towering over him. "She's like a billion fucking pounds, you motherfucker!"

Connor leaned away from me and looked into my eyes.

"It's you I love, Beth," he gasped, holding onto his crotch with one hand and his gut with the other. "Really! But I understand if you don't want to be with me anymore."

One of his hands reached out and was touching my knee. I stood in front of him for a moment with tears of anger and emotional pain in my eyes.

If I dumped Connor right then, Jane would get him and that fat fuck would win. No way in hell I was about to let that happen.

Best friend my ass! Even if I was keeping him out of spite, that asshole was mine! I took a deep breath and pushed his hand away from me, by kicking his shoulder lightly... ish. Then I crouched down in front of him.

"Look at me," I snarled. "You're staying with me. You can be friends with that backstabbing bitch, but if you so much as look at her in any kind of seductive way... you will be so sorry."

Unfortunately, for the next month Jane was bitchy enough (and Connor had been moronic and horny enough) to make out (and almost more) every time they saw each other when I was not around. He finally broke off the fucked-up relationship the day I found out about a more recent affair Connor had failed to inform me about, which was relayed to me in a very graphic note from Jane, taped to my locker.

That day Connor was waiting on the fence in front of my house after school. As soon as I saw him through the window on the bus, I took off my backpack. I kept a straight face as I jaywalked across my street into my driveway, where he greeted me with a goofy, unbrushed-toothy grin. Then I pulled the note out with one hand, and with the other, I socked him in the face with my backpack. He dropped the three feet off the fence, landing on his knees, the concrete ripping his only pair of jeans. I stepped closer, threw my bag at him, then read the note loud enough for a couple of my neighbours to hear. After that, he never saw her again.

And now, a year later, he was after Candice. And that pimple-faced freak wasn't telling him to back off, at least according to a guy I just met—a really *hot* guy who gave me butterflies just thinking his name.

Rudy.

CHAPTER 10
GOSSIP

As soon as I entered the resource centre on the fourth floor, three girls I had spoken to maybe once before ran up to me. One of them burst into tears and threw her arms around me, sobbing into my shoulder. Over hers, I saw Candice, who was careful not to make eye contact with me.

"Really?" I heard Fuzzy say to her. *"Really?"*

"Beth, I am so, so, so sorry," the girl bawled. "I know you were really close with your mom; you talked about her a lot."

Everyone in the room was staring at us. I patted her on the back and she stepped away. Then she looked around at all the pupils and screamed, "What are you all looking at?"

The other two girls had tears in their eyes, but didn't say anything. One just squeezed my hands and the other squeezed my shoulders.

Those were the gestures that got to me.

"Fuck," I breathed as my eyes welled up. "I have to go."

I buried my face in my hands, turned on my heel, and bolted toward the girl's bathroom. I threw myself against the door with my side, making it swing open and slam into the wall behind it with a loud *BANG!*

I hurried to the last stall and kicked it open, rushing inside it and slamming it behind me. It was a good ten seconds of fumbling with the lock before I gave up, leaning my back against the door and slowly sliding down to the floor. My bag landed with a *thump* next to me.

Hugging my knees to my chest, I shoved my face into my knees. I could feel the cold tile floor through my jeans.

"My life sucks, my life sucks, my life sucks..." I mumbled over and over again. I looked up and reached into my bag, pulling out a black permanent marker and scribbling "LIFE SUCKS" on the wall beside me. I ran my fingers over the ink to make sure it would not smudge. It didn't, so I added "really, really sucks" in smaller letters underneath it.

Everyone in the school knew who I was. Not because I was really smart (which I was not), not because I was a great athlete (which I was not), not because I was caught in the make-out closet with Connor's hand up my shirt (which I had), but because my mom had killed herself.

I should have known that Candice would go around telling everyone, making the suicide about her.

"Fuck," I almost yelled, hitting the back of my head on the door behind me. I was going to say it again, but I heard someone enter the bathroom.

"Beth?"

"What?"

"It's me. Candice."

"I know. What do you want?"

"Where are you?"

"In the last stall."

I heard her walk toward me and I pushed all my weight against the unlocked door. I felt her try to push it open, but when it didn't budge, she gave up.

"Can I come in?"

"No," I said flatly. She said nothing. "I can't believe you went and told all those people!" I cried, slamming my fists on the floor.

"It's big news, Beth," Candice said, as if that excused her behaviour.

"I know that," I scolded through the door. "But it's *my* news to share. That's if I want to even! God, it's you telling everyone about my epilepsy all over again! Everyone thought I was dying."

"So you want me to stop telling people about your mom?" Candice whimpered.

Picked up on that, did you?

"I never wanted you to start, Candice. Look, I know you like to gossip, but you have to learn the difference between 'gossip' and 'personal information'."

"Okay," Candice agreed. "I won't tell anyone else."

I let out a deep shuddering breath and eventually stood up. I grabbed my bag off the floor and pulled it onto my back, opening the stall door as I did.

Candice greeted me with a gentle hug that I stiffly returned. She took my hand as she let go and led me back to the resource centre room.

I avoided all eye contact when we entered it, spotting an empty desk between Connor and Fuzzy and slipping into the wooden seat. The two boys smiled at me and I shook my head. Recognizing the feeling of people watching me, I sighed and closed my eyes, waiting for this day to be over.

Drama was the next and last class of the day. Fuzzy had signed up for the class because I did, and Candice signed up for it because Fuzzy did. Connor had little to no interest in it, so he planted a very sloppy, very long kiss on my mouth before heading off to biology. Fuzzy put his arm around my shoulders, almost protectively, as we made our way through the gossipy hallways to our last class.

At the beginning of every drama class, everyone arranges the class chairs in a circle and takes a seat, waiting for their cohorts to arrive. There was a fainting couch, from a play a few years ago, that Fuzzy and I had sat in every day last year, so it was not a surprise that it was empty and waiting for us when we got there. It was basically permanently dibbed for the two of us. Candice always sat, grumpily, beside Fuzzy on a classroom chair.

As soon as everyone sat down, including our teacher Mr. Thomas (Mr. T, as everyone called him), we would go around the circle and talk about what we had done the day before, in order to get used to talking in front of other people. Nothing changed this semester, besides the fact that I did not want to go first. So Candice did.

"On break I did a lot of things," she began. "I read, and cleaned my room, and other stuff happened." Her eyes flashed over to me and Fuzzy on the couch. We both shook our heads. I don't think I had ever seen Fuzzy give anyone a look that cold, not even Connor. "That's all," Candice said quickly, glancing toward the guy beside her to start.

Before I knew it, beside me, Fuzzy was finishing up what he had done and then glancing over to me, his eyes giving me a worried look.

All eyes on me, I took a deep breath. Fuzzy put his arm around my shoulders, helping me stay calm.

"On the break, uh… my mom died," I announced, just barely above a whisper. Nobody moved. Nobody made a sound. "It happened the first day of spring break. There's a service on Sunday at two at St. Patrick's Funeral Home, if anyone wants to… you know… go."

The silence was starting to get to me when finally a girl said, "Someone told me, but I didn't think it was true."

Fuzzy and I threw a look at Candice, who was looking at the ceiling.

"How did she die?" a guy named Brett asked.

I cleared my throat. "She… it was…" *Why am I so nervous?* "It was her choice," I said cryptically.

A couple of people did not understand but knew it must have been bad by the horrified looks on my classmates' faces.

Unable to look at anyone, I put my face in Fuzzy's chest. He wrapped both of his arms around me and I felt his breath on my hair.

"She's a little overwhelmed right now," Candice told the class.

Thank you, Madam Obvious.

Comments and questions were flying at me from every direction.

"Why are you here?"

"Shouldn't you be at home?"

"Poor Beth."

"I can't believe a mom would do that!"

Nobody bothered to keep their voice down. Fuzzy held me tighter.

"What about you, Mr. T?" he asked loudly. "What did you do?"

The class quieted down, and (not leaving Fuzzy's embrace) I shifted my head to look at my teacher.

"I turned fifty," he said.

"Happy birthday," I sniffled.

"Thank you, Beth." Mr. T smiled, his eyes filled with pity. "I was going to do some improv today, but let's just… take it easy." He stood up, dismissed the circle, and walked over to Fuzzy, Candice, and I.

"Beth, can I talk to you?" he asked, blocking my view from the rest of the class on the other side of the room. I nodded, not wanting to move. Mr. T could tell that I was comfortable where I was, so he continued. "Are you sure that you want to do the school play with what happened?"

"Yes!" I exclaimed. "I need it now more than ever! I need something to do, and I've never gotten a lead before."

"Okay," Mr. Thomas said, holding up a hand to politely shush me. "I just don't want too much on your plate. Rehearsals start today at three-thirty."

"Thank you for your concern, but I'll be kay." I half-heartedly smiled as he walked away, and turned back to Fuzzy. I looked up at my friend and smiled; then my brow furrowed when I saw the look on his face. He was staring over the top of my head, looking very confused.

I looked over my shoulder and noticed everyone staring at me. To my surprise, it was Brett, whom I had never gotten along with, who approached me first. He bent down, pushed Fuzzy's arm off of me, and replaced it with his own. He wordlessly held me for a moment, and when he let go, every single person in my class followed his actions.

Every person bent down and put their arms around me. Some said nothing, others whispered words of encouragement in my ear. One girl actually kissed my cheek and said I was beautiful even when I was sad.

I can promise you this: It was the most beautifully sad moment of my entire life.

CHAPTER 11
REHEARSAL

After the bell rang, I stayed behind for rehearsal while everyone else left. Fuzzy was the last to leave, giving me an extra strong hug.

"Daniel, off you go." Mr. Thomas approached, holding a binder in his hand. Fuzzy grumbled something and slumped out the door. "All right Beth, here you go. Your script is in here. I've highlighted your lines. Why don't you flip through it while the rest of the cast arrives?" I took the binder from his hands and sat back on the fainting couch, smiling.

I opened it and ran my fingers over the black print, thinking, *I have so many lines! Yes!*

Someone sat beside me, and I glanced over and smiled—then did a double take.

"Hey, Beth." Rudy smiled at me. I was glad that I was sitting down, because I felt my knees wobble.

"Hey," I smiled, watching him take his binder out of his bag. I heard the classroom door open and looked over my shoulder to see who the next cast member was. My heart dropped when I saw that it was one of the school bullies who had made up a lot of seizure jokes at my expense. I cannot tell you how many times I had locked myself in the bathroom crying because of that bitch.

"Hey, Beth," she sneered.

"Hey, Lindsey," I scowled back at her, then remembered what I could do to piss her off. "Aren't you going to congratulate me? I got the part of Mimi." I raised my script so she could see it and waved it at her.

"Yeah," she snarled, and then replaced it with a deadly smile. "But I also wanted to say that I'm sorry to hear about—"

I stopped her before she could finish her sentence. There was still at least one person who did not know about my mom and he was sitting right beside me.

"Yes, thank you," I snapped, turning away from her quickly. I felt Rudy watching me. "What?" I asked simply.

"What was that?" he asked, nodding at Lindsey (who was now getting her script from Mr. T). "I know she's a bitch, but what's she sorry for?"

"Oh, I have epilepsy and over the break my seizures started again, after about a year without having one," I lied, shrugging.

"Oh, man, I'm sorry," Rudy frowned, patting my knee. I could feel the heat from his hand up and down my leg.

"Thanks," I smiled. There was a pause between us as we looked over our scripts some more.

"So, tell me about him," he said suddenly.

"About who?" I blinked, confused.

"Your boyfriend. Connor, was it?"

My brow furrowing, I shrugged and answered his question. "I dunno, he's nice enough. His mom is the art teacher here. Straight A's. We've been together about a year now."

"A year? Wow," Rudy repeated, looking impressed. "So, you guys are pretty serious?" I swear I saw disappointment in his eyes.

"Yeah, I suppose. Committed or whatever."

"You don't mind that he can be a total dick?" he asked, putting his arm across the back of the couch. "I mean, he was flirting with your best friend or whatever she is. That's not cool."

"Everyone has their baggage," I answered.

Why was I talking to this guy about my love life? For some reason I felt I could trust him, and that did not happen very often. Trusting anyone at all, ever.

"How old are you?" Rudy asked, changing the subject.

"Sixteen," I replied. "What about you?"

"Seventeen. I'm graduating this year," he announced, proudly.

"Lucky!" I moaned. "I can't wait to graduate and get out of here!"

"You don't seem like a girl who would stick around for long."

Now that I have a little sister to raise, I don't have a choice but to stay.

"Okay, cast and crew!" Mr. Thomas called, clapping his hands loudly, getting everyone's attention. During our conversation, about twenty other people had joined us in the drama room. "Let's get started."

He sat down behind his desk and everyone turned their seats to make as semi-circle around him. Rudy and I did not move the couch. We just turned around and pressed our stomachs to the back of it so we were facing our director. I could not help but notice that our sides were touching each other. I think Rudy noticed too, judging by the smile he gave me.

"Does everyone know everyone?" Mr. T asked, looking around the room. I at least recognized everyone, but considering the pitying looks they all gave me (except for Rudy and Lindsey) I was pretty sure that everyone knew my name. Rudy gave me a flirty smile and Lindsey looked ready to claw my face off. Mr. Thomas continued. "We all know the parts we have? Well, let's start from the beginning. Brett," he nodded at the guy sitting a few chairs to the left of me, "you start as Mark. Let's work on everyone's cues today. *Rent* is the loudest song in the performance and has basically everything to do with timing, so it'll take a while."

It really was very difficult. The beginning was mainly Rudy and Brett, which was fine. Even though there were only about four lines from everyone else, we'd all had to stay while we ran through the scene four times, before we were all told to go home and practise.

It was going on five and I was surprised to hear my stomach grumble as I headed down the hallway to the foyer. It was the first time I'd heard that sound since my mom died. I placed my hand on my tummy and wondered what to do.

Do I even bother trying to eat? I'll probably just throw it up anyway...

"You okay?" someone asked, tapping my shoulder.

I whipped around, my heart pounding. "What?" I gasped, as I faced Rudy.

"Your hand is on your gut. Are you okay?" he asked again. "You look queasy."

"Oh," I said, dropping my hand. "Tired," I lied. "And hungry, I think." I started walking again with Rudy beside me.

"Well, if you're hungry, there's that pizza place across the plaza," Rudy suggested, nodding in the other direction. "I could buy you a slice."

"No," I declined, a little too quickly. I was already flirting with the guy earlier; I did not want to lead him on (or have *him* lead *me* on). "I have to go home."

"Oh... all right, I guess," Rudy mumbled, stopping in his tracks. "Well, I'm going to get one," he told me, turning around. "See you tomorrow. Oh, and I'm sorry for being the one to tell you about Connor and what's-her-face flirting."

"Don't worry about it. I'm glad I know that I have to look out for them," I said over my shoulder, as I continued to the main entrance.

This isn't fair, I thought. *Now I have to look out for Connor and Candice, not just my little sister.*

As soon as I got home, I headed straight to Amy's room and sat down beside her on her bed.

"So, how was it?" I asked her. "How did you tell your friends?"

Amy looked up at me from the book she was reading and folded it closed in her lap. "It was weird," she answered, crossing her legs beneath her. *Marmee won't be here now to teach her to shave her legs,* I thought.

"Yeah, it was weird for me too," I said, putting my cold fingers under my butt to warm them up. "Telling my friends was—"

"No, I mean... it was weird how they already knew."

"What?" I was surprised. "You were careful not to tell anyone. Except Clair, who was sworn to secrecy."

"I know, I called her when I got home and she had only told her parents." She shrugged. "I don't know how anyone found out. But my teacher was awful."

"How so?"

"When I was out of the room, she told my entire class what happened... and *how* it happened."

"WHAT?! Are you kidding me?" I jumped to my feet.

Amy shook her head.

"She had no right!" I ranted. "God, that bitch!"

"I know, she's the worst," Amy agreed, wincing at my language. "My friends were heartbroken. Abby was wailing in my arms before the bell even rang for class. What about your friends?"

"Well," I took a deep breath and sat down again, "Candice went into some kind of shock and Fuzzy almost fainted or something." I made sure to leave out that we'd cried in each other's arms. "My teachers, actually the entire school staff, knew in a couple hours. As soon as Candice was out of earshot, she told anyone who would listen. She even played the victim card somehow. And I told my drama class because, well... they're the drama class." I left out the weird group hug, and my new friend who made my knees wobble. I just summed up the most depressing day at school ever.

I lay back on her bed, missing the wall by inches, and ran my fingers through my hair.

"Are you going to say anything at the funeral?" Amy asked me, pulling at her own hair.

"Yeah," I nodded. "I'm gonna talk about how she used to warn me about a scary movie, and then we'd have to turn it off because she'd get too freaked out. And about how she'll come back as a tabby cat. And how we used to get a coffee before we would head up island, and then she'd have to pee halfway up, so we'd pull over so she could go in the bushes."

By now my sister and I were laughing hard at the thought of those fond memories, but I stopped suddenly when I realized that there weren't going to be anymore made. The last memory I had of my mom was her calling every fifteen minutes to say goodbye to my sister and me getting annoyed because I wanted to watch a movie.

I was annoyed at my mom while she was popping every pill in her house.

Amy snapped me out of my morbid thoughts. "I'll probably write a poem. A short one, of course. Not Poppies Fields."

"Do you know if *Will* is going to say anything?" I asked coolly.

"I don't know," Amy shrugged. "What do you have against that guy? He's really nice. I mean, you called him Dad."

"I only called him that so he and Marmee wouldn't get divorced. The plan worked for a while. Before Will and Marmee moved to Matched Lane, they were going to get a divorce. They were still drinking a lot. Then they stopped fighting, kept drinking… then started fighting, then stopped drinking… then stopped fighting… and then separated."

Amy didn't say anything and I did not tell her about the diary I had found.

"Well, I'm going to work on the eulogy," I told my sister, sitting up.

"Okay," Amy said, stretching her legs out again and opening her book.

I left her room and headed to my own, where I sat down at my desk and prepared to write. I pulled my notebook in front of me and grabbed a pen from my desk drawer, which was askew. I held the tip of the pen less than an inch from the blank sheet, and stared blankly down at the light blue lines. A minute ago I was telling my sister what I was planning to write: funny memories and anecdotes. Now I had no idea. Why should I say something funny? Shouldn't it be mournful? If I said those things, it would literally be roasting my mom at her own funeral. I took a deep breath and began to scribble away. I wrote down memories, then crossed a couple out. At the very end of it, I wrote: "My mom loved a lot of things, and this song was one of them." Queue Tom Petty's "Free Falling".

I put down my pen and pulled my cell out of my pocket, quickly dialling my aunt's number.

"Hello?"

"Hi, Auntie," I said, stretching my cramped-up fingers. Looking at my clock, I saw that I had been writing for almost an hour.

"Hey, sweetie, how are you?"

"I'm okay."

"How was your first day?"

I summed up my day, almost like a copy and paste of what I had told Amy, and then added, "I just finished Marmee's eulogy."

"Really? Can I hear it?"

"Of course, that's why I called." I cleared my throat and read the whole thing through and through. Afterwards there was silence on the line from both ends while I waited for an opinion. I could not wait anymore. "Is it okay?"

"Sweetie, it's wonderful," she assured me, her voice catching.

"I'm glad you like it," I told her, feeling my shoulders relax. "I wanted you to hear it."

"I'm glad you read it to me."

"Dinner!" my dad called from the kitchen.

"I should go." I stood up. "Have a good night, Auntie. Say hi to Uncle for me."

"I will."

We hung up and I put my cell beside my notebook. I closed it quickly and shoved it into my backpack. I didn't want anyone to read what I was going to say.

"Dinner! Bethy, dinner!" my dad called again.

"I heard you!" I hollered back, leaving my room. As I spoke, the smell of mashed potatoes wafted its way through the house and my mouth began to water.

Amy was already at the table, holding a fork ready in front of a plate of potatoes, peas and chicken. It was a house rule that no one was allowed to eat until we were all seated at the table. I sat down across from Amy, and just to annoy her, *very slowly* shovelled a scoop of potatoes onto my plate. Knowing my evil plan, my sister rolled her eyes and more or less inhaled her food anyway. As I put a spoonful of peas on my plate, I remembered how we used to have to say grace at Marmee's house, after she and Will started going to AA. My sister and I never said it. We just sat there, our hands limply draped in each other's, while someone, usually Will, thanked God for all the food and stuff. I remembered that I actually had a cross in my room and made a metal note to throw it out later on and out myself as a Buddhist on Facebook.

"How was your day, Bethy?" my dad asked, picking up his fork and working on his own dinner.

My plate had the least amount of food on it as usual, and not because I had already eaten. A couple months ago, Connor had told me I was getting fat. Since then I had rationed my meals and tried extra hard in PE.

"You know," I shrugged, placing a couple of peas on my tongue.

"What about you, Amy?" Dad said, turning to my sister. He knew that was all he was going to get out of me. Amy told him about what her teacher did while she had been out of the room, telling everyone everything, and he had about the same reaction as me, minus the swearing.

"That's *awful!*" my dad cried, dropping his cutlery. "I should call the school! That woman is just terrible!"

"Whatever, Daddy, it happened. It's done." Amy sighed, not wanting a big scene.

It took a while for my dad to calm down. I had almost finished my dinner by the time his face had finally turned back to its usual colour under his big beard.

"Do you two have any homework?" he grumbled, snatching the dishes off the table once they were bare.

"No," I said. "I was practically kicked out of English, and psych was just catch up. I do have to go through my lines though."

"That's right, the play," my dad said, putting the dishes in the sink. "How was your first rehearsal?"

"Pretty good," I replied, smiling at the thought of sitting next to Rudy and him nudging me with his hip. "We went through the first scene today. I didn't realize I would have so many lines."

"Well, practise makes perfect," my dad pointed out.

"Well," I sighed, standing up and stretching. "No one is perfect so why practise?"

"Elizabeth..." he groaned in a warning tone.

"I'm kidding!" I laughed as I headed to my room. "Thanks for dinner."

I closed my bedroom door behind me and pulled my script out of my bag. I sat down on my bed, flipped it open to the first page, and saw that someone had scribbled on it just above Rudy's first line.

"Call me. 250-794-8529. Rudy."

Rudy gave me his number? What the hell?

I grabbed my cell off my desk, unlocked it, punched in the number, and texted:

-Rudy?

A few minutes later: -Beth?

-Yeah. Why did u give me your number?

A moment later: -I like you, that's why.

I gaped at the phone and snapped it shut again.

"What the f—" I started to say, but my phone rang, interrupting me. I looked down at the caller ID and saw the name "Connor" flashing up at me. Feeling a little disappointed, I answered it. "Hey, Connor."

"Hey, you," he said, before quickly adding, "Wanna have phone sex?"

CHAPTER 12
FRENEMIES

The rest of the week was basically a repeat of Monday. Sympathetic looks given to me by complete strangers in the hall, and strong sincere hugs given to me by classmates I had never spoken to before. Whenever either of these things happened, Candice always avoided eye contact after. I was practically kicked out of every class by teachers, and a few times I suddenly burst into tears and dashed into the nearest washroom to hide out.

Candice was no help at all. On Tuesday morning, she told everyone who would listen about how she told her dad about my mom's death:

"I was waiting at the dining room table when he got home and I asked for a hug, which I, like... never do, and he asked what was wrong, and I, like... *burst* into tears about Beth's mom. I don't know what I would do if I lost my dad. I'm not very close to my mom; I hardly ever talk to her... maybe I should call her?" She had memorized this speech. By the end of the day, Fuzzy and I had memorized it as well and would lip-sync her monologue behind her back. We were both surprised at how she had started to act. It was like Candice to try and make everything about her, but it was surprising that she was trying to get people to think that she was a victim when what had happened had *nothing to do with her*.

I was very thankful for Fuzzy. He was always giving me hugs or keeping a protective arm around me when Connor was not around. When my boyfriend was with us, Fuzzy would make a point of looking away or glaring at Connor's inappropriately wandering hands.

At Thursday's rehearsal, Rudy sat next to me again. My heart pounded in my chest when his hand brushed against mine as he turned the page in his script binder.

"Now, you two are aware that there's a kissing scene between your characters, right?" Mr. Thomas said as we were packing up. Mr. T was a friend of Connor's mom, so he knew I'd been in a relationship with her son for over a year. "We'll probably being going through that song next rehearsal."

"Wait, the... the what now?" I stammered, spinning around to face our teacher.

"Okay." Rudy grinned, cocking an eyebrow at me.

"I get to... I mean, have to... kiss Rudy?" I asked, grabbing my script and flipping wildly through the pages looking for the scene.

"Yeah, a couple times. The first is right... here." Rudy shrugged, flipping through his own script and pointing to a circled part in the second act. After everything that happened during spring break, I had completely forgotten that Roger and Mimi kiss!

I skimmed through it over his shoulder and glanced up at him. "Why is it circled?" I asked quietly, tracing my index finger along the pink highlight. "Won't it be a little awkward?" I asked, looking up at Mr. T.

"C'mon, Beth. It's not like I'm taking your shirt off," Rudy pointed out, not answering my question about the highlighted 'action'.

"Connor's not going to like this," I sighed, running my fingers through my hair.

"Neither will Daniel." When I gave him a confused look, Rudy explained. "Fuzzy."

I kept forgetting Fuzzy's real name was Daniel.

I shook my head and turned back to Mr. T. "Okay, thanks for telling us," I said, as Mr. T grabbed a satchel-type thing from beside his desk.

"Okay everyone, here Monday at three thirty," Mr. T said loudly, not realizing that almost everyone had left already. He turned around and left the classroom with the rest of the cast, leaving Rudy and I packing up our things.

"Hey, Beth?" Rudy asked as I zipped up my backpack.

"Yeah?" I answered, shrugging it on and turning to face him.

He was leaning against Mr. T's desk, with his head bowed, looking over at me from behind his long eyelashes. "I was wondering if you wanted to practise or something this weekend?" he asked, turning redder by the word.

My jaw dropped. "You want to practise… kissing? *Me?*"

Rudy nodded, a small smile playing at his lips. "It could be fun. And the lines need work too." He added quickly.

So much of me wanted to say yes, but there was Connor to think about and my mom's funeral was on Sunday.

"I'm sorry, Rudy," I sighed, running my fingers through my hair. "I can't. This weekend is no good for me."

"Why not?" Rudy asked, nearly pouting. He started walking over to me and I had to bite my lip to stop myself from *rehearsing* right then and there.

"Well, there's Connor. And I have plans."

"What kind of plans?" he pried, now a foot away from me.

"Unbreakable ones," I answered, noting that he did not question the fact that I had a boyfriend. "I have a boyfriend," I reminded myself out loud.

Rudy licked his lips and we stared at each other for a moment. He sighed and took a step back. "All right. See you tomorrow." He sounded defeated. Crossing the room, he grabbed his bag and walked out without giving me a chance to answer.

On Friday, all I could do was think about Sunday. I would be saying goodbye to my mom for good. She had been cremated. All Marmee was now was memories and ashes.

"How ya holdin' up?" Fuzzy asked at lunch.

I shrugged with one shoulder. "It's not easy."

"Tell me about it," Candice chimed in. "I have no idea what I'm going to wear on Sunday. I know dark colours, but I don't look very good in dark colours. They make me look too skinny."

"No one will be taking pictures of you," Fuzzy snapped. "Jesus."

Candice glared at him as a comeback. Or that might have her usual face; it was hard to tell.

"I meant to ask you how rehearsal was yesterday, baby," Connor asked, putting his arm around my waist and pulling me closer.

"Oh, it was good," I said, smiling. "Turns out there are a couple kissing scenes," I added under my breath.

"There are *what*?" all my friends said at once, gaping at me.

"Yeah. Between me and…" I glanced at Candice, "this guy. We're rehearsing on Monday."

"Wow. Is it like a peck or… ?" Fuzzy asked, leaning in.

"No, it's like a kind of like a… seductive peck."

"Can't wait to see it," Connor said, stealing one of my untouched fries.

"You're not jealous?" I asked, surprised.

"Well, it's not like you *like* the guy… and *I'm* the one who gets to have sex with you." He shrugged and smirked.

I exhaled angrily through my nose. Fuzzy looked at me with curious eyes.

"So are you looking forward to rehearsing it?" Fuzzy asked.

"Kind of nervous," I answered honestly.

"Why? Are you a bad kisser?" Candice asked.

"What? No!" I said. "There's gonna be a lot of people there and… stuff."

"You're really not afraid that you're a bad kisser?" Candice asked again.

"At least *I've* kissed someone, Candice, so just shut up, okay?" I barked.

"Well, of course you have. You're totally promiscuous."

We all stared at her, waiting for her to say that she was joking, but she just started texting someone.

"*What* did you just call me?" I growled.

"You heard me," Candice said simply.

"So, you're saying that she has casual sex?" Fuzzy said. "Really? She's been with Connor for over a year now."

"Yeah, but before him there was Aaron, Jake, and she was totally in love with Orlando,"

"Having a crush on someone and making out with a guy is not being a total whore, Candice! It's being a high school girl!" I snapped, thanking God that she didn't know about a make-out session I had with a girl named Allie the year before on a dare.

"Well, you are! You have sex all the time!"

"Yeah, but with the same guy! Ugh, whatever. At least I'm not a virgin." I grabbed my bag and stomped away from her, closely followed by Fuzzy and Connor.

"Guys!" Candice yelled after us, running to catch up. "What did I do?"

"You called your best friend a slut, Candice!" Fuzzy snapped over his shoulder.

"I didn't mean to hurt your feelings, Bethy," she pouted. "I'd never do that."

"Candice, just..." I stopped, turned around, and held up a hand to shut her up. "*Never* say that again. *Ever*. Even if you think it's true."

Tears welled up in her eyes and her lower lip quivered. "I'm sorry," she whimpered.

"Look, we're all aware of the tragedy of being you. But right now, let Beth be a victim, okay?" Fuzzy said quietly. He put his arm around my shoulders for a moment. Then he remembered that Connor was on my other side and took a step away from me.

As Candice began to scream at Fuzzy, I stepped away from them, and with a certain look, convinced Connor to skip the rest of school for me.

CHAPTER 13

THE FUNERAL

"Sweetheart?" My dad tapped his fingers on my door. "Sweetheart, are you ready?"

"I'll be out in a minute," I choked out and listened to him walked away.

It was early Sunday afternoon, and I was sitting on my bed, all dressed up and holding the wooden cross necklace in my hands that I still had not thrown out.

How could there possibly be a God if people had to go through such shit? Diagnosed with epilepsy at eleven, unsuccessful brain surgery at thirteen, bullied through middle school, dead mom at sixteen. That was not even the whole list. And that was just me; so many people had it much worse than I did. I had only started to pray because my mom did and I wanted to support her to help her stay in AA.

Fuck that. Just fuck it.

I tossed the crucifix in my trash bin and stood up just as my sister walked in without knocking. She was wearing a blue t-shirt and a dark blue skirt, beautiful, as usual. Her big blue eyes looked me up and down. I had chosen a dark brown blouse and a loose black skirt that billowed out down to my knees.

"I can't remember the last time I wore a skirt," I told her as she crossed the room to me.

"Neither can I," she said, reaching over my shoulders and taking my hair out of its usual twisted bun. "Wear it down. It really does look nice." She put the hair tie on her wrist. "Ready?"

To say goodbye? I thought, but just nodded and followed her out of my room.

My dad was standing at the top of the stairwell, wearing a black suit and dress shoes I did not know he owned.

"So, the three of us will be sitting at the front, girls," he instructed, as I put on my only pair of heels and Amy slipped on her black flats.

"Why?" I asked, patting down my hair and starting down the steps.

"Because that's where the family sits at a funeral," he told me.

"Bethy, you forgot this," Amy said, handing me a paper over my dad's shoulder. I took it. *How could I forget the eulogy?*

We made our way out of the house and clambered into Dad's huge van.

The drive to St. Patrick's Funeral Home was very quiet. I read over my speech a couple of times until I started to feel car sick and folded it back up.

We finally pulled to a stop across the road from the funeral home.

"I can't believe Will paid for all of this," Dad muttered, taking Amy's hand as we crossed the street. The parking lot was already full and I watched, surprised, as loads of people made their way inside.

There was a quiet buzz of conversation in the foyer, which held at least 60 people, too many vases of flowers to count, and a guest book propped up on a wooden desk.

I wove myself through the crowds of people to the book. *I'm her daughter; I should be the first to sign it.*

I took a pen out of someone's hand and leaned over the white and gold pages, which were already covered in signatures and notes of sorrow. I fought off the urge to scratch out, 'Will Smart, husband'.

"Shitty husband," I hissed, and then continued down the page and froze at the words: '*Terrance Morgan, older brother*'. I had never met my uncle before. I had heard stories, but never even seen a picture. Below that name read '*Mrs. K, wife of the late John Morgan*'. That was my mom's stepmom. The same situation with her: stories but no pictures. They both lived in Ontario, that much I knew. I finally signed my name on an empty line on the third page.

"*Elizabeth Marsere, first-born daughter.*"

I put the pen down and stepped away from the desk so that people could sign the guest book. I turned away from it slowly, scanning the crowd, hoping to see Terrance or Mrs. K, and then remembered that I had no idea what they looked like.

"Whoa. Almost didn't recognize you," Fuzzy said behind me. "Hair down and a skirt? Not very Beth."

I turned around to face him. "Could say the same thing about you." I saw that he was wearing a blue shirt, black dress coat, and a black, poorly styled tie. "That jacket's way too big for you," I observed, nodding at the sleeves, which covered his fingertips, as I straightened his tie.

"It's my dad's," he explained, blushing and looking me in the eye before pulling me into a gentle hug that was wonderful to receive.

I saw Connor and Candice approach me from the guest book area and stepped away from Fuzzy, who quickly wiped something away from his eye.

"You look nice," Candice complimented Fuzzy, who barely noticed her. He was suddenly very interested in the wall behind us.

Connor stepped between us and embraced me. He smelt like strawberries and I wondered if his mom had paid him to shower.

"How are you?" he asked, his voice full of concern.

I shook my head and stepped away. "It's too much." I shuddered.

"I know how you feel," Candice agreed.

What? Like how Ringo knew how Yoko felt when John Lennon was shot right in front of her? How? How do you fucking know how I feel, bitch? I screamed at her in my head, but I turned away from her instead.

"A couple of teachers from school are here," Connor informed me, nodding over my shoulder. I followed his gaze, and sure enough, there was the career counsellor and vice-principal, both holding large bouquets of flowers and staring out the bay windows. My eyes swept over the growing crowd of people.

"I don't know, like... *anyone* here," I exaggerated, as I spotted Aunt Melanie walking toward me.

"Honey, we're about to start," she said when she reached us. My heart started racing and I thought I was about to throw up.

"Okay," I nodded. I left my friends to find Amy and Dad. As I made my way through the swarm of people, I saw heads turning and heard people muttering things like: That's Beth. She's the first born. Poor thing. I felt almost famous in a way. People I did not even know existed knew my name and my situation. I felt like I was on the front page of a tabloid called *Morbid*.

I linked my arm around Amy's and Dad took her hand, leading us into a room with rows and rows of benches, a long thin aisle, and a tall podium at the very end of it. We walked down the aisle together and sat down on the bench at the front of the room, just like my dad said we would. My sister placed herself between me and my dad. My cousin Ellie sat beside my dad. Aunt Melanie sat beside her, and my uncle Mitch sat on the end of our seat. Family really did sit in the front.

I looked over my shoulder and watched more people file in. I could tell that there were already triple digits in the room. There were, literally, no seats left. People were leaning against the walls in the back. Many of them had tears streaming down their faces.

I spotted Connor and his mom sitting a couple of rows behind me, and behind them Fuzzy and Candice were talking. Well, Candice was talking; Fuzzy was staring straight ahead, expressionless.

Eventually a man stepped up to the podium and all the attention turned on him.

"We are here for Margret Smart-Morgan," he said loudly. There was no need for him to raise his voice. The room had gone dead quiet as soon as he opened his mouth. "She left us at the young age of 45 and we are here to celebrate those years. Her daughter Elizabeth would like to share a few words." He stepped away and I shakily got to my feet. I strode over to the podium and leaned against it to keep my balance. Taking a few deep breaths, I looked up just to have them taken away from me again.

"Wow," I said stupidly. "There are more people here than I thought." A couple of people chuckled, but I was not kidding. "My mom was an amazing person, a great friend too. As much as I'm going to miss her, I thought I'd share some fun stories I have about her, instead of sad ones…"

And so I told everyone about buying coffee before driving up island and her having to pee before we got home. I told them about how she would get scared before me, while watching scary movies. I told them about how she wanted to come back as a tabby cat in her second life. Finally, I said, "Marmee loved a lot of things, and she really loved this." I made my way to my seat as a song by Tom Petty and The Heartbreakers starting playing through hidden speakers. As I sat next to Amy, I caught myself mouthing the words to "Free Fallin'". I closed my eyes and leaned my head back. I remembered being picked up on a Friday afternoon and clambering into my mom's ugly blue Honda with Amy, slamming the doors behind us, and turning on the tape player. I had made a collection of mixed tapes to listen to on the drive and every one of them contained this song. And be damned if we didn't sing at the top of our lungs to the chorus of this song *every* time it came on.

"*And I'm FREE!*
Free Fallin'
Yeah, I'm FREEEEEE!

Free Fallin'!"

When the song ended, I opened my eyes and there were tears on my cheeks. I did not bother brushing them away. Beside me, Amy stood up and walked over to the stand. She looked far more composed than me.

"I, uh... I wrote a poem for my mom," she said, unfolding a crumpled piece of paper onto the podium. I know that the poem was lovely, but I do not remember it. I remember more tears, and a few chuckles. I do not remember the words at all. When she took her seat, another Tom Petty and The Heartbreakers song came on, "Learning to Fly". It too was on all of the mix tapes, as per her request.

When the song faded away, the man I had completely forgotten about stepped up again.

"As this service comes to an end, if there is anyone else who would like to say a few words, please do so now," he announced, looking around the room.

Slowly, Aunt Melanie stood up and turned to face the rest of the mourners, her hand clasping Uncle Mitch's.

"Uh... hi," she said, shyly. "I'm Melanie, Margret's sister. We looked exactly alike, but no... I'm not her. I don't mind if anyone sees me and says 'hello'. Thank you for your condolences." She sat down. A few people mumbled "you're welcome" and "sorry for your loss". There were no sounds besides coughs and sniffles for a moment, until my dad's stepmom stood up.

"I'm Nancy, Amy and Beth's grandma. Thank you all for coming and may Margret rest in peace," she said, just loud enough for people near her to hear. She sat back down and for a few more minutes no one said anything. A small part of me dreaded that Candice might have the nerve to say something, but nothing came from her section. I had a feeling Fuzzy had something to do with her cat-held tongue.

"Well, there are refreshments and snacks in the back room, through those doors," the man informed everyone, gesturing to a pair of double doors on the right side of the room. "Thank you all for coming," he added before stepping down and making his way to the foyer.

Slowly, everyone got to their feet and I felt my dad touch my arm. "You should greet people at those doors," he said quietly in my ear. I nodded and slipped away from him. I pushed my way through the crowd and stood beside the doors like my dad had suggested.

People I did not recognize or hadn't seen in ages stopped and said morose hellos and gave gentle hugs, followed by weak, forced smiles.

After what seemed like hours of greeting people, someone grabbed my elbow and pulled me mercilessly into the refreshment room.

"What the f—"

"I need to talk to you," Candice hissed, pulling me into a corner.

"Right now? Really? Candice, this isn't the best time," I started, yanking my arm out of her grip. Her big blue eyes were larger than usual and she looked panicked.

"It's really important," she wined, wringing her hands.

I glared at her for a moment, then groaned. "What's going on?"

"It's Fuzzy," she breathed, looking over my shoulder.

I crossed my arms and looked over my shoulder. I spotted him sitting alone at a table, watching me. He caught my eye and gave me a quizzical look. I replied with an eye roll, then looked back at Candice.

"What about him?" I asked.

"Doesn't he look so handsome in that suit?" she breathed, her panic turning into an unsuppressed grin of glee.

"It's like... three sizes too big for him, but sure," I shrugged. "Wait... is *this* what is so important? His *suit?*"

"No!" she cried, grabbing my arms. "Beth, I think I'm in love with him."

"Candice, I know," I nodded. Was she really bringing this up *now?* At my mom's funeral? Seriously?

"Wait, what do you mean you *know?*" she demanded, looking surprised.

"Come on man," I groaned, running my fingers through my hair, which I felt like pulling out. "It's been obvious to me that you like him for, like… two years."

"It, it has?" Candice stammered.

"Yeah," I started counting off points on my fingers, watching her bite her lip. "You're crazy possessive of him; you glare at every girl that talks to him, including me; and you constantly ask him who he's talking to or texting… and not in a curious way. In a 'Oh my God, who the fuck is she?' kind of way."

"Are you serious?" she gasped. "Does he know?"

"I don't know. But you should probably back off a bit. It's really annoying. Now, *if* you don't mind, I'm going to get back to my mom's funeral." I turned on my heel and bee-lined straight for Fuzzy.

"Hey," he mumbled, standing and wrapping his arms around me again. "How're you doing?"

"Ugh." I grumbled into his chest, embracing him.

"What was Candice going on about? You didn't look pleased to be talking to her."

"She is so selfish." I shook my head and stepped away from him.

"I know." He took my arm and helped me into the chair that he had been sitting on. I stared at the lace table cloth while he poured two cups of coffee and offered me one, which I took gratefully. "You're speech was wonderful."

"Thanks," I mumbled, taking a gulp of my coffee.

"Whoa," Fuzzy said, his jaw dropping.

"What?" I asked, taking another sip. "What's wrong?"

"Beth, that coffee is black. You take your coffee with, like... five packs of sugar."

I looked down into the mug I was holding and saw that the drink was as black as tar, not a faded brown. "I guess my taste buds died, too," I said flatly, taking another sip.

"Oh, Beth…" Fuzzy sighed, reaching across the table and taking my hand in his, running his thumb over my knuckles. "Your hand is freezing."

"Hey." Connor seated himself beside me, and Fuzzy yanked his hand off of mine as if he had just been electrocuted. "How're you holding up?"

"I'm drinking black coffee," I mumbled, lacing my index finger through the holes of the lace table cloth.

"Black? Really? Are you feeling okay?"

"She's at her mom's funeral; what do you think?" Fuzzy grumbled, and I shot him a look that summed up it up. *Not now.*

I smiled weakly at Connor, and saw Candice walking over to the table.

She placed herself beside Fuzzy and took his coffee out of his hands. He rolled his eyes and I pushed my nearly empty mug over to him. This annoying coffee exchange was done quite often in the cafeteria in the mornings or at lunch. Never at a funeral before, but at school it was not uncommon.

"How're you doing, Bethy?" she inquired, sipping at Fuzzy's coffee. "Ugh, this is bitter," she spluttered before I could answer her question.

"It's *coffee* Candice; it's *supposed* to be bitter," I said, as if speaking to a five year old about not putting fingers into electrical sockets. "You say that every time you take Fuzzy's coffee. If you want coffee to taste the way *you* like it, why don't you get some for yourself?" I snatched the coffee pot in front of me, and took my cup back from Fuzzy. Then I poured the cup three-quarters full, put the pot down, pushed the cup over to Candice, along with the cream and sugar packets beside Connor, and sat back in my chair again. "There you go. Make it the way you want and stop bitching about the tiniest little things. God!" I crossed my arms and glared at my best frenemy.

Candice, Fuzzy, and Connor were all staring at me, their jaws open just a little. I was just glad I had kept my voice down or far more people would be looking at me with the same expression.

"Beth, I—"

I'd had enough of her shit, so I stood up and walked away.

I made my way between small groups of people chatting quietly with each other. I spotted my aunt talking to my sister and a tall man standing next to her, smiling down at Amy. An older woman was standing on my aunt's other side.

"Hi," I waved, stopping beside my sister and wrapping my arm around her shoulders.

"Bethy, this is our uncle Terrance and Mrs. K," Amy said, gesturing to the man and the older woman, who grabbed my hands.

"Let me look at you." She smiled warmly, while she looked me up and down with a pair of kind brown eyes. I looked at her the same way. Mrs. K was my height with short curly grey hair. "You look so much like her," Mrs. K sighed, almost dreamily. I glanced over at my aunt and mentally compared our features. I had always thought that, besides our dark green eyes and brown hair, we did not share any physical similarities, but seeing as my mom had been beautiful, I smiled at the compliment.

"Thank you," I said, as she let go of my hands. I found it amazing that my aunt had stayed close to her father's widow, even twenty or so years after his death.

"Beth, it is so nice to meet you," my uncle Terrance then said, pulling me into a hug. "I'm so sorry about Margret."

"Me too," I choked out as our embrace ended. "How long are you in town?"

"About a week," he answered. "I'd love to get to know you and Amy better."

"We'd like that," Amy said beside me.

"We'll have the two of you over for dinner on Thursday; how does that sound?" Aunt Melanie suggested, glancing around the circle of her family.

"Sounds like a plan," I nodded, glancing at Amy who was smiling and nodding.

I suddenly felt a hand on my shoulder and heard my dad clear his throat behind me. Amy and I turned around to face him as he nodded at Mrs. K, Aunt Melanie, and Uncle Terrance.

"Sweethearts, we should get going soon. Guests are leaving too," Dad told us, looking at his watch. "It's past five now and we need to load all the flowers into the van still."

"W-what?" I stuttered, looking around at the vases surrounding us and remembering the rest in the foyer. "We are keeping these?" My dad nodded. "How is it already five o'clock?" I added under my breath.

"Yeah, the time did go fast for such a sad day," Amy agreed. "I'm going to go say bye to my friends; then I'll help with the flowers." She skirted off and my dad looked down at me. He put both of his big calloused hands on my small shoulders.

"How're you doing, Bethy?" he asked solemnly. I bit my lip and shook my head. I could not put how I was feeling into words. I had just said goodbye to Marmee. Everything felt so final. It was all over. There was nothing left to do but mourn and wait for things to get a little easier. "Well, go say bye to your friends, then help out Amy and me."

I nodded and turned away from him, almost walking into my aunt.

"Bethy," she said, hugging me quickly. "Before I forget..." she reached into her pocket and pulled out something sparkling. "Your uncle and I were cleaning out some more of your mom's things from her house, and as I was going down the stairs, I found this in the middle on the top step." She held up a diamond and gold banded ring. "It's yours now."

My jaw dropped and I stared at it. "Really?" I whispered, taking off the promise ring Connor had gotten me a couple months before and carefully replacing it with my mom's engagement ring. "Wow," I breathed, staring down at the ring. "Why was it on the step?" I asked, looking back at my aunt.

"My guess is that she wanted you to find it." Melanie smiled, hugging me again. "And hey, it looks like you're engaged," she joked, noticing what finger it was on.

I put the promise ring back on behind the engagement ring, to make sure it wouldn't slip off.

"Now it looks like I'm married," I smiled back, holding up my left hand for her to see. I gave her a tight hug and she kissed my forehead before letting me go. I walked over to Mrs. K and Uncle Terrance, hugging them both and telling them I would see them the following Thursday, before walking over to my friends who had not moved.

"Hey, guys," I said, pushing a lock of hair behind my ear. "I have to start putting these flowers in my dad's van, so I'll see you tomorrow."

"Okay, babe," Connor sighed as they all stood from their seats. He gave me a hug and a long kiss on the mouth. *That's appropriate.* "I love you."

"Uh-huh." I nodded at him, pulling away.

Candice gave me a small hug and whispered something about it being a really hard day for her.

A part of my brain screamed, *Throw her over the table and claw her face off!* I shook my head and watched her and Connor leave.

"Hey," Fuzzy said, wrapping his strong arms around my waist from behind; I rested my head on his chest and put my arms gently over his, squeezing them. "I'll help you with the flowers. There are crap loads, and since you dropped the high school wrestling team, you have hardly any muscles."

"Shut up," I laughed, hitting his chest playfully as he let go. "I have plenty of strength," I insisted, picking up the nearest vase and grunting under the weight.

"Why *did* you quit the team?" Fuzzy asked, grabbing another vase and following me through the doors.

"I told you, I lost interest in wrestling with guys when all they wanted to do was feel me up," I replied, "and no other girls would join the team."

"But you were really good," Fuzzy said, as we stepped outside and handed my dad the flowers we were carrying. He had moved the van into the parking lot, as close to the doors as possible. "I thought Coach Foster was going to cry when you told him you were leaving. You, like… *were* the team."

"Yeah, because I was pissed whenever they would grab my tits. Gave me all the more reason to tackle them."

Fuzzy laughed hollowly, and for the next half hour helped fill the van with the flowers that had been delivered or dropped off by people in honour of my mom. Once in a while, I would get stopped in the reception area by a lingering guest who wanted to tell me once more that they were sorry for my loss. I would nod and give the person a small hug before returning to the flower task at hand.

The longest conversation I had was with Holly, whom I had not even seen at the service.

"Hi, Beth," she called, as I stepped back inside for the last flower set.

"Oh, hey," I said, her sudden appearance startling me. She slowly approached me, as if she were nervous I might explode.

"I'm not going to ask how you're doing, because I'm pretty sure the answer is 'shitty'. I just wanted to say hello before I left and that I really am very sorry about your mom." She shook her head, red bouncy curls swaying around her shoulders.

I bit my lip, nodded, and then gave her a hug.

"Thank you," I moaned into her neck. "Thank you so much for handling the estate."

"It's okay, baby girl," she said, stroking my hair, which was messy from the amount of times I had run my fingers through it. "It'll get easier."

I nodded again and pulled away finally. "I need to get these flowers to my dad," I told her, reaching behind her and picking up a woven basket of lilies.

"All right," she said, following me outside but stopping me before we got the van. "Listen, Beth… before your mom died, I started planning a trip to China and she was going to go with me." I stared at her, confused. That's not something my mom would have done; she was more of a stay-at-home person. "So… I was wondering if I could take some of her ashes with me," Holly continued.

"Well, I don't see a problem with that," I said, starting to walk back to the van. "My aunt will have the ashes by the time I see her next week. I'll ask her then."

"Great," Holly smiled happily. "I don't leave until next month, so plenty of time."

"All right," I said, putting the basket in the van and closing the back door behind it. "I'll see you."

We hugged again and I scanned the parking lot for Fuzzy, who was standing beside his dad's Nissan Versa a few spaces away from my dad's Hummer. I walked over to him and wrapped my arms around his waist.

"Who was that?" he asked, hugging me back.

"A friend of my mom's," I answered, taking a deep breath. "Thank you Fuzzy, for coming today."

"Thank you for getting Candice to stop drinking my coffee," Fuzzy replied, chuckling. "That was crazy."

"She's terrible," I groaned, stepping away when I heard my dad call my name. "I'll see you tomorrow?"

"You bet, Beth," he said, turning to the car and unlocking the door.

As I got into my dad's van, I noticed the smell of sawdust had been replaced with the scent of a green house. I wondered if the smell of flowers would forever haunt me.

When we got home, Amy and I helped Dad bring all the flowers into the house. Vases took up every surface of the living room and dining room, and a pile of sympathy cards lay on the kitchen counter. I was grateful no one had brought daisies; they were my favourite flower and this would have ruined them for me.

I stood in the hallway between the living room and kitchen, taking in the smell of lilies and roses while staring at the cards. The next time I saw a lily would be too soon.

"Sweetheart? Are you listening to me?" Dad asked from the kitchen by the sink.

"Huh?" I said.

"What would you like for dinner?" he repeated.

"Nothing," I answered quietly.

"Honey, you have to eat something," he implored, crossing his arms.

"I can't." I shook my head. "I-I'm going to bed."

"Beth, it's seven o'clock."

"I didn't say I was going to sleep," I muttered, heading to my room.

"Beth…" my dad called after me, but I replied by closing my bedroom door.

I stripped out of my skirt and took my blouse off, pulling my favourite *The Beatles* shirt over my head and replacing the skirt with a worn-out pair of sweats decorated with penguins. I quickly and painfully dragged a comb through my curtain of hair, switched the bedside table lamp on, and turned the overhead light off.

Getting my copy of *Little Women* off my desk, I got into bed and leaned against the wall behind me. I carefully opened the thick book to the first page and ran my fingers over it. I had read this book so many times the pages were crumpled and my favourite parts were either highlighted or dog-eared. I flipped to where the bookmark had carefully been placed and began to read.

As I reached the part where Amy falls through thin ice while skating, a light tapping on my door brought me back to the twenty-first century.

My sister stepped into my room, closing the door quietly behind her. "Bethy?" she whispered, approaching my bed.

"Yeah?" I asked, marking my place with my thumb. She looked up at me and I could tell she had been crying. Not saying a word, I grabbed a pillow from the end of the bed and placed it beside me, then shifted over and pulled the duvet back. Amy climbed into bed beside me as I bookmarked the page, closed *Little Women*, and handed it to Amy to put on my desk. She did so and turned the lamp off as I lay down beside her.

We had not slept in the same bed for a couple of years, when we shared a room up at Marmee's. Eventually I had gotten so sick of my diagonally sleeping baby sister that I dragged a twin-bed mattress and tiny TV up to the attic and slept up there until Marmee and Will bought a bigger house on the other side of the lake. Even then, they rented the downstairs suite, where our rooms would have been, for a year. I bitched and moaned so much that they eventually gave in and moved us downstairs to separate bedrooms, for which I was very grateful. Unfortunately, Amy began to complain that I stayed up too late watching TV in the den, which was just outside her bedroom, so I was moved into the guest room down the hall from Marmee and Will's bedroom. They both snored so loudly that they could not hear me watching TV in my room at three in the morning, or Jane and I giggling when she would come up with us on rare occasions, or the one time Connor spent the weekend with me. He was set up to sleep in my old room, but he snuck into mine as soon as everyone was asleep. No one ever found out about that.

"Thank you," Amy mumbled into her pillow and I put my arm around her.

"It's okay," I assured her. "Everything will be okay."

It took a while, but eventually my sister and I drifted off into a dreamless sleep.

CHAPTER 14

NOT A RANDOM GIRL

"Hey," I greeted Candice the next day, as I stepped up to our locker, which she was rummaging through. "Lose something?"

"No, I just..." she started, then—as if realizing it was me she was talking to—stood up straight. For a moment, the look of concern on her face made me think she was going to ask how I was doing after saying goodbye to my mom the day before. I was very wrong. "Look, Beth... you're not going to tell anyone about my feelings toward Fuzzy, are you?"

God, you are unbelievable! I wanted to scream, but instead I shrugged.

"People already know," I said, taking off my backpack and pulling my English book out of it, then pulling my sweater off.

"You told?!" she hissed, rage very visible in her eyes.

"What? No." I rolled my eyes, shaking my head. I put my sweater on the third shelf of the locker, because Candice was already using all three hooks for her shit and freaked out if I ever moved anything. "I told you this yesterday. You already act so much like a jealous girlfriend, when a chick so much as *talks* to Fuzzy, that no one really needs to use their imagination to guess your feelings."

"I do *not* get jealous of girls who talk to him," she insisted as Fuzzy appeared at the top of the end staircase. "I just don't like it when some random girl drapes herself all over him."

An evil light-bulb lit above my head. Candice was always driving me up the wall, so why not give her a taste of her own medicine. I was prepared to not let up.

"Am I a random girl?" I asked, smirking.

"No, of course not," Candice said, turning back to the locker.

"Really?" I arched an eyebrow. "Let's put that to a test," I whispered as Fuzzy came into earshot. "Hey, Fuzzy," I said happily, wrapping my arms over his broad shoulders and staring up at him. "How're you doing?" I asked, leaning my body into his. Our faces were so close that he could have leaned down half an inch and be kissing me.

"Uh... I'm fine," he answered slowly, clearly unsure of what to do about my embrace. I had hugged him as a greeting before, but never like this, and never for this long. "How're *you* doing?" Fuzzy asked, remembering the day before.

"I'm doing okay, thanks." I nodded, biting my lip.

"Really?" he asked again, genuine concern on his face. He relaxed in my arms and wrapped one of his around my waist.

"No, no not really," I admitted, enjoying his warm forearm pressed against the small of my back. I leaned my head against his chest and felt him smell my hair.

Suddenly, Fuzzy jerked away from me and strode over to his locker, shaking his head.

I turned around to face Candice, whose pale, pimple face was as red as a tomato and scrunched up, as if she tasted something sour.

"What? I'm not a random girl, just a friend." I shrugged innocently. "By the way, Candice, I'm fine." I closed our locker door as the bell rang. "What with my mom's funeral and everything happening *yesterday.*"

Her mouth popped open, but before she could snap anything at me, I grabbed Fuzzy's arm, turned on my heel, and walked to English with him.

Candice, Fuzzy, Connor, and I were all sitting at our conjoined desks just before the second bell rang. Our teacher began to scribble bullet points on the blackboard, and Candice pushed a folded-up piece of paper across the desk and over to me.

```
I am NOT jealous! -C
```

I almost laughed and uncapped a pen to write back.

```
Sure, you're not. -B
```

I passed it back to her. She exhaled sharply and wrote furiously on the looseleaf sheet.

```
I'm NOT! Touch him all you want! See what I care!
-C
```

I looked up at her and whispered with a sneer. "Challenge accepted."

Her eyes went wide as I shoved the note into my backpack and ignored her for the rest of class.

The bell rang just as the teacher told us to read the first two chapters of *Lord of the Flies* and write a paragraph on symbolism. I wondered when I would get a chance to do it. I was planning to read through song lyrics and the scene I was doing at rehearsal after school.

I linked an arm through Connor's and the other through Fuzzy's after we exited the class room.

"I was so sure she was going to forget to assign homework," I said to them, as Candice fell behind.

"Totally," Fuzzy laughed. "She's usually not very good at keeping an eye on the clock."

"I hate English," Connor put in, oblivious to my other arm holding onto Fuzzy's. "How are you doing today?" he asked.

"Better," I said honestly, looking over my shoulder at a furious Candice, and mouthed "Not a random girl." Then I noticed Rudy a few steps ahead of her, watching me. "Well," I sighed, as I reached the top of the staircase, "I have Psych 101 now." I slipped out of their arms, stopping a few feet away from the landing.

"Okay," Fuzzy said, just as Connor grabbed the nape of my neck and pulled me into an awful, passionate kiss. I pushed him away and glanced over at Fuzzy, who looked startled, exasperated, and angry. Behind him I was surprised to see Rudy, whose face held the same expression.

I bit my lip and glared at Connor. "That wasn't appropriate," I snapped, spinning around and starting down the stairs.

"Hey!" Connor called, pushing through a couple of people and hurrying after me. Not wanting to fight in front of the entire west wing, I quickened my pace. "Hey, you were the one who said I need to be more impulsive. 'Get out of my shell', quote unquote." Without answering him, I hastened my steps even more and thought I had lost him, until he grabbed my arm in the middle of the foyer. I gasped and turned around. "Well? That *is* what you said. Why are you pissed, then?"

"That *is* what I said, but I didn't mean in the middle of a crowded school hallway," I told him, shaking his arm off of me. He quickly snaked his other arm around my waist and leaned in close.

"You mean not in front of your *good friend* Fuzzy," he hissed in my ear.

"No, Connor," I corrected. "I *mean* not in a crowded hallway. We can get in trouble for Pubic Displays of Affection; you *know* that. Your mom works here for fuck's sake!" I started squirming in his grip.

"Since when do you care about getting in trouble?" he growled. "Last time I checked, it turned you—"

"Shut up!" I cried, remembering a self-defence move Coach Foster had taught me once. I turned around with his left arm still around my waist, grasped his wrist, and lurched my upper body to the right, keeping my feet firmly planted on the floor. With the force and twist in the move, Connor ended up stumbling forward and landing unsteadily in front of me. My hands still gripping his forearm, I dug my fingernails into him and said, "Get to class, Connor." I stomped away, very thankful that I did not have to see him for another ninety minutes, then jogged to Psych 101 with barely a minute to spare.

I took my seat just as the second bell rang, fully aware that everyone was staring at me. I guess people had seen that. Most of the class was spent doodling in my notebook and trying to filter out my teacher's voice, seeing as today's topic was "depression" of all things.

"Beth?" Mrs. Jenkins asked, when the bell was about to ring. I looked up at her from a drawing of Amy I had been working on.

"Huh?"

"I was saying that you don't need to do the homework if it's too hard for you."

I glanced at the board behind her and read, "Homework: read chapter 10, Depression. Q-A 1-4." I swallowed and my eyes met hers.

"I think I know enough about that topic," I replied. "Thank you."

She nodded grimly, and as if on cue, the bell rang.

"Why does she get out of reading a whole chapter?" a guy behind me asked.

"She says her mom killed herself over the spring break," a girl replied. I recognized the voice as Lindsey, the girl who had been bullying me since sixth grade and had a minor role in the school play. "It's one hell of an excuse if you ask me," she continued as she left the room.

I thought I might throw up. I bit my lip as it began to tremble. Using my mom's death as an excuse? Did people really think that low of me?

"What's wrong?" Connor asked, as I came out of psych shaking with anger.

"Something Lindsey said," I snarled, clutching my textbooks to my chest as we were joined by Candice and Fuzzy.

"The bully?" Fuzzy asked as we headed to the cafeteria. I nodded, taking a couple of deep breaths.

"What did she say?" Candice asked. I was about to tell her, but stopped myself when I realized that Candice would probably agree, which would be a danger to her health.

"Forget it," I said, leading them over to our windowsill and tossing my pack and books onto it before jumping onto it myself.

"You sure?" Candice asked, climbing up and leaning on the wall behind her.

"Yes, now drop it," I said, irritably.

"I'm going to get you some water from the machines," Connor told me as Fuzzy settled himself beside me.

"Thanks," I called after Connor as he walked away. I knew how this was going to work. We would pretend the fight never happened, and he would be really nice to me for the rest of the day. Same every time.

"You okay?" Fuzzy asked, opening his lunch.

I just sighed and saw Candice roll her eyes. I held in the urge to slap her and leaned my head on Fuzzy's shoulder. I felt him stiffen, then relax underneath me a second later.

"Psychology kinda sucked," I whined, nuzzling into his neck, catching Candice's eye out of the corner of mine.

"No one would blame you if you dropped it. You don't need the class," Fuzzy pointed out. "You already have the credits you need for this year."

"My dad would care," I said, as Fuzzy took a large bite out of his sandwich. "That looks really yummy; can I have some?"

"Damn it," Fuzzy grumbled, shrugging his shoulder violently, making me sit up just as Connor joined the three of us on the windowsill and handed me a bottle of water.

"Thanks," I said, twisting off the cap. I tilted my head back to take a gulp of the beverage and saw Candice scowling at me.

I swallowed the water and turned to Fuzzy. "Do you think I'm a random girl?" I asked him.

"Um... no," he answered slowly, confused by my question. "You're a weird girl who says random things, but *you're* not random."

"I'll take it," I said, not giving him an explanation as to why I had ask such a... well... random question.

"Do you have rehearsal today?" Connor asked, digging into his backpack and pulling out his lunch.

"Yeah," I nodded. "Right after drama."

"You wanna come over after?" he asked with a full mouth. Fuzzy stiffened beside me.

"Maybe," I said, taking another sip of water.

"Well, let me know. I'll make sure my sheets are—"

"I'll let you know, Connor," I said loudly, twisting the cap back on the water bottle. I stretched out my legs in front of me, placing one on top of Fuzzy's knees, and started to eat my own lunch. Glancing at the clock above the side doors, I was happy to see that there were another twenty minutes before the bell would ring for resource centre. I closed my eyes and rested my head on Fuzzy's arm again.

"Beth?" muttered Fuzzy, as I put my lunch back in my bag.

"I'm tired," I mumbled. I was not surprised when he did not protest to my napping place. I *was* surprised when the bell woke me up, because I hardly ever fell asleep in school, unless it was English. I sat up straight and hopped off the sill so that Fuzzy could get down.

"Hey, can I talk to you?" he asked.

"Yeah, of course," I said, pulling my hair out of its bun just to twist it up again.

"Bethy, are you coming?" Connor called from the door where he was waiting with Candice.

"I'll meet you up there, okay?" I called back, waving.

Candice rolled her eyes and angrily pushed open the door, exiting dramatically. Connor shot Fuzzy a curious look and followed her.

"What's up?" I asked when they were gone.

"What are you doing?" he demanded quietly.

"What do you mean?"

"You've been all... handsy today," he told me, waving his hands in the air in front of me. "What's going on? Are you, like... breaking up with Connor or something?"

"Why would I break up with Connor?"

"Well, for starters, he's an asshole who doesn't—" He stopped himself. "That's not the point." He took a deep breath. "This morning... what *was* that this morning? I thought you were going to kiss me."

Before I could stop myself, I actually laughed. Fuzzy's face fell into a look of hurt.

"Oh, shit, no... that's not what I'm laughing about," I explained, putting a hand on his arm. "It's just... kissing you in front of Candice would have been a tad too far."

"You're not answering my question, Beth. Why was your mouth an inch from mine?"

I took a deep breath and the truth shot out of me.

"I'm using you to piss off Candice. She doesn't like it when *random* girls touch you, or look at you, or talk to you, or say your name... so to get back at her for the way she behaved at my mom's funeral, and the way she's been acting lately, I was going to be touching you as much as possible."

"Really?" Fuzzy said, stunned.

"Yeah." Guilt flooded through my body, as the second bell rang. We both started moving toward the door while I looked down at my hands. "But I'll stop. It's obviously annoying you."

"No!" Fuzzy said, a little too quickly. "I mean, if the intention is to annoy Candice, trust me, she's been getting on my last nerve too."

I grinned over at him and linked my arm through his. I noted that he had not asked why my actions would annoy Candice and figured that he already knew about her feelings.

"We need to hurry," I said, letting go of his arm and starting to jog up the nearest staircase.

"Really?" Fuzzy laughed, following me. His legs were so long that he was going up the steps three at a time while I broke into a run. "You're going to run to the fourth floor from the first?"

"What? Afraid I'll beat you to class?" I smirked over my shoulder at him.

"Challenge accepted," he said, bolting in front of me.

"Shit!" I darted after him.

Toe to toe, we raced up six flights of stairs until we reached the fourth floor. He may have had long legs, but I was quick on my short ones. Our class was at the end of the hallway, and I raced down it, listening to the *smack smack smack* sound of our sneakers hitting the linoleum floor below us. I was three doors away when Fuzzy grabbed me from behind, and still running, lifted me up. He started to slow down, and I was trying my hardest not to let out a squeal as he stopped just before the resource centre doors. He turned around so that we were both facing the staircase again and put me down. I whipped around, just in time to see him take one more step so that he was right in front of the RC room.

"I win." He grinned, cheekily.

"You cheated," I huffed, pretending to be pissed.

"No rules were set before the contest of speed began," he pointed out smugly, grasping the door handle. He turned it, then looked down at the knob, confused.

"Open it," I said, adjusting my backpack, which had almost fallen off during our race.

"It's locked," Fuzzy explained, frowning. Then his eyes went wide. "Oh, shit. The teachers are doing that thing where if you're late they lock the door so you can't sneak in and avoid detention."

"Aw, fuck," I groaned, just as the door opened. We both looked at our feet and stepped inside as Mrs. Alberns handed us detention slips.

"I have rehearsal," I told her quietly, feeling every eye in the class room on me.

"Oh, so you'll be here after school anyway," she said, taking the slip and tossing it into a recycling bin by the door.

"I have rehearsal too," Fuzzy lied, trying to hand her back the yellow piece of paper.

"Nice try, Daniel. I'll see you after last class." She pointed to our desks, which we both slunk over to.

"That's what you get for cheating," I whispered, taking off my bag.

"Cruel and unusual punishment?" Fuzzy hissed back, staring glumly down at the detention slip.

"Over actor." I giggled as Connor slipped a note onto my desk.

```
What were you two talking about? - C
```

```
Your birthday is next month, I can't tell you. - B
```

```
Oh. Lol. - C
```

I rolled my eyes. Connor had not laughed out loud.

I looked up from the note and nearly jumped when I saw that Candice had turned in her seat to glare at me with eyes as cold as ice. I shrugged. *What?*

"I'm not talking to you," she hissed and turned back in her seat.

Candice still was not talking to me when drama class started. Fuzzy had an arm around my shoulders, as usual, and she was shooting daggers at him the entire circle time, until it was my turn. As usual.

"Well, it was my mom's funeral on Sunday," I said glumly. "It went well. I saw a lot of people, met my mom's brother for the first time... I have a house full of flowers now."

"Fuzzy looked so handsome!" Candice said loudly beside me. Every head in the room turned to look at her with wide, disbelieving eyes. "I'm serious, he had this suit on and everything. And I wore this dress that—"

"Candice!" Fuzzy barked, making her shut the fuck up and stare at him, shocked. I was glad he said something, because I could not seem to close my dropped jaw.

There was silence in the class room until Mr. T looked at me and said "Beth?"

"No," I choked, "just move to Fuzzy."

"I went to her mom's funeral," Fuzzy said. "It was very nice. Somber, but nice."

"Beth was wearing a dress. It wasn't dark blue with a shawl to match, but she looked okay," Candice told the class.

It was a good thing Fuzzy had his arm around me, because I almost threw myself at her to rip out her ugly mousy hair and claw out her eyes.

The rest of the class was all working on improv, with fun games in pairs. Fuzzy and I were obviously together. We enjoyed watching Candice wander aimlessly around the room looking for a partner. No one wanted anything to do with her.

It was our turn to improvise in front of the entire class. We stepped up onto the small stage by the class windows and turned to each other.

"And... go," Mr. T called over to us.

"Are you all right?" Fuzzy asked, as we started a game called Questions Only, in which the whole conversation has to be made out of questions. The first person to voice a statement loses and they are replaced on stage with the next partners.

"You mean, am I crazy furious right now?" I asked, throwing a quick glance down at Candice.

"Why wouldn't you be?"

"Did I deserve to be treated like that?" I asked, sitting on the edge of the stage, placing my elbows on my knees and propping my chin into my hand.

"Why the hell would you deserve to be treated with such insensitivity?" Fuzzy asked, sitting beside me and rubbing my back.

"How should I know?" I asked, turning to face him.

Fuzzy, clearly out of relevant questions to ask, and knowing he would lose the game if he said a statement, asked: "Did I really look handsome in my dad's suit?"

I burst out laughing and smacked his chest.

"I've got nothing," I said, hopping off the stage. "You win."

Joining our laughing classmates, we sat down on our fainting couch and watched the next Questions Only presentation.

The rest of class went faster, after watching everyone make fools of themselves on stage. It felt good to laugh again—real belly laughs, snuggled up with my best friend.

When the bell rang for the end of class, everyone left except Fuzzy. I had rehearsal and he was avoiding detention. Leaning against him, I flipped through the pages in my script to find the scene we would be been doing that day. My heart jumped into my throat when I remembered it was a kissing scene with Rudy. I bit my lip and felt myself turn red. I vaguely heard someone enter the room behind us.

"What's wrong?" Fuzzy asked, seeing my expression. "Are you okay?" He looked down at my script and snatched it from my grasp. "You have to kiss someone today?"

"I think you mean *get* to kiss someone," Rudy said behind us. "Hey, I'm Rudy," he said, sitting at my feet and reaching over me to shake Fuzzy's hand.

"Daniel," Fuzzy said, his voice low. "You're kissing Beth today?"

"Well, my character is," Rudy said, pulling out his own script. I heard a low growl come from Fuzzy.

"Fuzzy, you better get upstairs before you get locked out again," I told him, sitting up straight so he could stand. "I'll see you tomorrow."

"Fine," Fuzzy sighed, standing and taking a glance at Rudy, then back at me. "See you." I smiled as Fuzzy left and Rudy took his spot next to me.

"Hey," he said, reading over my shoulder. "How was your weekend? Did you miss me?"

I half smiled. "It was all right. And yours?"

Rudy chuckled a bit and nudged me with his shoulder. "It was uneventful."

"Okay, you two, let's get into the auditorium," Mr. T called from his desk. "Everyone is waiting for our stars. We don't have a lot of time today. Probably only one read through."

The two of us grabbed our things and headed to the stage, where we would share our first kiss in front of the entire cast and crew. My heart pounding and palms sweating, I stole a glance at Rudy. He looked nervous, but had an excited smile on his face.

We followed our teacher through the large double doors of the auditorium and set our bags down in the second row, while the props managers (students in ninth grade who wanted extra credits) ran around the stage, setting up a few chairs and small decorations here and there.

"Mr. T, this is the first time we're doing this scene, why are there props up already?" Rudy asked the director as he sat down, placing a clipboard on his lap.

"I didn't ask them to. They're just sucking up," he muttered, scribbling something down on his clipboard. "Well, get on up there." He motioned for the two of us to get up on the stage.

Rudy glided over to the stage steps and went up them quickly. I followed after him, but not before Lindsey tried to trip me as I walked past her seat. Her earlier comment about my mom came back to me and I had to take a deep breath before I could continue up the steps.

I joined Rudy on the stage and made sure my script, which was shaking in my nervous grip, was on the correct page. I worried my lip and looked up at him, noticing that his light eyes were dancing with excitement. I took a deep breath for the umpteenth time that day, waiting for our director to tell us to start the scene.

"And... go," Mr. T called out. The music started and Rudy pulled me to the centre of the stage.

The scene starts out soft and nearly lonely as the two characters open up to each other and tell the truth about the night they met, obstacles they had had in the past, and their current battle with AIDS. At least, that's how I heard it.

At the second to last lyric in the song, Rudy took my hands in his and pressed them into his chest. I could feel his heartbeat and dug my fingernails into the fabric of his t-shirt, stepping closer to him.

One more lyric and he'd be kissing me...

The damn note wouldn't end!

"Here goes, here goes, here goes..." we sang together, and then he slowly lowered his mouth to mine. Rudy folded his strong arms around me; I moved my hands into his dark hair and kissed him back with fervour.

Everyone disappeared. I never, ever wanted this moment to end. I had forgotten what a real kiss felt like, after a year of being with Connor. It felt really, really—

"I said 'cut'!" Mr. Thomas' voice cut into our musically induced kiss, and Rudy pulled away from me. "Okay, as great as you two sang together..." he sighed and I saw him fight back a laugh, "it's supposed to be a gentle kiss that lasts *maybe* five seconds. That, uh... wasn't."

My cheeks flamed, and I saw Rudy smirk slightly and nod at the helpful critique.

"All right, anything else?" Rudy asked, fidgeting with his script.

"Yes, actually," Mr. T said, consulting his clipboard and not bothering to hide a smile this time. "Beth, I understand that this is an... anticipated scene, but maybe calm down a bit?" I could tell that my face was bright red and heard laughter coming from the rest of the cast and crew. "All right, all right!" Mr. T scolded them as if he, too, hadn't just been amused at my expense. I suppose it *was* a little funny. "Would you two mind doing it again?"

Rudy and I nodded and started back at our marks. The music started and Rudy began to sing.

"That was great, you two," Mr. T praised when we finished with a three-second kiss. "We'll go through it again tomorrow. I have dinner reservations and I'm already late. I should have cancelled today's rehearsal. So... everyone head home." Rudy let go of me and hopped off the stage. "Oh, uh... the props... Lindsey and Beth, stay back and put the props away. See you tomorrow."

I hopped off the stage as well and watched Rudy and everyone else leave, wishing we could go through the scene a million more times. While I started picking things up off the floor, including a grey backpack someone had forgotten in the second row, Lindsey started stacking up the chairs on stage. While we got along in front of others by putting on polite masks, we would really rather be with other company and tonight was no different.

"What's your hurry?" she called over to me as I crammed some granola bar wrappers into a trash bin. "It's not like you have any homework to do."

I looked over at her, stiffening. "What's that supposed to mean?" I demanded, remembering my English assignment.

Lindsey turned to face me, smirking. "Name one assignment you've had since you got back from spring break." My jaw dropped. "That's what I thought," she sneered, turning back to her project at hand.

At that moment, I moved on from the 'sadness' stage of grief to 'anger'. I felt it everywhere. Surging through my body like an unwanted virus.

Next thing I knew, I was striding toward the stage, leaping onto it, and tackling Lindsey to the floor as I screamed, "You bitch!" Lindsey let out a yelp of surprise before swearing profusely. "You think I'm using my mom as an excuse to get out of doing homework?" I shrieked, as she rolled onto her back, attempting to get up. I lunged on top of her and straddled her waist, pinning her to the floor.

"Get off me, you crazy bitch!" she cried, clawing her long nails down my arms.

"No!" I yelled, shoving her shoulders to the floor. "Answer me! Is that *really* what you—Ow!" I snatched my right hand away as she dug her teeth into it.

"Yes!" she snapped, kicking her legs. "It's totally something you would do," Lindsey added, reaching up and grasping my hair, tugging it hard. I stretched my leg out so I would not roll off of her and raised a hand above my head. Unfortunately, someone grabbed my fist before it met her perfect plastic nose. This action was quickly followed by another arm being wrapped around my waist and lifting me into the air.

"Oh, God! Thank you, Rudy!" Lindsey gushed, climbing to her feet.

"Put me the fuck down!" I bellowed, swinging my legs in the air.

"I heard what you said, Lindsey. It's a good thing I came back for my bag," Rudy said in a deadly calm tone. "You better leave before I let Beth go."

"I could take her," she snapped at him, grabbing her bag and throwing it over her shoulder.

"You wanna bet, bitch?" I screamed, squirming even more violently in Rudy's grasp.

Lindsey turned on her heel, jumped off the stage, and ran out of the auditorium, swearing at us over her shoulder.

Rudy put me down as soon as the doors closed behind her and I whipped around, shoving his shoulders hard.

"What the hell, Rudy?!" I nearly screamed as he stumbled back a bit. "She just said one of the *worst* things—"

"I understand that," Rudy nodded. "But what could your mom possibly have done for you to be able to use it as an excuse to get out of doing homework?" I gasped, remembering that he was the only person who did not know. "Hey, I'm not saying that you do. I'm just wondering what she could have done to make Lindsey believe such a stupid thing."

I bit my lip and shook my head. "She left," I managed to say without my voice cracking. Rudy let out a small moan of sympathy and cupped the side of my face with his hand.

"Oh, Beth..." he sighed, stepping closer to me.

I felt a sob about to escape my lips. I swallowed hard, looked him in the eye, and whispered, "I have to go. Sorry." Stepping away from him and his confused, beautiful face, I hopped off the stage, grabbed my bag, and hurried out the doors. As soon as I stepped outside, although I did not stop walking, I did stop holding in the tears that desperately needed to be freed.

CHAPTER 15

THE BATHROOM PICNIC

The following day I decided to skip Psych 101. Lindsey had made a valid point, after all. I probably could get away with anything due to my current circumstances, so why not skip a class or two? It wasn't like I did it often. But to my surprise, I got caught in the act. Apparently, Fuzzy had also thought today was a good day to skip second class and hang out in the deserted cafeteria.

"What're you doing here?" we said at the same time.

"Skipping class," we both replied.

"Won't tell if you don't," Fuzzy said, even though it was obvious that I would never rat on him. I nodded in agreement and we settled ourselves on the windowsill where we ate lunch every weekday.

One of the great things about my friendship with Fuzzy was the fact that we could sit in total silence, not exchanging a word, and be completely comfortable. That was the case right now. I reached into my bag and pulled out a book. I lay down on my back and propped my legs up on the wall Fuzzy was leaning against, my feet by his head. Fuzzy pulled out his phone and started to text or check Facebook or something. I raised my arms and began to read.

A little while later, just as I was turning a page, I glanced over at Fuzzy. His hands were in his lap but his eyes, looking pitiful and a little angry even, were on me. I lowered my book to my stomach and looked into his unblinking gaze.

"Fuzzy?" I asked quietly. The cafeteria was so silent that it seemed wrong to speak at a normal volume.

"Yeah?"

"What are you thinking about?"

He paused, and then answered, "Suicide."

I blinked in surprise. Not a lot of people actually said the word. Usually they beat around the bush or tried to say it politely, with phrases like, 'took her own life,' or 'self-destructed' or the more usual 'killed herself'. Hardly ever did I actually hear 'suicide'. Leave it to Fuzzy to be blunt.

"You're not planning to—"

"*What?* God, no! Jesus, Beth!" Fuzzy exclaimed, clearly offended. "I would never do something that selfish."

I sat up on my elbows. "*Excuse* me? My mom was *not* selfish!"

"How would *you* word it then? Because she *clearly* wasn't thinking about anyone but herself when she did it! I just don't know how she could do this. Leave you like that. She could have—no, she *should have* stayed here with you and Amy, but instead she just gave up. It's just wrong. She could have tried harder."

"She did try!"

"Not hard enough," Fuzzy argued. "Your mom left you. She had a choice and she left you and Amy."

I said nothing. Fuzzy had just said out loud what I had been thinking for days, but felt too guilty to say aloud.

"Some people say that it's brave," I mumbled.

"How is it remotely brave?"

"Because she ended it without knowing what happens on the other side. People have said that they don't want to be alive, but they're too afraid to die."

"That is horse shit, Beth," Fuzzy said flatly. "Completely false. Being too afraid to keep on living makes you a coward. Ending your life when there are people who love and count on you, that makes you a coward *and* selfish."

I closed my eyes and felt tears leak out of the corner of them, slowly trailing into my hair. "I don't want to remember my mom like that," I whispered.

"Then don't. But you can't lie to yourself and say what she did was brave just to save face."

My heart in my throat, I slowly opened my eyes and looked over at Fuzzy. He was leaning forward, his face barely a foot from mine. I stared into his eyes. "Why didn't she love me enough to stay? Did I do something wrong?" I pursed my lips and gulped back a sob.

Fuzzy's eyes went wide. He put one arm behind my shoulders, the other under my knees, and lifted me, pulling me onto his lap. Then, having given voice to the last thing I'd kept bottled up, he held me while I cried into his chest.

The next day at lunch, before we entered the cafeteria, Connor took my arm and gently pulled me aside.

"Hey, can we talk?" he asked, brushing my bangs out of my eyes.

"Yeah, sure." I shrugged, looking over at Fuzzy, who was watching us from the doorway with Candice. All day I had been hugging him whenever Connor was not around, snuggling into his chest, and he always wrapped his strong arms around me in return. "What's up?"

"No, not here." Connor shook his head, glancing over at Fuzzy too. "In private."

"Okay," I said, hitching up my bag. "Where did you have in mind?"

"Well, the closet if it's not occupied," Connor suggested. I agreed and waved at Fuzzy as Connor took my hand and led me down the hall. Fuzzy gave me a small wave, a look of disappointment on his face, and Candice rolled her eyes. I think I heard the word 'typical' escape her lips. *What a bitch.*

"So, why are we going to the closet?" I asked, as we approached the closet door, taking my hand out of his.

"I just want to talk, baby." He knocked loudly on the closet entrance. There was no reply, so he swung the door open and I followed him inside, closing it behind me.

"About what?" I questioned, as we both took off our backpacks and tossed them carelessly to the floor.

"What's going on between you and Dan?" Connor demanded, whipping around to face me. It was like a Jekyll and Hyde effect: The look on his face was suddenly so angry that I was afraid he might actually hit me. "I've heard you're, like… snuggling with him or something in the halls? What the hell is *that* about?"

"I can explain," I said, backing away from him slightly. "Really, I can."

"Then go ahead, Beth," he snapped, crossing his arms and scowling at me. "Enlighten me."

I took a deep breath and told Connor the truth. How Candice was selfish at my mom's funeral, about her feelings toward Fuzzy and how inadequate she makes me feel, so I had decided to use Fuzzy to get under her skin. That was it. When I finished my explanation, I found myself holding my breath, waiting for Connor to react.

"So there are no romantic feelings between you two? You don't want to be, you know… *with* him?"

"No! God, no," I said flatly, shaking my head. "That would be like incest."

"For you maybe," Connor snorted.

I took another step away from him when a flash of anger shot through his eyes. When I bumped into the wall behind me, I decided it was time to get out of the not-so-secret make-out closet.

"Are we done here?" I asked meekly, as he crossed the room toward me.

"Don't be stupid," Connor laughed as he leaned against me and kissed my neck. He grasped the bun my hair was in and tugged the elastic out roughly, making my hair tumble down to my waist in waves. "Stop wearing your hair like that, Beth. How many times have I told you that?" Connor scolded. He put one hand above each of my shoulders and stared down at me. "Also, don't ever, *ever* humiliate me in public like you did yesterday in the foyer. Pull that wrestling bullshit on me again and you'll regret it."

I gawked up at him, stunned. What was wrong with him? "What's your damage?" I nearly yelled, pushing his hands away from me.

"Excuse me?" Connor exclaimed, grabbing my upper arms.

"You've been so *weird* lately! You've always been, like... territorial or whatever, but now you're grabbing me and far more aggressive in bed than I would like—"

"Are you saying I'm bad in bed?" Connor tightened his grip on my arms.

I winced, and—pissed off that he didn't let me finish—didn't answer his question. "Let me go or I will show you a wrestling move that has to do with your balls and my knee," I hissed through my teeth. The death grip on my arms slowly relaxed and I shook away from him. "And there's nothing wrong with the way I wear my hair," I added, snatching up my bag and starting for the door. As my fingers touched the doorknob, Connor spoke from the corner I had left him in.

"Since spring break ended, you and Dan have become a lot closer. And since your mom died, you've been... doing stuff more. I guess I feel threatened by Dan. But now that I know you don't care about him *that way*, I'll calm down. I promise."

"Fuzzy is my best friend, Connor. I need him. He has been there for me since I was twelve, not just since Marmee died. I need comfort and he gives it to me!" I hollered, turning back around. Connor was leaning against the wall, his arms crossed stubbornly.

He started to point an accusing finger at me. "Since your mom died, the only *comfort* you've been asking for is sex, Beth!" he yelled back. "Can you blame me for being concerned about what kind of 'comfort' Dan might be giving you?" He air-quoted 'comfort'.

"What?" I breathed, taken aback. "What are you implying?"

"You know exactly what I'm implying, Beth." Connor shook his head. "You're *my* girlfriend and—"

"Yes, your *girlfriend!*" I yelled over him. "Not your fucking property!" I yanked open the door, and before storming out of the closet, added, "I am not sleeping with Fuzzy, and I am not speaking to you." I slammed the door.

The fact that Connor assumed I would, and was, betraying him hurt my already fragile feelings. Our entire relationship, I had always been faithful, unlike him, and according to Rudy he was bound to do it again.

With tears in my eyes, I ran down a hall to the nearest bathroom to lock myself in a stall before I started to cry. I pushed myself against the washroom door, which swung open and closed behind me. Unable to see through my tears, I leaned against the wall opposite the sinks and mirrors, putting my face in my hands and choking back a furious sob.

"Uh…" I heard someone say in front of me.

I peered through my fingers and caught the reflection of Rudy in the mirror above a bathroom sink. He looked my reflection up and down, a look of bewilderment and surprise on his face.

"What are you doing in the *girl's* bathroom?" I demanded, wiping my eyes and dropping my hands to my hips.

"I'm not," Rudy answered, slowly turning off the rusty sink tap and drying his hands on his jeans. "What are you doing in the *boy's* bathroom?" he asked, turning to face me directly. "You could get in a lot of trouble if you're caught in here."

"Huh?" I said stupidly. I looked around the tiled room, and sure enough, I was standing right next to a row of four urinals and three stalls, which were considerably narrower than the ones in a girl's bathroom. "Well, fuck." I swore, and started to leave.

"No wait," Rudy said, catching my fingers with his. "Have... have you been crying?"

"No," I replied, the warmth of his touch flooding my whole body.

"Were you about to?" he asked, entwining our fingers together.

"Yes," I nodded slowly.

"About your mom?" Rudy guessed.

"No. About Connor," I sighed "He's being a total dick. He thinks I'm—"

Just then the bathroom door started to open, replacing Rudy's warmth with panic, but he gently and silently pushed me into the handicap stall, following me in and locking the door. He helped me stand on the toilet so that I was perched on the U-bend. He quickly joined me so no one would see our feet.

We listened as someone took off a bag and dropped it on the counter. Then a zipper being undone.

BANG!

I jumped so violently that I almost slipped as the bathroom door was thrown open and slammed closed again.

"You!" I heard Connor's voice yell. "Are you screwing Beth?" My jaw dropped.

"Dude! I'm pissing here!" I heard Fuzzy snap indignantly. "Wait, are you freaking serious? How could you even ask me that?"

Connor had just interrogated me on this. Now he was trying to go all Jack Bauer on Fuzzy, who was half a foot taller than him and on the rugby team? Way to pick your fights, dumbass.

"Are they talking about you?" Rudy breathed in my ear. I nodded. "Are you cheating?" I shook my head, shooting him a dirty look.

Connor started to explain the reasons behind his suspicions. "You two are really close, Dan, and she's been very, you know... active lately. And you're always hugging her—"

"Jesus, Connor, her mom just died!" Fuzzy yelled. At these words, Rudy almost fell into the toilet and had to grab my shoulders to stay on his feet. I was pulled forward by his weight, and even though our faces were suddenly inches apart, I didn't dare look at him now that he knew. Now that officially *everyone* knew. "*You're* sleeping with Beth! *I'm* comforting her! *Candice* is, is, is... well... making things worse for Beth. I don't know what the hell has gotten into her lately..." I heard a urinal run, and footsteps, then a tap being turned but no running water. "Damn it, I hate this bathroom! What sink works again? Oh, yeah." Water running. "Now, Connor, listen, I am not—"

"Okay," I heard Connor say, relief in his voice. *What? Why couldn't he believe* me *when I told him?* "Just wanted to make sure."

Son of a...

The water stopped running and I heard Fuzzy put his bag back on his shoulders. The two boys started walking to the door.

"You're an asshole, Connor. I don't know what Bethy sees in you."

The door closed.

Rudy and I were now alone in the poorly tiled bathroom.

Fighting the urge to run from the conversation I knew I was about to have, I slowly looked up from my sneakers and met Rudy's gaze.

"Your mom's dead?" he said slowly, his eyes wide.

I had told him that she had left; I had not really gone into detail about how.

"Yeah, she is," I nodded. "It happened over spring break. She, uh... killed herself."

Rudy took in a sharp breath and pulled me into a sudden hug. The movement was so strong that I almost lost my footing on the toilet seat.

"Beth, I am so, so, so sorry for you. God, I am so sorry."

"Rudy?"

"Yeah?"

"Can we get off the toilet now?"

"Huh? Oh!" Rudy seemed to have forgotten we were standing on toilet, locked in a bathroom stall together.

He let go of me, lightly stepped down, then reached up and lifted me effortlessly off the toilet. He placed me directly in front of him and stared down at me with concerned, focused eyes, as though he was trying to read my thoughts. Neither one of us went to unlock the stall.

Standing inches apart, his hands still on my waist, Rudy asked, "Why didn't you tell me?"

I took a deep breath, and as quietly as I could, began to explain.

"Everyone at the school knew me as the chick who has seizures, but now everyone knows me as the chick whose mom killed herself. I wanted one, *just one*, person to know me as just another girl. Absolutely nothing weird, fucked up, or broken about her. Just a girl. A plain, ordinary, girl. Then you came along and had no idea about my past or present, so I... I didn't lie necessarily. I just didn't tell you everything. I was vague. You knew me as Beth, a girl co-starring in a school play with you, so I took advantage of that." I said this all very quickly, and was almost panting as I waited for Rudy to say something back. Anything. "Please, don't be mad. Please?"

Rudy, tracing his fingers lightly along my midriff, shook his head a little. "I'm not angry at all," he said soothingly, and I relaxed, "I know what it's like to lose someone you love. Not my mom, not like that, granted. I can't even *imagine* the pain you're in."

"Who did you lose?" I asked, trying to concentrate on his voice, not his fingers, which were now curled into my belt loops.

"My papa," he replied, his answer echoing through the old room. "My dad's dad. He had cancer. My family is all really close, so it was really hard." His voice cracked a bit and he wrapped his arms around my waist, pulling me into him. I couldn't help but flashback to the kiss we had shared on stage not twenty-four hours ago. I hugged him back, wondering why (despite the odd location) being in his arms felt so right. "So Connor thinks you're cheating on him. And you're not, right?"

"No!" I exclaimed, a little louder than I meant to, stepping away from him. "The closest I've come to cheating on him was yesterday when we kissed, and that was for the play." There was silence for a moment. We continued to hold each other.

"Beth?"

"Yeah?"

"I could never find you plain or ordinary. Even if I didn't know you were messed up."

Thinking that what he had just told me was the nicest thing anyone had ever told me, I took a little step back and looked up into his kind eyes.

"Rudy, I'm really, *really* fucked up. Like… bad."

Rudy moved his hands up to my shoulders and squeezed them gently.

"And yet, here you are. At school, even though most people would be shut up in their room crying. You may be messed up, Beth, but damn you are *strong*." He gripped my shoulders tighter, as if letting go might allow me to float away. My lip trembled and eyes stung. I hung my head so that Rudy wouldn't see my weakness. Strong people don't cry. "Hey, hey… Beth… no." Rudy slipped his hands into mine and linked our fingers together. He bent his knees so he could look up at me, and wiped away a tear that had escaped from my eye. "I was trying to make you feel better. What can I do, Beth? What can I do to make things better?"

I had known Rudy for about a week, and things were moving faster than a speeding bullet. We had gone from strangers in an abandoned stairwell to confidants squished together in a narrow bathroom stall. I had never felt so much trust toward anyone in my life and I did not even know his last name. I didn't know his favourite colour or if he had any siblings. For all I knew he could be a secret millionaire, or worst case scenario, a distant relative of Charles Manson. But trust was hard to come by, so I grabbed it and held on tight.

"There's nothing you can do, Rudy," I said, letting go of his hands and sliding down the wooden stall wall behind me, resting my elbows on my knees. I inched away from the toilet so my side was pressed against the door of the stall. Rudy copied my movements, but stretched his legs out on either side of me and into the stall behind. "There's nothing anyone can do," I sighed, reaching into my bag and pulling out my uneaten lunch. "It happened and there is nothing to do but move forward. Oh! My dad packed me wine gums!" I grabbed the pack of my favourite candies. "That was nice of him."

"Can I?" Rudy nodded at the bag, with a guilty mooching look in his eyes.

"You're the only one of my friends who actually asks. So... yes." I laughed, putting the bag between his sprawled legs and my feet. He leaned over to take one but I smacked it out of his hand, taking it from him.

"What?" he said, taken aback.

"Not the green ones. Those are always mine." I put the green wine gum in my mouth. "Always have been, always will be."

"Get used to disappointment," Rudy smirked, snatching one up and licking it as if to claim it.

"But... seriously? The green ones are—"

The first bell rang for the end of lunch, cutting off the end of my sentence and filling my gut with disappointment. I was having fun with Rudy. I did not want to go to resource centre, where Connor would be waiting to either apologize or act like he had done nothing wrong. Fuzzy would be there to tell me what Connor had accused him of, and Candice would be there to play the role of anthrax-covered pickle on the crap sandwich that was my life.

When I did not start to stand up, Rudy looked at me quizzically. "Don't you have class?" he asked, raising his eyebrows.

"I could ask you the same question," I shot back, picking up a wine gum.

"Beth, are you skipping class?" Rudy gasped in fake horror. "That's not very—"

"Are *you*?" I interrupted, throwing a black wine gum at him. It bounced off his perfect nose, making him laugh.

"I don't have a class," he told me. "Free block. You?"

"Resource centre, but I'm not in the mood to go. It'll have too much drama in it, which is the class after that one."

"Don't you do, like… nothing in RC?"

"You'd be surprised at how dramatic nothing can be," I replied.

With that, I skipped class with Rudy. We spent ninety minutes sitting on a bathroom floor, comparing notes on each other's lives.

Turns out he was *not* a millionaire and had two sisters and a brother. His favourite colour was blue, and as far as he knew, he was not a relative of Charles Manson.

When Rudy ran out of questions regarding Marmee, or rather could not stand the look of pain on my face when I answered them, he moved on to questions about Connor. Although there was not much to tell, the more information I gave him the more violently Rudy would rip up a sheet of toilet paper into bits. I could not help but be flattered by his jealousy.

"Connor's an asshole." He scowled at the tiny pile of confetti of toilet paper on his lap.

"I know," I agreed, packing up the leftovers of my lunch.

"Then why are you—"

"I don't know," I snapped, tired of the repetitive question. "The bell for last class is going to ring in a moment," I said, standing up and stretching. I rubbed my ass, which had fallen asleep. He did the same, handing me my backpack.

"I'll see you at rehearsal?" he asked, unlocking the door and holding it open for me.

"It's a date." I smiled. He beamed down at me and I left the bathroom.

The butterflies in my stomach felt more like hummingbirds.

CHAPTER 16
DINNER AT AUNTIE'S

The following Thursday, my sister and I had dinner with Aunt Melanie, Uncle Mitch, Uncle Terrance, and Mrs. K. I will not deny that I was rather nervous. This was the first time I would be able to say more than "nice to finally meet you" and "it is such a tragedy" to my two long-lost (in a way) relatives.

Amy and I had decided that we would head to Auntie's house right from school and meet each other there. Too many people from school took the bus. I needed to get away, so I ended up walking. Unfortunately, Connor (whom I still was not speaking to) took it upon himself to walk with me, rewording the question "Why aren't you talking to me?" in as many ways as he could think of. I finally caved when he yelled it in Spanish.

I whipped around to face him, my long ponytail catching him across the face. "Seriously?" I cried, "You really don't know why I'm mad?"

"Finally she speaks," he sighed, rolling his eyes. "Please, explain what put your panties in a twist."

"If you ever want to see my twisted panties again, you will never roll your eyes at me again," I snapped, putting my hands on my hips.

"Okay, okay," Connor said, raising his hands in mock surrender. "Why are you upset?"

"Oh, let me think…" I said sarcastically, tapping my chin with my index finger while looking up at the sky. "Well, it could be because you accused me of cheating on you when I've only ever been faithful. Or it could be because, after I answered you *truthfully*, you still took it upon yourself to interrogate Fuzzy while he was trying to use the bathroom. Maybe it's because you flirt with Candice right in front of me, even though she is the ugliest thing in the world. Or maybe because you keep insulting the way I wear my hair or, or, or because you're so judgemental, and you won't leave me alone when I clearly want some space, some time to think about us, or—God, what *now?!*"

Connor had stepped closer to me until he was barely three inches in front of me. "What is it? What do you need to think about?" he insisted, his brown eyes full or worry. "Are... are you going to leave me?"

My shoulders slumped and I shook my head. "But things have to change," I told him. "*You* have to change."

"I will. I will," Connor said in a pleading tone. "I love you, Bethy. God, I love you so much." When I said nothing in return, he took a step away me. "Do... do you love me?"

I do not know why, but Rudy popped into my head when Connor asked me that. Mentally scolding myself, I forced myself to speak. "Of course, Connor. Of course I love you," I told him. "I just... you have to understand how much I'm going through."

"I do," Connor said eagerly. "I know exactly what you're going through."

He struck a nerve and I snapped. "No, you don't!" I yelled. "I hate it when people say that! You don't know anything that I'm going through, let alone *exactly* what I'm going through! You don't know *shit!*" I poked him hard in the chest.

"Don't yell at me!" Connor shouted back. "I worded it poorly, lay off!"

"Don't fucking make excuses and don't tell me what to do!" I pushed him, making him step back a couple feet. Anger flared in his eyes and he shoved me right back.

Caught off guard, I stumbled back but lost my footing, falling hard on my ass. "Ah!" I cried out, just as Connor crouched beside me.

"Oh, crap… oh Jesus! Beth, I'm sorry! I don't know what got into me, I just—" I swatted his hands away as he tried to help me to my feet. "No, Beth, please, I'm sorry!" he babbled. I pretended not to notice his voice crack.

"Connor, just go," I grumbled, pushing myself to my feet. "Whatever. It's fine. Connor, I'm up. Stop *touching* me! God!"

"Do you want me to kiss it better?" Connor cooed, as if I were two years old.

"Oh my God!" I cried out in exasperation. "What is your problem? You go from grovelling for me to talk to you, to pissed off, and then back to grovelling like *that.*" I snapped my fingers. "You have, like… a rare case of bi-polar disorder or are you PMS-ing? Just go home, Connor. Now! I have to get to my aunt's house." I turned on my heel and marched away, so angry I was shaking.

What a fucking asshole! He actually shoved me! Granted, I pushed him first and kind of deserved it, but he had at least sixty pounds on me. Not to mention the fact that I'm a girl. I should have jumped back to my feet and tackled him to the ground like I had learned from wrestling. I wished Fuzzy had been there to beat him up afterwards. Or better yet, Rudy.

We had not seen each other outside of rehearsal, but we always hung back and talked for a bit. Okay, more like flirted, but it was totally innocent. The amount of chemistry there was between Rudy and I, and the lack thereof with Connor, was beginning to stress me out. Since our bathroom picnic, Rudy was always the one I was thinking about. He was who I thought about when I zoned out at the dinner table and when I was trying to fall asleep at night. That used to be Connor… or Mr. Wolfe, the incredibly sexy social studies TA that every girl swooned over and every boy hated.

"Beth! Bethy! Bee-eth!" I heard Amy's voice and looked around. I had been so wrapped up in my own thoughts that I had walked right past my aunt's house, where Amy was now waving at me from the driveway.

I waved back at her to let her know that I had seen her without screaming her name, and made my way over to her.

Amy greeted me at the front door and ushered me inside.

"What took you so long to get here?" she questioned as I shrugged off my backpack and hoodie. "I thought you were heading here right after school."

"I did," I told her, untying my sneakers. "I just got caught up in something."

"Was that something falling? Because you have dirt on your bum." Amy giggled, brushing dirt off the back on my jeans.

"More or less." The implication was not a stretch. Amy knew I was very accident prone. The year before I had broken my arm walking backwards and falling off the school stage. "Is Auntie here?" I asked, setting my things beside the door.

"They're all outside on the back patio," Amy nodded, leading the way to the back door.

"If we're heading outside anyway, why did I bother taking my shoes off?"

"We don't want to track dirt through the entire house, Bethy," Amy sighed.

It struck me then that Amy had become very tidy since spring break. Her room was always spotless, and she was doing dishes right after dinner. She used to be a total slob, even compared to me. There would always be dirty clothes to wade through and glasses sitting around in her room.

I stopped walking and Amy, hearing my lack of footsteps, turned to face me. "You coming?" I looked my little sister up and down, taking in her appearance.

Amy used to wear no makeup at all and now she had a layer of foundation and so much eye makeup on that she vaguely resembled a blonde, blue-eyed raccoon. Her regular boot-cut jeans were now replaced with skin tight ones and she was wearing a t-shirt with the logo of a band I had never heard of.

How had I not seen these changes? Was I so wrapped up in my own shit that looking over my sister had actually slipped my mind? That made me officially the worst sister in the world. When did she buy skinny jeans? When did she start wearing makeup? Where did she get the money for them?

"What?" Amy said, a look of annoyance on her face. "Why are you looking at me like that?"

"Like what?" I said. "I'm not looking at you like anything."

"Okaaay..." She dragged the word out while turning back around and starting toward the back door again. Her hair, which I could see she had used a flat iron on, swayed from side to side just below her shoulders.

Amy led me onto the back patio where Auntie Melanie, my two uncles, Mrs. K, and (to my surprise) Holly were all lounging.

"Hey, sweetie." Auntie Melanie beamed as I bent over to give her a hug. She looked too comfortable in her deck recliner to get up.

I hugged them all in turn, and seeing Amy take the last seat available, I sat on the ground beside Uncle Terrance. He told me about pranks he used to pull on Marmee and Aunt Melanie, stories about the grandpa who died before I was born, and about his own family. I had no idea I had so many cousins. Eventually, there was a break in the conversation and the semi-awkward silence was broken by Holly.

"So, I'm going to China next week and Margret had asked me if she could come. Before she died, of course." Everyone stared at her, waiting for her to continue. She looked nervous and was wringing her hands. She shifted in her seat and went on. "I would like to bring her. Or some of her, I suppose. If that's all right," she added hastily. I remembered agreeing to this at Marmee's funeral and glanced over at my aunt, who was keeping Marmee's ashes in the den. She looked almost grim for a moment before she nodded.

"Okay," she nodded. "If that's what Meg wanted."

She stood up and walked back inside, with Holly behind her looking nervous. A minute passed without anything else being said, so I wordlessly stood and entered the house as well.

I found Aunt Melanie in the kitchen with Holly, holding a brightly coloured box.

"So, how do we do this?" Holly was saying.

Auntie put the box on the counter and bent over to open a cupboard beside her. She pulled out a Ziploc bag and grabbed a spoon from the dish rack. Auntie pulled the box closer to the sink and peeled open the bag.

"Can you open the box for me?" she asked Holly, who complied by delicately opening the lid.

From where I was standing, it looked like the box was full of tissue paper, but when Auntie put the spoon inside it and pulled out a pile of dust, I knew differently.

I was looking at my mom. My hand flew to my mouth as I watched a spoonful of ashes being transferred into the Ziploc bag Auntie was still holding.

What part of my mom was that? I thought, as my aunt took another spoonful. *Was that her nose? Her hair? Her eyelashes?*

After three spoonfuls of my mom was put into the plastic bag, my aunt zipped it up and Holly put the lid back on my mom's… coffin, I guess. I briefly wondered whether my aunt was ever going to use that spoon again, while Holly thanked her and took the bag from her hands.

I slipped into the bathroom and listened as Auntie returned the box to its rightful place in the den and both of them went back outside.

I closed the lid of the toilet and sat down, rubbing my eyes wearily. I was not sure how I felt about what I had just seen. That dust... those *ashes*... were not *really* my mom. Not anymore, at least. Now my mom lived on in memories, not in a solid body. Holly had told me that she wanted to take a part of my mom to China and I had not had a problem with it... but now I was not so sure.

"Well, it's too late now," I mumbled to myself, wiping my damp palms on my jeans. "The ashes are packed and ready to go."

I left the bathroom and tried to smile as I joined everyone outside again, but ended up staring at my fingers most of the time.

"Sweetie?" Auntie Melanie said, snapping me back to the present.

"Huh?" I said stupidly, looking up at her. She raised her eyebrows as if to say, *you can do a little better than that.* "I mean, yes?"

"Are you ready for dinner?" she asked slowly, as if she were repeating this simple yes or no question for at least the second time.

"Yeah, for sure. Totally." I nodded, standing up. I looked around and noticed that everyone had gone inside already. Had I fallen asleep or something?

My aunt served my favourite dish of all time: macaroni and cheese with salsa. None of that Kraft Dinner shit with cheese powder; this was real cheese with bread crumbs added to the sauce. I loved this dish so much that I had once yelled at Connor for telling me he preferred cheeseburgers and curly fries.

"How can you say that?!" I had cried, grabbing his arm. "Have you not tasted—"

"Yes, I have and it's not my favourite." He had shrugged, giving me a look that asked, *What is the big damn deal?*

I had crossed my arms after that and glared daggers at him. Knowing I could not change his mind, I had snubbed him and scoffed: "Well, then, you're... stupid."

I laughed now at the memory of the lamest comeback in the world and felt everyone look over at me.

"Sorry," I giggled. "I just... ha ha... made myself laugh."

"How? What happened?" Uncle Terrance asked me while Auntie placed more pasta on my plate. I guessed she had noticed the weight I had lost. I smiled at her, and still giggling, told my family about the stupidest argument I had ever had. Everyone was laughing when I finished the story, which I thought was funny because... well, it *wasn't* funny.

"Bethy," my aunt gushed, "it's just macaroni and cheese."

"No, no, Auntie." I shook my head. "This is not 'just' anything. This is my favourite kind of pasta with *cheese* and *salsa*. That is not a 'just'. It is amazing and anyone who says differently is stupid," I told her, in the most serious tone I could muster. I took a large bite of the pasta and smiled at my aunt after I swallowed. "Thank you for dinner, Auntie."

"Of course, sweetie. Anytime."

When it was time to head home, Amy and I had to say goodbye to our uncle Terrance and Mrs. K for the last time. They were leaving for Ontario the next morning, so it was a given we would not be seeing them for a long time. Hugging them each in turn, we agreed to stay in touch, and if we were ever in the area, to stop by for a visit.

Saying goodbye to Holly was a little different. Although I was sure I would see her again, I was saying goodbye to a part, or parts, of my mom for good.

"Please, choose a place that my mom would have liked when you spread her?" I requested, giving her a hug.

"I would not have it any other way," she whispered in my ear as she wrapped her arms around me.

With one last wave to our family, Amy and I descended the driveway and made our way to the nearest bus stop.

"Baby sister?" I asked, timidly.

"Hmm?" She looked over at me, her bangs covering her left eye completely.

"How... how are you doing?" I asked as nonchalantly as I could. "With everything, I mean, not just Marmee. Like school, friends... boys, maybe?"

A small smile played at Amy's lips at the word 'boy' and my heart skipped a beat.

Oh no, please not a boy. Please.

"Well, actually..." she glanced over her shoulder, as if making sure that no one could overhear us talking. "There's like... one guy, Matt, who's really cool."

Well, shit.

"Oh, yeah?" I said, trying not to sound bitter. "How old is he?"

"He's in my grade."

"Aren't you a little young to have a boyfriend?" I asked before I could stop myself.

"I never said he was my boyfriend," Amy corrected me sternly. "I only said he was cool."

"Fine, fine. Sorry," I said, feeling a little better. "Calm down, I'm just teasing."

Amy made a sound that resembled a puppy attempting to groan for the first time and I could not help but laugh.

Amy was going to be turning thirteen on May 7th, about a month from now. I guessed that was the appropriate first-boyfriend age. As long as Matt was not repeating the seventh grade for the third time, and therefore way too old to be anywhere near my sister, I would be okay with it.

Not ecstatic. But okay.

When we got home I quickly showered, brushed my teeth, got into my pj's, shouted "Night!" from my bedroom, and pulled out my copy of *Lord of the Flies* from my bag. I had to read an assigned chapter for English and so far, I hated the book was a passion.

I kicked my backpack over to the door and my cell phone toppled out of one of the pockets, skidded across the floor, and bumped into my desk.

"Oh, shit," I hissed, picking it up and inspecting the screen for any damage. It was completely unharmed, so I unlocked it and gasped when I saw how many texts and missed calls I had. The in-boxes were almost full and all but one text was from Connor.

```
-Beth, I'm sorry. Are you still mad?

-Bethy are you hurt?

-Why are you ignoring me??

-Reply dammit

-Sorry that was mean
```

These went on for over sixty messages. The only one *not* from Connor was, thankfully, from Rudy.

```
-I enjoyed our picnic the other day
```

I smiled, remembering eating my lunch on a bathroom floor, and replied:

```
-So did I ☺
```

I put the phone on my desk beside me and started reading the assigned chapter.

As I was beginning to get irritated at all of the biblical symbolism in *Lord of the Flies*, my phone began to ring. Expecting it to be Connor's usual "Night night, I love you, want to have phone sex?" I answered it very curtly.

"Yeah?" I grumbled, not looking up from the pages. If I faked it in bed, I could fake it on the phone too.

"Uh, hey. Is this a bad time?" a voice that was not Connor's asked.

"Who—"

"It's Rudy."

I smiled that he was calling instead of texting me. "No, no. It's a perfect time," I replied. "Just reading."

"What are you reading?"

"*Lord of the Flies*," I groaned, leaning back in my chair.

"Right. Grade eleven curriculum." He laughed a little. "How are you liking it?"

"I'm not," I answered. "The boys are really mean and it's so biblical it could be a copy and paste."

Rudy laughed again and began to agree when a *beep* sound went off in my ear. I pulled the phone away and looked down at the screen where Connor's face was grinning up at me with an incoming call. I bit my lip before pressing 'ignore' and returning my attention to Rudy.

"Beth, you there?" he was saying.

"Yeah, yes, I'm here," I told him, getting up and climbing onto my bed. "An alarm on my phone went off," I lied, settling back on the pillows. "So, how're you doing? Wait, do you know what happens in chapter four of *Lord of the Flies*?"

"Yeah? Why?"

"Because, if you tell me, we can stay on the phone longer," I explained, grinning at my ceiling.

I heard Rudy smile while he explained that Piggy's glasses break, Ralph spots a ship, the fire goes out, and finally the boys kill a pig and make up a chant about hunting.

"Gross," I said, my nose wrinkling at the thought of little boys chanting about killing poor, innocent animals.

"Yeah," Rudy agreed. "Anyway, do have any more homework?"

"No, you just did it all for me."

Rudy and I talked until nearly one a.m., and even then, the only reason we stopped talking was because my battery died.

Yawning as I plugged in my cell, I smiled. I was looking forward to going to school the next day for the first time since spring break.

CHAPTER 17

THE FALL

When I got to school the next morning, I poked my head into every open classroom, hoping to see Rudy. I had no luck.

Pouting a bit, I didn't even notice Connor walking up to me while I was opening my locker door.

"Why didn't you answer my texts? Or call? Are you mad at me?" he began questioning without so much as a hello.

It actually took me a moment to remember what I was supposed to be mad at him about. *Oh right, he pushed me around and accused me of cheating.*

"Look, Connor," I started, turning to face him. He reached behind me and gently put his hand on the back of my neck. Thinking he was going to pull me into a kiss, I rolled my eyes and leaned away from him. "No, Connor, will you just listen?" I started to bat at him, trying to get his attention.

"Calm down, Beth," he sighed, grasping the bun my hair was in and tugging on it. "I'm trying to take this thing out of your hair. There we go, much better."

My jaw dropped while he pocketed my hair tie and my hair twisted out of its bun, tumbling over my shoulders.

"Are you fucking serious right now?" I hissed, narrowing my eyes. "You hate my hair that much?"

"What? No baby, I don't hate your hair," Connor said calmly, brushing my bangs out of my eyes. "I just can't stand that Goddamn bun."

"Shut *up*!" I cried, resisting every urge I had to hurt him. "*You* try and have hair down to your waist and wear it down! It gets hot, it gets tangled, and my hair is actually heavy." I reached over and shoved my hand down into his front pocket to retrieve my elastic, all the while Connor grinned wickedly down at me. "There is nothing wrong with the way I wear my hair, Connor. I can't believe we're even having this argument again."

"We've had it before?" Connor asked, bemused as I pulled my hair into a ponytail.

"The closet? You accused me of cheating? Then you told me I needed to stop wearing—"

"Oh, yeah, I remember now. Anyway, you didn't answer my earlier questions," Connor whined. "Are you still mad at me about yesterday? Is that why you didn't call?"

"Connor, can't this wait until later?" I asked, returning to my locker. "I mean, we're at school."

"You avoiding my questions is basically answer enough."

I gathered my books in my arms and closed my locker door. My breathing quickening as anger made its way through my body, I pulled him into a corner for privacy, even though the corridor was empty.

"Connor, I was really pissed off yesterday and for a good reason. Not to mention the fact that yesterday you said you would give me some space, time to think. The opposite of what you're doing now. I had basically slept the whole thing off until you brought it all back and rubbed it in my face before class even started!" My voice was getting a little louder and a more high pitched as I spoke.

"So, you're not mad?" Connor assumed, gleefully. He leaned in to kiss me, but I brought my books in front of my face and he ended up kissing *Lord of the Flies*.

"I am now!" I corrected, wiping the cover of the textbook on his shirt. "Pulling the elastic out my hair for the second time in a week. If you don't like it, go ogle Candice's stringy, mousy, thin, short hair. I'm sure you already do anyway."

"What is that supposed to mean?" Connor's eyes narrowed.

"You know exactly what it means." I hissed. "He *saw* you flirting with Candice during my audition."

"Who? Dan?" Connor questioned, his brows furrowing. Not wanting him to know about Rudy, I shook my head.

"It doesn't matter," I sighed. "The point is, you're at it again. I'm supposed to be the only girl you have eyes for, but for some reason they don't burn whenever you look at her."

When Connor didn't deny my accusation, I surprised myself by walking away instead of screaming at him further and hitting him over the head with my books.

I stormed down the nearest staircase, my chest heaving. Connor may not be acting on his feelings for Candice, but they were there. But that was exactly what was going on for me as well. I was getting butterflies in my stomach just thinking about Rudy and I had known him barely two weeks, while Connor had known Candice since the beginning of tenth grade.

Oh God, what was I going to do? Where the hell was motherly advice when you needed it? Oh, yeah.

I was so wrapped up in my thoughts that I collided right into Fuzzy, who had been looking down at his phone while climbing up the stairs. He must have been in mid-step when I walked into him, because he was unable to steady his weight, which I had counted on to keep us upright. Instead, Fuzzy teetered back and reflexively grabbed my arms for support, making me fall into him.

We both cried out in horror as we began to fall down half a flight of stairs, tumbling over each other and rolling onto the third floor landing. Gasping for the air that had been knocked out of us, we lay spread eagle on the ground a few feet away from each other.

Coughing and groaning profanities, I reached my arm out to find Fuzzy.

"Are you okay?" I wheezed, when my fingers found his arm.

"Y-yeah." He coughed, neither of us attempting to sit up.

"S-sorry about"—he gasped— "that."

"Don't worry about"—I gasped—"it." I started to wiggle my toes. "Try moving a bit. Make sure nothing's broken." My right ankle was throbbing.

"Just my good mood," Fuzzy groaned. I saw him move his arm to see if there was any pain. "Fuuuuuck. I can't believe that just happened." He rolled onto his stomach, while I bent my knees.

"Are you okay?" he asked, pulling himself up onto all fours and crawling over to me.

I slowly propped myself up on my elbows. "Yeah, I think so." I touched the back of my head where I felt a goose egg forming. I hissed in a breath through my teeth.

"Oh, crap, Bethy... I'm really, really sorry," Fuzzy said, getting into a squatting position, wrapping a strong arm around my waist, and pulling me slowly to my feet. "Let's get you to the nurse's office."

I looked up at him, about to protest that I had suffered through worse injuries than a stupid bump on the head, when I noticed a pretty bad cut just above his left eye.

"Oh, Fuzzy!" I gasped, reaching up and tracing my fingers just above it. "You're bleeding pretty badly."

"Am I?" Fuzzy used the hand that was not currently resting on the small of my back to touch his forehead. "Oh, Jesus."

"Let's get you cleaned up," I said, searching his face for any other injuries.

Just then we heard Connor's annoyed voice echo through the stairwell.

"I'm supposed to be the only guy *you* have eyes for too, you know."

I looked up the staircase we had just fallen down and saw my boyfriend gripping the handrail hard and glowering down at us.

"What are you talking about?" Fuzzy asked, letting me go and bending down to collect the textbooks and binders we had dropped during our fall.

"You were holding—Dude, you're bleeding!"

"I know," Fuzzy growled, wiping away some blood that had gotten in his eye. I pulled a few looseleaf sheets of paper from a binder he was holding, folded them up together, and gently pressed it against his cut.

"What happened?" Connor questioned, making his way down to us.

"We fell down the stairs," I told him, favouring my left leg. I turned Fuzzy around and walked with him down the hallway.

"Can I help at all?" Connor asked, walking beside me. Fuzzy had one arm around my waist to help me limp, while I was pressing the paper, now nearly soaked through, to his forehead.

"Yeah, actually, you can," Fuzzy said, stopping. He reached over and shoved all of the books he had been carrying into Connor's arms. "Here. Take these to our English class, tell the teacher what happened and that we'll either be late or might not make it. That way we won't get detention."

Connor held the books to his chest, nodded, and sprinted to the staircase we had just come from, while Fuzzy hummed the *Mission Impossible* theme song.

"Shut up," I laughed, as Fuzzy pushed open the door to a boy's bathroom and helped me inside.

"Morning, Dan—hey, whoa!" A guy, whose name I think was Brandon, was standing at a urinal. "Dude, no chicks in here!"

"Never mind the fact he's *bleeding*, asshole," I snapped, pushing myself up onto a counter. Settling between two sinks, I smirked. "It's not like you have anything I haven't seen before."

I grabbed a few paper towels from a dispenser, and pulling Fuzzy in front of me, replaced the sheets of paper I had been holding to his forehead. I dropped the used ones into the sink.

There was complete silence in the bathroom while I cleaned Fuzzy's wound. I hate how much a head wound bleeds. Fuzzy's brow furrowed and he looked over his shoulder at Brandon, who was still at the urinal.

"Dude, did you stop mid-stream?" he asked, biting back a laugh.

"I can't piss around girls, Dan," Brandon snapped at him.

I giggled and took Fuzzy's chin in my hand to turn him to face me. "Will you stop bleeding?" I demanded, replacing the paper towel with a new one.

"I'll try, but I don't think it works that way," he said, closing his eyes tight as if concentrating very hard. "Did it stop?" he asked, opening his eyes again.

"You're not trying hard enough," I laughed.

Fuzzy's expression turned into a sad smile. "I've missed that," he said, looking into my eyes.

"Missed what?" I asked, confused. He reached up and touched my cheek.

"Your laugh. You used to do it so much."

We were silent for a moment until Brandon grumbled, "Screw it, I'll go use another one."

I grinned as Fuzzy cocked an eyebrow, lowering his hand from my face. Over Fuzzy's shoulder, I watched Brandon zip up his jeans and grab a backpack off the floor. Fuzzy put a hand on either side on my thighs, caging me in as Brandon stood beside us, washing his hands.

"So Beth, is it true what they've been saying about you?" Brandon asked, rinsing his hands under the tap.

"That depends on what they've been saying this time." I shrugged, feeling my heart beat faster in my chest. I kept my eyes on Fuzzy's wound.

"You know... about your mom," Brandon filled in, turning off the water.

"I don't think that's any of your damned business, Brandon," I snapped, seeing anger flash through Fuzzy's eyes.

"Shit." Brandon shook his head, grabbing some paper towels to dry his hands. "So it is true. How did she—"

Before he could finish the dreaded "how did she do it" question, Fuzzy lunged at Brandon and had him against the wall. Fuzzy kept him pinned there with his forearm across his chest.

"Finish that sentence and I'll kick your sorry ass," Fuzzy growled, towering over him. "Go on. I dare you." At six foot and change, sharp eyes, and a bloody gash on his brow, Fuzzy must have looked so terrifying that Brandon *could* have peed in front of a girl.

"Fuzzy," I said in a warning tone, "he's not worth it. Let him go." Honestly, I was touched that he cared so much about my feelings.

Fuzzy shoved Brandon once more before letting him go and returning to me. I watched Brandon grab his bag and hurry out the door just as the bell for first class rang.

Fuzzy was breathing heavily and grasping the counter on either side of me so hard that his knuckles were white.

With one hand, I dabbed at his forehead with a damp paper towel, while with the other I gently unclenched his left hand, holding it in my own.

"Fuzzy, calm down. It's okay," I said softly.

"No, it's not." He nearly snapped. "Sorry, it's… it's just he had no right to ask you that question."

"I know, but you didn't need to resort to violence. On school property no less," I explained. "I could have told him off."

"I know," Fuzzy groaned, hanging his head. I nudged his chin up again. "I'm sorry, it's just… ugh!" he stomped his foot in frustration.

"You were defending my honour. It was kind of sweet."

Fuzzy grinned up at me as I took the towel away again. The bleeding had mostly stopped now, but I decided to hold the paper there for a bit longer. I wasn't in the mood for English class.

"Hey, did I tell you that Connor followed me into the bathroom the other day and accused me of sleeping with you?" Fuzzy asked me suddenly. I shook my head, sighing.

"No, *you* didn't."

"What? *He* told you?"

"No, I overheard you two arguing."

"You were listening behind the door?"

"Kind of." I shrugged.

"Kind of?" he raised his eyebrows.

"I was in the stall behind you guys." I took off the paper towel.

"Oh." He nodded as I threw the paper away and lowered myself off the counter. "Hang on, wait… what? You were where?"

I took a deep breath and explained to him why I had been in the bathroom and that when I heard him come in I had barricaded myself in a stall. I left out Rudy completely. I couldn't help but notice that his jaw was clenched while I was telling him this.

"Beth, Jesus, I don't understand." Fuzzy sighed, not bothering to hide his exasperation as we made our way out of the bathroom. I was still having trouble walking, so he gently put an arm around my waist so I could lean against him. "Why? Why are you still with him?" He pushed the swinging door open with his hip and we headed for the staircase.

"Fuzzy, you've been asking me that question for months now," I said, getting annoyed. We reached the bottom step. "Why do you keep asking me that?"

"Because," Fuzzy began, stepping around me and facing the stairs, "he proves time and time again how much he doesn't deserve you, *and* you've yet to give me a real answer to the question." He crouched and motioned for me to get on his back. I swung my legs around his sides and locked my arms around his broad shoulders. Fuzzy grasped my thighs, stood up, and made his way effortlessly up the stairs.

Connor would never do this for me, I thought after a moment.

"Beth, glance over the last few months. Even before your mom died. When was the last time you were happy with him? Not happy with him *around*. When were you last happy because of him?"

I bit my lip as I wracked my brain. There were times when he made me feel nothing, instead of pain. But happy?

"I don't remember," I choked, my eyes stinging. "He's my boyfriend and I can't remember the last time he made me happy." I buried my face in Fuzzy's shoulder. We reached the fourth-floor landing and Fuzzy slowly lowered me to the ground. I leaned against a handrail behind me, keeping my injured leg off the floor. "We used to get along so well," I continued quietly, staring at my shoes as if they had the answers to every problem I had. "He made me laugh, he listened when I needed to vent, he—"

"Cheated on you," Fuzzy interrupted, leaning against the wall opposite me, bending one of his legs at the knee and propping his foot on the wall behind him, before continuing. "And made you feel insecure; I'm pretty sure you suffered from an eating disorder last year because of him."

"Fuzzy!" I snapped indignantly, even though he wasn't wrong.

The first time Connor had seen me in only my underwear, he had said: "You look thicker than I thought you would." I basically stopped eating after that.

"I still can't believe he said that," Fuzzy groaned, pinching the bridge of his nose and shaking his head. "I mean, Jane was a cow and you have the best body in school."

I blinked back tears. *Why couldn't Connor say things like this to me?* I resisted the urge to run to the nearest bathroom and lock myself in a stall.

Fuzzy stepped over to me and gently embraced me. One arm around my shoulders and the other around my waist, he held me tight to his chest.

"I'm so sick of this," I told him, my voice muffled against his shirt. "I'm sick of aching, and the loneliness. I'm sick of problem after problem piling up in my life."

We stood there in complete silence, Fuzzy's fingers now entwined in my hair. I held onto my best friend so tightly that my fingernails were digging into his back.

"Isn't that girl dating Connor what's-his-name?" we heard a girl below us ask. Fuzzy's grip on me, if possible, tightened even more to prevent me from whipping around and causing a scene.

"Yeah, she is," answered another girl, as a group of gossips walked by us. "But since her mom died she's been all over, like… every single guy in school."

"I heard she's pregnant with Mr. Wolfe's baby," said a blonde, who didn't bother to keep her voice down.

I saw red. I saw fucking red. I was breathing fast through my nose, my hands clenched into fists and my heart pounding in my chest.

"Bethy," Fuzzy whispered, sympathy in his voice. He relaxed his grip and I pushed away from him, tears of anger caught on my eyelashes. "Bethy, they're full of BS."

"You don't understand!" I cried, not caring that there were classes in progress. "You don't get it! No one does!"

"Help me understand then, Beth," Fuzzy implored, taking my fists in his big hands. "Please, I want to know what is going on inside your mind."

Holding in a sob, I nodded slowly and started to limp back down the stairs.

"Bethy? Where—"

"Let's talk where no one can hear us," I said, gesturing for him to follow me. Because my ankle was still rather tender, I did not want to walk all the way outside, so I slowly led the way to the library on the third floor. We tiptoed past the school's stereotypical grouchy, old librarian and into a room attached to the non-fiction section.

"You think no one will find us in the study hall?" Fuzzy whispered, glancing into the nearest cubical.

Fairview High's study hall was designed a little differently than other ones. Instead of ten-foot-long tables to share with classmates, there were about twenty cubicles about half the size you would see in an office building. Final exams were often held in there.

"No one uses the study hall, Fuzzy; you know that," I pointed out, walking tenderly to the cubical farthest from the door and pulling a second chair into it.

I sat down and put my foot up on the desk, elevating it to prevent swelling. Fuzzy sat in the chair I had pulled up and wheeled closer to me.

"So? Talk to me," he said, leaning forward with his elbows on his knees.

I took a deep breath and pulled out my hair elastic, nervously running my fingers though my hair.

"Okay," I began, leaning my head back to stare at the ceiling. "I feel... empty and scared and alone and... and sad. Not to mention confused and abandoned. I want to scream and cry until my throat is sore and my ears are ringing, but I can't because then people will see that I'm not the brave girl they think I am and I'll start a new chain of gossip. 'Oh, I heard she locked herself in a closet and cried during last class' or something like that. I'm pissed because she left; I'm scared because other people will leave me now. I'm empty because she's gone and, and..." my throat tightened and my eyes stung. I took a deep shuddering breath and looked at Fuzzy. He was looking at me with unshed tears of his own. He reached over, took my hand, and cleared his throat.

"Why are you confused?" he asked quietly.

Before I could stop myself I muttered a single word: "Rudy."

"What's a Rudy?" Fuzzy blinked, looking confused.

"Now a what. A who," I mumbled, staring at my lap. "He's this guy."

Fuzzy stiffened and drew his hand away from me. "He's confusing you?" His jaw muscles clenched as he spoke. "Wait, I've met this guy; he's on the rowing team? He's in the play with you. You… kiss him."

"It's not important," I mumbled, shaking my head. *I shouldn't be talking to you about another guy I have feelings for.*

"No, Beth… I want to know what's going on. I told you this. Please, tell me," Fuzzy insisted, trying and failing to sound relaxed.

I stared into his blue eyes before finally giving in. Maybe talking about it would help me understand it myself?

"So, he's in that play," I told him, twirling a lock of my hair between my fingers. "He plays my love interest, Roger. We get along really well and we… well, we like each other. We talk for ages, and he makes me laugh even though sometimes I feel no joy at all. He's a really great guy." I smiled just thinking about him.

"Have you kissed him?" Fuzzy grumbled, leaning back in his seat and crossing his arms.

"Kind of," I nodded. Fuzzy raised his eyebrows at my vague answer. "There's a kissing scene in the play, remember?"

Fuzzy nodded. "So, what about Connor? What are you going to do about him?"

"God, Fuzzy, we were just talking about him! Can't we *not* talk about—"

"The boyfriend you've had for over a year?" Fuzzy snapped, a tone he usually saved for Candice. "No, we kind of need to talk about him. He makes you want to cry, yell, and kick something; while Rudy makes you happy, even though your mom just died. Yeah, sounds like a really hard decision." He said the last part with quite a bit of sarcasm in his voice. "At least you can do something about this."

"Fuzzy, it's not that easy," I groaned, running my hands down my face in frustration. "Connor is fucking terrible when it comes to serious conversations. He cuts in and won't let me get two words into it."

"So you're just going to let him believe that you still love him while you're rather fond of a co-star?" Fuzzy said with a note of bitterness on his tongue. "I've got to say, Beth, that's not very cool. No matter how much of a dick Connor is, it's not fair to him to be in a relationship with him when you want to be with another guy."

"So either way, I'd be the bad guy," I said. "Dump Connor to be with another guy. Bad guy. Stay with Connor, longing to be with someone else. Bad guy."

"I don't really care why you dump Connor, just as long as you do," Fuzzy shrugged. "He doesn't—Beth, don't roll your eyes at me!"

I had not even realized that I was. "Fuzzy, I've heard you say this like a million times in the last week alone. I'm getting a little tired of hearing it."

This time Fuzzy rolled his eyes. "You just said you're—and I quote—'longing to be with' another guy. You don't think that's a reason, among many, to leave him? No, let me finish! You're not being fair to yourself or... and I can't believe I'm about to say this... Connor. You can't stay with him while wanting to be with someone else."

"Where's all this fucking wisdom coming from? What do you even know about relationships? You've only been kissed and that was on a dare like three years ago!" I snapped, my voice raising and breath heavy.

Fuzzy said nothing for a minute. He just stared at me. "Really, Beth?" he finally said, tilting his head down a bit. "You're going to lash out at the one person who's helping you and not trying to get something for themselves out of it? You choose me, really?"

My breath caught and my lip quivered. He was right. I began to tremble even though I was not cold. Then, without thinking, I crawled onto Fuzzy's lap. I wrapped my arms around his neck and brought my knees into my chest. Without hesitating or questioning me, Fuzzy held me and rocked me back and forth gently.

Finally, just like I had told Fuzzy I wanted to do, I cried.

I cried for my mom. I cried for my sister. I cried for my dad. I cried for Mr. Darcy. I cried for yelling at Fuzzy.

But mostly, I cried for me… for my loss. I finally allowed myself to feel woebegone in front of the only person I knew would not judge me.

My entire body was shaking with gut-wrenching sobs. My throat hurt and my eyes stung. I was grasping onto the front of Fuzzy's shirt, but my fingernails still dug into my palms.

"Please," I gushed into his chest. "Please, Fuzzy, I don't want to anymore!"

"Don't want to what, Bethy?" Fuzzy whispered in my ear, rubbing my back gently.

"I don't want to hurt. I don't want to be brave anymore. It's too hard. Please, don't make me!" I rasped in return. "I can't, I can't, I can't." My heart began to pound so furiously that I was sure it was going to burst from my chest. Terror swept through my body and I started to hyperventilate. "Fuzzy, I think I'm having a heart attack! Fuzzy, I think I'm dying. No, no, no, no…"

Fuzzy slowly pulled away from me. He lowered us from the chair to the floor, leaning himself against the wall, all the while keeping me on his lap.

He took both of my small hands in one of his. With his other hand, he tilted my head up to look at him, so that I was looking into his eyes.

"Bethy, listen to me," he said calmly, though I saw he had been crying as well. "You're not dying, you're having a panic attack. My sister has them all the time."

"What, what do I do?" I gasped, my palms sweaty in his.

"Breathe with me and think of something that calms you. Breathe with me, Beth. In... and out. That's right. Again."

My chest rose slowly then relaxed with his. I thought of listening to *The Beatles* and reading.

In and out. In and out. In and out.

I was calming down. My heart rate slowed and my breathing slowly returned to its normal pattern. My throat was raw from the sobs I had let out and my entire body felt like I had just run a marathon without any training. I leaned my head into Fuzzy's neck and softly thanked him.

"You're the best," I said, wiping my eyes with the back of my hand. "Thank you, Fuzzy. Really."

"Don't even mention it." Fuzzy let go of my hands. "Beth?"

"Mmm?"

"I can't feel my legs," Fuzzy mumbled.

"Oh!" I slid off his legs and stood, gingerly testing my ankle (which was feeling better) and stretching. "How long have we been here?" I asked, looking around for a clock, while Fuzzy shook his legs to return circulation to them.

Just then a bell in the hallway rang to signal end of first class.

"Does that answer your question?"

"Yeah," I sighed, "We missed all of English. And Connor has our books."

"Well, Beth," Fuzzy said, as I looped my arm through his offered one, "looks like we have to be brave and face the hell that is high school."

"Will you help me through it?" I asked, as we made our way out of the study hall.

"Every step of the way."

CHAPTER 18
DISCUSSIONS

By the end of rehearsal on the following Monday, we had officially gone through every scene in the play. It had not been a complete run through, but the show was coming together. Lindsey had a tendency to glower at me during and between scenes (whether because Rudy and I had become very close or because I had a lead role, I couldn't tell), but otherwise I was getting along with all of the cast.

"Hey!" I heard someone call out behind me, as I walked through the courtyard on my way to the bus stop. I turned around and watched as Rudy hurried over to me. "I was looking for you," he said when he reached me.

"I thought you'd left," I said, beginning to walk again. Rudy matched my pace.

"Since we met, have I ever left a rehearsal without saying goodbye to you?" he asked, raising an eyebrow at me.

"Good point." I smiled.

"Hey, do you want a ride home?" Rudy asked when we reached the sidewalk. "I can tell that you've hurt your ankle and I think your bus stop is like five blocks away."

Since the fall the previous Friday, I had been keeping my ankle elevated whenever I could (such as stretching my legs over his lap while waiting for the cast to arrive that afternoon).

"Are you sure? I don't want you going out of your way just to take me home."

"Seeing as I don't know where you live, I don't know if you'll be out of my way." He shrugged. "But I want to drive you home."

"You're cheeky," I laughed, shoving his arm.

He grinned at me and shrugged. "But you like me anyway."

"Okay. I could use a ride home."

"Great," Rudy nodded. Surprising me, he took my hand in his and started to walk us to the student parking lot. Instead of pulling my hand away like I knew I should have, I entwined my fingers with his and smiled at the warmth he was sending up my arm.

Rudy slowed down beside a black BMW and pulled out his keys. I let go of his hand and stood beside the passenger-side door, waiting for him to unlock it.

"What are you doing?" Rudy asked, from the driver's side, looking over at me quizzically.

"Uh, waiting for you to open the door," I said, pulling on the handle to make sure it was not already unlocked.

"That's not my car," Rudy laughed and nodded at the truck beside the BMW.

It was an old, large, blue Nissan pickup truck. There was rusting around each wheel and door handle. The windshield had a thin crack down the centre, and there was a noticeable indent in the passenger's door where it looked like another vehicle may have driven into it at one point. Was this thing allowed on the roads?

Rudy unlocked the door and pulled it open with ease. I made my way around the BMW and watched him climb into the passenger side and clamber over the gear shift, settling in the driver's seat. I followed him in and closed the door behind me, placing my book bag at my feet.

"You need to close the door harder than that," Rudy said as he put the keys in the ignition. I opened the door again and slammed it shut, making the whole cab rock a bit. "Much better." He smiled, looked in the rear-view mirror, and started the truck. He put it in reverse, as it roared to life, and slowly pulled out of the parking lot and onto the street. "I know it's not much," he said, after I gestured for the first turn he had to take, "but I love this truck. My papa and dad helped me pick it out actually. Really, it's a hunk of junk but…" his voice trailed off and he shrugged.

"I love it," I told him honestly. He shot me a sceptical look. "No, really, I do. It's got character and sentimental value. I think it's perfect. But… why did you get in through the passenger door?"

"The driver's side won't open," Rudy shrugged, grinning now that he believed me.

I was about to tell him that that did not surprise me, but I bit my lip and held in the rather rude comment. Rudy reached over and put his hand gently on my knee, squeezing it gently.

Even though I gave directions for Rudy to take the long way home from school, the drive still ended way before it should have. He pulled into my driveway and I smiled when I saw that my dad's van was not in it. I unbuckled my seatbelt.

"Do you want to—" I began, but my phone started to ring. I pulled it out of my bag and saw Connor's stupid face grinning up at me from the screen. I ignored the call and put the phone back in my bag. "Sorry," I said, straightening up and turning to face Rudy. He was holding onto the steering wheel tightly and his jaw was tense. "Rudy, do you want to come in? My dad's not home. We can watch a movie or see what's new on YouTube?" I surprised myself with the invite.

I saw Rudy glance down at my bag where I had just replaced my phone after Connor's call. He turned to face me and I inched closer to him.

"I don't know," Rudy said, glancing down at my mouth. He reached over and tucked a lock of my hair behind my ear, then leaned closer to me still and slid his hand over mine.

My heart was pounding and both of our breathing was erratic. Even though I knew he was a good guy, the best guy, I wanted him to say yes and come inside with me. I wanted him to kiss me for real, not on a stage. I was finally giving in to my feelings for him.

Still staring at my lips, Rudy took a deep breath and leaned away from me.

"I should go," he said quietly, closing his eyes and running his hands down his face.

Didn't see *that* coming.

Humiliation swept over me. I felt my face turn red and I snatched my hand out from under his.

"Okay," I said, unable to hide my disappointment and embarrassment. I bent down and grabbed the strap of my bag.

"Beth, it's not that I don't want to, because I do. It's just… I shouldn't," Rudy explained hastily, watching me with pained eyes.

"Are you being serious right now?" I exclaimed, my voice involuntarily rising. "The first week I met you, you asked if I'd be willing to practise the kissing scene with you. You knew I had—have—a boyfriend then!"

"And you said 'no' because you knew it would be wrong," Rudy pointed out, his voice rising like mine.

We looked away from each other and took a few deep breaths to calm ourselves down. I did not like talking like this to Rudy.

"I want you to kiss me, Rudy," I admitted quietly, chancing a glance over at him.

"And I will. Just not today," Rudy promised, smiling at me.

It took all of my willpower to get out of the truck then without kissing him anyway.

I made my way to the front door and looked over my shoulder when I reached it, raising my hand in a small wave before entering my house. I closed the door behind me and listened to Rudy start the truck up again and back out of the driveway slowly.

I walked up the stairs, dropped my bag with a *thud*, and kicked off my sneakers. I glanced around and noticed my sister in the living room, at the computer she shared with our dad. She was staring at the screen, deep in thought.

"Hey," I greeted, entering the room. She jumped and turned at the waist to face me.

"I didn't hear you come in," Amy said, laughing a little. I shrugged and walked over to her, leaning on the back of her chair.

"What's going on? You look like something's bothering you," I said, looking at the screen over her shoulder. I saw that she was on Facebook, reading a rather long message.

"You know that Honesty Box thing? Where the person is anonymous?" she asked, glancing over her shoulder at me and then back to the screen.

"Sure." I nodded.

"Well, for the last, like... two months, I've been getting these messages from someone saying that I'm beautiful and I inspire them to be a better person," she explained, scrolling up the page. I saw that, indeed, the messages had been going on for a while. I read one dated a few days before.

Amy,

I watch how beautiful and brave you have become over the last couple months. You're absolutely stunning and I hope one day to deserve a person like you.

"That's flattering. Creepy, but flattering," I said, voicing my opinion. "Have you replied or anything?"

"No. I wouldn't know what to say."

"Do you know who it is?"

"I have a few ideas, but I'm not sure," Amy replied.

"Well, let me know," I said, pushing off her chair and starting to the leave the room.

"Who was that guy?" Amy asked, just before I entered the hallway. I froze.

"What guy?"

"The guy who dropped you off," Amy persisted. "With the blue pickup."

I turned to face her. "Oh, that's Rudy. He's in the play with me." I waited for her to say something but she just nodded and turned back to the computer. "I've got some homework to do. I'll be in my room."

I grabbed my bag off the floor and brought it to my room, closing the door behind me. I dumped everything on my bed and picked up my phone. I did not feel like getting another scolding from Connor the next day, so I quickly called him back.

"Hey," he said. "Why didn't you answer earlier?"

No 'hi' or 'how are you', but since I had been wishing Rudy would kiss me when he called, I let it go.

"I was talking to my sister. I didn't want to be rude and answer the phone," I lied.

There was a pause on the other line before Connor finally said "All right."

"How's your evening been?" I asked, grabbing my copy of *Lord of the Flies* and settling down on my bed, propping a pillow against the headboard and leaning against it.

"Wish you were here, honestly," he sighed. I heard a door close in the background and knew what he was about to ask. Not in the mood for phone sex, I quickly started talking about something that was a complete turn off.

"So, what do you think of *Lord of the Flies* so far?" I asked, cringing. I really did not want to talk about the novel.

"I hate it," Connor replied flatly.

"Of all the things we agree on." I almost laughed. "I have to read those chapters and I have a bit of psych to do, so I should go."

"Why didn't you do it during resource centre?" Connor asked. "The whole point of the block is to get homework done."

"I was studying my lines for the play," I told him.

"Oh," Connor sighed. "Okay. Fine."

"I'll talk to you tomorrow?"

"Yeah, sure. Wait, Beth?" Connor said hurriedly, before I could hang up.

"Yes?"

"I just thought you should know something," he began. I heard him lie down on his bed. The *squeak* sound of the twin mattress was very distinguishable. "I told her."

"Told who what?" I urged, confused. What was he on about?

"I told Candice about, you know, that thing," he murmured.

"Connor, what are you *talking* about? What thing?" I racked my brain for something he might tell her that I did not want her to know. "She's such a blabbermouth. You know the whole school will know by tomorrow afternoon," I emphasized.

"I told her how I feel," Connor admitted. "I told her that I have a crush on her." All the air left my lungs and my jaw dropped. "I'm not going to act on it, I promise. I told her because… actually, I don't know why the hell I told her, but I did. Beth, are you still there?"

"Yes," I uttered, barely whispering. I knew I should not be mad. Half an hour ago I was pissed that another guy would not kiss me. The thing was, I was not pissed. I was hurt. "Um, I have to go."

"Beth," Connor hastened. "I'm sorry. Please, don't go. I'm sorry. Please, we can talk about this."

"Goodbye Connor," I broke in, quickly hanging up the phone and shoving it under my pillow.

I took in a deep, shuddering breath and pulled my knees to my chest. Why was I not angry? Three months ago I would be pulling my hair out and screaming at him, enraged out of my mind. But now I just felt small and hurt. What did that say about me? What did that say about us? What did it say about us that we both had feelings for other people? I actually believed Connor when he said he was not going to act on his feelings for Candice (unless you count telling her that they existed), but I *really* wanted to act on the ones I was having toward Rudy. Not long ago, I almost did.

I tilted my head up to look at the ceiling. "Marmee, I need you," I whispered.

Taking a few more deep breaths, I grabbed my books and started my homework.

A little while later there was a soft knock at my door and Amy poked her head in. "Dinner," she told me and left as I slid off the bed and stretched.

I joined my dad and sister in the dining room, half of my mind still on the phone with Connor and the other half still reading my psych textbook. I sat down across from Amy and put a corn on the cob on my plate and a baked potato beside it.

"How was your day, Bethy?" my dad asked as he served himself.

"Typical Monday," I shrugged.

"And how is the play coming along?" he continued, handing the gravy boat to Amy. Being a vegetarian, I skipped the gravy.

"It's going really well, actually." I smiled, taking a bite of my mashed potatoes. "We're planning for opening night to be at the end of May."

The rest of the dinner conversation mostly revolved around Amy: how her thirteenth birthday was two weeks away and what she wanted to do. She asked for some money to take three friends out with her for dinner and a movie. My dad consented and told her that she could set up a futon in the den so they could sleep over afterwards. Seeing Amy smile at her birthday plans coming together absolutely made my day.

After dinner was done, Amy and I did the dishes, then I took a quick shower. As I stepped into the tub, I realized that I only had five more weeks of rehearsals with Rudy. My breath caught and dread overtook me. I didn't want it to end.

I turned off the taps, wrapped myself in a towel, brushed my teeth, and hurried into my bedroom. "Night, guys!" I called out (my code for 'I'll be in my room from now until morning so leave me alone') and closed the door behind me.

Throwing the towel into my hamper, pulling on a tank top and sweat shorts and crawling onto my bed, I pulled my phone out from under my pillow and unlocked it.

There were five missed calls, four from Connor and one from Rudy.

I skipped over all of Connor's voice-mails and went straight to Rudy's.

"Uh, Beth, hey. It's me. Rudy. Can you call me back? Yeah, um... bye."

I quickly dialled his number and held my phone to my ear, my heart beating nervously.

"Hey, you called," Rudy answered, sounding surprised.

"Have I ever missed a call from you and not called you back?" I smirked, basically repeating what he had said to me earlier that afternoon.

He laughed. "Listen, Beth," he began, and then sighed and all the humour disappeared from his tone. "I'm sorry about the whole thing in the truck. I really did want to kiss you."

"I know." I nodded even though he could not see me.

"It's just—"

"I have a boyfriend, I know."

"No, that wasn't it. Not exactly, at least," Rudy claimed. I could almost see him running his free hand down his face. I felt like he was there.

"What do you mean?" I asked, folding back my duvet and sliding beneath it. I rearranged my pillows so they were flat on the mattress and slowly lay down on my back, closing my eyes and listening to him breathe on the other line.

"Connor had just called you," he said. "His face was in my mind. It was the fact that you might have been thinking about him that made me not want to do it. Really I'd prefer you don't have a boyfriend at all, but I want to be the only thing you're thinking about when I kiss you for real," Rudy continued. I smiled at his confession. "Believe me, I really, *really* wanted to but—"

"No, Rudy," I cut in. "I understand now. And you were right to do that. It'll happen. Just not today."

I heard him smile. "Thank you," he said. "So, what are you up to for the rest of the night?"

I glanced at the clock. It was only eight.

"I'm going to read," I told him, eyeing the stack of books on my bedside table.

"*Lord of the Flies?*" Rudy asked, laughing a bit.

"Good God, no!" I chuckled. "I'm thinking a re-read of Harry Potter is in order." I snagged my copy out from between *The Hobbit* and *The Lottery*. I traced my fingers along the worn cover of the book. I didn't want to hang up the phone yet. "Do you—"

"Will you read to me?" Rudy asked, surprising me.

"Yeah, of course," I grinned, opening it to the first page. "Ready for the awesomeness that is the third Harry Potter book?"

"Will you put on voices and pronounce all of the spells correctly?" he requested hopefully. I could hear a shuffling sound, along with squeaks in the background, and I assumed that he was laying down on his bed.

"How else would I do it, Rudy?"

"Then, yes... I am ready for the awesomeness that is Harry Potter."

"All right." I cleared my throat. "Chapter one."

CHAPTER 19
CONSQUENCES

The next morning I found Connor waiting for me at my locker, wringing his hands.

"Um, hey," he said, when I reached him. "Are you kay? You look really tired."

"I was up late," I replied, tonelessly. I reached past him and started to open my locker. I had been up until about two in the morning, before I finally stopped reading to Rudy and turned off the light.

"Beth, listen... I'm really sorry about yesterday," Connor said almost pleadingly, watching me place my bag on the bottom of my locker. "Look, no one's going to be home this afternoon—"

"Connor, do you *really* think I'm going to be in the mood to, you know, *be* with you this afternoon?" I hissed, grabbing my English book and binder.

"No, you didn't let me finish." Connor held his hands out in front of him, his palms up as if surrendering. "I just want to talk. We need to talk and you know that. You've been really busy with the play and at home, and we haven't really had time to ourselves. Please, *please* talk to me?"

I closed my locker door and leaned against it, sighing. I had already told Rudy that I would hang out with him after school, but I guessed I probably should talk to Connor about all this bullshit.

"Fine," I moaned, closing my eyes and hanging my head. "I'll be there a little late though, around four thirty."

"Why? You don't have rehearsals on Tuesdays," Connor questioned, leaning against the locker beside mine.

"I already told someone I'd hang out after school and I don't want to ditch them altogether," I said, rolling my head to face him. "I'll be there at four thirty."

"Promise?" he whispered, his brown eyes imploring.

"Hey, Bethy," I heard Candice's unusually chipper voice behind me. "Whatcha guys talking about?"

I pursed my lips and breathed out hard through my nose. Not looking at her, I nodded at Connor and pushed off the locker.

"Hi Candice," I grumbled, walking past her and hurrying to the English classroom. I was going to be half an hour early but I did not care.

I took my usual seat and pulled my phone out of my pocket.

-I can't hang out for too long today.

I sent the text to Rudy.

-Why? The reply came about two seconds later.

-I agreed to talk to Connor.

-K.

I knew I was disappointing him, but Connor was right. We had to talk.

The day went by a lot faster than I expected, probably because I was dreading the end of it. Basically the entire day Fuzzy was giving me concerned looks and asking if I was all right, while Candice kept flashing me smug smiles. Connor did not say anything to me. He probably feared that, if he gave me an opening, I would tell him I would not be coming over. He was probably right.

At the end of drama class, Candice threw me one more look that made me want to punch her in the taco and Fuzzy pulled me into a corner away from where the students were collecting their bags.

"What's going on with you today?" Fuzzy demanded, crossing his arms and staring down at me. "You're being weird."

"Oh, gee, thanks," I snapped, copying his posture. He cocked an eyebrow. "Sorry. That was rude. I've just got some stuff to do." I relaxed and my shoulders slumped.

"Connor," Fuzzy growled, "I'm going to kick that boy's ass one day."

"Just leave it. I can handle this." I shook my head, walking around him to gather my things. Mr. Thomas was motioning us to get going. "I've gone through worse, right?"

"If you need to talk…" Fuzzy said, holding the door open for me and following me into the hallway.

"I know. I'll give you a call," I nodded, giving him a grateful smile, and turning to the exit attached to the parking lot.

"Beth, where are you going?" Fuzzy asked, staring after me. I could not tell him that I was planning to meet Rudy at his truck, so I shrugged.

"I told you I have stuff to do," I replied. "I'll see you tomorrow." I slipped out with a few other students taking the same exit as me.

Rudy waved at me when I spotted him leaning against the tailgate of his truck. I sped up and stopped about a foot away from him. I looked him up and down, taking all of him in. I absolutely loved his big blue eyes.

"Hey," he smiled, pushing off the truck and taking a step toward me. I took a little step back, which I hoped he did not take personally. We had to be careful, gossip spread faster than wildfire in high school. He looked around the parking lot. School had just let out, so there were still quite a few students around us. Rudy saw me glance around and nodded in understanding. "Where should we go?"

I nodded for him to follow me. We walked side by side across the soccer field and a couple of rain drops landed on my face. Rudy and I both glanced up and watched rain clouds gather above us.

"Oh, crap, that's going to be more than a drizzle." Rudy voiced my own thoughts. He took my hand and we ran the rest of the length of the field and stopped underneath the bleachers.

"It's not an umbrella, but it'll do," I shrugged, letting go of his hand and bending down to put my bag on the ground. When I stood up again, Rudy was inches from me. I had barely gasped in surprise before his hands were in my hair and he was pressing his mouth against mine.

"Finally," I sighed into his kiss, pushing myself into him.

I grabbed onto the front of his hoodie, and felt his hands run down my back and settle on my waist, pulling me as close as I could get to him. I ran my fingers through his dark hair and twisted the curly locks around them. Rudy's grasp moved from my waist to my thighs, lifting me off the ground. I wrapped my legs around him and he pressed me against the wall of the bleachers. Rudy's hands roamed up my sides, while I ran my hands down his neck and arms, stopping at his impressive biceps.

I have no idea how long we made out, hidden from the sight of the track team, but it was not until the phone in Rudy's pocket started ringing that we pulled away from each other just a bit. We were both panting heavily and our eyes were wide with lust-like wonder.

"Wow," I gasped, my hands running up into his hair again.

"Yeah," Rudy agreed, grinning. He leaned in to kiss me more but his phone went off again. He groaned. With my legs still wrapped around him, he reached into his back pocket to pull out his phone. The word 'Mom' was flashing on the screen as he answered the call. "Hey, mom." Rudy gave me an apologetic look but I shrugged and squeezed him tighter with my legs. He shot me a look that read *please don't do that* and I grinned at him. I bent in and started to kiss his neck and he let out a small groan. "No, mom, I'm fine. I just, uh… stubbed my toe." I bit back a laugh and kissed up his face to the tip of his nose. "Yeah, I should be home soon, why? It's *what?*" His eyes went wide and much to my disappointment, he slowly lowered me to my feet. When I looked up at him in confusion, Rudy looked down at his left wrist as if checking a watch.

I gasped and dove for my bag. I pulled out my phone and saw that I had about five minutes to get to Connor's house.

"Shit," I cussed, shoving it back in my bag and pulling the strap over my head. I watched Rudy finish up his conversation with his mom and hang up. "I have to go," I told him meekly, stepping up to him.

"I know." Rudy nodded and kissed me quickly. "I'll see you tomorrow?" I smiled up at him and nodded. I started to walk past him, but he caught my arm. I looked over at him, expectantly. "Beth?"

"Yeah, Rudy?"

"I really like you."

My heart skipped a beat. "Me, too." I blurted. Rudy laughed and bent down to kiss me again. "No, no," I said, "I really have to go. I promised I'd talk to him. I don't want to be thinking about him around you."

Before he could say anything else, I slid my arm out of his gentle hold and started to run to Connor's house.

My boyfriend may live only a five-minute run from the high school, but the rain had still basically soaked through my clothing by the time I reached the steps to his front door. I stood completely still at the bottom of it, staring at the entrance to his house. I had decided not to tell him about what happened between Rudy and me. I mean, we were going to end up breaking up soon anyway, with the way things were going between us, so why hurt him (as much as he fucking deserved it)?

Taking a deep breath, I carefully walked up the stairs and slammed my hand against the door. I wanted inside away from this freezing rain.

"Oh my God!" Connor cried when the door finally opened. I pushed past him and kicked off my flats. "You're soaked!"

"Am I?" I said, taking off my bag and following him into his bedroom. He put a towel on the bed and sat beside it. I slowly sat down next to him, thankful that he was not expecting me to lie down on the towel.

"Are you cold?" he asked quietly.

"No," I replied, wringing my hair out on the towel. "We should just talk, I think."

"Yeah," Connor choked. I looked over at him. I had never seen him look so guilty. Not when he told me about Jane (each time with Jane) or when I told him off about expecting too much from me when we first started seeing each other. "Beth, I'm so sorry. I shouldn't have told her. You were so right. You told me that she would tell everyone and she more or less did. God, and the way she was looking at you today was driving me crazy. I'm sorry I even have these feelings for her! I don't get it, Beth! What's wrong with me? You're such an amazing girl and I keep screwing things up. God, I'm so sorry."

Connor never called me amazing. He made me feel mediocre at best, which was why the look of total despair on his face was very surprising. His lip was even trembling. I actually felt... bad for him. I watched him as he leaned forward, put his elbows on his knees and his face in his hands.

"You're not the only one who fucks up, Connor," I whispered, staring at him.

"What are you on about?" he asked, twisting to face me, his eyebrows raised. I said nothing. I immediately regretted saying anything. I should have just left and that would be the end of this joke of a relationship. "Well?" he shot, suddenly angry. I winced at his loud voice in the quiet empty house. I hated it when his moods would suddenly change from hot to cold in seconds. Unfortunately it was a side effect of one of the medications he was on for his ADHD, so there was never any warning when it might happen.

"I kissed someone," I admitted, keeping eye contact.

His face was stone cold. He stared at me unblinkingly, not moving.

At least thirty completely silent seconds went by before he finally moved and it was not what I was expecting.

Connor raised a hand and brought it down hard, connecting with the left side of my face.

I let out a cry of pain and surprise as the force of his slap threw me off the bed. I hit my head on the hardwood floor and rolled onto my back groaning.

"Connor," I began, but before I could say anything else, Connor was straddling me.

"Who was it?!" he yelled, grabbing my shoulders and shaking me. "Was it Daniel? Was it?!"

"No," I whimpered, truly scared of the man glowering down at me. "No, no it wasn't Fuzzy!"

"Then who was it?!" Connor bellowed, shaking me again. I groaned in pain when the movement caused my head to smack against the floorboards. "I make it pretty clear that you're mine!" He grabbed my wrists with one hand and pinned them above my head. "Who tried to take you from me?!"

He spoke like I was an object, not a girl who had been dating him for over a year. I tried to squirm out of his grasp. He raised my wrists off the floor and then slammed them back onto the floorboards. I had never seen him this angry before.

With his free hand, he started grabbing me without mercy. He'd always been a little rough, like he was too excited to touch boobs, but I knew this was because he genuinely wanted to hurt me. Or claim me. Both. "These are mine!" he shouted in my face, spit flying from his mouth. His hand went down farther until he was palming my crotch. "So is this!" he continued, the zipper of my jeans digging into me as his palm ground against me.

"Please, Connor, stop!" I trembled, my hands clenching into fists and my legs flailing beneath him.

"Who was it?" He used his free hand to shake me again. His enraged face blurred as tears started to fall from my eyes. I felt them trickle across my temples and into my hair. "Who was it, Beth? Who did you fuck? Who took this from me?"

"It didn't... it didn't go that far, Connor! It was just a kiss!" He grabbed my jaw and made me look him into his inhuman, rage-filled eyes. "Ow, ow!" I sobbed. "Please, please, Connor! I didn't—"

"Who was it?!" he bellowed. He grasped the neck of my shirt, pulled it to the side, leaned in, and bit my shoulder. I actually felt his teeth puncture my skin.

"I can't tell you!" I screamed, kicking my legs beneath him. There was no way I was going to narc on Rudy. It was a mutual kiss, making it just as much my fault. I deserved this. I had done him wrong.

"What do you mean, you can't tell me?" Connor snarled, his teeth gritted.

My shoulder ached and I was pretty sure I was bleeding.

"I can't tell you." I panted for breath under his weight.

He let out a furious growling noise and started to fumble for the button of my jeans. "Tell me, Beth."

"Connor, w-what are you doing?" I gasped, pulling at the grip he had on my arms. "Connor, no! *Please*, it was just a kiss!" I felt his cold fingers on my stomach. I began to kick my legs harder. "Please, Connor, don't do this!" He was trying to pull my soaked jeans down, with only one hand, but the wet fabric was practically glued to my skin. He let go of my wrists and I started to hit and claw at him. "Get off! Please, Connor! I'm sorry, I'm sorry!" I sobbed, reaching down and trying to take the waist of my jeans out of his grasp.

"What?" he snapped, shoving my hands away. "You can beat the shit out of me in public when I cheat on you, but I can't get a little favour?" By now my jeans were at my knees.

"Please, Connor, I don't want to!" I begged, sobbing into my hands. I cried out when I felt him bite my leg. "Stop, please." I heard him unbuckle his belt. "No!"

Just then, we heard the front door's deadbolt unlock.

"Fuck, you're lucky," he grunted, getting to his feet. I sat up and started pulling my jeans back up with shaking hands; it was difficult and uncomfortable.

I avoided Connor's furious eyes as I stood up and wiped mine. The left side of my face was hot and the places where he'd bitten me throbbed.

"We'll talk later," he spat. "Just get out."

I opened the bedroom door just as Bob was entering the foyer.

"Hi, Beth," he smiled. "Are you okay?" he asked as I shouldered my bag, which I'd left in the hall.

"Yes," I croaked, pulling on my flats. "I'm just leaving." I forced a smile that tore at my heart.

"Are you sure?" Connor's dad pressured. "You don't look great."

"I have to go," I sputtered, hurrying past him and running down the steps two at a time.

My wrists aching, the back of my head throbbing, and the left side of my face on fire, I started to run toward the nearest bus stop, but before I could get halfway there, I burst into tears. Crying so hard out of fear and pain, I fell to my knees and threw up in some bushes next to a nearby tree.

'You deserved it,' a voice in my brain, which sounded quite a bit like Candice, said. *'You did something wrong and you needed to be punished. He was right about you beating him up in public when he cheated on you. It's only fair.'*

I agreed. I knew two wrongs did not make a right, but it was fair.

I tried to even my breathing and looked down at my wrists. There was reddening around them. There would be bruises there soon.

I stood, sniffled, and pulled my phone out of my bag. I scrolled through my contacts as I continued to the bus stop and tapped 'Marmee'. Holding the phone to my ear, I listened to a robot tell me that the number was now out of service. Confused, I hung up and entered the number into the touch key pad. Halfway through the second ring, I remembered that I no longer had a mom to help me decide what to do. You would think after a month of her being gone, I would have taken her number out of my phone... or at least remembered that she was gone. A fresh wave of tears began as I pocketed my phone and reached the bus stop. I ignored the stares I was receiving from people and waited for my ride, quietly crying.

CHAPTER 20
BRUISES   Blutergüsse, Prellungen

The next morning I woke up after next to no sleep. I rolled onto my back and called to my dad that I was awake. Staring up at the ceiling, I listened to him walk down the hall to Amy's room. I raised my hands above my face and inspected my wrists. There were dark blue and purple bruises around them. How was I going to hide them in school today?

I got out of bed and crossed the room. I pulled on a pair of jeans and a long-sleeved shirt. I put a watch, which my mom had given me years ago, around my wrist; it didn't mask the marks completely, but it helped.

"Good enough," I grumbled, looking down at myself. I took a quick glance in the mirror and my jaw dropped. "Oh my God." [kiefer]

There was a very prominent purple bruise just below my left eye. Panicked, I grabbed my rarely used make-up bag and applied a layer after layer of cover up. Still not good enough. I added another two layers before it was faded enough to leave my room.

Knowing I was going to miss my bus if I did not hurry, I quickly brushed my teeth, shoved on a pair of sneakers, grabbed by bag, and ran down the stairs. "See you later!" I hollered and closed the back door behind me. [brüllen, rufen]

I jogged to the bus stop just in time to watch it come to a stop. I jumped on, swiped my bus-pass, and took a seat in the back. When the bus pulled away, I relaxed a little. Good, I had missed running into Amy. I needed time to think of a story for my black eye.

I could not believe I had a black eye. Honestly, what the fuck? I kissed another guy and Connor attacked me, hit me across the face, and then tried to force himself on me! I began trembling and wrapped my arms around myself. All night, whenever I had closed my eyes, I felt his fingers on me or his teeth on my leg. In the end, I had cried myself to sleep. I shouldn't have told him. I'm sure there were secrets he was keeping from me.

Relief swept through me when no one was at my locker that morning. I quickly shoved my things into it and removed my usual textbook and binder.

"Hey Beth."

I actually screamed. I'd had nightmares about that voice and the things it had said to me the day before. I spun around, staring at Connor with what must have been a look of terror. "Hey, calm down, I'm not going to hurt you." He was standing way too close to me. I could feel his breath on my neck. I could not back up any farther without actually stepping into my locker. "I shouldn't have handled things the way I did yesterday. That wasn't right. It doesn't look like you're bruised or anything, though." I wanted to scream at him. *Not bruised or anything? Like that makes it all right? Tell him he's an asshole and that you never wanted to see him again!* "Beth, tell me who it was." I just barely shook my head. Connor's eyes flashed with anger. He slammed a hand down hard on the locker beside my head, making me grimace. "Beth, I'm serious, tell me! What it Daniel?"

"What's going on?" We both turned out heads to see Fuzzy walking up to us, a confused and angry look on his face. "Beth? What's going on?"

My wide eyes shot back to Connor who was glaring at my best friend. What was he going to do?

He ended up grabbing my face and kissing me hard, as if claiming me. I actually cringed at his touch. He pulled back violently and stormed away from us without a word.

Trembling, I closed my locker and pressed my forehead against the cold metal of the door.

"Beth?" Fuzzy said softly from behind me. "Come on, we need to talk." He gently took one of my hands in his hand and led me into an empty computer lab. He closed the door behind him and waited for me to start talking. When I remained silent, he let out a loud sigh. "Bethy, what the hell was that?"

"What do you mean?" I said, staring at my feet and clutching my books to my chest.

"I have *never* seen you look that scared before! You actually look pained for him to be touching you! I know he stinks sometimes, but honestly, what happened? And that look he gave me? What the hell was that for?" Fuzzy ranted, gesturing at the door.

"We got into a fight yesterday," I mumbled, shuffling my feet. "I was afraid he was still mad."

"Must have been one hell of a fight," Fuzzy grumbled, leaning against the wall. "What was it about?"

I hesitated before answering. "He thinks I kissed you."

"But you didn't."

"I know that."

"Why does he think that then?"

I finally looked up at him. "Because I did kiss someone, but I wouldn't tell him who. I kept denying that it was you, but he wouldn't listen. And, really, I can see why. We are really close."

"You kissed someone?" Fuzzy asked, a look of surprise on his face. "Who? Wait—it was that Rudy guy, wasn't it?"

I nodded. "Yesterday after drama class we met up and made out. Then I went over to Connor's place, because he wanted to talk about how he told Candice about his feelings for her, and I was not planning on telling him." I sat down in a nearby computer chair. "But he was really beating himself up and I had just acted on feelings I have toward Rudy, so I told him, thinking that it was just going to end us but... stuff happened."

"What stuff?" Fuzzy asked slowly, sitting beside me.

"We fought. He got mad. Whatever, it's over." I ran my fingers through my hair, which I had not even bothered to put up in its usual bun. "I'm going to break up with him; I just don't know how." I glanced at Fuzzy and noticed that he had gone white. "What?"

He reached over to me, took my hand in his, and turned it over. He had seen my bruises, so the long sleeves had been useless. "Beth," he breathed, tracing his fingers along them gently. He suddenly stood and started to the door. "I'm going to *kill* him."

"No, Fuzzy!" I shot up and hurried between him and the doorway. "He got mad, that's all!" A flash of Connor pulling down my pants went through my mind and my knees buckled a bit. I put a hand on Fuzzy's broad chest, which was heaving. "He got mad and I deserved it. No, listen! When he cheated on me with Jane, I kicked his ass in the middle of the street. I kind of deserved it, in an eye for an eye kind of way. Please, leave him alone. For me."

"Bethy, no one should ever hurt you," Fuzzy snapped, glancing down at my wrist. "You'd tell me if he did more?"

"Yes," I lied, just as the bell for English class rang. I turned to open the door that we had come in through, but Fuzzy stopped me.

"Wait, did you just say that Connor admitted to having feelings for Candice?"

"Yeah," I groaned, rolling my eyes. "That's why she was so fucking smug yesterday."

"Jesus," Fuzzy sighed, pulling open the door for me.

"Yeah, I know." We made our way to our first class.

At our desk during English, the facial expressions that were exchanged would have been funny had they not been at my expense.

Candice was smirking smugly, glancing from me to Connor once in a while. Fuzzy was glaring at Connor, who would glare right back when he was not scowling at me. I tried to remain clueless to these looks and copied down the notes off the board without actually reading them. Just before I left for psychology afterwards, Connor gave me another one of his rough kisses that seemed full of anger. I had a flashback of him grabbing at me and yelling that I was his. He was marking his fucking territory.

Psych went by faster than I thought it would. Usually I paid attention in that class. Instead, I skipped forward to the chapter in my textbook about PTSD or flashbacks. I did not get much out of it, but it was interesting nonetheless.

As I was leaving for lunch, I bumped into Rudy. For the first time that day, I smiled.

"Hey," I grinned up at him. "Are you... are you here waiting for me?"

"Well, yeah," he shrugged. "I thought we could have lunch together or something."

I bit my lip and looked around. Students were filling the hall and were bustling around, making their way outside or to the cafeteria. "I don't think that's a great idea," I said quietly, thinking about what Connor might do if he saw me talking to another guy. Rudy looked disappointed. "It's just, I always eat with Fuzzy and Candice and, ugh, Connor. So..."

"I see," Rudy nodded, looking down at me. He reached into my arms and snagged my psych book out of my grasp with a cheeky grin on his face.

"What are you doing?" I demanded, laughing.

"This book is being held hostage until after rehearsal today," he told me, tucking it in between a few books of his own. He bent down closer to my ear and whispered, "And there's a ransom."

"Don't worry, I'll pay it." I half smiled, then walked to the cafeteria where my friends would be waiting.

While the four of us sat on our windowsill eating away at our lunches, I could see Connor still giving Fuzzy the stink eye. He was still completely convinced that I had kissed my best friend and I understood why. Connor was also torn about how to act around me. He seemed to have three different personalities: one felt guilty about what he had done the day before, another was disgusted with me, and the last was acting very territorial. This included a hand down the back of my pants while glaring at any guy who walked past us. I was not sure which personality I hated the most. Whenever he touched me I would flash back to when he attacked me and would have to remind myself that he was provoked, kind of.

By the end of lunch I had barely eaten a thing. Fuzzy was sure that I had downplayed what had actually happened and Candice remained oblivious to everyone but herself.

In resource centre I could not do my psych homework because Rudy had my textbook and nothing had been assigned in English. I pulled out my script and read through a scene that I was having difficulty with and knew we would be rehearsing that day.

Before walking to drama class, Connor slammed an angry kiss against my mouth. I could have sworn he actually made a growling noise after pulling away and storming down the hall to his biology class.

"What is with him today?" Candice asked as the rest of us headed down the stairs. "He's been so grouchy."

"It's probably a side-effect of the medication he's on for his OCD or ADHD," I suggested quickly. "Best not to mention it."

Fuzzy glanced at me over Candice's head. "Yeah, must be it."

The drama class assignment was to produce and perform a quick scene about teenage pregnancy, which seemed to be very popular. Just the week before, a tenth grader had twins.

"Choose your 'mates'," Mr. Thomas air quoted when he finished describing the project. "You have twenty minutes."

I saw Candice turn to Fuzzy, who was always afraid to turn her down because of her guilt-tripping abilities. The last time they had been partnered together, he had politely told her that he would not kiss her on stage, even though they were playing a married couple.

Fuzzy had not meant any offence toward her or any intention to hurt her feelings, but she did not speak to him for three days. And, for some reason, silent treatment from the ice queen, no matter how immature it was, was torture.

So, to save him from a class of agony, I grabbed the front of his shirt and pulled him close to me.

"Oh, baby, stupidly don't wear a condom, while I irresponsibly don't use any form of birth control, and rock my world!" I nearly shouted in an exaggerated seductive tone.

Fuzzy, surprised at my ability to say those words while looking him in the eye with a straight face, decided to play along while everyone stared at our improvised performance.

"Oh, yes, girl I hardly know," Fuzzy said just loud enough for people to hear. "Let me practise unprotected coitus on you."

I bit my lip to suppress a smile and lay back on the fainting couch we were sitting on. "So how does this sex thing work? I skipped Sex Ed," I said.

"Let me show you," Fuzzy replied, leaning over me.

"And scene!" Mr. T called out just in time, because I could not hold in my laughter any more. Fuzzy promptly cracked up beside me, along with the rest of the class (except for Candice, of course).

"How... how did you do that?" Fuzzy gasped between chuckles. "Without laughing, I mean."

"I could ask you the same question," I giggled, watching a guy offer Fuzzy a high five.

"Yeah, it was real witty," Candice snapped. "Not inappropriate at all."

"Candice, that was the assignment," I pointed out. "Besides, we were acting."

"Yeah, I think we might get an 'A' on this assignment," Fuzzy nodded, glancing at Mr. T for confirmation of his suspicion.

"Two thumbs up," our teacher said. "Borderline inappropriate," he semi-agreed with Candice, who gave us a smug smile and did not talk to us for the rest of class. What a shame.

When the bell rang, I stayed in the drama room waiting for rehearsal to start. I grabbed my script and lay down on the fainting couch, reading through that day's scene again.

"Hey, you."

I put the script down and pulled my legs to my chest, just in time for Rudy to sit down and grin over at me.

"Hey back," I grinned, wishing I could kiss him. Wait... no one was in the room, what was stopping me? Besides my suddenly abusive boyfriend scowling at me in the back of my mind, I could not think of any reason not to.

Connor had a way of making me feel small and pathetic. With just one look he could ruin a great day. If he was going to be an asshole, I may as well do something to deserve the treatment, which I kind of did.

After taking a quick glance around the room, I grabbed Rudy's head and pressed a soft kiss against his lips. I slowly pulled away and smiled at him.

"Well, thanks for that, but I still have your book," he kidded, putting his hands over mine and pulling them away from his face, just as Mr. T walked in.

"Well, it's just the three of us today," he announced, standing in the doorway.

"Why?" I asked.

"Probably because we're the only ones in the scene," Rudy shrugged, still looking at me suspiciously.

"Grab your things, we'll be practising in the auditorium today," Mr. Thomas told us. I grabbed my book bag and Rudy snatched up his backpack. We listened to our director rant about how "They signed up, so they may as well show up."

The three of us headed to the auditorium and Mr. Thomas sat in the front row with a clipboard in his lap, while Rudy and I ascended the steps to the stage. We placed our bags and scripts on the edge of the stage and stood on our marks.

"And go!" Mr. T called up to us and we began our scene.

Still with a bit of stammering, Rudy and I tried our best to get through the candle song. I thought it was one of the best songs in *RENT*. It was the first time we'd done it using actions, not just singing it at each other, scripts in hand, so that made it a little harder, with more than just the words to concentrate on.

"And scene!" Mr. T said. "You guys did a great job! Honestly, I was a little worried about this one." Rudy chuckled at the comment and I made a note to try and run through it to get even more praise from my favourite teacher in the school.

We ran through the scene three more times before our director told us that we were done for the day and hurried out of the room, saying that he didn't want to miss the new episode of *Big Brother*. I waved as he left the auditorium and Rudy called out "Bye!" just before the door closed behind him.

That's when I realized that I was alone with Rudy. A memory of Connor demanding to know 'who I'd fucked' flooded my memory and I closed my eyes, breathing deeply like Fuzzy had shown me during my anxiety attack in the study hall.

I headed backstage where I'd left my book bag, willing my heart to slow down. Just as it was reaching its normal rhythm, I felt Rudy's arms slowly wrap around me from behind.

"Hey," he breathed into my neck, just above the same shoulder Connor had chomped down on the day before. A shiver ran up my spine as his stubble grazed my bare neck. "How are you?" he asked as I turned to face him.

Walk away! I thought, staring into his sky blue eyes. *Just go!*

"I'm fine." I choked out somehow.

"Yeah, you are." Rudy grinned and I rolled my eyes.

"Dork."

What are you doing?! Do you not remember what happened yesterday?! Just walk—

Rudy bent down and kissed me gently… longingly even.

What had I been thinking about just now?

He kissed me so passionately that my knees went weak. I stumbled a couple steps, my back ending up pressed against the wall behind me. I moaned into his mouth and ran my hands up his arms, which were braced on either side of me. Rudy ran his fingers through my hair and down the side of my face. His fingertips grazed my hidden black eye and I inhaled sharply through my nose and stiffened.

Rudy stopped and stepped away from me slightly, his eyebrows creased.

"Are you all right?" he asked slowly, eyeing my face for any hint of a lie.

"Yeah." I nodded, trying to pull him back to me. "Yeah, I'm totally fine."

His eyes narrowed and he took my hands off of him firmly.

"Ah!" I gasped, pulling my tender and bruised wrists to myself.

"Beth?" Rudy whispered, concern laced in his tone. "What's going on?"

I bit my lip and shook my head. "Nothing." I insisted. "It's nothing." I grabbed by book bag off the floor and started across the stage to leave.

"No," Rudy said, grabbing my elbow to stop me. He rolled up my sleeve and I tried to pull away but the damage was done. He had seen the bruises. "What happened to you?" he demanded, lightly tracing the purple and yellow finger-shaped marks on my skin. I hung my head and was grateful that he couldn't see my black eye or the bite marks.

"Nothing," I lied again. "Connor was mad. I told him about, about the kiss—"

"He did this to you?!" Rudy shouted, his strong voice echoing through the room.

"I deserved it." I shrugged. "I cheated on him."

"So he *bruised* you?" Rudy fumed, his fists clenched at his sides. "Did he... do anything *else* to you?" he hissed through gritted teeth. I didn't say anything. "Did he?!"

"I, I deserved it," I stammered finally.

"He's a dead man," Rudy growled taking a step to the edge of the stage.

I grabbed his arm and shook my head hard, my ponytail whipping back and forth. "I deserved what I got," I said, emphatically. "I shouldn't have done what I did. I beat him up when he cheated on me so, really, it's only fair."

"Fair?" Rudy nearly spat. "Fair?! Beth, if you think that that is acceptable behaviour over a kiss, you're wrong! If that was *all* he did, imagine how bad he could hurt you if he lost control again!"

"He wouldn't do it if I don't have it coming!"

"Have it—" Rudy ran his fingers through his hair, then down his face in frustration. He huffed a sigh, "Beth, you are so naive! I thought you were smarter than this!"

That pissed me off. "Just because we kissed doesn't mean you have the right to judge me! You barely *know* me!" I yelled.

"You're right! I *don't!*" Rudy shouted back. "You have to figure out your priorities: your health and safety, or your screwed-up relationship with the world's biggest asshole. You are literally in danger, Beth, and you know it." He grabbed his backpack and jumped off the stage. "Let me know what you decide." He added over his shoulder, leaving me alone with nothing but my thoughts and conflicted tears of anger and hurt.

You don't understand, Rudy. This is what he did when all I did was kiss you; if I tried to dump him, far worse things would happen to me. Or even to you.

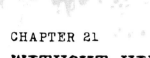

CHAPTER 21
WITHOUT HIM

The rest of the week was nearly unbearable. The only time Rudy would talk to me, let alone look at me, was in rehearsal and then it was only when we had to direct lyrics toward each other. On Friday when we sang the candle song, he was distant and wasn't even looking at me half the time. I'm pretty sure Mr. Thomas thought he was trying a new tactic for the song, making Roger shy or something.

Besides rehearsal, the few classes we had apart, and when I was at home, Connor never left my side. He continued to try to get the name of whoever it was I cheated on him with. It was scary at first, his brown eyes threatening, but by Friday afternoon I just wanted to tell him to shut up. If I was going to tell him, it would have been when he tried to rape me earlier that week. I considered breaking up with him when he shook my arm and told me that there was no way he was ever going to let anyone take 'what was his', but he had me too scared to do anything that might make him angry. Breaking up would have done that.

Every night I texted Rudy about, well, anything: apologizing for the way I spoke to him, telling him that my relationship with Connor was more than meets the eye, that I thought he sounded great with Brett earlier, what I'd had for dinner, wondering if he wanted to listen to me read *Harry Potter* again… He never replied.

My black eye had faded into a very nearly invisible yellow. Unless you were looking for it, you couldn't see it. My bite marks were gone, but I could still feel the ghost of them.

I felt like I was in a million pieces and I was awful for it. I should have been broken up about my mom being dead, but instead, here I was on a Saturday morning, staring at the ceiling and grieving the loss of a boy I wasn't even with. What was wrong with me? I should be awake and taking advantage of the fact that my dad wasn't home and my sister and I could blast music that he hated and drink his good coffee.

Slowly I sat up and tossed the covers off of me, my books slipping off the end of the bed with a *thump*. "Whoops." I said in a monotone voice, swinging my legs off the bed and standing up. I stretched and yawned loudly before picking up what had fallen off my bed.

My script. And it had landed open on "Light My Candle". It was a sign or something. I had to get perfect at this song, and Rudy would be really impressed and then *have* to talk me, to say 'Wow, you did great today!' or something. At this point, sadly, I would do anything for a thumbs up from him.

I left my room, still in my cherry-decorated sweat-shorts and tank top, and knocked on Amy's door.

"Hey, what are you up to?" I asked her after entering her room. She was sitting up in bed, writing in a notebook with her hair in an adorable ponytail at the top of her head.

"Not a lot," she said, sitting upright and rolling her shoulders, making them pop. "What's going on?"

"I need a favour," I told her, stepping over a pile of dirty clothes.

"What is it?" she asked, standing up.

"I need your help with a song." I held up my script, which I had been hiding behind my back.

"I've only seen the movie once, Bethy," Amy told me, tentatively. "Which song is it?"

"'Light My Candle'," I said. "I have the music downloaded, so it'll kind of be a karaoke thing."

"All right." Amy shrugged. "I might not be any good, but it can't hurt and I'm not in the mood to do homework."

We headed into the living room and I entered the flash drive with the RENT soundtrack into the family computer, which my dad had left on, and then handed Amy a photocopy of the lyrics.

"So, am I Roger or this Mimi chick?" she joked and I gave her an 'oh, shut it' look.

I started the music and pointed at my sister to give her the cue to begin.

"Oh, what did you forget?" she sang... sort of.

"Got a light?" I mimed holding up a candle.

Eventually she got pretty into the song, even though she was completely off key, and by the time we were acting out the part where Mimi and Roger are searching for her stash, Amy was attempting to rap and waving her arms around calling me 'son'.

Laughing so hard that I was close to tears, I stood up and paused the music. "Oh my God, Amy! You just made Roger into a wannabe gangster," I nearly howled. "I seriously need to learn these lyrics, man!"

Taking a deep breath to calm her laughter, Amy nodded. "Start again?"

"Okay."

I restarted the music, and with as much dramatic flair as my little sister could muster, she raised her arms up and sang/bellowed *"What did you fooorrrrrrgeeetttttt?"*

"Got a light?"

She sang as opera-ish as she could and I remained as professional as I could, considering the circumstances.

We were nearly flawless until, when Mimi is on all fours singing the lyric *'They say I have the best ass below Fourteenth Street'*, our dad walked in.

"What the—what?" he sputtered, looking from me to Amy, who was standing above me, her arms up above her head, doing jazz hands.

My sister and I exchanged a devious glance. We knew how uncomfortable this would make him, and so continued as though he wasn't there as a single audience member. He stared at us with an expression that could only be translated into "Oh dear God!" and "the horror!" I was pretty sure I heard him choke when Amy sang that she didn't recognize me without handcuffs.

When the song wrapped up and I mimed snatching a stash away from my sister, we turned to Dad as straight-faced as we could.

His face was pale underneath his beard and bushy eyebrows.

"That's not an appropriate song," he finally said, crossing his arms.

"She has AIDS, too," I said without hesitation. "Don't worry, Dad. It's a love story."

Amy burst out laughing and I hugged my dad quickly, just to make it weirder, and skipped off to my room, humming.

It wasn't until I closed the door and was sitting on my bed, singing quietly, that I realized that that was the first time I'd smiled since Rudy and I had fought.

"Thanks, Amy," I whispered.

On Monday I went to school, looking forward to showing off just how much I had practised over the weekend. I just barely got my homework done, but had spent *hours* on my lines. Unfortunately, at rehearsal, Rudy barely looked at me unless we were on stage.

Connor continued walking me to all of my classes, my hand gripped firmly in his. It might have looked endearing to anyone who saw, but I knew what was going on. I was on a leash.

"What is up with you?" Fuzzy asked me on Tuesday, as I watched Rudy make his way through the flood of students in the cafeteria. My heart fluttered when he briefly looked over his shoulder at me before snapping his head back to his food tray. It was one of the very rare moments when Connor had left my side for a millisecond. "Beth?"

"Huh?" I asked, tearing my eyes away from Rudy's back and to my best friend, who was sitting across from me on the windowsill, his eyes narrowed and arms folded over his chest. "What's going on?"

"That's what I'm asking," Fuzzy said, shaking his head. "You're being weird again. You've been really... distracted the last couple of days. Didn't hear from you once over the weekend."

"I've just been really busy, Fuzzy," I said, showing particular interest in the wrappers that had contained my lunch. "You know, the show and homework and stuff."

"Beth, talk to me," he said, taking my hand in his gently. "Please, I know something is wrong." His eyes searched me. "Is it Connor?"

"Is what Connor?" my boyfriend asked, swinging himself up beside me on the sill. I yanked my hand away from Fuzzy's and placed it, more out of habit than anything else, on Connor's knee.

"Nothing, don't worry about it." I faked a smile toward the both of them and glanced back toward where Rudy was sitting.

His chair was empty and the food on the tray in front of it was hardly touched.

The next day was the first time since our fight that Rudy made contact with me outside of *RENT*... and it was through Connor.

My boyfriend was glaring at a teacher's assistant that I had smiled at, out of reflex, when suddenly he fell to the floor with an *oomph*, his binder and textbooks spiralling out in every direction.

Connor was not a clumsy person and I'd seen no '*wet floor*' sign, so I looked around the crowded hallway for the reason for his sudden gravity hug. I looked over my shoulder and saw Rudy five feet away, staring down at Connor while walking backward with a smug smirk on his face. He glanced up at me and raised his eyebrows as if to say *I'm not even sorry* and turned back around, striding to his next destination.

Connor got to his feet, snatching his textbooks up off the floor. "Someone tripped me," he snarled, looking around for the guilty culprit who was now long gone.

"Are you all right?" I faked concern, just as Fuzzy joined us with Candice trailing him.

"What happened?" Fuzzy asked, glancing back and forth between Connor and I, making it look as if he were watching a tennis match.

"Nothing," Connor snapped, pulling me to him and crashing his lips to mine.

I knew better than to push him away, so I stood completely still until he had, ugh, claimed his territory. I wished I had the courage to break up with him, the guts to tell him off, but what Rudy had said still haunted me.

If I angered Connor with more than a kiss, what would he do? I was sure he wouldn't be pleased with me if I broke his heart, no matter how small it was.

"Elizabeth! Hey, Elizabeth?" I heard someone call from down the hall the following morning. Only one person called me that and I hadn't spoken to him since the previous semester.

Hoping there was another Elizabeth in the corridor, I turned around to watch my old wrestling coach heading my way, and unfortunately, looking directly at me. I had heard through the grapevine that his team wasn't doing too well without me on it, so I was pretty sure I knew what he wanted to talk to me about, but he took me by surprise.

"Can I talk to you for a moment?" he asked once he had reached me. Beside me, Connor grabbed my bicep tight and glared up at our physical education teacher.

"Yes, you may," I said, snatching my arm out of Connor's grasp.

Coach Foster smiled and crossed his arms over his chest. He was rather tall, with light brown hair and a lean body. I knew that a lot of the female staff (and a few male faculty members) where fond of looking at him.

"I know you don't want to join the team again, and since some of those boys are horny dogs, I can respect that, but I'd like to ask you a favour."

"What's that?" I asked, smiling up at him.

"I was wondering if you'd be interested in showing a few wrestling maneuvers to the ninth grade girls' PE class that I'm teaching." He shrugged at the suggestion. "I'd write you a note to excuse you from the class you'd be missing, don't worry. You're the best female wrestler I've had..." He started the flattery approach, but I was already sold.

"Yeah!" I nodded excitedly, nearly bouncing on my feet. "Which period? Which day?"

Coach looked a little surprised at my eagerness, then grinned. "Third period and does tomorrow work?"

"Thursday? Yeah, sure! I'll bring my gear." I agreed "Who will I be grappling with?"

"Graham. He's already said he would," Coach Foster told me. "I thought it would be neat to show how to dislodge someone significantly bigger than yourself. It's simply physics and they never believe me at first."

Graham was a good guy; one of the only guys on the wrestling team who didn't try to feel me up.

"Okay, great! I'll see you tomorrow."

The warning bell for Psych went off and Connor put his arm around my shoulders, spinning me around and away from Coach Foster.

"Why would you say yes to that?" Connor growled, practically pulling me down the stairs to my class.

"You didn't have a problem with it last year," I snapped, nearly stumbling on a step and grabbing the rail beside me to prevent another fall down the stairs. "Slow *down*, Connor! Damn!"

"Well, last year you didn't cheat on me," Connor said, stepping beside me and pressing me into the wall with his body.

"*You* cheated on *me* and I didn't stalk you to every class," I hissed, pushing at his chest. "Connor, people are staring—"

"What's going on?" Fuzzy's voice demanded from a few steps above us. "You okay, Beth?"

Connor glared up at him while I nodded. "Come on, Beth, you'll be late." He grabbed my wrist and dragged me to the door of my next class.

Great. More bruises to look forward to.

The next day, I helped set up the wrestling mats in the gym while the girls PE class changed into their work-out clothes.

"I heard about your mom," Coach Foster said, adding a fourth mat to the floor beside mine. An eight by eight square lay at our feet. "I'm sorry that happened."

I nodded at the floor but said nothing. There was never a proper response to that. I could not say 'it's all right', because obviously it wasn't, and I couldn't say 'thank you', because all they had done was acknowledge that my mom was gone.

Graham and I made our way to the sidelines of the gym to stretch. "You think you'll be able to beat me?" he goaded jokingly, bending down and grasping his ankles.

"I've done it before." I smirked as I put pulled my arms behind my back, clasped my hands together and locked my elbows while arching my back. "Simple physics." I shot a glance over at him and added in a quieter voice, a note of warning in my tone, "Don't throw this because you feel sorry for me." I had no doubt he knew about my mom.

Graham gave me a small nod of understanding and sat down. I sat in front of him and we helped each other stretch while the girls filed into the gym and looked around the set up curiously. Once all the students had piled into the gym, Graham and I joined the coach who was standing in front of the mats, facing them.

"All right," Coach Foster clapped his hands and rubbed them together, the sounds echoing loudly throughout the room. "Today we are going to do something different."

"Thank God,"

"I am so sick of volleyball!"

"And capture the flag!"

"I know, it's getting so freaking bor—"

"Hey!" the coach said over the sudden complaints. I wondered if I had been that annoying in ninth grade. "We're going to be doing some wrestling." The girls looked intrigued and I smiled at their interest. "There are different forms of wrestling that people do, whether competitive or not, and in some cases, they can be helpful for self-defence. These are two of my best wrestlers: the adorable heart-throb is Graham and the badass beside him is Beth." He waited for his students to finish laughing before he continued with his lesson. "The kind of wrestling they're going to demonstrate and help you girls with begins with one of these two on all fours." He glanced over his shoulder at us and raised an eyebrow as if to say '*choose*'. Automatically my opponent and I raised our fists in front of us and counted to three. I spread my index and middle finger out and Graham kept his hand clenched in a fist. He mimed smashing my 'scissors' with his 'rock' and I rolled my eyes. I stepped onto the middle of the makeshift wrestling mat and got down on my hands and knees, with Graham standing beside me. "The goal," coach continued, "is to get your opponent on their back for three seconds straight. Yes, Beth does have a disadvantage, but she has won against him before. It's simple physics, girls. You'll see. Any questions?" he asked everyone, as Graham got down on his knees. None of the girls said anything, so coach turned to us, and squatting down beside the mat, muttered, "When you're ready." I nodded and he slapped his hand down on the hardwood floor. "Go!"

Graham's left hand shot under my torso and snatched my right forearm, pulling it to him. My shoulder hit the mat and I tensed my left arm to keep some leverage. He swung his right leg over my hips just as I was bringing my right knee up to my fallen shoulder, making it harder to roll me onto my back. Graham steadied himself on top of me, most of his weight on my waistline, and his right arm braced a few inches above my head. I pulled my left knee up so that my hips were sort of in a mid-twerk position, and with my free arm, I grabbed his right wrist and pulled it to my side. Graham fell forward onto his right shoulder, most of his weight now either off of me or only on his right side. His left arm was still wrapped around my body and my left arm remained in his determined grasp. By now, both of us were grunting with the effort of tensing as many muscles as possible, and panting for the same reason. I hooked my right ankle over his shifting right leg, and with all my might, pushed off with my left arm and leg, shoving against him in one motion. The momentum made Graham roll onto his back. His arm was still wrapped around me so I rolled with him, my back against his front, and I arched my back using the upper part of my body to push his shoulders into the mat while keeping my feet braced on either side of his kicking legs.

Over our grunts and panting, I heard the coach slap the mat beside us three times and shout out, "We have a winner!" Graham and I relaxed our muscles, and totally wiped, I remained sprawled on top of him until the coach grabbed my arm and pulled me to my feet. "With at *least* a forty-pound disadvantage, Beth wins in less than a minute! *Told* you she was a badass!"

The girls, whom I had actually completely forgotten about, were either clapping or saying, "That was so cool!" as Graham stood up, rubbing his shoulder.

After bringing us each a bottle of water and giving us a five-minute break, the coach clapped Graham on the shoulder and said to us, "Again, but this time I'll be getting you to pause so I can point out where the physics come in."

Graham and I went through it twice more before Coach Foster instructed the girls to partner up with someone relatively their size and try some of the moves we had demonstrated. Most of them wanted Graham to help, for an excuse to have any contact with one of the school's best athletes. He also wasn't hard on the eyes. Maybe that's why Connor didn't support me wrestling with him?

For the girls who were more serious about learning the moves, I went around and helped out by giving pointers, or even have them get on all fours while I slowly took them down, explaining what I was doing the entire time. I instructed them on how to hook an ankle with the instep properly or how the closer your knee is to your elbow, if you are on your front, the more leverage you would get.

At the end of class, the girls thanked both of us and coach asked if I would be willing to come in again.

"Yeah, sure. You'll have to clear it with my resource centre teachers, but I'd love to," I told him, helping Graham stack the mats and lean them against the wall beside the not-so-secret make-out-closet. I saw Graham glance at it and smirk, as if remembering something fondly.

"All right, I'll do that," Coach smiled and squeezed my shoulder. "Thanks you two."

"No worries, it was fun," Graham replied and waved as his headed to the boy's change room.

I hurried into the girl's locker room and quickly changed, washed my face, and stuffed my gym clothes into the bottom of my bag. By the time I was done, I had less than two minutes to get to drama class.

I yanked open the change-room door, darted through the gym, and ran up the nearest staircase, two steps at a time. Rounding the corner to the east wing of the second floor, I bumped into Rudy. More like ploughed into him actually.

The force of my sprinting and him hurrying to his next class sent me stumbling back, and Rudy grabbed my arm to prevent me from falling. I grasped onto his arm and righted myself. I knew I should have let go of his bicep, but I only loosened my grip. It had been a week since I had touched him outside of rehearsal and I revelled in it.

"Rudy," I began, breathlessly, not really knowing what I was going to say.

"Beth, don't." Rudy shook his head and let go of my arm. My fingers trailed down his until they swept over his fingers gently. He hooked his pinky around mine. "Not here. Not right now."

"Then when? Where?" I asked, my voice going up an octave.

Rudy let go of my finger, ran both of his hands through his hair, and then heaved a sigh. He really did not want to talk to me. "We can talk after rehearsal," he said just as the final bell rang. "Damn. I'll see you later." And he hurried away… just as Connor's mom came out of the classroom beside us.

"Oh… hi, Beth!" Lynn said, smiling at me. "How are you?"

Clearly she had not seen me and Rudy together. "I'm all right," I said. "On my way to drama."

She held up a file she was carrying. "I'm just about to drop off some set design ideas to Mr. Thomas; I'll walk with you." She started down the hallway. Alone in the corridor with a mother figure would be a perfect time to bring up boy problems, unfortunately the boy I was having a fucking problem with was her son. "How are you actually doing, Beth? Like… *really feeling?*"

"Um, kind of stuck," I said "Like I've hit rock bottom and can't even go up."

"Oh, honey," Lynn sighed, stopping outside the closed drama room door, putting her hand on my shoulder, and looking me in the eye. "You are not stuck; I know you feel that way, but it'll lessen. You just need to talk. You can always come to me and there's always Connor too. That boy doesn't plan to ever leave your side."

I know that's supposed to be comforting, but there couldn't have been a worse thing to say.

"I can give those to Mr. T, if you like," I said instead, nodding at the file.

She could tell I was changing the subject but gave me the artwork anyway, and after giving me a quick hug, watched me enter the classroom.

After I somehow found a way to leave Connor without being beaten to a pulp in the process, she wouldn't give me the time of day. While I was still with him, at least I still had her.

Throughout drama class, all I could think about was what I was going to say to Rudy. Thankfully the class was just improv games and we basically all made asses of ourselves for a little over an hour.

"Hey, you okay?" Fuzzy asked while the class was packing up. "You were pretty quiet for a game day."

I nodded. "Mm-hmm," I crossed my legs Indian style on the fainting couch and faked a yawn. "I'm just tired."

"All right," Fuzzy said, pulling on his backpack. "Let me know if I can help you with anything." I smiled at my best friend and made a show of taking my script out of my bag. I could not remember a single time when I wanted Fuzzy, of all people, to leave. "Okay," he said. "I'll see you tomorrow, I guess." I nodded and watched him leave the classroom.

I flipped through my script for a bit, waiting for the rest of the cast to arrive. Once everyone was present, Mr. Thomas had everyone pull a chair into a circle formation like we do at the beginning of every drama class. I watched Rudy, wishing that he would sit next to me, but Brett, the boy who played Mark, plopped down next to me instead and smiled politely as a greeting. Rudy frowned slightly at him before seating himself next to our director. We all stared at Mr. Thomas, waiting for instructions as to what we were going to be doing that rehearsal.

"So, the auditorium is being used by the jazz band today," he began, taking his trusty clipboard out of his briefcase, along with a pen, clicking it so that he was free to scribble away notes. "I thought we would do a sort of table read again. By now I'm hoping you all know your solo lines? Good, good. Well, today we're going to put the song "Rent" to the test. It's mainly cues that have been found to be the most difficult to memorize, so let's see how we do. Everyone, sit on your scripts." The sound of rustling papers filled the room as everyone sat up a bit or leaned to the side and slipped the pages under their butts. "All right, we have the music," Mr. T held up his iPhone, which he had plugged into a pair of speakers. "We are going to get this perfect today. You ready?" There were mumbles and nods and the director made eye contact with the boy sitting next to me. "Go ahead, Brett."

Beside me, Brett cleared his throat and gave himself a slight shake, as if his character were taking over his voice and body, and started his monologue. "We begin on Christmas Eve…"

Because Mimi doesn't have any direct lines until a little later in the play, but does have to join in for a few lyrics in the song we were practising, I allowed myself to watch Rudy as he and Brett sang together/at each other as they mimed throwing posters and screenplays into a fire. If anyone had come into the classroom near the end, they would have thought that they had stumbled across a cult that sat in circles, singing about having AIDS and no money to pay for (you guessed it) rent.

Our throats were raw after four takes, but Mr. Thomas was beaming. "Well done, all of you!" He grinned, clapping his hands.

"That was fantastic!" He flipped through his notes for a few minutes, giving a few suggestions to anyone with solo lines while the rest of us pulled our scripts out from under us and put them back in our bags. "All right, everyone! See you all on Monday."

Rudy followed me out of the classroom and we walked away from our co-stars, ignoring the tension between us until we were hidden away in an empty staircase

"So?" Rudy said after an awkward thirty seconds of anxious silence. "What do you want to say?"

I was a little taken aback by his wording. That was kind of rude. "I, I miss you," I admitted quietly.

He sighed. "Then stop spending time with *him* and you'll have more time for me." He looked nearly pained saying these words to me.

"Rudy," I groaned, feeling so frustrated that I could have stomped my foot. "I can't! There's more to it than that!"

"Then explain it! I want to understand!"

"It's him mom, okay?!"

Rudy blinked a couple times. "What?"

"Lynn. Connor's mom. She's like my mentor. She's the mother I never had even when I *had* one. If I leave Connor... I lose her." My lip trembled at the thought and I swallowed hard. "I can't, Rudy. She thinks of me like another daughter and I need that. I need her."

Rudy's face softened and he took a step closer to me, his posture relaxing.

"Beth, she'll stay. If she truly feels like you're one of her own, she'll stay," he whispered, kissing my forehead lightly. "You have such an abundance of love." He pulled away. "Don't give it to the wrong person."

I closed my eyes and sighed, fighting the urge to lean into him. It's lucky I did, because when I opened my eyes, I was alone in the stairwell.

I could have told him about the way Connor was behaving and how he was scaring me into staying with him, but I knew nothing good would come of that. Not that any good was coming from *not* saying anything either.

CHAPTER 22
RED

After I opened up to Rudy about Lynn, and that she was really the only reason I was still with Connor, he began to text me again. It started with this text:

```
-what time is rehearsal today?
```

I knew for a fact that he knew the schedule by heart. Then they slowly became more personal:

```
-have a good day
```

```
-shame we don't have a class together
```

When I received a text from him, asking if I would like to hang out over the weekend, I knew that I was back in his good graces. He still was not pleased when he saw me in the halls with Connor (or worse, saw him kiss me) but I assured him that I was planning on leaving him soon. Just not yet.

The next two weeks with Rudy went by so fast that I actually double glanced at my phone when I read that it was the first of May.

"When did that happen?" I muttered, putting my phone back in my bag after answering a text from Connor. No, I would not be seeing him that evening.

"When did what happen?" Rudy asked, as we entered the pizza shop not far from the school after rehearsal.

"When did it become May?" I asked him, standing beside him in the line.

"This morning, I think." Rudy smirked down at me.

"Oh, shut up. You know what I mean." I nudged his arm with my elbow, grinning at him.

"I know," he laughed, taking a step forward. He took my hand in his and squeezed it. "Time has been flying by with you." He pulled me in front of him and wrapped his arms around my waist. "I like you."

"I like you, too." I smiled up at him and stood on my tiptoes to kiss him.

"Can I take your order?" the person behind the counter asked loudly.

I turned around in Rudy's arms and ordered a single slice of cheese pizza, while Rudy ordered a pepperoni.

The guy handed us our dinner on cardboard plates and we both handed him five dollars. He kept the change without asking if we wanted it. Exchanging a look, Rudy and I left the pizzeria.

"Hey, can I ask you a question?" Rudy said around a mouthful of pizza.

"Besides the one you just asked? Yeah, sure," I joked, heading over to a nearby park bench.

"Now, you don't have to answer, but I was wondering…" Rudy paused as we took a seat. I watched him while nibbling on my pizza. "What, what was your mom like?"

I had not expected that. No longer hungry, I put the slice back on the plate in my lap and stared down at my feet.

"Well, um…" I cleared my throat, wiping my sweaty palms on my jeans. "She was, or I thought she was, a happy person. She was always laughing and joking around. She loved coffee and grapefruit juice. She was fun. She was actually an alcoholic for a long time. She hadn't had a drink in, like… three years or something." I threw my pizza and its plate in the trash can beside the bench and drew my knees to my chest. "Needless to say, it was a shock when my aunt told me what she had done. I had just talked to her the night before. My mom, I mean, not my aunt. I had been watching this musical called *Fiddler of the Roof* when she called the first time."

"The first time?" Rudy repeated. I glanced over at him. He had finished his pizza and was turned at the waist to look at me, one arm along the back of the bench around my shoulders.

"Yeah. She must have called, like... ten times that night." I nodded, looking back down at my knees. "She was trying to get ahold of Amy to say goodnight. Or goodbye rather. And it was getting so *annoying*. I was trying to watch a movie and she just kept calling and calling. I was like, 'She's not here, I'll get her to call.' Turns out Amy was spending the night at a friend's house. When I told Marmee that, she sighed and said something like, 'Okay, tell her I said nighty-night,' and I was like 'Okay, can I watch my movie now?'" I buried my face in between my knees, hiding my upcoming tears. "Can you believe that? I was annoyed at my mom while she was planning to kill herself. How terrible is that? And over a stupid movie! Actually, the movie wasn't that bad, but still!" Rudy's hand ran through my hair. "My last words to her were: 'I love you. 1, 2, 3, bye'."

"1, 2, 3, bye?"

"Yeah, we used to say it to each other every night. Kind of like a 'you hang up first' sort of thing." I sighed. "So, yeah... that was my mom. She was a cool person."

"I'm really sorry, Beth," Rudy said, pulling me close to his side.

"Yeah," I sniffled, wiping my eyes on my jeans. "So am I."

"Why do you have to have brown hair?"

Connor's question confused me the next day at lunch. Fuzzy and I turned to face him, while Candice's eyes remained glued to her phone.

"What are you talking about?" I asked, as he swirled a lock of my hair around his finger.

"Well, it's just so... plain. I mean, I like how long it is, that's sexy, but it's so brown. Why can't you have blonde hair?" Connor asked in almost a whiny tone.

Over the past two weeks, Connor had accepted that I had kissed another guy, that it was not Fuzzy, and that I was not going to tell him who it was. This had ended the almost violent kisses in the hallways between classes, but the kisses that had replaced them were just plain, rude bluntness.

"You want me to dye my hair?" I asked, pushing his hand away from my head.

"Well, yeah," he shrugged, not realizing that I was rather insulted. Or he did and did not care. "I mean, blondes are hot."

"You realize that *you* have brown hair, right?" I heard Fuzzy start to cuss, but he was drowned out by the bell signalling the end of lunch.

"I think Connor has a point," Candice voiced, surprising me. She had been listening? "Your hair is boring."

With that, she pocketed her phone, grabbed her bag, and hopped off the windowsill. Connor slid off after her, leaving Fuzzy and I gaping after them.

"They want change?" I grumbled angrily, pulling the strap of my bag over my head and resting it on my shoulder. "I'll show them fucking change."

Fuzzy helped me down and walked beside me as we made our way to resource centre.

"You're not actually going to dye your hair, are you?" he asked, eyeing my curtain of 'boring' hair curiously. "I think it's beautiful." I glanced at him and he turned pink. "I mean, pretty, um... fine the way it is."

"Well, I think I do need a change," I shrugged, watching Connor and Candice talk as they reached the landing above us.

"Oh, like your life hasn't changed drastically enough over the last month and a half," Fuzzy said, almost sarcastically, clearly frowning upon the idea of me changing the way I look.

"At least I would be able to control this change," I pointed out. "If I fuck up I have no one to blame but myself. Who knows, maybe a new look will end my status as the-chick-whose-mom-killed-herself."

Fuzzy looked at me with compassion and did not bring the subject up again.

During resource centre, I quickly texted Rudy that something had come up and I would not be able to see him after school. He answered quickly.

```
-Is everything okay?

-Yeah

-Is it Connor? Are you seeing him?

-Nope. Don't worry. I'll make it up to
 you tomorrow.

-Awesome. Now stop texting in class.
```

I stifled a giggle and tucked my phone in my pocket.

After drama class, I gave Fuzzy a quick "bye" before darting out the door and straight to the nearest drugstore. I walked down the aisle of hair dye selections, looking for a shade I liked. When I found it, I saw that my hair was far too dark to get it to that colour, so naturally, I snagged a container of bleach and purchased them together, then bussed home.

Knowing I only had about two hours before my dad and sister would be arriving home, I threw myself into the bathroom and stripped down to my underwear so I wouldn't get anything on my clothes.

Taking the bleach out of the plastic bag, I read the instructions that I had found on the Internet, and (turning the bathroom fan on and pulling on the gloves) applied the bleach to my dark brown hair. Trying to avoid getting it on my scalp, I twisted and turned and tousled my hair until all of it was covered with the shit.

    I sat on the edge of the tub, waiting for the chemicals to seep into my locks. When my nose started to burn from the smell, I tore off the gloves, took off my underwear, and jumped into the shower, rinsing the poison out of my hair.

    When I was sure it was all gone, I turned off the water and wrapped a towel around myself. I grabbed Amy's hair dryer and used it for a good ten minutes before my hair was completely dry. I wiped my hand across the fogged up mirror and stared in shock at my reflection.

    "Holy shit."

    My hair was platinum blonde. I mean like, Beth Chapman blonde. Dragon chick from *Game of Thrones* white. Not to mention the fact that my hair was fucking fried!

    I had about an hour before Amy would be arriving, so after digesting the fact that I was "blonde", I opened the actual hair dye, made the mix, put on the gloves, and massaged the colour into my white hair. Following the directions, I pulled a hair tie off the door handle and pulled my hair into a bun at the top of my head. By now the fan had made the stench of bleach fade, so I did not have a problem staying in the bathroom and waiting for twenty minutes for the colour to settle into my hair.

    Just when I was considering making a dash to my bedroom to grab a book, the timer on my phone went off. I repeated the process I had done with the bleach until the water running down my body and swirling into the drain was clear, then stepped out of the tub and wrapped the towel around myself again. I dried my hair, tousling it with my free hand trying to hurry up the job. Unable to wait anymore, I put the drier away and used the palm of my hand to clear the mirror in front of me. My hair was now stop-sign red, except for the front, where I supposed I had not put enough of the dye. It was neon pink instead. I fucking loved it, but I still was not satisfied.

Pulling my hair into a low ponytail, I grabbed the pair of scissors that my dad used to trim his beard and cut. A good eight inches of bright red hair fell into the sink. Instead of tumbling in waves down to my waist, my no-longer-split-ended hair now ended about an inch below my collarbones.

Grinning, I gathered my cut hair into my hands and flushed the strands down the toilet. I took off the towel and put the clothes that I had abandoned on top of the toilet back on. I put all of the empty boxes and used gloves into the pharmacy bag, grabbed the wet towel off the floor, and hurried to my room.

About twenty minutes later I heard my dad walk in the front door and start to remove his work boots. My heart began to speed up. He was not going to like this.

"Beth? Are you home?" he called from the foyer.

"Yeah, in my room!" I hollered back. Running my fingers nervously through my hair, I sat on my bed with my homework spread out in front of me.

He knocked lightly before entering. I slowly looked over at the doorway when he did not say anything. I watched his eyes widen in surprise and anger.

"What did you do?" he asked, so quietly that I wished he had yelled.

"I dyed my hair," I said lamely.

"Why?"

"I needed a change," I shrugged. He stared at me for what felt like an eternity.

"If you ever do that to your hair again, you'll have to cut it this short," he scolded, holding his index finger and thumb about an inch apart from each other. I actually laughed.

"No, I won't." I shook my head. "It's just hair."

I could tell he was about to yell at me, but just then, Amy appeared beside him in the doorway.

"What's going on?" Then she spotted me. "Bethy! I love it!" she squealed and ran over to me, hopping up onto my bed and stroking and inspecting my red and pink hair.

Our dad stormed off while Amy and I chatted excitedly.

The next day, I walked into the high school with my shoulders back and my head held high for the first time in ages.

By the time I had reached the lockers, I was feeling very good about my new look. I had turned a few heads on my way up, and for the first time since spring break, it was not because of my mom.

"Hey! That's not your locker!" I heard Fuzzy cry out from down the hall. He didn't even recognize me. Awesome. "Get out of—*Beth?*" Smirking, I turned to face him. "Whoa. You're... red."

"I know, right?!" I squealed girlishly, clapping my hands. "Isn't it great?" I spun around so that he could get a good look at the new style. When I finished the 360 degree turn, I looked up at him expectantly.

"It's fantastic," Fussy grinned, stepping closer. "That *is* change. Can I touch it?"

"Yeah, of course."

He reached out and gently ran his fingertips along my fluffy hair. "Your hair was really dark, how did you get it this bright?"

"Bleach," I answered simply. He looked down at me, stunned.

"You *bleached* your hair? So you *were* blonde at one point?"

"For about ten minutes, yeah." I laughed. Fuzzy looked at something over my shoulder and dropped his hand from my hair. I looked over and saw Connor striding toward us.

"What did you *do?!*" he yelled, stopping mid-step.

"You said my brown hair was boring and this is anything but," I replied, flipping my hair over my shoulder.

"Are you kidding me?" Connor gawked, still rooted to his spot. "I suggested blonde, not firetruck red and neon *pink*. Christ, you cut it, too." He noticed the new length. "I told you I liked that it was long."

"It still *is* long," I snapped, getting sick of his attitude. *"I* like it and it's not going anywhere, so get used to it." I snatched my books off the bottom of the locker, slammed the door, and stormed away from him, but not before I heard Fuzzy offer his opinion:

"Dude, I think it looks great."

"Shut the hell up, Dan!"

I still had twenty minutes before English was going to start, so I decided to get a coffee from the cafeteria. Just as I was handing the cashier a five dollar bill, Rudy came out of nowhere and handed her a ten.

"Where the hell did *you* come from?" I gasped in surprise, taking a step away so that he could get his change.

"I was looking for you. I missed you yesterday," he replied, pocketing the five dollars he got back and picking up two empty paper coffee cups. "I take it you were busy with your hair last night?"

"Yeah," I nodded, taking a cup and filling it with a medium roast. Rudy copied me while I added cream and sugar. "What do you think?" I found myself nervous about his reaction.

He held up his index finger and swirled it around in front of him, wordlessly asking me to spin around. I put my coffee on the counter beside us and turned.

"I love it," he beamed, his eyes boring into mine. Feeling a flutter of butterflies in my stomach, I forced myself to look away before I kissed him right there. I nodded toward the door and we left, sipping on our scalding hot coffees. That was the thing about the coffee in the cafeteria, it was either kind of warm or way too hot.

"Beth, I have to ask you something," Rudy said, taking my hand and pulling me into a classroom. He looked around quickly to make sure that it was empty before turning back to me while I closed the door. "Did you—" He stopped, sighed, and nervously ran a hand through his hair. "Did you do that for him?"

"What do you mean?" I asked, not following. He grimaced, as if asking this question was actually painful. I adjusted the books I was holding to my chest. "Rudy, what are you talking about?"

"Your hair. Is it red because of Connor? Did he ask you to do that?" he sputtered, talking so fast I was surprised I understood him.

"Kind of," I replied. "At lunch yesterday, he told me that my brown hair was boring and how he wished I was blonde. So naturally, I went home and dyed it red and pink. Oh, and he hates everything about it." Rudy set his coffee on a desk beside him and removed mine from my hands and placed it beside his. "I was drinking that," I complained, reaching to pick it up again, but Rudy was kissing me before I could stop him.

I knew I should not be letting him kiss me when the risk of being caught was so high, but at the moment, I really did not care.

"I can't help it," Rudy whispered, pulling away from me. "I don't want you changing anything about yourself for him."

"But I did," I blinked. "Well, sort of at least. I mean, I wanted the change, but I knew this was exactly what he *didn't* want, so I did it."

"I mean don't change anything to make him *happy*, not piss him off," Rudy smirked, tilting my chin up and kissing my neck. "Besides, something tells me that you would have done this eventually anyway."

"You're probably right," I agreed. "I just wanted to control the changes in my life."

"I can understand that."

I tilted my head back to give him better access to my throat, and just as the thought of jumping on one of the desks and making out started to form in my brain, the bell for first class rang. I gasped and stepped away from him, eyes wide. "You kissed me," I accused, grabbing my coffee.

"I know," Rudy chortled, picking up his as well. "I couldn't help it."

"What do you mean 'you couldn't help it'?" I hissed, trying to remain annoyed, but his smile was infectious.

"All right, I could have helped it, but I didn't want to," Rudy admitted, lifting a shoulder in a half shrug as he opened the door for me. I could not stay mad; after all, I had wanted him to kiss me. I glanced around the hallway we were entering and was relieved when no one saw us leaving the classroom, which could have been bad.

"I have to get to English and it's on the fourth floor," I said, nodding to the stairs. "Thanks for the coffee."

"Wait," he took a giant step, blocking my way and spilling some of his coffee onto his fingers. "Ow, damn it! How is it still hot? Anyway, will I see you after rehearsal today?"

I glanced around the corridor again to make sure it remained deserted before nodding and stepping around him, bustling off to class.

Still flustered from kissing Rudy downstairs, I pushed my way into the English room just as the second bell rang. I made my way to my seat beside Connor and sat down, ignoring the glare he was giving me. However, I was enjoying the jaw Candice had dropped when she saw me.

"Where did you go?" Fuzzy asked, leaning over to me. I gestured to the coffee I had just put down and opened the textbook to the page number written on the white board. "Coffee took you that long?"

"Yes, coffee took that long."

While our teacher went on to assign the reading of a scene from *Hamlet*, and the figuring out of what the fuck the characters were saying, I found myself thinking about Connor. I had just been kissing another guy in the same building, and here I was sitting next to him in class and I felt nothing. There was no remorse in my heart, just longing for another guy. I wished I was still in that classroom with Rudy, not here with a stupid assignment (everyone knows what happens in *Hamlet*). I surprised myself with the thought.

I zoned out completely, staring down at the pages in front of me without actually seeing them.

"Beth?" our teacher said from the front of the class.

"Yes?" I jumped at my name being called.

"Can you explain to us what happens in *Hamlet* Act one, scene one?"

"Sure. Bernardo comes down..."

That afternoon was one of the first ones I had without plans in some time. No rehearsal. Rudy was busy, Fuzzy had rugby, and I hadn't seen Connor since the end of RC. A tiny bit of me was looking forward to the time I could have alone with my thoughts; the rest of me was terrified of the thoughts I'd be having. Try as I might not to think about it, my mom was still at the forefront of my mind.

I wasn't in a hurry to get home, due to that fact my dad was still pretty pissed about what I did to my hair, so instead of going home right away, I wandered to the library after drama class. No one ever went there after school unless they really had to, so it was more or less a guarantee that I would be alone there, other than the librarian who was going deaf and disliked students with a passion.

I made my way into the non-fiction section, which led to the study room Fuzzy and I had been in when I had my first panic attack. I was reaching up for a biography of Marilyn Monroe when someone grabbed my wrist, hard. I inhaled sharply and tried to tug free when Connor snarled, "We need to talk," in a tone I'd only heard him use once before.

Who tried to take you from me? I make it pretty clear that this is mine!

"No," I breathed and tried harder to get away from him. Connor reached behind me and opened the study room door. He pushed me inside and closed the door behind him, releasing the grip he had on me. I shook my head. "No, Connor, let me out." My heart was in my throat.

"You need to stop, Beth," he said in a low voice that was just as terrifying as his threatening growl. "You need to stop telling me off in front of people. You need to stop openly going against what I've asked you to do. Your fucking spite is going to get you in trouble."

"I, I didn't," I said, feeling myself shrink away from him. He took an angry stride toward me and I backed away quickly, the back of my legs bumping into one of the desks. "No! I mean, I didn't *mean* to; it was—I was angry. I needed something I could control since my mom died—"

Connor's eyes flared and the next thing I knew, one of his hands was around my neck and I was bent backward across the desk. The grip he had was firm, but loose enough that I could still breathe. I smacked at his chest and neck until he grabbed my wrists with his free hand, holding them together against my chest. I tried in vain to kick my legs, but he had me in such an awkward position that I couldn't land a good strike. *He wouldn't try something at school... right?*

"Because of your impulsive decision to fucking ruin your hair, I look like I'm dating some weird Emo chick."

"Please—"

"People think you're weird enough as it is; this didn't help. Now listen closely—stay still, Beth, don't make me hurt you—from now on, if you want to do something about your appearance, you run it by me first."

"You're hurting me, Connor!"

"Do you understand?" he spat, tightening his grip on my throat.

I attempted to nod but ended up exhaling a weak, "Yeah."

Connor slowly let go of me and stood up straight. "Good," he said, and before my eyes, he changed back into the boy I met last year in a computer lab, asking me for help on getting his backpack unstuck from the wheel of his chair. Innocent and goofy. "I'll see you tomorrow." He smiled and left the room.

I stayed where I was, sprawled out on a study desk. I traced my shaking fingers over my neck, appreciating the cool touch to the burning skin.

"He's going to kill me," I told my non-existent audience.

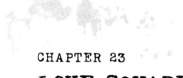

CHAPTER 23
LOVE SQUARE

That Friday in Resource Centre, one of the TA's came over to my desk and crouched beside me.

"Beth?" he asked in a near whisper, so as not to break the concentration of my classmates.

"Yeah?" I looked up from my script.

"The school therapist just called up. She'd like to talk to you."

My brows furrowed "Why?"

He eyed my hair. "You know why, Beth."

I leaned closer to him. "I don't want to talk to a complete stranger about—"

"Beth please, Theresa could really help you."

I huffed angrily, closed my script, and shoved it in the bag at my feet. "I don't need help," I hissed, standing up and striding out of the room.

Cursing under my breath, I stormed down three flights of stairs to the school therapist's office, stopping in front of her door.

Why should I talk to someone I had never met about my problems? I already had Fuzzy and Rudy. I was about to turn around and go to the library instead when the door opened and a middle-aged, friendly looking woman appeared in the doorway.

"Elizabeth?" she asked, looking me up and down, her gaze lingering on my hair.

I grimaced. "Don't call me that," I told her, brushing past her and placing myself on a couch across from a large oak desk.

"What should I call you then?" asked Theresa, calmly closing the door and sitting in her desk chair.

"Beth," I muttered, slouching back into the couch, crossing my arms in a self-hug.

"Okay, Beth." Theresa nodded, picking up a clipboard and scribbling something down on it. "Tell me about yourself."

"Why?" I questioned. "I don't know anything about you."

"What would you like to know?" Theresa tilted her head a little to the left.

"I dunno." I shrugged with one shoulder. "Where are you from?"

"Ontario, you?"

"Doing a *quid pro quo* thing?" I asked, raising my eyebrows.

Theresa shrugged this time, as if to say, *Why not?*

"I'm from all over the island," I said.

"What do you mean?"

"When my parents divorced they moved to different parts of the island and changed houses a lot, so all over," I explained. "What's your favourite food?" I pulled a question out of my ass.

"Cookies," she said, writing on her clipboard, as she spoke again. "What's your favourite subject in school?"

"Drama," I told her. "Why did you choose such a nosey profession?"

Theresa glanced up at me and smiled. "I think it chose me."

"What do you mean?"

"Beth, my turn." She pointed to herself with her pen. "Quid pro quo, remember?"

I rolled my eyes. "Whatever."

"How did your mom die?" she asked, her eyes locking with mine.

I stared at her for a beat. "I wouldn't be here if you didn't already know," I said, flatly.

"You're right, I do," she nodded. "How does it make you feel, that everyone knows? Even complete strangers, like me?"

I bit my lip in contemplation. "Violated, maybe? I don't know. I mean, I was stupid enough to tell Candice. I should have known that a few seconds later everyone would know."

"And who is Candice?"

"Quid pro quo, doctor." I shook my head. "What do you call a love triangle with four people involved?"

Theresa gave me an odd look. "Is that riddle?" she asked slowly.

"No, I'm serious. There are four people."

"Then a square, I guess," she answered, drawing a square in the air with the tip of her pen. "Why? Are you in one?"

"Yeah," I nodded, thinking of Connor, Fuzzy, and Rudy.

"I've seen you with the brown-haired boy. His mom is a teacher here."

"Connor."

"And the tall red-haired boy?"

"Fuzzy," I nodded. She raised her eyebrows at the name.

"Who else?" she asked.

"He's in the school play with me."

"I see... and you like all of these boys?" she asked, pen poised above the clipboard.

"Well no, not all of them," I said, forgetting the quid pro quo. "I've been with Connor for over a year now. I get butterflies just thinking about Rudy, and Fuzzy likes me, I think... and I can't stop leading him on."

"You didn't answer my question," Theresa said after a few moments of silence. "Do you like all of these boys? You only mentioned having feelings of any kind toward Rudy. You said that you've been with Connor and—Fuzzy, was it?—likes you. Do you actually like them though?"

I did not say anything for the rest of the session. I was in Psych 101 and I knew that I had just made a Freudian slip. I was actually a little tempted to tell her about Connor and how he had been treating me lately. He hadn't touched me in a violent way since the incident in the study room, but that didn't mean I was any less afraid of him.

When the bell for last class rang, I stood and Theresa handed me a card.

"Email me to set up another appointment, Beth."

I took it and left with no intention of ever emailing her, but I will admit that she gave me motivation to say something I would have otherwise bottled up inside.

As I slowly made my way to drama class, I took out my phone and started a new text message.

-need to talk to you after school

Just as I was reaching the art and entertainment hall, my phone chirped with Rudy's reply.

-where?

-under the bleachers

-OK. 3:30

That would give me half an hour to get there after class ended. Hopefully that would be enough time for me to figure out what the fuck I was going to say.

"Hey, Bethy."

I gasped and shoved my phone in my bag.

"Connor, hey," I greeted my boyfriend (or whatever he was by now). "Wait, what are you doing here? You need to be on the fourth floor for bio." We were standing just outside the drama room door.

"Well, you had to leave RC early," Connor shrugged, stepping closer to me. I took a step back, in hopes of avoiding him, but ended up hitting the lockers behind me. "And I wanted to give you this."

He pressed his mouth against mine and I had to force myself not to grimace, but I did not kiss him back. I had not returned a kiss since he attacked me... the first time. God, his breath was disgusting. He pulled back, looking concerned. Hardly two months ago, I would have wrapped my legs around his waist by now.

"Are you okay?" he asked quietly, not stepping away. "Are you thinking about your mom? You were in the therapist's office for a while." I swallowed and nodded. I was wondering if she would think I was a total whore. "I'm sorry, Beth," Connor whispered, leaning in to kiss me gently.

"Ahem."

I turned my head so that Connor's mouth touched my neck instead of my lips. Fuzzy was standing a couple feet away, glaring at Connor who was still slobbering on my throat.

"Dude, she has to get to class."

"She can always skip," Connor said, looking up and winking.

Of course. I was sad. He thought that meant he would get laid. Christ.

Fuzzy strode over, grabbed my arm, pulled me to him, opened the classroom door, and practically shoved me inside.

"Cock blocker!" Connor yelled at Fuzzy before the door was slammed in his face.

By now people were used to our dramatic entrances, so only half of the class was staring at us as we made our way to the fainting couch.

"Where's Candice?" I asked, taking off my bag and setting it on the floor.

"Bathroom," he answered. "She would have loved to see that PDA." He jabbed his thumb at the door.

"Yeah, totally." I laughed. "She does like to give me a good scolding or scowl."

"That's not her scowl. She always looks like that," Fuzzy smirked, making me laugh, which I stopped abruptly when Candice came in the room just as the second bell rang.

During circle time and the rest of class, I tried to think of what the hell I was going to say to Rudy. I wanted to tell him that I had no feelings for anyone but him, but how could I tell him that and still be with Connor? I found myself looking down at the promise ring Connor had bought me after about five months of dating. It was a simple white gold band that probably cost about eighty dollars. I remembered the day that he gave it to me.

It was a Saturday and he came over midmorning with a big grin on his face. I was frowning, because I had just found out that things had gone a little further with Jane than he had told me.

"We need to talk," I said grimly, watching him take off his backpack and rummage through it. He froze and looked over at me.

"That doesn't sound good." He sighed, sitting down next to me on the bed and avoiding my eyes.

"Jane sent me an email last night," I told him, showing him a printed copy of it. "She thought I deserved to know what actually happened when you went to break it off with her. Apparently, you did more than just... talk."

"Damn it, Jane," Connor moaned, scanning the email.

"Is it true, or is she a fat fucking liar now, too?" I snapped, my heart beating furiously.

That is when Connor pulled out a small velvet box and put it down in front of my crossed legs.

"What the hell is this?" I questioned, not opening it.

"Look." Connor nodded at it. I did and stared down at the band. It was plain, nothing special about it. "I saw it and it made me think of you. It's a promise ring." I didn't bother telling him that promise rings usually contain some kind of jewel, but I did let him take it out of the box and put it on my left ring finger. "Are we good?" he asked, kissing my cheek.

"Did you get one of these for Jane?" I whispered.

"No way, babe." He shook his head. *"You're my girl."*

"Hey, Beth? You okay?"

"Huh?" I started, looking up at Fuzzy who was staring quizzically down at me.

"The bell rang. Do you have rehearsal or anything?"

I looked around to see that everyone was leaving or had already left. Mr. Thomas waved goodbye to us from the door and left with a couple students.

"No, I don't. I was just thinking." I shook my head, rubbing my eyes.

"Don't hurt yourself," Fuzzy joked, sitting down next to me with a sigh. "I'm so glad it's the weekend."

"Then why are you still here?" I laughed, gesturing around the now empty class room.

"Because you're here," he said, looking at me like I had asked him a rather absurd question. He glanced down at his watch and groaned. "But I do have rugby practise. I should go. Sorry, Beth." I waved his apology away and watched as he stood and picked up his bag. He waved at me from the door. "Have a great weekend."

"You too." I smiled.

Before the door could close behind him, I heard Fuzzy swear loudly and shout, "Leave! Her! *Alone!*" just as Connor strode inside, looking pissed. I hurried behind the fainting couch, leaving it between us. I had not seen him this angry since he attacked me.

"I know who it was, Beth," he snarled, walking closer to me. I am pretty sure my heart stopped beating for a second.

He knows about Rudy? How?

"What do you mean?" I asked, trying to sound impassive.

"I know who you kissed," Connor continued, now about four feet away from the couch.

"Connor, leave her alone," Fuzzy repeated. I had not noticed that he had stayed. He seemed uncertain of what to do.

"Mind your own damned business, Dan!" Connor yelled at him over his shoulder.

"Connor," I said as calmly as I could. He glared at me, but I had his attention. "I want you to leave me alone for a while. You're very—"

"You better not be dumping me!" he snapped, taking a jerking step over to me.

"No, no," I whimpered, shrinking back, submitting like a small dog. He was really scaring me. "You're just on really thin ice."

"What did *I* do? *You're* the slut! You thought I wouldn't figure out you were hooking up with Daniel?" he yelled, gesturing angrily at Fuzzy, who was standing not far away from him with a startled expression on his face. That was when I realized that Connor had not figured out whom I had kissed; he had more than likely not taken his OCD or ADHD medication that day and was looking for an outlet for his anger. If he skipped even one day, his mood swings could be awful. His attack on me was evidence of that. "How long has it been going on? How long have you been *whoring* your—hey!"

Fuzzy had rushed over to Connor and shoved his shoulder blades hard, making him stumble forward and bump into the couch in front of me.

"Don't talk to her like that, you asshole!" Fuzzy shouted, watching Connor spin around to face his opponent. "She deserves way more respect than you give her, dickhead!"

Connor hurried over to Fuzzy and shoved him. "She's *mine*, Daniel!" he bellowed, pointing at me. "And you can't have her!"

Fuzzy grabbed the front of Connor's one good shirt and yanked it hard. "She doesn't belong to anyone, Connor!" he hissed, bringing his arm back.

When I saw Fuzzy's hand clench into a fist, I jumped over the couch and ran over to him.

"Fuzzy, *stop!*" I cried, grabbing his arm and pulling on it. "Just let him go." Breathing heavily, Fuzzy lowered his arm and Connor shoved him away. "Fuzzy, sit down and breathe. In and out, remember?" Grudgingly, Fuzzy did as I asked and I walked over to Connor, who was straightening out his shirt. "Connor, that was, that was—"

"He almost punched me!" Connor snapped, glaring over at Fuzzy. "I can't believe you hooked up with him."

"You *shouldn't* because I *didn't!* Jesus!" I shouted, throwing my arms up in exasperation. "I told you that, over and over again. The person I kissed was not him, and I'm not going to tell you who it was."

"But the way he acted in the hall before class, all possessive and stuff," Connor spat. "What was that?"

"That was his way of saying, 'You shouldn't be doing this in the middle of a hallways two seconds before class starts.'"

"What about the way he—"

I stopped him, cutting my hand through the air between us. "Connor, this is the last time I'm going to say this," I said, my eyes boring into his. "There is nothing between Fuzzy and I besides a strong friendship. That's it. If you bring it up or question it one more time, we're done." I hope I hid how terrified I was while I said these words.

Connor gaped at me for a second before a flash of anger went through his eyes and he left the classroom without another word.

My entire body relaxed and I turned to Fuzzy, who was smiling at me grimly.

"Honestly, I hope he brings it up again," he said, without a single note of humour in his voice. He looked down at his watch and sighed. "Three thirty already? We should—where are you going?"

When Fuzzy had told me the time, I had run across the room, grabbed my bag, and slung it onto my shoulder. "I have to go. I'm going to be late."

"Late for what?" Fuzzy asked curiously, his eyes following me.

"This, uh… thing. Have a good weekend," I answered lamely, rushing out the door and leaving him staring after me.

I made my way to the bleachers, silently thanking someone that rugby practises were held on the north field.

I saw Rudy standing beneath them, checking the time on his phone. "Hey," I waved at him when I knew I was close enough for him to hear me without raising my voice.

"Hey. I was getting worried," he said, pocketing his phone and embracing me.

"Why?" I asked, confused.

"Usually you're right on time and you weren't this time, I guess," he shrugged, blushing a little.

"I'm sorry about that. The weirdest thing happened in the drama room and I got held back," I explained, rolling my eyes.

"So, what did you want to talk about?" Rudy asked, pulling away and gazing down at me.

I realized that I had not had any time to figure out what I was going to say, so I took a deep breath and improvised. "When, when I'm around you I feel butterflies in my stomach, and my heart speeds up when I see you." Rudy slowly began to grin. "When I'm around Connor, I feel disappointed and lonely, because I'm not with you. When I'm around Fuzzy, I feel comfort and friendship." Rudy's grin widened. I took a hold of the front of his shirt. "I've never been so excited to get to school, just to catch a glimpse of you in the halls or between classes. I'm pretty sure you're the best thing that's ever happened to me."

Rudy ran his hand up my back and traced the line of my jaw with his index finger. "What are you trying to tell me?" he whispered, his blue eyes full of emotion.

"I really like you and no one else," I breathed. "I only want you."

"Thank God." Rudy grinned, then pulled me in and (still smiling) kissed me. Smiling right back, I locked my arms around his neck and pushed myself into him. Not expecting that, Rudy stumbled back and tripped over the backpack he had left by his feet, bringing me down with him. "Shit!" he cried out, as he landed hard on his back with me on top of him, and a whoosh of air left his lungs.

"Oh crap, Rudy, are you okay?" I sat back on his lap, my legs on either side of him.

"Uh-huh," he grunted, coughing a few times. "So, does this mean you left him?" he asked, referring to Connor.

I sighed and shook my head. "No, I'm sorry. Not yet."

Rudy pushed himself up onto his elbows. "What? But, Beth, with what you just said, I thought you'd…" I slowly lowered myself onto him and kissed him gently, running my fingers along the shadow of stubble on his jaw. He sighed against my mouth and lowered himself back to the ground, running his fingers through my hair and down my back. "All right." Rudy gave in when I slowly started unbuttoning his shirt. "I know I'll get the girl in the end." It was past five when Rudy suggested that we head home.

"Do you want a ride?" he asked, taking my hand and pulling me to my feet.

"Sure, I'll take you up on that," I replied, straightening my shirt and patting my hair down. I picked up my abandoned book bag and shouldered it while Rudy buttoned his shirt back up and grabbed his backpack, pulling it on. I followed Rudy to the school parking lot where his old truck was one of the only ones left sitting. He pulled himself into the passenger seat and I clambered in after him.

"Mind if I put on a bit of music?" Rudy asked, pulling out his iPhone and gesturing to the USB port in the recently installed CD player.

"Yeah, go for it," I smiled, pulling off my bag and putting it at my feet. Rudy pushed his backpack behind his seat and started the truck, then handed me the phone to plug in. I did. Just as we were pulling out of the lot, the music from the last song Rudy had listened to started blasting from surprisingly good speakers.

Rudy froze and stared at me, slowly turning red while "Ain't No Mountain High Enough" serenaded us. Finding his embarrassment extremely amusing, I bit my lip to try and hold back my grin, but failed.

"I, I don't know how that got on there," he lied quickly, still staring at me. "Really, I don't know." He continued to sputter excuses until, to put him out of his misery, I started singing along with the song. Rudy seemed stunned for a moment before bursting out laughing, and singing the boy's part of the duet.

"Thanks for not giving me a hard time," Rudy said, turning down the volume when the song ended. "I have a lot of music on my phone, not just that stuff."

"I like that song," I defended, laughing. "Besides, I think everyone has music on their phone or computers that they like but won't admit to anyone."

"Oh, yeah? Like who?"

"I have more Taylor Swift on my phone than I care to brag about," I admitted, shaking my head. "And I know that Fuzzy has the song "Downtown" by Petula Clark. Granted, I put it there, but he hasn't deleted it so…"

Rudy laughed and pulled into my driveway. "So, are people home or anything?" he asked, searching the rest of the driveway. I nodded over at my dad's van.

"Yeah. My dad probably got home a while ago," I told him, disappointment in my voice.

"All right, I guess I'll see you on Mon—is that your phone?" he cut himself off and I strained my ears. I grabbed my bag and rummaged through it when I recognized the alarm, set to remind me to take my nighttime anti-seizure medication. "Who's calling?"

"No one," I told him, silencing my alarm and pulling out my pill box. "It's an alarm."

"For what?" Rudy inquired, watching me pour half a handful of pills into my cupped palm, then tossing them in my mouth and swallowing without any water.

"Remember how I told you I'm epileptic?" I asked, trying to ignore the bitter taste left on my tongue by the medicine. Rudy nodded, his eyes gazing into mine. I unbuckled my seat belt and turned to face him. Turning off the engine, Rudy did the same thing. "I have to take about fourteen pills a day to manage the seizures."

"Wow," Rudy breathed, shaking his head. "How long have you been having them? The seizures, I mean."

"Since I was eleven," I answered, tucking a piece of hair behind my ear. "I've had the brain tumours or whatever since I was born, but they didn't start affecting my health until I was eleven."

"Christ. You were so little. You must have been terrified," he sympathized, compassion in his eyes. "How did it happen?"

"One day when I was at the computer, my right arm just stopped working. I couldn't move it. I tried to hide it from my dad, because I didn't want him to worry about me, but apparently the right side of my face had gone completely limp as well, so when he saw me he freaked out."

"Understandable," Rudy nodded. His rapt attention was making me uneasy. Whenever I talked about my seizures with Connor, he would call me woebegone and make me feel really selfish for thinking about my health, but Rudy was staring at me like he wanted me to continue. I pulled my knees to my chest and locked my arms around them, then stared down at my fingernails and continued.

"I started throwing up and I couldn't walk right because the muscles in my right leg were starting to go too," I remembered, picturing my dad helping me into the computer chair, while my sister stared at me in confusion and horror behind him. "I was crying, and to make me feel better, he kept telling me that it happens to everyone. Then he carried me to his van and we drove to the hospital. We waited for hours and finally the doctor said to take me to the downtown hospital. I had a nap and dreamt about having my arm amputated. Dad called my mom, who drove down. When I was finally admitted, my eyes started going back and forth really fast and everything got blurry and I tried to hide it again. My dad saw through it. I started barfing again and had my first seizure. I was in the hospital on and off for about two weeks. It took ages for my muscles to start working properly again. I had tiny seizures about three or four times a week."

"Was there nothing the doctors could do?" Rudy asked quietly.

"Kind of," I replied. "I had brain surgery when I was thirteen but it didn't work, obviously. It made the seizures worse but less frequent. They hurt way more and last longer and are really violent, but I have maybe two a month. Usually when I fall asleep or am stressed out or haven't eaten enough or something."

"Are the tumours benign?" Rudy asked, sounding worried this time.

"Yeah. Turns out there were about six more than the doctors thought, though." I finally looked up at him and he was staring at me intently. I wanted to comfort him. "Don't worry, Rudy. I'm fine. Besides the fucked-up brain and the fact that I'm emotionally damaged in so many ways it's unreal, I'm totally fine."

Rudy reached over and wrapped his arms around me, pulling me to him. I leaned my head onto his chest and he kissed the top of it.

"Beth, I think you're the bravest person I've ever met," Rudy said into my ear. "Thank you for telling me your story. I know that wasn't easy."

I looked up at him and kissed his lower lip lightly. "If you ever want to know something about me, just ask. I can't remember the last person I trusted as must as I trust you." I sighed and slid a little away from him. "I'm sorry, Rudy, but I should head inside. I'll talk to you later?"

"Yeah, of course," Rudy said, watching me pick up my bag and shoulder it. "Have a good night, Beth."

I smiled at him over my shoulder as I stepped out of his truck, closing the door behind me. I knew that if I looked back I would just want to get back in his truck, so I bee-lined straight to the front door, closing it quickly.

"Is that you, Bethy?" I heard Amy call out from the living room just as I entered the foyer.

"Yeah," I shouted back, kicking off my flats and treading up the stairs, missing Rudy already. I made my way over to my little sister, who was at the computer, staring at the screen pensively. "What's going on?"

"I got another message," she told me, pointing at the monitor. "He's talking about how pretty my hair is this time."

"That is so creepy," I shuddered, giving her a small hug from behind. "You do have very pretty hair, but still…"

"Yeah," Amy nodded in agreement.

"Is Dad here?" I asked, straightening up and looking around.

"No, he went out with a few friends. He'll be back later."

"All right. Well, I'm gonna go read for a bit. Let me know if you need anything."

"I'm fine." She repeated what I had just told Rudy two minutes ago.

Besides being emotionally damaged in so many ways it's unreal, I believe you.

CHAPTER 24
RUN

The next day Connor invited himself over and I was surprised to meet a new personality of his that I was *very* un-fond of: Clingy Connor.

I was sitting on my bed, attempting to do my homework but ending up daydreaming about Rudy and me under the bleachers, when Connor walked into my room without knocking and lay down beside me.

"Hey, beautiful." He grinned up at me. I rolled my eyes at his line.

Over the next half hour or so, I concluded that Connor had become clingy in such a short time span because he came to realize that he was losing me.

I was trying to concentrate on my homework (for real, this time) but kept getting distracted when he would tell me how much he loved me or how pretty I was. To some girls this would be swoon worthy, but I knew his true colours, and when he reached to touch me I could barely stop myself from recoiling. He was completely suffocating me.

Eventually I got so sick of him that I gathered up my psych textbook, got off the bed, told him I had to use the washroom, and darted into it. I slammed the door, but unfortunately there was no lock on it, so I yanked open a drawer in the counter, which would only allow the door to open about three inches, making entrance impossible.

I took a few deep breaths and climbed into the tub. Sitting cross-legged, I opened the psych book and continued to read about the placebo effect.

I had been in there for five minutes, *maybe*, when there was a tap on the door.

"What?" I groaned in exasperation, hanging my head in defeat.

"Bethy? Are you okay in there?" Connor's voice filtered into the bathroom.

"What?" I said again, confused this time.

"I've been standing out here and I don't hear you peeing," he explained, like this act of voyeurism was completely normal.

"*What?!*" I exclaimed, astounded and dumbfounded. "Connor, *go away!*"

There was silence for a moment while I stared at the door in disbelief. Just when I thought I could not be any more shocked by the way he was acting, Connor actually tried to come in, again without knocking. Thankfully, with a *thunk*, his entrance was blocked by the drawer.

"Bethy, let me in," Connor whined, not closing the door.

"Are you kidding right now?" I cried. Then I saw two of his fingers slip between the door and its frame and start to inch the drawer closed. "Are you fucking serious?!" I clambered out of the tub, shoved the drawer closed, threw open the door and screamed in Connor's face, "BACK OFF, YOU FREAK!"

Connor looked stunned at my sudden outburst and blinked. "Oh, were you pooping? I didn't hear you flush."

I let out a scream of frustration and shoved past him to my room just as my dad yelled from the living room, "Leave her alone, Connor!"

When I entered my room, I stubbed my toe on my computer chair and let out a string of curse words. Connor rushed over to me and wrapped his arms around me from behind.

"Oh Bethy," he cooed. "Are you okay? Do you want me to kiss it better?"

I elbowed him in the gut and he stumbled back a bit. "You're so overwhelming!" I yelled, spinning to face him. "No, I don't want you to kiss my fucking toe! God! Just, just, ugh!" I threw my arms in the air. "I'm going for a run."

"Great!" Connor grinned excitedly. "I'll come."

I smirked, looking him up and down. He was wearing cargo shorts, a sweater, and sandals. Worst running gear ever.

"Ooookaaaay..." I dragged the word out and grabbed my gym bag. I changed into my workout clothes, and after Connor asked if I needed help tying my shoelaces, we made our way to the nearby running and bike trail.

After stretching for a few minutes, I put the ear-buds to my iPhone in and started my running playlist. "Ready?" I asked Connor, trying my best not to laugh at the thought of him running in that get up. I knew I would lose him in about a minute.

"You bet, Bethy," Connor nodded. "Let's go." He began to jog, while I stayed back for a few moments before bursting into an all-out sprint, barrelling past him.

Note how inferior you feel right now? You used to make me feel that low all the time. Suck it, dick.

Leaving Connor way behind, I flat-out ran over a kilometre before slowing to a stop in front of a public water fountain. Not the most sanitary water supply, but I was parched. I took my headphones out and looked around the paved trail, seeing absolutely no one. And I did not give a fuck. Bending down to take a sip of water, my phone chirped. I pulled it out of my sleeve and rolled my eyes when I saw that it was Connor calling.

"Hi," I said.

"Beth! What the hell?" Connor panted on the other line. "You left me in the freaking dust!"

"How far did you get?" I asked, glancing back the way I came.

"I dunno, like... half a K. And I still have to run back."

"Well, you don't have to *run* back," I pointed out. "Besides, you wanted to come. And you know that I'm faster than you."

"Whatever," Connor sighed. "I'm going home."

"Go ahead, see ya later," I said, preparing to hang up.

"Yeah," he grunted and the call was disconnected.

Well, Clingy Connor was gone.

Good?

CHAPTER 25

HEROS

"He actually said, 'Were you pooping?'" Fuzzy asked on Monday, gawking after I told him about Connor's behaviour on Saturday.

"Yup," I nodded, leaning on the locker next to his. "It was ridiculous."

"What would make even a nut job like him act like that?" Fuzzy asked rhetorically, closing the door. "Do you want to get a coffee before class starts?"

"Yeah, sure," I agreed, turning to the main stairwell. "And he thinks he's losing me, that's why."

"And he's right, right?" Fuzzy prodded, matching his stride with mine. With me at only 5'3" and Fuzzy at 6'4", his regular pace was much faster than mine. "I mean, after the stunt he pulled on Friday..."

I dodged his question, because I did not know how to explain without bringing up Rudy.

"What about you?" I asked, "How was your weekend?" Fuzzy narrowed his eyes at me for changing the subject, but started to tell me about his Saturday rugby game.

"So, how's the play coming?" Fuzzy asked eventually, as he paid for our scalding hot coffees. "You've had rehearsal almost every day."

"Not *every* day," I corrected, putting lids on both of the cups and two sleeves on them to protect our fingers from potential blisters. "We have a full day on Saturday though."

"You have to come to school on a Saturday?" Fuzzy gawked again, taking one of the cups from me.

"Yep," I nodded. Honestly, I was really excited to have a whole day with Rudy. "Anyway, it's coming along really well. It'll be opening first week of June."

"So, like… three weeks?"

"Yeah," I nodded, my heart falling a little. I didn't want it to be over. I glanced over at Fuzzy to see if he had caught my fallen expression and panicked when I saw him tilting the cup at his mouth. "No! Fuzzy, don't drink it yet!" Fuzzy spat out the morning brew and swore so loudly it echoed down the corridors, scaring a few ninth graders who were mingling by the vending machines. I hurried over to the soda machine, pushed in a dollar and pressed the button for a bottle of water. I snagged it from the dispenser and handed it to Fuzzy, who was cursing coffee past his burnt tongue.

"Thanks," he said gratefully, twisting the cap off and taking a swig. "Seriously, why do they do that? Make the coffee so freaking hot!" he panted, taking another gulp and actually gargling the water. When he spoke, it sounded like he had a small lisp.

"I don't know Fuzzy, I don't know." I tried not to laugh at the way the ninth graders were staring at us. "Come on dude, we have to get to class." Fuzzy angrily threw his coffee cup into a nearby garbage can, and followed me back up to the fourth floor for English.

"You're late," Candice said as soon as we sat down. I set my coffee on the desk in front of me, next to my books.

"No, we're not." I shook my head when Fuzzy looked at me with a worried expression. "The bell hasn't even rung yet."

"Well, you're usually earlier than *this*," she scoffed, arching an eyebrow at me. "Maybe that hair dye leaked into your brain so you can't tell time anymore."

"Hey, Candice, would you like some of my coffee?" I pushed the cup toward her, speaking as calmly as possible, while under the desk I was squeezing my hands into fists.

"Nope." Fuzzy reached over her and took the cup out of her reach. "That's mine." I looked at him quizzically and he shook his head as if to say, *Don't start something; it's not worth it.*

"Well, you take yours the same as I like mine," Candice shrugged and took it from his hands. I am pretty sure she tried to bat her eyelashes at him.

"I just said 'no', Candice," Fuzzy said, just as she took a sip. Her eyes went wide and she almost slammed the cup on her desk.

"Something wrong?" I asked, biting back a smile. She shook her head violently and grabbed Fuzzy's unfinished water bottle, chugging what remained in it. While I watched her try to hide her failed flirting attempt, someone tapped me on the shoulder. I turned around and saw Connor looking down at me. He nodded at the door and left. I got to my feet and followed him.

"Hey," he said, once I joined him at the end of the hall, away from all the bustling by the lockers and classrooms. "I know we only have, like... five minutes before class starts, so I just wanted to ask you something real quick." He looked very nervous.

"Yeah, go ahead," I agreed, crossing my arms over my chest protectively. "What's going on?"

Connor took a deep breath and ran his fingers through his hair. I was surprised to notice that it had been washed recently. I briefly wondered if he had brushed his teeth too.

"Have you always been like this?" he asked so fast that it sounded like one word. I blinked in confusion. Should I be offended? "I mean, on Saturday you were standoffish and you literally ran away from me. And the hair. Have you always been this way?"

"I guess not." I shrugged and leaned against the wall behind me. "I've got a lot going on. What are you getting at?"

"Nothing." Connor shook his head. "I was getting worried that I'd fallen in love with the wrong girl." My breath caught in my chest and thought I might throw up.

Sticks and stones will break my bones but words will never hurt me. What bullshit.

As if he had not said something terrible, Connor bent over, gave me a quick kiss, and headed to class. He had brushed his teeth.

If he was afraid he had fallen in love with the 'wrong girl', who was his other option? I did not understand why his words were affecting me so much. I had no right to be upset with him when I had extremely strong feelings for Rudy and was actually acting on them.

Still feeling as though I had been punched in the gut, I went back to the classroom just as the first bell rang. I took my seat, but not before seeing a shit-eating grin that Connor and Candice exchanged. Fuzzy caught my eye, glancing from Connor to Candice, and gave me a quizzical look. I shrugged. I had an idea, but I pushed it out of my mind. It was not fair of me to be upset with Connor when I was cheating on him.

Our teacher began her lesson, going over more of *Hamlet*. I pretended to take notes in my spiral-bound notebook when really I was sketching pictures of Mr. Darcy. I jumped when I felt a hand on my knee. I looked over at Connor, who gave me a crooked smile in return. I grabbed his hand and pushed it off my leg, but he caught my fingers and tried to place my hand on his crotch. With an annoyed huff, I pulled my hand out of his grasp and smacked his groin. I did not do it hard, just hard enough for him to jump in surprise and shoot a very pissed look at me.

"Not appropriate," I hissed at him, and returned to my doodles.

When I exited my psych class later that day, I was surprised to see Fuzzy waiting for me.

"Hey," I grinned at him. "How's it going?"

"Fine," Fuzzy said, giving me a half-hearted smile. "Can we talk?"

"Uh, yeah, sure. You want to go to the library or the gym? It's pretty crowded in the halls right now."

"Let's go to the study hall," Fuzzy suggested. I nodded and we weaved through our classmates to the third floor.

"So, what's up?" I asked, taking a seat on a desk in the same cubicle we shared the day of my panic attack.

"What happened during English?" Fuzzy nearly demanded. "I mean, you practically ran out of there. Didn't even say bye to me."

"Ugh, sorry about that," I apologized, twisting my hair into a messy braid over my shoulder. "I had to get away from Connor. He tried to get me to grope him under the desk and I smacked him in the crotch." Fuzzy's eyes went wide in surprise. "Not the first time he's done that, either. And after that look he shared with Candice... I just had to get away."

Fuzzy sat in the chair beside me and spun it to face me. "Do you know what that look was all about?"

"No, but I have an idea. In the hallway, he said that he might have fallen in love with the wrong person."

"You don't seem too bothered by this," Fuzzy observed, searching my face for a look of annoyance or anger.

"I'm over it," I shrugged. And I was. "People get crushes on other people even if they are in a long-term relationship."

Fuzzy suddenly looked very hopeful and stood up, standing about a foot away from me. "Do you have feelings for another person?"

I broke eye contact with him and slid off the desk. "We need to eat our lunches and we can't in here. Let's head to the cafeteria." I slunk past him, and feeling awful, left the room.

He didn't follow me.

Despite how terrible the day was going, it went by rather quickly, and the next thing I knew, resource centre was over and drama class was about to start.

Fuzzy and I were sitting next to each other on the fainting couch. He seemed very stiff around me and was very interested in watching the rest of the class set up the chairs for circle time. It felt so awkward not to be joking around with him, while waiting for the final bell to ring. Without thinking, I reached over and took his hand in mine. I did not link my fingers through his, just held it gently, palm to palm. I watched him, waiting for a reaction. Fuzzy squeezed my hand and I slid it out of his. He smiled at me and wrapped his arm over my shoulders. It was not joking around, but I would take it for now.

"All right, class," Mr. Thomas said, taking a seat in the circle beside Brett. "Instead of talking about what we did last night, we're doing something else." He pulled a red rose out of his jacket pocket and I couldn't help but wonder if he carried it with him everywhere. "We're going to pass this around and name who our personal hero is. This can be a fictional character or someone in your life, or someone you've never even met. I just thought this might be a neat exercise." Everyone nodded and mumbled in agreement, and Mr. T handed the (what turned out to be a plastic) rose to Brett.

It was amusing hearing who people looked up to. One guy said that Forrest Gump was his hero, which I thought was adorable. When Candice handed it to me, I froze. My hero used to be my mom, but I couldn't say that anymore. I stared down at the flower and ran my fingers over the petals.

"Paul McCartney," I finally said. "He's very talented and he's a vegetarian. He's my idol. Or Louisa May Alcott." I handed the rose to Fuzzy.

"Dwight Schrute from *The Office*," he said simply, and handed it to the girl sitting beside him while the class chuckled.

When the rose was returned back to Mr. Thomas, he cleared his throat. "My hero is in this room," he admitted, fingering the stem. "She's only sixteen and she's been through more than most people go through in their entire lives." He looked up at me and my throat tightened. "Beth, you're my hero."

Even if I could talk, I had no idea what to say. I was about to attempt to say something like "thank you" when a girl named Pam shouted out: "I'm changing my hero! Beth's my hero, too!"

"Mine, too!" Fuzzy and about ten other students raised their hands and smiled down at me.

For the second time in three months, I received and gave hugs to everyone in the class. It was the most touching moment of my life.

CHAPTER 26
SEIZURE

"As happy as I am to see you, I still can't believe we have to have a rehearsal on a Saturday," I complained Saturday morning, as we ascended the front steps to the main foyer.

"I can't believe you agreed to meet an hour earlier than it actually starts," Rudy kidded, opening the door for me and following me inside. I took his hand and we started for the auditorium.

"What do you mean you can't believe it? There's no way I would have said no." I nudged his shoulder. "I like spending time with you... and kissing you." Rudy smiled down at me and pulled open the auditorium door.

Hand in hand, we walked down the aisle until we were in front of the stage. I turned to face him and lifted myself up so that I was sitting beside the floor lights. Rudy stepped forward so that he was between my legs and wrapped his arms around my waist.

"Beth?" he said quietly, his blue eyes boring into mine.

"Yeah?" I brushed the back of my hand over his stubble. *Seriously, how does a seventeen year old grow this?*

"I don't want to hide us anymore."

My shoulders slouched and I looked at my lap. "Rudy—"

"No, Beth. I really, really like you and I want to be able to kiss you in public and not have it needing to be scripted. I'm sick of hiding." He leaned his forehead against mine.

"It'll happen, Rudy," I assured him in a whisper. "Just wait for me?"

Rudy nodded. "You know I will."

I placed my hands on his cheeks and pressed my mouth against his. "Rudy, how do you grow this shadow so perfectly?" I demanded, feeling the rough hairs against my palms. "You're seventeen for Christ's sake."

"Maybe *you're* not trying hard enough," he joked, leaning into me. I leaned back until I was lying down and Rudy was on all fours above me. "Do you not like the scruff?"

"Oh, no, I love the scruff," I shook my head. "If I were a boy, I'd want to look just like you."

Rudy cocked an eyebrow down at me and laughed. "Weird, but thanks."

"Can we make out now?" I asked, holding onto the front of his black t-shirt.

"That's a giant 'yes'," Rudy laughed, meeting me in another kiss.

Half an hour later, Mr. Thomas and the rest of the cast and crew were mingling around waiting for rehearsal to begin. Rudy and I sat about a foot apart on the stage, pretending to be going through our lines and notes.

"Okay, people." Mr. T clapped his hands, the sound echoing in the auditorium. "We are going through the entire play today—yes, Lindsey, the entire play—and if you forget your line, do your best to recall it or just say 'line' and I'll help you with it. I'll be taking notes and nit-picking throughout the performance, and I apologize in advance for that. All right, everyone got it? Good." He took a seat in the second row with a clipboard in hand. "Places!"

We all scrambled to our marks for the first scene.

Just then, I felt one of my epileptic seizures coming on. I tried to will it away and listen to what Mr. T was saying, but the point was moot. White hot fiery pains shot up the entire right side on my body and my heartbeat became so frantic I thought my heart was going to burst out of my chest. No one who was here had seen me have a seizure before. No one knew what to do. I was fucked. I was going to die. *I'm fucked and I'm going to die*, I thought in a loop. My breathing became erratic and I felt my right arm seize up and my hand warp itself into a messed-up fist, my fingernails digging into my palm.

"No! Help!" I screamed. I started to lay down before I fell and hit my head.

"Beth? Beth? Are you okay? What's happening?" I heard a thump and Rudy's worried face loomed above mine. "Beth? Is this a seizure?"

"Don't let me die," I pleaded, before I lost the ability to talk. My eyes rolled into the back of my head. Pain coursed through every vein in my body as if they were full of lava instead of blood. My back arched and my limbs began to jerk uncontrollably. All I could think was *I don't want to die! Please! Please, stop! I'll do anything, just make this end!*

I could hear the cast and crew talking on the stage and Mr. T arguing with Rudy.

"Rudy! Back up! Give her some space!"

"Should I call 911?"

"No, Mr. T, she needs me!"

"What the hell is going on?"

"She's faking."

"I remember her telling me that she doesn't need any paramedics after a seizure, unless she hits her head or if it goes on for over two minutes."

"Well, how long has it been?"

After what seemed like an eternity, but was really more like forty seconds, my body slowly stopped seizing and my muscles gave out. Feeling as though I had just run a marathon while on fire, I gasped for the breath I'd lost while I had been 'faking' a seizure.

"Beth? Beth, can you hear me?" Mr. Thomas asked, towering over me.

"Y-yes," I wheezed.

"Can you move?" a very pale Rudy asked.

"No." I exhaled. "I can never move the right side of my body after a seizure." I winced at the aftermath, feeling hot pins and needles roaming over my body.

"Do you need an ambulance?"

"No, no. I just need to rest for a bit."

"All right," Mr. T said, nodding at Rudy. I felt a cold arm slip underneath my knees and another snake beneath my shoulders. Rudy picked me up effortlessly and held my limp body against him.

"I'll take her to the drama room and watch over her," he told Mr. T, and then my neck gave out and my head lolled back. I could see an upside down Lindsey, looking extremely pissed off, glaring at me

Yeah, I faked a seizure so Rudy could carry me like a damsel in distress to the drama room, I thought sarcastically.

"Okay, we'll do the scenes you two aren't in," Mr. T agreed.

Rudy turned away from him, carried me across the stage, and nudged the backstage door open with his hip. Then he carried me down the hall and into the open-doored drama room, kicking the door closed behind us. He made his way to the fainting couch that Fuzzy and I sat on every day and gently lay me down on it, straightening my head so that my neck was not tilted at a strange angle. He pulled a chair over to the couch and sat in front of me.

"Jesus Christ," was all he said while I lay there, still panting.

"Are... are you okay?" I asked with difficulty. My lungs still felt very tight.

"Am *I* okay?" Rudy said, shocked that I had asked a question like that. He did not know that I usually asked anyone that after they had seen me have a seizure for the first time. "Jesus, Beth." He leaned forward and took my right hand in both of his. "You really can't move this?"

"Nope," I replied. "It just feels really hot. Kind of like I've been holding a cup of boiling coffee for too long."

He ran his hand up and down my arm and stretched out my fingers. "Oh God," he gasped. "Your hand is bleeding."

"That happens. It's normal." I tried to calm him down, but his breathing was sounding panicked. I tried to wave it away with my left hand. "No one was holding my hand while I was seizing, so my fingernails dug into my palm and I ended up clenching my fists so tight my fingernails broke the skin."

I watched Rudy use his sleeve to wipe the blood away and kiss the tiny cuts on my palm. "Oh, Beth," he croaked. "I'm so sorry this crap happens to you."

"It's been going on for years now. I'm used to it," I shrugged with one shoulder.

"No, Beth." He shook his head. Standing, he picked me up again and sat down on the couch with me curled up in his lap, holding me to his chest. "I mean *all* this stuff. Everything, all of it, it's too much." Rudy rocked me gently back and forth. I was not sure whether it was to comfort me or himself. "I'm so sorry. So sorry," he continued to repeat.

Seizures tend to drain out any energy I had, so I was not surprised when my eyelids became heavy and my head leaned into him.

Next thing I knew, I heard a door close and felt Rudy shift beneath me.

"What's going on in here?" Mr. T asked as I sat up, quickly wiping drool off my chin.

"I was comforting her and she fell asleep," Rudy told him, as I slid off his lap.

I glanced at Mr. Thomas (who looked entirely unconvinced) and stretched my crazy sore right arm and rubbed my neck. I was able to flex my fingers again, although they were still weak. My leg was stiff but I would be able to walk. Not well, but I could do it.

"How're you feeling?" our director asked.

"All right," I told him truthfully. "I can rehearse, but I'm really spent."

"Okay," he nodded. "Everyone is on a break right now, so be on stage in fifteen, you two." We both nodded and watched him leave, closing the door behind him.

"You really okay?" Rudy asked, doubt in his voice. He stretched his arms above his head.

"Yeah," I yawned. "Tired, stiff, and weak, but I can move so I can take it." I slowly stood and retrieved my water bottle from my book bag.

"Hey, Beth?" Rudy said, looking down.

"Mmm?" I said, gulping down some water.

"You drooled on me." He laughed, pointing at a wet spot just below his shoulder. I flushed but giggled. "Don't worry about it."

I found it odd that it was damned near impossible to snuggle with Connor, but I had just napped on Rudy's lap for a good hour, not to mention drooled on him, and he was not freaking out; he was laughing. He had comforted me and was not expecting sex. He just wanted to hold me, to take care of me. This man was… amazing. I watched him work out a kink in his neck, rubbing it hard and wincing a bit. He had sat in an uncomfortable position with me while I slept and put a damp spot on his shirt. A swell of affection toward him filled me and I kissed his cheek tenderly.

"Give me one week, Rudy," I said, touching his face. He stared at me as if he could not believe what I was saying. He said nothing, just waited for me to assure him that his thoughts were on the right track. "One week and then I'm yours. I would do it sooner, really I would, but I need to figure out how to do it. Seven days, then we can stop hiding."

CHAPTER 27

IGNORANT BLISS

The next day, Connor invited himself over again to help me with my lines. I quickly discovered that 'help me with my lines' actually meant 'skip to the kissing scene and see how far he could get'.

We were sitting on my bed, cross-legged, facing each other, when he leaned in to kiss me. Without thinking, I tilted back away from him. Unfortunately, he took that as a sign to lie down on top of me. His mouth on mine, he pushed me onto my back. Because of the lines we had just exchanged, I thought of Rudy.

Rudy's rough hands running up my sides, his lips on my throat, his shadowed jaw tickling my skin, his nimble fingers unbuttoning my jeans... *Wait, what?*

My eyes snapped open and I came back down to earth. Connor was touching me; Connor was slobbering on me; Connor was trying to unbutton my jeans.

I was disgusted with myself. "No," I grunted under his weight. I turned my face away from him and swatted at the hand trying to undress me.

"What do you mean 'no'?" Connor questioned, putting hands on either side of my shoulders and pushing up off of me.

"I mean 'no'," I repeated. "I'm not feeling it."

"Since when do you not feel it?" he scoffed. "You always feel it." God, his breath reeked. When was the last time he had brushed his teeth?

"You mean I've been feeling it since my mom died," I snapped, pushing him off of me until we were both sitting up again.

"Beth, she's still dead," Connor said, as if I had forgotten.

My jaw dropped. *Remind me why I don't love him, again?* I raised a hand above my shoulder to slap him, but Connor jumped off the bed, out of my reach.

"No, no, Beth! That's, that's not what I meant!" he stammered, his hands in front of him, his palms facing me.

"What else could you have meant with a comment like that?!" I snarled, my hand still prepared for a strike. "You don't have to *remind me* that my mom is dead! I'm reminded every morning when there's no text saying 'have a good day', every night when she doesn't call to say goodnight, and every weekend when she's not there to pick me and Amy up! Once and a while I get a moment of ignorant bliss and forget... where I still feel sad but I get to forget why! I know she's gone, Connor, and talking about her won't bring her back. Keep her out of your mouth!"

He blinked at me. "I was surprised. Hands off, I promise."

My jaw clenched and I slowly lowered my hand.

Do it! Do it now. Do it! Dump him!

I did not follow my own advice.

"If you ever say something like that again..." I growled in a warning tone.

"Never again," he promised, crawling back onto the bed.

My heart still pounding with fury, I grabbed my script, opened it, and turned on the radio beside my bed. Katy Perry's *Thinking of You* was playing, a reminder that I was a fucking coward.

That evening, I sat on my bed re-reading my copy of *Little Women*, at the part when Jo refuses Laurie, when there was a soft knock on my door.

"Yeah?" I said, dog-earring the page. Amy poked her head in and looked at me with sympathy in her big blue eyes.

"Bethy, can I come in?" she requested, even though she was already closing the door behind her.

"Of course," I said, the corners of my mouth lifting. My little sister had been thirteen for a little over a week and it killed me inside that she had already been through so much. I was so damned proud of her.

"Bethy, what's wrong?" she asked, sitting down on my bed beside me.

"What do you mean?"

"I could hear you crying from my room." She gestured in the direction of her bedroom. "The walls are thin but still…"

I wiped the back of my hands over my cheeks to discover that they were wet. I had not even realized that I was crying. I was quiet for a moment.

"I have to…" my voice broke, "I have to break up with Connor." Amy nodded and waited for me to continue. Apparently this was not a surprise. "I don't love him anymore and he's mean and disrespectful, but I still don't want to hurt him. He makes me unhappy but, but…"

"That other guy *does* make you happy?" Amy finished as a question.

"What?" I gasped, my eyes widening. "How did you know about him?"

"I've seen him drop you off, remember? And you text way more than you used to, and you're always smiling after rehearsals. You must really—"

"His name's Rudy," I admitted, picking at my duvet cover. "I met him first week back after spring break. He makes me feel really… safe. Yesterday I decided that I'm going to dump Connor by Saturday. I like Rudy *so much*, but I don't want anyone to get hurt." I buried my face in my hands and began to weep again.

My baby sister pulled me into her until my head rested in her lap while she gently braided and unbraided my hair—something Marmee used to do.

"Amy?" I croaked, after my full-on sobs finally subsided.

"Yeah?"

"When did you grow up?"

She paused and thought about her answer.

"I guess the same day you did," she told me, her tone full of sadness.

I rolled onto my back so that I was looking up at her. "I'll still take care of you," I promised, sitting up a bit.

"I know," Amy nodded.

That was the moment it hit me that, while I may be the new mother figure for Amy, I could still talk to her about boys like normal teenage sisters do.

"Hey, Beth? What do you say that we watch *Little Women*?" Amy suggested, braiding my hair once more. "I know we only watch it on Christmas Eve, but it sounds like you could just use a break from everything right now."

"*That* is exactly what I need," I agreed. "A young Christian Bale to stare at."

Halfway through the movie and our second bowl of popcorn, I remembered something from ages ago that I hadn't thought to ever bring up again. Pausing *Little Women* I turned to face Amy.

"Hey, I like this part," she protested, reaching for remote.

"Hang on, I just wanted to ask you something," I said, holding it out of her reach. "Did you ever find out who was sending you those secret messages? You know, the secret admirer or whatever?"

"They haven't stopped." Amy said, grabbing a fistful of popcorn. "I get like three a week."

"Any idea who they're from?"

"A few." Amy shrugged. "I'll let you know when I find out. Now press play!"

I did, and once again, my sister and I cried as Jo refused Laurie.

CHAPTER 28

PLAY MISTY FOR ME VERSUS DIRTY HARRY

Monday morning came round and Fuzzy and I decided to get a (possibly fatal) cup of coffee before class.

"Whoa, it's packed in here," Fuzzy acknowledged as we entered the cafeteria. "Are they selling pot brownies instead of muffins now?"

I laughed as we stood in line with tired students, almost squished together. "I don't think so, but it *is* a Monday morning."

"True," Fuzzy nodded, pulling out his wallet and checking the amount of cash he had.

Someone nudged in beside me but I didn't take any notice until I felt a finger loop itself around my pinky. I didn't need to turn my head to see that it was Rudy subtly lacing his finger around mine. I smiled and stole a glance at him. He was looking at the chalkboards above the counter, reading what the specials of the day were.

"Beth, are you listening to me?" Fuzzy said, waving a hand in front of my face. "You in there?"

Rudy started to let go of my finger, but I squeezed it and he stayed where he was.

"Sorry, I zoned out," I apologized. "What were you saying?"

"I was saying that maybe I should get a Coke instead. It might be safer for my tongue."

"Really? A coke at eight thirty in the morning? You know, the coffee might not be scalding hot today." I shrugged. "Might be cold instead."

"Yeah, you're right," Fuzzy agreed, wrapping an arm around my shoulders. "As usual." I would have laughed, but out of the corner of my eye I saw Rudy glowering at where Fuzzy's arm was draped. He stepped closer to me, our arms now pressed together.

Well, this was awkward.

I paid for a coffee after Fuzzy did and Rudy let go of my fingers when I picked up the Styrofoam cup the cashier handed me. I stood beside Fuzzy, who was carefully pouring the wake-up juice into his own cup.

"Well, it's not steaming," I observed when he handed me the canister.

"But that could mean that it's practically frigid," Fuzzy stated, adding cream and sugar and placing a lid on the rim.

"True," I said, filling my own cup. When I put the pot down and reached across the counter for a lid, I felt a body press against the back of mine.

"Sorry," Rudy's voice said in my ear, his scruff tickling my cheek. He took a cup lid, and before leaning away from me, placed a quick kiss on my neck. I gasped and whipped around to face him, but he had already taken a step away and was looking at me with a glint in his eyes.

"Whoa, personal bubble much?" Fuzzy exclaimed, pushing his way to my side and handing me my coffee, to which he had added a lid. I realized that Rudy and I had been staring at each other and I placed a palm on Fuzzy's chest. "Seriously, dude," Fuzzy said to him, "you couldn't have waited a second?"

"No, no, Fuzzy, it's okay," I said. "It's Rudy. The guy I'm in the play with."

Fuzzy's eyes flashed and he looked Rudy up and down. I saw Rudy do the same.

"All right," Fuzzy nodded, taking my arm. "Let's go." He started to drag me out of the room.

"See you at rehearsal?" Rudy called after me.

"Of course," I waved with my free arm.

Once Fuzzy and I were in the hallway, I pulled my arm out of his grasp and stood on the spot, glaring at him.

"Beth, what are you doing? We're going to be late for English," Fuzzy asked, doubling back to me.

"Fuck English," I snapped. "What the hell was that?"

"What the hell was what?" Fuzzy blinked at me, taking a sip of his coffee. He did not wince, so I gathered that it was (for once) just right.

"Why were you so rude to Rudy just now?" I demanded, gesturing down the way we came from. "You basically dragged me out of there as soon as I told you who he was."

Fuzzy stepped closer to me. "You said he's confusing you," he said, referring to the day I'd had my panic attack in the study hall. "Why should I be polite to him?"

"Because he's my friend," I replied, deciding it was better not to go into further detail. "You should be nice to my friends."

"I'm not nice to Connor," Fuzzy retorted, not missing a beat.

"That's different."

"Why? Because you're sleeping with him?"

"No, because he's a dick."

We stared at each other for a moment, trying to hold back our smirks. "Listen, Fuzzy," I said, giving up and letting my smile spread. "Rudy is a really nice guy and it's important to me that you like him."

Fuzzy looked at me curiously for a moment and I knew he was wondering if there was more to the friendship than I was letting on.

"You're right," he sighed eventually. "Again. I'll be friendlier next time I see him, I promise."

"Thank you," I smiled, marching past him and starting up the stairs.

"Where are you going?" Fuzzy asked, following me.

"English class." I took a gulp of my coffee. It was just right.

"But you *just* said 'fuck English'," Fuzzy quoted, jabbing his finger to where I had been standing when I said those words.

"It's more like... fuck *Hamlet*," I shrugged, continuing up the stairs. "I mean, everyone knows what happens in the end."

Fuzzy stopped mid-step and stared at me. "Why? What happens?"

"Kind of like what happened at the end of *Les Mis*," I answered, sipping my coffee.

Fuzzy's brows furrowed as he tried to remember the ending on the play. "Everyone... bursts into song?" he guessed slowly, following me.

"No!" I laughed. "Basically everyone dies."

Fuzzy laughed and strode along beside me up the stairs. When we reached the classroom, Fuzzy stopped abruptly in the doorway. I slammed into him and jumped back to avoid getting coffee all down my front.

"Dude!" I huffed, slurping the liquid caffeine from the gap in the lid. "Move," I said to his back. He did not listen, but thankfully, I was small enough to squeeze between him and the door jam.

I stopped in my tracks as well when I saw what was going on at our desk. Connor and Candice were leaning toward each other over the desk, their foreheads were nearly touching and Candice was smiling at him, what I assumed was flirtatiously, while Connor seemed to be sharing a story with her.

"You okay?" Fuzzy asked behind me. I closed my eyes and took a deep breath. I had literally been rolling around on the floor with Rudy on Saturday. I had no right to get pissed at Connor. Candice on the other hand...

"Yeah," I nodded, turning around and pushing him back into the hall.

"What are you doing?" Fuzzy asked, bumping into a couple of students who were hurrying to class before the bell rang.

"Fuzzy, I apologize, but I need to use you," I explained, downing the rest of my coffee and tossing it into a nearby trash can. Fuzzy copied me. "Connor can get away with that, but Candice can't." I pointed at the classroom with a shaky hand.

Fuzzy took a deep breath and nodded in understanding. He handed me his books, turned around, and squatted. I hopped on his back, wrapped my legs around his waist, and my arms around his shoulders. He cupped his hands under my butt, straightened his legs and sighed.

"You know, if I didn't enjoy having you pressed against me, while holding your ass, I might have a problem with this," Fuzzy told me as we made our grand entrance into the English classroom. Candice and Connor looked up when one of Fuzzy's long gangling legs bumped into an empty desk and he cussed. "Ow, shit."

Candice's expression was priceless. Her normally pale face was beet red and the frown she almost always wore deepened even further. When I saw Connor's face, I felt mine fall. The look had me convinced that there would be a screaming match the next time we were remotely alone.

"Yeah, this wasn't a good idea," Fuzzy whispered, bending his knees so I could slide down his back. I put his books on his desk beside Candice, and sat at my own.

"Morning," I greeted, giving Connor a sheepish smile. Connor pushed his mouth against mine and I had to fight the urge to shove him away and slap him in a crowded classroom. Instead, I slid a hand between our chests and gently pushed him away. "I know what you're doing. Stop it," I stated. Fortunately, class started before Connor could protest and accuse me of anything.

Sure enough, during lunch, Connor found Fuzzy and I hanging out at our lockers and rounded on us.

"You have *no right* to put your hands all over her!" Connor yelled at Fuzzy who stared down at him, unfazed. Instead, he rolled his eyes.

"Dude, calm down. It was a piggy-back ride, not a doggy-style ride," he grumbled. He would have continued, but I punched his arm.

"Fuzzy! Shut up!" I snapped, then turned to Connor. "Connor, before your mind runs amok, just let me say *again:* Fuzzy and I are friends. That's it."

"Yeah," Fuzzy nodded. I glanced at him and noticed that he had an evil smirk on his face. "Friends. Like you and Candice." He stared at Connor, waiting for a reaction. He got one.

Connor's cheeks flushed. "Like me and Candice?" he echoed, his eyes shifting from me to Fuzzy and back again.

"Sure. You two get along really well. That's all, right?" Fuzzy continued, crossing his arms over his chest. "There's no added romantic feelings. Beth shouldn't have a reason to accuse you of sleeping with Candice, should she?"

"Fuzzy, that's enough," I butted in. Not only did I not want to know the answer to that question, but Rudy and I had come dangerously close to just that on Saturday so, again, I had no right to get pissed if I found out the truth. "That's enough, both of you."

Fuzzy opened his mouth to protest, but his phone started ringing in his pocket. He pulled it out and stepped away to answer it, keeping an eye on me and Connor all the while.

"Come over after school," Connor said, taking my hand in his. "I know you have rehearsal, but come over after. Please?"

It would give us the privacy for me to break up with him.

"Um, I'm not sure when it's going to wrap up, but if it's not too late I will," I told him.

He smiled and bent down to kiss me, but I stepped away from him.

"Beth, what the hell?" he exclaimed, yanking on my hand and pulling me toward him. "Why can't I kiss you lately? Do you realize that we've never even gone this long without… you know. What is wrong with you?!" He squeezed my fingers tight with his.

"Connor, let go!" I hissed. "You're hurting me!" When he did not let go, I looked over my shoulder at Fuzzy, who was looking at us curiously. "I haven't felt like it in a while. Pressuring me into it won't help!"

Connor let go of my hand and I pulled it to my chest, flexing my fingers.

"You're right," he sighed. "I'm sorry. We'll talk tonight?"

I nodded and he turned away, walking down the hall just as Fuzzy joined me.

"You okay?" he asked, staring after him.

I merely nodded and said nothing for the rest of lunch break.

I had another wrestling lesson with Coach that day. Graham and I demonstrated some self-defence moves, which could be used on attackers, for the ninth grade girls, who were still excited to be doing something that was not throwing a bouncing ball through a hoop or hitting a not-so-bouncy ball over a net in the hopes that the other team would be unable to hit it back to them.

"Hey Coach," I said, once all the girls had partnered off to try the moves themselves. "What gave you the idea to teach them this instead of your usual lesson plan?"

The coach scratched the stubble on his face with bitten-down fingernails. "My niece."

"What do you mean?"

"This conversation is in confidence, agreed?"

"Uh, yeah, sure."

Coach sighed and told me that his fifteen-year-old niece had been attacked on her way home the month before.

"Oh my God, is she okay?" I asked, shaking my head in shock.

"Yes, she's all right for the most part. Shaken up a good deal, though." Coach nodded, putting his hands on his hips and looking around at the class, learning how to defend themselves. "I can't help but think that if she had known how to dislodge an attacker, she wouldn't have gone through all that. So, with your help, along with Graham, I'm trying to help prevent another girl from getting into a similar situation."

"That's good of you, Coach," I said. I wanted to give him a hug, because a lot of people paid rather expensive lessons to learn these things, while he was teaching it in a public school PE class.

"Thanks, Beth. Now, could you go tackle Graham from behind? He doesn't know it's part of the lesson plan."

Fuzzy stayed behind when drama class ended the next period. Candice, on the other hand, bolted. She had been giving me the cold shoulder, all because of the piggy-back stunt. For once, I did not give a flying fuck.

"Are you actually going over to his place after rehearsal?" Fuzzy asked, once the drama room was empty, except for a few straggling students gathering their school things.

"Like I told Connor, if it doesn't run too late," I replied, knowing where this conversation was going. "Look, I know what you're going to say, we've had this conversation a billion times—"

"What conversation?" Rudy's voice sounded as he appeared beside Fuzzy. "Hey, Fuzzy."

"It's Daniel," Fuzzy corrected in a cold tone. I raised an eyebrow at him and he rolled his eyes. "I mean, most people call me Daniel. It's so good to *see* you, man!" Fuzzy gave Rudy a huge hug, which was awkwardly returned. Well, at least he was being more polite.

"Okay, *Daniel*," Rudy said after Fuzzy let him go. "What conversation are we talking about?"

I bit my lip, wondering if Fuzzy would figure out what was going on between Rudy and me if I brought up Connor.

"My boyfriend is a dick and I plan to end it with him tonight after rehearsal," I said, noting the look of surprise on Fuzzy's face. "That's why I'm going over there, not because I'm in the mood for—" I shut up when I saw Rudy's face flush and jealously flash through his eyes. He turned around and made his way over to the fainting couch.

"You're really dumping him?" Fuzzy asked, unable to hide his amazement.

Not wanting to talk about Connor anymore, I nodded. "That's the plan. You should get going, Fuzzy. We'll be starting soon."

"You're right," Fuzzy agreed, retrieving his bag off the floor. "You'll let me know how it goes? Give me a call tonight?"

I nodded again and joined Rudy on the couch after the door closed behind my best friend.

Rudy turned at the waist to face me, a very serious expression on his face. "That guy," he pointed at the door Fuzzy had just gone out, "is quite sure that he'll be your boyfriend by the end of the month."

I was stunned for a second before I started to laugh. "What? No! Fuzzy and I are just friends!"

"And so were we until two and a half weeks ago," Rudy shrugged, gesturing between us. "Trust me. The *moment* Daniel finds out that you're not with douche-dick-stick, he'll be trying to kiss you."

"He knows I don't feel like that," I assured Rudy, crossing my legs.

"Does he? Does he really?" Rudy questioned. "Have you flat out told him, 'Dude, I don't like you like that'?"

"Well, not flat out," I admitted. "But he *knows*, Rudy, honest."

Rudy ran a frustrated hand over his face. "You are going to—"

"Connor? What are you doing here?" we heard Mr. Thomas say by the door. "Did Beth forget her homework or something?"

Hoping that it was a different Connor looking for a different Beth, I turned in my seat to look at the door, where sure enough, the same Connor was standing in front of Mr. T.

"No, I thought I might watch the rehearsal today," he shrugged, not really sounding interested.

Mr. T seemed to have a silent battle going on in his head. If it were any other student, he would tell them to hit the road, but Connor was a co-worker's son and the co-star's boyfriend. So, unfortunately, he caved to Connor's request.

"Right, yeah. Just… don't be a distraction."

"Don't worry about it," Connor said and made his way over to us. The last time he was in this room he had been accusing me of cheating on him, and Fuzzy was about to punch him in the face. Now, sitting stiffly beside me was the guy I was actually cheating on him with.

Kill. Me. Now.

"Hey, Bethy," Connor said when he reached us.

"What are you doing here?" I asked, knowing that I sounded quite rude.

"Whoa. Nice to see you, too," he huffed, leaning forward to kiss me. I attempted to back away from the kiss, but he grabbed my face in both hands and held me in place.

Keeping my hands at my sides, I scrunched my eyes closed, wrinkled my nose, and kept my lips pursed, but still he kissed me. I was sure Rudy was going to leave, but surprisingly, I felt his fingers weave through mine.

When Connor finally gave up on trying to get me to kiss him back, he let go of me and took a step back. "Fine," he grumbled as my face relaxed. Then he noticed Rudy, who was hiding our hands behind a couch cushion. "Who's this?"

"This is my friend Rudy. He plays Roger. Rudy, this is Connor." I introduced them, feeling very uncomfortable.

"Oh, you get to kiss my girl here," Connor nodded, remembering the scene he had 'rehearsed' with me. "Hope you haven't copped a feel or anything," he laughed.

I bit my lip and exchanged a quick glance with Rudy, who was biting back a grin. He had done more than cop a feel in the recent past.

"I'd never do that... on stage," Rudy said, with a hint of humour in his voice.

"Good, good," Connor mused, clapping him on the shoulder.

I was not sure whether to laugh at how absurd it was or scowl at the fact that Connor was not even the *tiniest* bit jealous that Rudy had been kissing me for over a month.

"I didn't know Lindsey was in the play," Connor voiced, watching the rest of the cast and crew file into the drama room.

"Ugh, yeah," I groaned, slouching into the back of the couch. My heart sped up when Rudy inched a little closer to me and our knees touched. "She, she plays Joanne."

"She must *love* that," Connor said sarcastically, sitting on the other side of me.

"Yeah. She's been a delight."

"All right, people," Mr. T called from his desk. "To the auditorium!" he added dramatically.

We all gathered our sweaters, bags, and books and followed him out of the classroom, across the hall, and through the door that entered the back stage.

"Where should I sit?" Connor asked, his eyes wandering the auditorium.

"Mr. Thomas usually sits in the second row or so," Rudy told him, taking my bag from me and setting it down next to his.

"Cool," Connor said, smiling. "I'm really looking forward to seeing this, Bethy," he added.

I gave him a tight-lipped smile but said nothing.

Thankfully we were not going through the kissing scene that day, just parts that Mr. T still thought needed work. With the amount of complaining coming from Lindsey, she did not agree.

"We have been through this one a *million* times," she bitched to Brett while backstage, "I mean, it's not even that good a scene; I always half-ass this one."

"Which is why we need to work on it," Brett, Rudy, and I all said together.

She turned bright pink, flipped me off, and watched the rest of the rehearsal in silence.

I was really hoping that it would go on late, so I could postpone the upcoming break up, but Mr. T had dinner plans and we had wrapped up by five thirty.

"So, you're heading to his place then," Rudy pondered, joining me in the backstage corner in which he had left our bags.

"Like I told Fuzzy, I *said* I would." I pulled my sweater over my head and shouldered my book bag.

"Are you gonna…?" He let the question drag out, bending over to get his own bag.

"That's the plan," I nodded, my heart pounding and tears stinging my eyes.

"What's wrong?" Rudy fretted, worry on his face. "Did I say something wrong?"

"No, no," I choked, waving my hands at my face to cool myself down. "I'm just scared. And the fact that his mom, Lynn, will hate me soon is starting to sink in."

"I know, Beth." Rudy wrapped me up in a hug and placed a kiss on top of my head. "It'll be okay. I promise. And his mom won't hate you. You're like one of her own, remember?"

"Beth? Are you *coming?!*" Connor's annoyed tone shouted from the seats.

Rudy's arms stiffened around me and I took a small step away from him. "Yeah! Yes," I called back over my shoulder. I took another step away from Rudy, but he closed the distance between us and wrapped one of his long-fingered hands around my tiny forearm.

He opened and closed his mouth a couple times, as if he were having difficulty wording what he wanted to say. "Please, don't sleep with him," he finally breathed, so close to me that I felt his breath on my neck. He looked away from me, as if embarrassed.

My eyes widened with surprise. "Rudy, I... do you... no, no, of course not." I shook my head, touching his scruffy jaw gently. He visibly relaxed and I gave the corner of his mouth a quick kiss. "Rudy, I have to go." He nodded and slowly let go of my arm, so I could make my way to my soon-to-be ex.

"So, what did you think of the scenes you saw?" I asked Connor as we headed to his house. I had just realized that I had not been over there since he had attacked me, and I needed something to take my mind off the inevitable panic attack.

"Me?" Connor shrugged, kicking a small rock on the sidewalk and watching it bounce into the road. "Not really my thing."

I exhaled sharply. "What?"

"I dunno, didn't really like it," he explained, either not caring about or not seeing the look of hurt on my face.

"Connor, I have been working on that play for almost *two months* and all you can say about it is 'it's not your *thing*?!" I exclaimed, hurt turning into anger.

"Hey, it's the same thing as your aunt's macaroni and cheese and the movie *Dirty Harry*."

"Don't you *dare* bring Clint Eastwood into this!" I snapped.

"I'm not, I just think *Play Misty For Me* was better."

"There was no awesome monologue in *Play Misty For Me*," I argued.

"At least there weren't crap sequels!" Connor shot back.

"Oh my God, you're useless!" I cried, throwing my arms up in exasperation. "*And* wrong!"

By now we were standing on the bottom step of the staircase that led to the front door of Connor's house.

"To each his own," Connor mumbled, stalking up the stairs and opening the door, closing it with a *snap* behind me.

I pulled off my bag, slipped off my flats, and followed Connor out of the foyer. He started to enter his room, but I backed away from it, flashes of the last time I had been in there going through my mind.

The bite on my shoulder, the bruises on my wrists, the slap that had sent me falling to the floor. *"Who did you fuck?!"*

"No, I'm not going in there." I shook my head and crossed my arms over my chest.

Connor looked quizzical for a moment, as if forgetting what had happened, then seemed to deflate a little. He shut the bedroom door. "Sure." He had the decency to look somewhat ashamed, like a dog that was caught chewing on a new sofa. "What about the living room?"

I nodded in agreement. "That'll be fine."

We shuffled into the open living room. A large couch sat by an impressive bay window, an old striped recliner was placed in front of a huge flat-screen TV, and a lone kitchen chair was abandoned by the fireplace. I bee-lined to the couch and sat Indian style on it. Connor grabbed an afghan off the floor and laid it on my lap before sitting beside me.

"Beth," he said quietly, taking my hands into his and pulling them into his own lap. He ran the pads of his thumbs over my knuckles. "Before we say anything, I just want to remind you that I love you so much." I didn't say anything. "Did you hear me? I love you."

"Mm-hmm," I acknowledged. Connor stiffened, clearly expecting me to return the sentiment.

I remembered the first time he had said the 'L' word.

We had been dating for about three weeks and were snuggled up on the same couch with the same afghan too, watching (of all movies) The Blair Witch Project. *Connor had been staring at me with his big brown eyes while I had been slowly curling into a tighter and tighter ball, terrified, and unable to look away from the TV, which must have cost a small fortune. When Connor muttered something I didn't catch, my eyes flicked over to him for a second.*

"Did you say something?" *I hissed, my attention already back on the TV.* "Are you serious?" *I almost yelled at the dumbass on the screen.* "You threw away the map?!"

"No, nothing." *Connor cleared his throat, but did not stop watching me.* "Beth?" *he said a few minutes later. By then, I was hugging my knees tight to my chest and hiding one eye beneath the afghan.*

"Yes?" *I nearly squeaked.*

"I love you."

My head turned so quickly to stare at him that my neck made a snap sound.

"What? What did you say?"

"I love you."

I blinked at him a couple of times before shaking my head. "No, you don't."

"What? Yes, I do." *He sounded irritated.*

"Tell you what," *I negotiated then,* "if you still think you're in love with me in a week, you can say it again. In the meantime, no, you don't love me."

Connor had gaped at me when I turned back to the TV and finished the movie.

I hated the ending.

"Beth, where do we start?" Connor asked. "We clearly need to talk about what's going on between us."

I shrugged. "I don't—"

"Hey, you two." Connor's mom suddenly walked into the living room with a big smile on her face. "Oh, Beth, it's so good to see you. You haven't been here in ages! Why is that?" She bent down to give me a hug and I looked at Connor over her shoulder. He knew damn well why.

"Oh, you know," I said, as she pulled away and took her seat in the recliner. "There's the play and school... just been really busy."

"Well, I hope to see more of you soon," she smiled. "How are you holding up?" Her face showed gentle concern.

I realized that after I left Connor, I would never be able to lean on her again. I was going to lose my mentor. My throat tightened. *Oh, fuck.* I was not going to cry. I could not stay with a guy I could not stand because I adored his mom.

"Oh, sweetie, come here," Lynn cooed, opening her arms to me. I stood up and stumbled over the afghan to her. I tangled myself in her arms. "I know... I know," she said gently. "Things will get better and easier, I promise."

I was going to miss her so much.

Knowing that I was about to lose my shit, I stood up straight and cleared my throat. "I have to use the bathroom," I mumbled, nearly choking on the words.

I dashed out of the room and across the hall, into the main bathroom. I closed the door and chain-locked it, then leaned against it taking deep breaths. I recalled the day that Connor had punched the bathroom door in a rage because his sister was taking up too much time getting ready for school. The door-jam had split where the deadbolt had been and his dad had to install the chain lock later that day, not wanting to risk another chunk of wall coming out in a fit of ADHD rage. Connor had not gotten into trouble, because his parents saw that he had not taken his medication that morning.

I crossed the room and gazed at myself in the mirror. My eyes were big and shining with unshed tears. I inspected my hair, which was losing its colour with every shower I took. All of the red had faded into a bright pale pink and the streaks in the front, which had been neon pink, were now almost white. I still liked it.

"Beth, are you all right in there?" Lynn's voice broke into my thoughts through the door.

"Y-yes," I replied. I flushed the toilet without having used it and turned on the taps. I blinked rapidly and took a few deep breaths. "You can do this," I whispered, turning the water off. "Quick, like a Band-Aid."

I exited the bathroom and joined Connor on the sofa again.

"You'll join us for dinner, right, Beth?" Lynn asked, poking her head in from the kitchen.

"She'd love to," Connor answered. I bristled. He could not tell me what to do.

"Excellent," Lynn beamed and left us alone again.

"Connor, you don't get to tell me what to do," I said, crossing my arms. "I'm not a dog. You can't tell me to stay."

"I just did," Connor said. "Besides, you always stay for dinner."

"Connor, I think we need to talk," I said after a moment's pause.

"Let's go outside?" Connor requested, nodding in the direction of the back door.

I licked my lips nervously and stood up. We padded through the kitchen, out the back door, and onto the porch. We went to the far side of it where trees surrounded us, so that Lynn would not be able to see us through a kitchen window. I leaned against a railing with my back to the house.

"What do we need to talk about?" Connor asked, standing beside me, gazing out at his backyard.

"I think you know." I did not look over at him.

"Don't, Bethy," Connor said with an almost begging tone. Did he really need to make this harder than it already was? "Please, don't do this."

He placed an arm on either side of me, caging me in. I started to panic. Lynn may be inside, but she could not see us. He would not try anything here... would he?

"Connor, you know that we're not doing great," I whispered. "We haven't been in a long time."

"I understand that," Connor said in my ear. How he made that sentence sound almost threatening was beyond me. I felt his breath on my neck. "But you're just going to give up?"

That pissed me off. I whipped around to face him. "Give up?" I yelled in a whisper. "If I were giving up, I would have dumped you after you slapped me, after you tried to force yourself on me, or when you held me down on the study-room desk."

"You made me angry. I wasn't thinking," he said, as if that excused him of his actions.

"So you gave me a black eye and held me down while I cried and begged for you to stop? And after I screamed, you *bit* me? I had no idea you were so—"

Connor clamped a hand down on my mouth to quiet me. "Beth, I said that I was sorry about that," he hissed, clearly angry that I had brought up the attack. "You've *got* to stay with me. We've been together for over a year and you're just going to throw that away? I love you—Ew!" He yanked his hand away after I gave his palm a big St. Bernard lick. "Beth! God!"

Connor's OCD kicked in and he hurried to the bathroom to wash his hands in scalding hot water for exactly two and a half minutes.

"Is everything all right?" Lynn stepped out onto the porch, drying her hands on a kitchen towel. She looked too motherly.

I could not do it. Not today.

"I have to go," I sighed, running my fingers through my hair. I was pissed at my cowardice.

"Dinner?" Lynn gestured at the kitchen. I walked past her into the kitchen. If I hurried I could leave without having to say goodbye to Connor. He was too busy counting.

I know it sounds mean, but it was true.

"I'll have to rain check," I told her. "Thank you, though."

"Don't worry about it." She waved off my apology. "More for me." She gave me another hug and I embraced her in return, holding on a few beats longer than I would have had I not known that this could be the last hug I ever got from her. I let go and Lynn turned back to the kitchen, saying something about her lasagna needing to be checked on.

"Bye, Connor!" I shouted, in the direction of the bathroom, and then I left the house.

I texted Rudy and Fuzzy when I reached my bus stop ten minutes later.

```
-couldn't do it. Not today. -B
```

```
-why not? -R
```

```
-are you kidding?! -F
```

```
-saw his mom. It would suck to lose her too. -B
```

There was a couple of minutes where I got no incoming messages, so I sent another out.

```
-I started to but I couldn't get a word in -B
```

```
-Are you still with him? -F
```

```
-will you still dump him on Sat? -R
```

```
-I'm still with him but he knows it will end soon.
 Shit went down today is all. I would have done
 it but lynn was in the next room. -B
```

-it better be soon. Tomorrow will be interesting
—F

-see you tomorrow. —R

-ya —B

CHAPTER 29
GIRL TIME

Tuesday morning I was surprised to see that Connor and Candice had beat me to the lockers, and that Connor was holding a small bouquet of tulips. Although my heart did not belong to him anymore, I could not bring myself to tell him I hated tulips.

"For me?" Candice was saying, as I approached behind Connor.

"Uh, no. These are for Beth," Connor said, holding them out of her reach.

Her face fell and then turned into an all-out scowl when she noticed me walking toward them.

"Oh, hi," she greeted me with a huff. She was pissed that my boyfriend had brought flowers to school for me and not for her? I wanted to slap her. "Connor brought *you* something." Oh my God.

Connor turned to face me with a hopeful look on his face. He held out the flowers as if they were a peace offering. Three months ago I would have been so moved by this gesture that I would have grabbed them, then shoved him into the nearest closet, and skipped the first class. But now... I wanted to throw them away. And that made me feel like a complete bitch.

Reluctantly, I took them and thanked him quietly.

"You're welcome," he said, just as softly.

I squeezed past him to the locker but did not miss Candice saying, "What did you have to do for those?" under her breath. It took all of my willpower not to throw the flowers at her and scream, "What the fuck is *wrong* with you?!"

"Connor, do you want to talk tonight?" I asked, snagging my copy of *Hamlet* off the floor of the locker where Candice had carelessly thrown it. I turned back to my (sigh) boyfriend.

"No," he said grimly. I knew immediately that he was avoiding confrontation. "No, I don't want to talk."

"Fine." I shook my head and closed the locker door.

"Beth, we can hang out if you want," Candice offered, putting on her most fake friendly voice. This surprised me. I could not remember the last time I spent time with her outside of school. I glanced over at Connor who looked just as taken aback.

Candice had always been self-absorbed, but she had never been a flat-out bitch before. She was always giving people backhanded compliments that could make or break your day. She liked being the centre of attention—that much I knew—but this was becoming extreme. It seemed that the more attention I was receiving from our fellow students (no matter how unwanted it was), the angrier and more unbearable she became toward me. She was morphing into a completely different person, one I really couldn't stand to be around. But instead of dumping her, I kept her around in the hope that the old her would come back. Maybe some one-on-one time would bring back how we used to actually laugh together?

"Um... yeah, okay" I shrugged. "What did you have in mind?"

"Shopping downtown, maybe?"

"All right, I guess." There was an awkward silence during which we all stared down at our shoes. "I have to use the bathroom," I mumbled, starting down the hall. "I'll see you in English."

The first thing I noticed when the door swung closed behind me was a freshman girl, whom I had seen in the halls, sitting beside the radiator with her face in her hands. I heard her sniffle and reached behind me to lock the door to give her a semblance of privacy.

"Hi," I said quietly, approaching her tentatively.

She jumped and stared up at me. The assumption that she had been crying was correct. Her eyes were puffy and red. Her gaze flicked down to the flowers I was holding and then back up to my eyes. "Hi," she croaked. She had either been crying really hard or for a really long time.

I bit my lip and handed her the tulips. "Here," I said, holding them out to her. "You look like you could use some cheering up."

"No, those are yours." She pushed them away from her.

"All right." I crouched down in front of her and placed the bouquet in her lap. "I'll just leave these here. You can take them and pretend that a really hot guy gave them to you and make whoever hurt you crazy jealous, or you can leave them here so another girl can do the same thing."

The girl cracked a smile and wiped her cheeks with the back of her hands. She stroked the petals gently. "Thank you."

"Of course." I straightened up just as the bell rang. "Also, word from the wise, next time you need to cry, lock the door or use a stall. In this high school rumours spread like wild fire, and doing this can start one."

Her eyes went wide. "Are you going to tell?"

"No, no, of course not." I waved her question away. "Your secret is safe with me." I went to the door and unlocked it. Before I opened it, I added over my shoulder, "I hope everything works out for you."

"Thank you," she said, getting to her feet. "And I'm sorry about you mom."

"Fucking Candice," I grumbled, yanking open the door, not at all surprised that a ninth grader knew.

When I took my seat next to Connor at the group's English desk, Connor eyed me strangely.

"What?"

"Where are the flowers?" he asked.

"I gave them away," I explained, opening my binder to a blank page of paper and finding where we had left off in *Hamlet*.

"You what?" Connor spluttered. "I paid for those."

"Connor, as much as I appreciated the tulips, I know you didn't pay for them," I said glancing over at him. "You picked them out of your dad's garden."

"What makes you think—"

"The stems were taped in a sandwich bag and there was not plastic wrapping," I told him. "It was a really nice gesture, but the girl needed them more than I did."

"Plus, she hates tulips. Beth's favourite flowers are daisies," Fuzzy put in. I shot him a look, which he ignored. "What? You'd think that a boyfriend of over a year would know that."

Connors shoulders seemed to both stiffen and slouch at the same time. Thankfully, before he could say anything back, class started.

After Psych 101 ended, I told the group I would meet them in the cafeteria for lunch, and that I was going to stop at the vending machines for a soda. Really we had just walked by them and I had seen Rudy counting out some change.

"Hey," I said, bumping his thigh with my hip. I stared at the drink selection, pretending to ponder over which drink to get.

"Hey back." Rudy smiled. "Damn, do you have a quarter? I'm jonesing for a Gatorade and I only have a buck fifty." I pulled my wallet out of my bag and unzipped the change pocket. "So, exactly what happened last night?" Rudy pried, watching me dig through the mountain of change I carried around, looking for a quarter.

"Well…" I looked around to see how many people were nearby. Not many and no one I knew so I continued. "I was about to do it, but Lynn got home and I fucking *love* her so I nearly broke down there. She's my mentor and I remembered that I'd be losing her too. Then we went outside while she made dinner and I started to do it again, but he shut me up and I ended up leaving." I pushed two dimes and a nickel into Rudy's open palm. He was looking at me with a worried expression. "What?"

"How did he... shut you up?"

"I didn't sleep with him, if that's what you mean," I said, watching him enter the change into the slot.

"I just wasn't sure," Rudy mumbled, selecting blue Gatorade. We watched as the bottle was pushed onto the shelf inside the glass and was lowered to the drawer at the bottom with a *ka-thunk* sound. He retrieved it and I stepped up to get my own drink. "So are you doing it tonight?"

"I was planning to," I said, inserting two dollars into the machine and pushing down on the Diet Iced Tea button. "But when I asked to see him, he said no."

Rudy stopped with his drink halfway to his mouth. "What do you mean 'no'?"

"I mean," I began, bending down to get my own drink, "he's avoiding confrontation. He may as well clamp his hands over his ears and sing *'La la la, I can't hear you therefore you are not breaking up with me'.*" Rudy sighed and took a swig of his beverage. "Don't worry, it'll get done," I assured him, touching his arm.

"So, what *are* you doing tonight?" Rudy asked as we made our way to the cafeteria.

"If you can believe it, shopping with Candice."

"Actually, I can't. I'll need pictures for proof." He reached over behind me and shoved open the door, quickly kissing the back of my neck. "Talk to you tonight?" he whispered in my ear.

My heart pounding in my chest, I stammered. "Yeah, yeah, yes. I'll call you."

"Great," he said and walked away.

I weaved my way through the crowded lunch room and over to my friends. I swung my bag onto the windowsill and pulled myself up, settling beside Connor.

"That took a while," Connor said, taking the iced tea from my hands because I was having trouble opening it. "Did you get diet? Good."

I flushed and looked away from him, catching Fuzzy's eye. He looked furious.

"Dude, she's not fat!" he barked. "She's like ninety pounds; she doesn't need to *diet!*"

Connor handed me my now open bottle and shrugged. "I was just saying."

"No, no, you were *implying*," Fuzzy continued. "Does it make you feel like a man, putting her down like that? Does it?"

I reached over and touched Fuzzy's clenched fist. "Fuzzy, it's okay," I said calmly. He began to protest, but I shook my head. "Just not here, okay?"

Fuzzy's jaw twitched before he jerked a nod and began to devour his sandwich like he wanted to cause it the most pain possible. I leaned away from him and opened my own lunch.

The rest of the day went by fairly quickly. Probably because I was dreading spending time alone with Candice.

"So, where are you two going?" Fuzzy asked, after almost going into shock when I told him about my plans. Drama class had been dismissed and we were making our way out of the high school.

"Just downtown. Window shopping and stuff," Candice told him, as I shifted the shoulder strap of my bag. "It's been a while since I've had any time for girl talk."

"I don't think I've ever used the term 'girl talk'," I said, shoving open the doors of the main entrance and holding it open for Fuzzy and Candice. "Like... ever."

Fuzzy laughed and walked with us toward the bus stop. It was barely a five minute bus ride downtown and a new bus came by every two minutes or so.

"When are you guys going to read the next two *Hamlet* scenes?" Fuzzy was asking, just as the bus rounded the block with our stop on it.

"I already did it," I said and Fuzzy rolled his eyes as if to say, *Of course, you did.*

"Oh no!" Candice squealed, pointing up the street. "Our bus!"

I was going to tell her to calm the crap down, another one would be arriving soon, but I knew she just wanted the drama.

"Just run down to the next one. He'll stop for you." Fuzzy gestured down the road to another stop about half a block away.

"Bye," I waved as we took off.

"Call me!" Fuzzy yelled at me.

"I will," Candice and I hollered back. Candice gave me a *why would he want you to call* look.

Sure enough the driver did see us rushing to the next bus stop and slowed for us to hop on. I swiped my pass and made my way to the back of the bus, Candice (collapsing beside me) was still winded from our sudden run.

"So, what do you want to buy today? New jeans? T-shirts? Bras?" I asked after a minute of silence between us.

"Of course, you need more sexy bras for Connor," Candice scoffed.

I bit my lip to hold back retorts: *At least I have a reason to wear revealing underwear* or *At least I'm a D cup and not still wearing a training bra at seventeen.*

Feeling claustrophobic with her in such a confined space and nothing to distract me from her, I grabbed the yellow chord above me and yanked on it. The 'next stop' sign lit up.

"What the hell?" Candice said, annoyed. "Centre of downtown isn't for another three stops."

"Oh well," I shrugged, standing up. "Road less travelled and shit."

We held onto the rails and made our way to the back doors of the bus, waiting for it to come to a complete stop before pushing them open. We stepped down onto the sidewalk and looked around to check out some landmarks.

"Where are we?" Candice asked, more to herself than to me. I took a step toward the shop right in front of us. "What are you doing?"

"I heard you only have to be sixteen to get something done here, not eighteen," I said, taking another step.

"Beth..." Candice said in a warning tone.

"Hey, *you* don't have to get anything done, but I always wanted one," I told her sternly and pushed open the door to the tattoo parlour. Candice squeezed in before the door could close behind me and we looked around, taking in the surroundings.

There was framed artwork all over the walls and on the coffee table in front of a leather sectional couch were at least five photo albums. There was a glass display case used as a cashier's desk, filled with different body piercing samples and the term used for them.

So that's what a Prince Albert is.

"Can I help you?" a bald guy behind a desk asked. I looked behind him and saw three tables that looked kind of like dental chairs after they have been completely reclined, a door with a sign that read 'bathroom' in graffiti-like font, and a curtained-off area.

"Yeah, sure," I said, "I've heard that you only need to be sixteen to get a piercing here?"

"That's true. I'll just need two pieces of ID and there's a bit of paperwork you'll need to fill out, darlin'."

The guy was taller than Fuzzy (which was saying something) and had tattoos crawling up his arms, across his chest, and up his neck. The wife-beater he was wearing did nothing to cover the large ship's anchor on his right peck. Had his voice not been so kind, and the term of endearment cute, I probably would have considered him threatening.

"Beth..." Candice warned again. I glanced over at her. She looked scared.

"Candice," I sighed, rolling my eyes and putting my IDs on the desk, "you don't have to stay." I took the clipboard and pen from the employee.

I filled out my name, address, age, and gender and agreed that I would not blame the parlour if anything got infected. I quickly signed it and exchanged papers with the tattooed guy for my BCID and student card.

"All right, Elizabeth," he said, looking over the sheet. "I'm Todd and you want... a belly button ring?"

I nodded and pointed to a shiny hoop with a blue gem dangling from it that had caught my eye in the glass cabinet. "I'd like that one, please."

"All right, come with me." He gestured for me to follow him behind the desk and farther into the parlour. I heard Candice say my name once more before I was behind the curtained area with Todd. Looking around, I saw another dentist's chair and a table with needles, gloves, hoops, cotton swabs, and rubbing alcohol. "Just lie down there," Todd told me. I took off my bag, placed it beside the chair, and climbed on. "Roll up your shirt?" Getting nervous, I rolled the hem of my shirt up until it was touching the underwire of my bra.

"Is this gonna hurt?" I whispered, watching Todd get ready.

"Not gonna lie, darlin', yes, it will. But only for a moment." Todd pulled on the gloves and spilt some rubbing alcohol onto a cotton swab. He stroked my navel with it for a few seconds and held up the loop I wanted. "The blue one, right?"

The colour reminded me of Rudy's eyes. I nodded and swallowed hard. I was getting scared now.

"Okay, when I count to three, I want you to take a deep breath and then slowly let it out," Todd instructed, positioning himself beside me. I felt one hand above my belly button and cold metal touching the inside of my navel.

"Yes," I nodded.

"And don't move."

I nodded again.

"All right, on three. One, two, three."

I took a deep breath through my nose, felt a sharp pinch, and released the air slowly, feeling a hook concave into my flesh and rise back up to break through the skin half an inch above my belly button.

Todd quickly replaced the hook with the ring and snapped it closed. "All done," he said, standing up and tearing off the gloves.

"Really?" I said, sitting up. I looked down and sure enough, there was a shiny loop jutting out of my stomach. "Thanks!" I beamed, excitedly.

"No worries." Todd smiled back, handing me my bag as I stood and rolled down my shirt again.

We went back to the front desk where Candice was waiting with narrowed eyes just for me. She said nothing as I paid, and Todd gave me a sheet of paper telling me how to take care of a new piercing. I thanked him again and we left the shop.

I promptly stopped Candice and held up my shirt so that she could see my new bling. "What do you think?" I asked, grinning.

"Makes you look like a slut," she sneered.

"What?" I gaped, dropping my shirt.

"You heard me." She crossed her arms. "You look like a slut."

I looked down at what I was wearing and then back up at her. "So... flats, skinny jeans, a t-shirt with *The Beatles* logo on it, and a hidden piercing makes me look like a slut?"

"Well, yeah." Candice lifted a shoulder. She was not even kidding. What was I saying? She did not know how to kid.

"Thanks, *friend.*" I glared at her. "I like it."

"You shouldn't."

"I'm going home," I snapped, waving a dismissive hand at her and turning on my heel. Ignoring her "What? Why?!" I walked away from Candice for the first time and did not look back.

I had honestly hoped that this little outing would rekindle our friendship, but it seemed that she was getting off on making me feel bad about myself. I felt a huge urge to break off our relationship, but I knew that it would somehow backfire, and with a power only Candice seemed to have, I would end up feeling guilty for wanting to get away from her.

Manipulation at its finest.

CHAPTER 30

I KNOW IT WAS WRONG

The following morning, I slept in by about ten minutes, which was very unusual for me. It had taken me ages to get to sleep. Thoughts of Candice would creep into my thoughts and my heart would pound harder in anger, then my stomach would sink due to the fact that I was a slut... just because of a belly button piercing.

At one point, I had rolled over onto my front to try to get comfortable and ended up muffling a cry of pain into my pillow. Note to self: Do not put all of your weight onto a new piercing.

"Beth! Are you up yet?!" my dad hollered from the kitchen at about 7:15. "You'll miss your bus!"

"Oh, fuck!" I exclaimed, sitting up so quickly that I fell out of bed. Clambering to my feet, I tore off my pj's, and paying no attention to the clothes I was grabbing, quickly dressed. I had to bite down on my lip hard to stifle a cry of pain when my fitted t-shirt caught on the hoop I had forgotten about. I pulled on a hoodie and zipped it up, gathering all of my previous night's homework and shoving it into my book bag.

I threw myself out of my room, ran to the bathroom, rinsed my mouth, and bolted out the front door, calling over my shoulder, "Have rehearsal after school, might be late. Bye." It all came out so quickly that it sounded like one long word.

I just barely reached the bus stop on time, but thankfully I did get to school my usual twenty-five minutes early. As I marched up the stairs to the lockers, I braided my hair over my shoulder and wrapped a hair tie, which I had found in my pocket, around the end. When I got to the fourth floor, I was surprised to see that, once again, Connor and Candice had beaten me to school, and somehow, Fuzzy had as well.

"How did yesterday go?" Connor was asking Candice.

"Why don't you ask *her?*" she jutted her chin over his shoulder at me. Connor and Fuzzy looked over, seeming curious.

"All right... how did yesterday go?" Connor asked again, a little cautiously this time.

"I was having a great time until she called me a slut." I shrugged, even though it still bothered me. I angled past Fuzzy to get to the locker Candice was rummaging through.

"What?! Why would you call her that?" Connor demanded, outraged.

"Because," Candice whipped around to face them, "she went and got her belly button pierced and now she looks like a slut."

"You did what?" Connor and Fuzzy both said, gaping at me. Connor looked pissed and Fuzzy seemed impressed.

I pulled up the hem of my shirt. "Apparently this piece of metal makes me a hussy."

"I think it looks great," Fuzzy complimented, just as Connor grabbed my elbow and pulled me toward a usually empty classroom.

"I need to talk to you," he growled, pushing open the door and dragging me inside. "Out!" he snapped at a ninth grader who was using one of the computers. The kid jumped up and ran out of the room, closing the door behind him. He rounded on me. "Why the hell would you defile your body like that, and without asking me?"

I yanked my arm out of his grip and crossed it over my chest with my other one. "What makes you think you have any right to tell me what I can and cannot do to my body?"

"I'm your boyfriend."

"So? This is *my* flesh." I pointed at my belly button. "And this is *my* hair." I grabbed my braid and shook it. "I can, and have done, whatever the crap I want to do with it."

"Do you not remember the little chat we had in the study hall after you screwed up your hair?" he almost growled. "Don't change your appearance without asking me, Beth!"

"Can you see my belly button ring right now?" I asked.

"No."

"So what's changed, then? I don't look any different. It's *hidden*, Connor; no one knows I have it. What's the problem?"

"It's the principle of the thing, Beth!"

"Face it, Connor, I win this one," I said. "One more thing, I never want you to use your body to steer, push, pull, or drag me anywhere ever again." I swung the door open and went back to my locker where Fuzzy was waiting for me, leaving Connor to wonder what the hell had just happened.

"Are you okay?" Fuzzy demanded, straightening when I was beside him. "Did he hurt you?"

"Just my feelings," I grumbled, unzipping my hoodie and hanging it up in the locker. I turned back to Fuzzy. "You know what I realized—Fuzzy, what are you doing?" For no reason, Fuzzy had gathered me in his arms and held me against his chest.

"Beth, why would you wear a white shirt with a red bra?" Fuzzy asked, his mouth right beside my ear.

"Huh?" I pulled away the tiniest bit, and sure enough, my bright red bra was completely visible though my t-shirt... so much so that you could see the pattern of little pink hearts on the cups. "Oh, shit. I didn't have time to even look in the mirror this morning," I explained, horrified. "Wait, why were you looking at my boobs?"

"Teenage boy."

"Oh, yeah."

Fuzzy let go of me and I grabbed my hoodie from the locker, pulling it on again and doing up the zipper.

"Today I guess you do look like a slut," Fuzzy joked. I punched him. Fuzzy suddenly lowered his voice. "Really, Beth, what did you and Connor talk about?"

I sighed and rolled my shoulders. "He's just mad."

"Why?"

"Because I didn't ask for permission to get my belly button pierced." Fuzzy opened his mouth to start bitching about him, but I held up a hand. "Don't worry. I put him in his place."

"Are you gonna do it tonight?"

I looked over my shoulder to make sure Connor had not exited the classroom that I had left him alone in. "I don't know. I have rehearsal." I retrieved my needed schoolbooks from my locker and closed the door to it.

"Do it after," Fuzzy shrugged. "Or even do it before." I didn't say anything. "You *do* want to do it, right?"

"Yes, Fuzzy, I really want to do it. I really do, but I don't think today is going to work is all."

Sure enough, Connor dodged me all day. He even skipped the classes we had together (which was really stupid considering his mom worked at the school).

"I'll do it for you," Fuzzy was saying, just as Rudy joined us after drama class had let out.

"Fuzzy—"

"No, really, I have it all planned out. I write 'fuck' on one hand and 'off' on the other—actually, I'd have to get you to write on my right hand—and then I'd walk up to him, tap him on the shoulder, say 'Beth is breaking up with you'… and then beat him up," Fuzzy explained, miming a few jabs and upper cuts in the air.

I laughed and shook my head. "Fuzzy, even if you are serious, I'll have to pass. After a year of dating, I think it should come from me."

"*Then* can I beat him up?" Rudy laughed with me, but Fuzzy remained completely serious. "I'm not joking."

It was getting hot on the couch, being squeezed between two guys, so I took off my hoodie and shoved it in the bag at my feet.

"Whoa," Rudy gaped. "Going for a new look?"

"What?" I blinked at him. He seemed to be straining to keep his eyes on my face.

"Beth! Jesus!" Fuzzy yelled in a whisper, grabbing the pillow beside him and shoving it at me. "Your bra, remember?"

"Oh, balls," I moaned, hugging the pillow to my chest and looking around the room wildly. There were only a couple of other people in the room with us and they were absorbed in the conversation they were having.

"Have you been walking around like that all day?" Rudy asked.

"I've had the hoodie on, but it's getting so hot," I complained, using my script to fan myself.

"You are such an over-actor," Fuzzy laughed.

"Says Mr. Pot to Mrs. Kettle," I said, whacking him with the papers.

"So, are you going to dump the douche tonight?" Rudy asked as Fuzzy attempted to wrestle the script out of my grasp.

"That was the plan, but he's been avoiding me all day and there's rehearsal," I said. "Now that I think about it, I kinda dumped him this morning."

Shocked, Fuzzy loosened his grip and I fell back into Rudy.

"And you didn't think to mention this?!" Fuzzy exclaimed a little too loudly, and a little too accusingly.

"I said 'now that I think about it'. It's just the way I worded something when we were arguing in that classroom."

"What did you say?" both boys asked in sync.

"That I didn't want him to touch me again, basically."

"What?!"

"He's always grabbing my arm and, like… dragging me somewhere. No 'hey, will you come with me?' or even guiding me with a hand on my back. It's always my elbow or my bicep." I held up the arm Connor had grabbed me by earlier, and sure enough, there were a couple of finger-shaped bruises on it. "See? So I told him that I never wanted him to grab me again. Does that count as dumping?"

Rudy chimed in, "I think dumping is more like... 'I never want to *see* you again!'"

"You've never been dumped before, have you?" Fuzzy asked me slowly.

I shook my head. "No, just flings that just, you know... fizzled. No one ended it, it was just like... 'That was fun, bye'." Just then my phone started to ring in my back pocket. I pulled it out and saw Connor's face grinning at me with the contact name "Douche Dickface" at the top. I shot a look at Fuzzy, who was fighting not to laugh. "Stay away from my phone, Fuzzy," I grumbled.

Fuzzy defended his action. "Put a pass code on it."

I rolled my eyes and answered the call. "Hi."

"Hey, baby Bethy-wums," Connor cooed. I wrinkled my nose at the weird/sappy term of endearment. "Whatcha doin'?" I heard him start to chew something loudly.

"I'm waiting for rehearsal to start," I replied.

"I missed you today."

"Then maybe you shouldn't have skipped the classes we have together?"

"That's fair," Connor agreed. I could tell his mouth was full and waited for him to continue to talk, but all I heard was muffled munching sounds, and Connor's computer mouse clicking, and a keyboard being tapped. Well, this was annoying.

"What's he saying?" Fuzzy mouthed, my frustrated look obviously not hidden in the slightest.

I pulled my phone away from my ear and handed it to him. Fuzzy took it and listened to Connor eat and do whatever he was doing on his computer. Fuzzy covered the mic part on the phone and looked at me, horrified. "What is he *doing*?" he demanded. "Is he—"

"He's eating and fooling around on his computer," I snapped, taking the phone back. "Connor?" There was no reply, just more eating. "Connor? Damn it, Connor!"

Fed up, I hit 'end call' and put my phone back in my pocket.

"What the hell just happened?" Rudy asked, his brows furrowed. He looked from me to Fuzzy and back again, waiting for an answer.

"That was Connor," I told him.

"I gathered that," Rudy said slowly.

"He was eating," Fuzzy inserted.

"So?"

"And he forgot I was on the phone," I grumbled. "All I heard was him chewing and doing shit on his computer. Not the first time he's done that."

"But... but *he* called *you*," Rudy said, confused.

"Yup." I nodded. "Where is Mr. Thomas? We've usually started by—Goddamn it." My phone ringing again interrupted me and I pulled it back out.

"What?"

"Why did you hang up?" Connor demanded. "What did I do?" By the way Fuzzy and Rudy were looking at me, I could tell he was being so loud that they could hear him.

"Nothing," I answered. "Literally nothing."

"So you hung up on me?"

"You forgot I was on the phone!" I cried. "And I didn't feel like listening to you eat."

"You could have said something to get my attention."

"I called your name, is that not enough?"

"Obviously not."

"Look, Connor, I knew you were on your computer and I knew you'd forgotten about me, so what was the point of staying on the line?" No reply. "Damn it, Connor... look, can we see each other tomorrow?"

"I have a field trip and probably won't get back until about five."

"Whatever. My sister is spending the night at a friend's house and my dad is working late. Come over when you can." I exchanged a knowing look with Rudy.

"All right." I heard Connor grin. "Privacy... nice."

I sighed in exasperation. "Yeah, privacy," I echoed. "I'll talk to you tomorrow."

"All right. I love you."

"Okay."

I hung up, dropped my phone into my bag on top of my hoodie, and dragged my hands over my face.

"So, Friday will be dump day?" Rudy asked after a few beats. I nodded into my hands.

"Why not tomorrow?" Fuzzy asked.

"I'll have more time on Friday. He'll have questions and there will be yelling. And I won't have to see him first thing the next morning." I shrugged. "Jesus."

I sat back up and jumped, letting out a small gasp when I felt someone slide their hand up the back of my shirt.

"What?" Fuzzy said, looking around for something that would have gotten that reaction out of me.

"Um..." I said, distracted by the feel of Rudy's fingertips tracing up and down my spine. "It was just a shiver. You know, someone walking over my grave." I glanced at Rudy who was pretending to study his script with a small, cheeky smile on his face.

"Sorry, people, sorry!" Mr. T suddenly burst into the room. "My daughter needed a ride to her piano lesson."

"Is that what they're calling it now?" Fuzzy joked.

"You can leave now, Daniel," Mr. T said, gesturing to the door that he had just come through. "If you wanted to hang out with the cast, you should have joined the play."

"See you later," Fuzzy said to me, getting to his feet. "See ya, Rudy."

"Bye," Rudy nodded. I gave Fuzzy a small wave as he strode out the door.

Pretending to have an itch on my back, I pushed Rudy's wandering hand out of my shirt so that I could put my fleece back on. Lindsey already gave me enough shit; I was not giving her this too.

"Hey." Rudy held me back while everyone filed into the auditorium. "No one is at my house this evening. Do you…" he cleared his throat nervously. "Do you want to, like… hang out?"

"Oh, wow. Um…"

"It's just, whenever I drive you home we end up staying in my truck for like an hour and I thought… I mean, the truck is kinda cramped."

"Yeah, yes, Rudy," I said quickly. I didn't want anyone overhearing this conversation. They would get the wrong idea, or the right one, which would be bad. "I'll come over to your house."

Rudy grinned down at me and we hurried to the auditorium before Mr. Thomas got suspicious.

We did a run through of the second act. It took us about forty five minutes, and while Mr. T was giving everyone personal nitpicks on their performances, I could tell Rudy was itching to get out of there. He was literally inching toward the door.

"Okay, next rehearsal is on Monday. We'll be re-doing act one and a run through of the second act as well," Mr. T wrapped up while everyone gathered their things.

"See you tomorrow, Mr. Thomas," I said, as Rudy and I left the drama room.

Rudy was unusually quiet on the way to the parking lot and getting into the truck. I finally decided to ask what was wrong. Did he regret asking me to come over?

After the third vicious slam of the passenger door, it latched and I turned to Rudy. "Are you all right?" I asked, buckling my seatbelt.

He glanced over at me and smiled. "Oh, yeah, of course," he assured me.

"You've just been really quiet."

"I'm... uh," Rudy turned a little red while he started the truck and steered us out of the parking lot. "I can't remember if I cleaned my room."

I let out a laugh. "I couldn't care less," I told him, putting a hand on his knee. "As long as it's not your mom that cleans your room, it's totally fine."

"I'm seventeen," Rudy said. "Of course I clean my own room."

"Good." I smiled. "Connor turned seventeen last month and his dad still does his laundry," I added. I pulled my phone out of my bag and sent a quick text to my dad, saying that rehearsal was going to run late and I would not be home for dinner. As soon as I sent it, I realized just how alone Rudy and I were going to be and my pulse sped up with nervous excitement. I glanced over at Rudy and he seemed to have the same gleam in his eyes.

We drove in a comfortable silence, listening to the unspoken words between us.

Rudy lived across town from me in a quiet neighbourhood I had never been to before. His house had a long driveway leading up to a front deck with a variety of garden flowers decorating the border of it.

Climbing out of the truck, I stared up at the two-story house in front of me. "I love it!"

Rudy closed the truck door and showed me inside his home. "My dad built it from the ground up." There was pride in his voice.

"No shit." I gaped, my gaze sweeping over a large dining room with a bay window, a small kitchen with an island, and a carpeted sitting room with fantastic wicker furniture. Directly in front of us was a steep staircase. "Speaking of your dad—"

"Don't worry," Rudy said, taking my hand and leading me up the stairs. "No one will be home until about ten."

"Where are they?" I asked as Rudy showed me down a hallway, passing a bathroom and about three bedrooms. We reached the very end of another extremely narrow hallway, which opened into a large bedroom with a window facing the backyard.

"Family dinner a couple towns over," Rudy replied, letting go of my hand and gathering a couple articles of clothing off the floor. "I couldn't go because of rehearsal."

"Sure," I nodded, smirking at him as I scanned his room. *"That's* why you couldn't go." A Blink-182 poster was tacked beside a rugby one above a small desk with a laptop resting on it. My heart rate sped up again when my gaze landed on his unmade queen-sized bed.

"You want to watch a movie?" he asked, turning on his laptop. "Listen to music?"

"Music is good," I said a little too quickly. My palms were sweaty and I wiped them on my jeans. I took off my flats and put them next to my bag.

"What did you have in mind?" Rudy inquired, opening iTunes. "Silverchair?"

"Who?"

"Blink-182?"

"Umm…"

"Our Lady Peace?"

"Oh my God, I love them! My first favourite band. Besides The Backstreet Boys, of course."

"I thought you'd be an NSYNC girl," Rudy joked.

"NSYNC didn't have AJ," I replied.

"What about Coldplay?" Rudy laughed.

"Sold." I smiled.

Rudy pressed the space bar on the keyboard and *Viva La Vida* began to play softly, just loud enough for us to hear the lyrics. He walked over to where I was standing in the middle of his bedroom. "I'm glad you agreed to come over," he said, pulling me into his arms, placing one hand on my lower back, and the other on the nape of my neck.

I wrapped my arms around his sides and pressed a kiss to his mouth. "Me too."

"Is this all right?" Rudy asked me, searching my eyes for any hint of uncertainty. "You're sure you want to do this?"

"Yes," I moaned, running a hand up his muscular chest. "Oh my God, yes."

Both wanting the same thing, we stared at each other for a few moments. I reached up and unzipped my fleece, tossing it carelessly over my shoulder.

"I like this new look," Rudy smiled at my chest, appreciating the red bra visible beneath my shirt. "Only for me though." I grabbed the back of his shirt and pulled it over his head. Mine quickly joined it on the floor. "You got your belly button pierced?" Rudy breathed, staring at it and tracing a finger around my navel, careful not to touch it.

"Yeah," I said, kissing his chest. I trailed gentle kisses up to his jaw. "Do you like it?"

"It's crazy hot," he told me, wrapping his arms around my waist and lifting me off the floor, carrying me to his bed.

Laying down on my back, my head resting on a pillow, I ran my fingers through his hair. I remembered guessing that, if it grew out, it would be kind of curly. I was right.

Slowly, Rudy lowered himself on top of me, his bare skin pressing against mine. He ground himself against me gently (something I was not used to), and kissed me tenderly but (somehow) passionately at the same time. I reached between us and blindly unbuckled his belt. Rudy hissed in a breath between his teeth and wrapped an arm beneath me, unclasping my bra.

He slowly began to kiss down my body, his hands following his lips... my chin, my neck, between my breasts, my abdomen. "You're good at that," I whispered. I don't think he heard me, the sound of my heartbeat had to be louder than the music. He unbuttoned my jeans, gradually pulled them down my legs, and tossed them onto the floor, where they landed silently by our shirts. "Now you," I insisted, sitting up on one elbow and gesturing to his own pants. He stood beside the bed then and took them off as I requested. Both of us now only in our underwear, he crawled back on top of me.

"You're sure?" Rudy asked again, getting a condom from inside his bedside table.

"I told you... yes." I touched his shadowed face.

With his strong arms around me and his body covering mine, I had never felt so naked and so safe at the same time. *Please, never let this moment end.*

I am not proud of what happened next, which I am guessing is quite obvious. I could have said no. We could have told ourselves that we only had to wait until the end of the week, and then I would be single and it would not be so wrong. I should have gone home. I should have left Connor before anything with Rudy happened.

But, to be honest, all that I could think about while Rudy and I were together for the first time was:

I can't wait to do this again.

CHAPTER 31
UP ALL NIGHT

The next morning I woke up with a huge grin on my face. It quickly faltered due to the giant pang of guilt that ploughed into my gut. I had slept with Rudy and now I had to go to school and face Connor.

Oh God, I thought, climbing out of bed. *If Connor finds out, he'll kill me. A kiss gave me a black eye, hair-dye equals being held down by the throat... what would mind-blowing sex come to?*

Careful not to put on a shirt that was as transparent as glass, I got ready for school. After I was done brushing my teeth and hair, I made my way into the kitchen where my dad handed me a bowl of oatmeal.

"How was last night?" he asked, while packing lunches.

"Hmm?" There was no way he knew. He *couldn't*.

"Rehearsal," my dad specified. "You got in pretty late."

My shoulders relaxed. "Yeah, sorry about that," I nodded, quickly shovelling my breakfast into my mouth and putting the bowl in the sink. I turned on the hot water tap and let the bowl soak. "There are a few people who aren't taking direction well, but we're working on it."

"When's your next one?" my dad asked, just as Amy joined us. She frowned at the oatmeal and grabbed a banana from next to the fridge.

"Monday," I answered. "It'll probably go late too, actually. We're running through the first and second act."

"All right. Just make sure to remind me the day of," my dad noted, handing me a plastic bag with a lunch in it. He handed another to Amy, who took it and looked over at me.

"Let's go," she said. "We're gonna miss the bus."

"You're taking the early bus?" I said, walking into the foyer and stepping into my flats, then grabbing my bag off the stairs. "Why?"

"Cuz."

On the bus, we sat in seats facing each other and I took in her heavily made-up eyes and flat-ironed hair.

"You look different," she told me, looking me up and down.

"*I* look different?" I said, eyeing her pointedly.

"Yeah..." she said slowly. "It's probably your hair. The red and pink keeps fading."

"Maybe."

There were only a few stops until mine when it clicked why Amy was going to school so early. It was that "cool" boy. Matt.

When my stop was next, I yanked on the yellow chord and listened for the *bing* sound, signalling my stop. "Say hi to your boyfriend for me," I sing-songed.

"He's not my boyfriend!" Amy declared angrily.

"Okay," I laughed, standing up. "See you tonight."

"Bye," Amy huffed, slouching into her seat. I pushed open the back door, stepped down onto the sidewalk, and headed to school.

Great, now I was alone and had no one who could distract me from the emotional battle going on inside me. I could not tell what was winning: guilt or happiness.

I always slept with Connor so that I could stop feeling anything. Being numb was my goal when it came to sex, and now I felt happy. I guess it really does depend on who you're with. Connor made me want to cry and hit something, so it only made sense that someone who made me smile and made me feel whole and loved would have a different effect on me in the bedroom.

I had actually snuggled with Rudy afterwards and I usually hated cuddling. At least I thought I did. We had lain in each other's arms, not talking... just smiling and kissing softly. Now that I thought about it, that was the first time I had let someone completely undress me, too.

When I entered the school, I realized that if I concentrated hard enough, I could still taste Rudy's lips on my tongue. A smile spread across my face, and knowing that the group would be at the lockers or be arriving soon, I decided to go down to the cafeteria. I just wanted to think about Rudy without distractions.

After purchasing a cup of coffee, I stood in front of the table that held the lids, cream, sugar packets, and other assorted paraphernalia. Using a swizzle stick to stir the liquid caffeine, a strong arm wrapped around my waist from behind. I did not have to turn around to know it was Rudy placing a kiss on my temple.

"Hey, you," I could hear the smile in his voice. I grinned, put a lid on my cup, and turned to face him.

"Hey, yourself," I said. He bent down to kiss me, but I remembered where we were and sidestepped him. He gave me a hurt look. "It's D-Day *tomorrow*," I reminded him. "Come on, let's find an empty classroom."

We found our way into the classroom that we had kissed in the day after I dyed my hair, and Rudy closed the door behind me.

I held my coffee out to him. "Want a sip?"

Rudy arched an eyebrow. "Beth, I go to this school too. I'm not temperature testing your coffee for you," he said, taking the cup out of my hand and setting it on the desk next to me. "Besides, I'm more of a tea guy."

I ran my hands up his chest and laced my fingers through his hair. It really was getting long. "How was the rest of your night?" I asked him.

"I can't believe how well I slept," he said, grinning. "Granted my pillow still smelled like you, so that probably had something to do with it."

"What do I smell like?" I asked, resisting the urge to lift my arm and sniff my armpit, in case that was the smell he was referring to.

"You smell like... peppermint," Rudy replied, taking a whiff of my hair. "What do I smell like?"

"Rain," I answered right away.

"Rain? I remind you of bad weather?"

"No," I laughed. "You remind me of the way the air smells right before a beautiful rainfall."

"Are you calling me beautiful?"

"I think you are." I nodded.

"But I'm a dude."

"I know that." I giggled. "You're just a beautiful person." Rudy put his hands on my hips and tilted his head, staring into my eyes as if he were trying to read my thoughts. I hooked my fingers into his belt loops. "You wanna skip first period with me?"

He gave me a pained look and groaned. "I can't," he whined. "It's getting way too close to graduation to start skipping classes."

"Graduation?" I echoed as if I had never heard the word before. I had completely forgotten that he was in twelfth grade. "That's right. Grad. Are you... where are you going to go after?" I asked timidly.

A look of sympathy and understanding stole across Rudy's face. "You're worried that I'm going to leave," he said. It wasn't a question. I did not say anything, just looked down at my feet. "Don't worry, I'm not going anywhere. My plan is to go to the local university and study to become an engineer." He placed an index finger under my chin and tilted my face back up to look at him. "Besides, I *just* got you. You think I'd leave now?"

"You're not just staying here because of me, are you?" I asked suspiciously. I did not want to be in the way of the plans for his future.

"No, you're a bonus though." He kissed my forehead. "I don't want to leave my family either."

"I don't want to be holding you back from what you really want."

"You're not." Rudy chuckled an assurance. "I've had this plan for years, okay?"

"Okay," I finally nodded.

The bell was due to ring in about three minutes when I joined Fuzzy, Connor, and Candice at the lockers on the fourth floor.

"Where've you been?" Connor demanded in an accusing tone.

I held up the coffee cup in my hand. "I didn't sleep well last night and didn't want to wait for caffeine. And I missed my first bus."

"Here." Candice handed me my English and Psych 101 textbooks from our locker.

"Oh, thanks," I said, surprised that she had just done something in the least bit helpful.

"Hey." Connor took my elbow in his hand and I stared down at it pointedly, and then back up at him, telepathically reminding him of our conversation the day before. He pulled his hand away and asked quietly, "Are we still on for tomorrow?"

"I was actually thinking we could meet at the diner a few blocks away from my house first? Grab some dinner or something?" I suggested. *You can't kill me in public.* I took a sip of my drink. It was the perfect temperature, meaning that it must have been scalding when I had bought it.

"What are you two doing tomorrow?" Candice asked, putting her nose where it did not belong.

"I don't think that is any of your business, Candice," Fuzzy said, making her flush and glare up at him.

"Thank you," I mouthed at him. He just smiled and shrugged in a *don't mention it* way.

The bell rang before Candice could start scolding Fuzzy for basically calling her nosey, and the four of us made our way to English.

Now that we had completed *Hamlet*, we were assigned a paper to write on our thoughts about the play. We also had to choose one character we felt we might be able to relate to and explain why that was. I thought that, for such a mundane class, it was a pretty neat assignment.

"I'll give you fifty dollars if you write mine for me," Fuzzy bribed, once class was dismissed.

"You didn't read it, did you?" I questioned, narrowing my eyes at him.

"You told me how it ends so I sort of... skipped it," Fuzzy admitted, having the decency to look a little ashamed.

"You didn't read it at all?" Connor gaped. "You read *Lord of the Flies* front to back, but you didn't read *Hamlet*?"

"*Lord of the Flies* was interesting and I couldn't understand what the hell was going on in that play."

"First of all, that book was almost as awful as *Catcher in the Rye* and you could have used the Elizabethan dictionary in the library... or this thing called Google," I said.

"Will you write it, or not?" Fuzzy sighed.

"Not." I shook my head. "Read it. Besides, we have completely different writing styles."

"She has a point," Candice piped up. "*Your* papers are good, Fuzzy."

I looked at her and let out a sharp breath through my nose.

"C'mon, I'll walk you to class," Connor said, putting a hand on the small of my back and steering me toward the staircase. I let him, because I knew I was dangerously close to slapping Candice, who was being glared at by Fuzzy. "I actually really liked *Catcher in the Rye*," Connor told me, as we started our way down the stairs.

"What? How?" I exclaimed, weaving through a few ninth graders who thought it was a good idea to stand in the middle of a staircase between classes.

"I felt that—Would you guys mind *moving?*—I could relate to Holden."

I glanced over at him. "You realize that's a bad thing, right?" I said slowly. "He's a gigantic douche."

"Yeah, I just felt he understood me."

"Mark David Chapman said the same thing about Holden Caulfield."

"You say the same thing about Jo March!" Connor declared angrily.

"Mark David Chapman didn't read *Little Women* a billion times and then kill John Lennon!" I snapped back. Now we had stopped in the middle of a staircase and I was aware of a few people staring at us.

"So you're saying that, because I can relate to a *fictional character*, I'm going to kill Paul McCartney?!" Connor flat out yelled. Now we had an audience.

"No!" I shouted back. "I'm *saying* that, if you were to say you could relate to any character in any book, it *shouldn't* be Holden Caulfield. That is not something to brag about!"

"All right." Connor took a deep breath and rolled his shoulders, standing at his full height. "Who would you say I relate to?"

I looked him up and down, putting great thought into the answer. I was about to say Mr. Darcy from *Pride and Prejudice* when I remembered that at least Mr. Darcy gets the girl in the end. "Severus Snape," I finally decided.

"From *Harry Potter?*"

"No, from *War and Peace*." I rolled my eyes.

"How the crap am I like Snape?"

"Your hair is greasy and I spend an awful lot of time trying to figure out if you're a good guy." As soon as it came out of my mouth, I knew that I was not one to talk. Connor glared at me.

Connor attempted a comeback and failed horribly. "Yeah, well, you're like, like that girl from that other book."

"Okay... I have to get to psych; I'll see you at lunch," I said slowly, talking as though he were five, and started heading back down the stairs again.

That was a really stupid fight but Catcher in the Rye *really was a terrible book*, I thought, as I took my seat, avoiding the eye contact of classmates who had seen our heated exchange.

When the lunch bell rang to signal the end of class, Annie stopped me at my desk.

"I heard the fight you had with Connor," she said sheepishly.

"Yeah, you and half the school," I moaned, leaning on the desk beside hers.

"Is everything okay?" she asked, concern in her eyes. "I mean, you two have been together for a long time. Some people have been saying that you got engaged after your mom's funeral."

My jaw dropped. "What?!" I cried, standing again. "What? Why? Why would someone start a rumour like that?"

"Well, for starters you're wearing the evidence," Annie said, pointing at my left hand.

"It's just a promise ring," I said. "He got it for me, like... a year ago."

"That's an awful big promise ring."

"It doesn't even have any diamonds on it." I laughed humourlessly. I brought my hand up for her to inspect and my shoulders slumped when I realized what she was talking about. I had been wearing my mom's engagement ring since her funeral. Of course people would jump to that conclusion. "No! Shit!" I cussed. "The diamond ring was my *mom's*," I told Annie, who was gazing at the large solitaire-cut ring. "Connor got me the plain white gold one."

"You didn't answer my question, though," Annie said, shifting her gaze back to mine. "Is everything okay? I'm gonna guess no, seeing as you just freaked at the mention of an engagement rumour."

The chirp of my phone receiving a text saved me from having to answer her. I pulled it out of my bag and read the text from Connor:

-r u coming?

"That's him now," I said reluctantly, putting the phone back in my bag. "I should get going."

"Beth," Annie touched my arm, "if you need someone to talk to, I'm here."

"Thanks, Annie." I smiled sincerely at her and left the classroom. I sure did get that offer a lot.

"Hey, what took you so long?" Connor asked when I climbed onto the windowsill in the cafeteria beside Fuzzy.

"Got caught up in psych," I said, taking out my lunch.

"Oh," Connor said, watching me.

"You know, almost everyone heard about your fight," Candice informed us, looking from me to Connor and back again.

"Well, it was really stupid and I'd rather not talk about it." I waved her off. *Least of all with you.*

"You compared me to Snape, Beth," Connor snapped. I heard Fuzzy snort with laughter beside me. "You have something to say, Dan?"

"Dude, it's the dumbest argument I've ever heard of, and it really sounds like Beth handed your ass to you." Fuzzy tried to hide a laugh and failed. "So why are you bringing it up?" Then he looked at Candice. "Wait, why would *you* bring it up? What's your game?"

"I don't have a *game*," Candice huffed. "I just thought they should know."

Her voice was getting so annoying that I wanted to cover my ears and sing at the top of my lungs. It would actually be good practise for *RENT*. Instead, I just turned back to Connor. "Did you hear that there's a rumour going around that we're *engaged*?"

Connor looked at me, stunned. "You didn't know that?"

"And you *did*?"

"Well, yeah. You're wearing an engagement ring."

"Why haven't you denied it?"

"Because we're going to get married one day anyway, so why stop it now?"

My eyes went wide and I swear my heart skipped a beat. Beside me, Fuzzy choked on his water and I saw Candice stare at Connor with a look of shock on her face.

Feeling pretty close to having panic attack, I stammered that I had to use the bathroom. I grabbed my bag, hopped off the windowsill, and hurried to the nearest girl's bathroom.

"No, no, no, no, no..." I breathed, slamming a stall door behind me and locking it with a shaking hand. I dropped my bag beside the toilet and slid down the wall, running my fingers through my hair. *Deep breaths*, I remembered Fuzzy instructing me, as I pressed my hands against my hammering heart. There was just no way I was going to marry a guy who reminded me of Snape. I was breaking up with him the next day and he was pre-proposing to me! He thought I planned to spend the rest of my life with him?

Yeah... no.

Breathe in through the nose and slowly out through the mouth. I did that a few times until my heart rate had returned to normal. Then I ran the back of my hand over my forehead, which was beaded with cold sweat.

I got to my feet and gathered my bag up off the floor. Exiting the stall, I saw the girl I had given the tulips to days before standing at the sinks.

"Oh, hi!" she said brightly.

"Hey." I gave her a small wave.

"Is it your turn to be crying in bathroom?" she asked tentatively.

"What? Oh, yeah, I'm fine," I lied. "Just a lot going on."

"You sure? You look pretty pale," she pressed, tucking a lock of black hair behind her ear.

I was about to tell her that I was okay again, but suddenly an all-too-familiar feeling shot up the right side of my body. "Oh fuck, not now," I whimpered, grabbing onto the counter beside me. Tulip girl rushed over to me and took hold of my left arm. I saw her take it, but could not feel her touch because of the electric volts charging through every muscle in my body.

"Oh God, you're *so* not okay! What's wrong?" I only had about ten seconds to explain what was about to happen before I would lose the ability to speak, so as calmly as I could, because she looked like she was about to pee her pants, I explained what was about to happen.

"Listen, I have epilepsy and I'm about to have a seizure—no, I need you to listen—I'm going to lie down, but I need to put my head on something soft," I said, noting that my right arm was beginning to shake. I slowly descended to the floor.

"Oh God, oh God, oh God," Tulip chanted, getting on her knees beside me. "Oh shit. Here, use my lap." She sat back on her heels and helped me lower my head onto her legs. Just in time, too, because that is when the fire in my body exploded and I thought:

Great. I'm gonna die on a bathroom floor. Karma really is a bitch.

Suddenly the room seemed to shift and Tulip started yelling for help. I wanted to tell her to stop, because (despite the fact I was sure I was about to die) I knew my partial seizures only lasted about a minute.

"HELP!" she screamed, "Please! Somebody HELP!"

I heard a door bang open and another girl cry out, "Oh my God! What happened?"

"She's having a seizure! She fell off my lap and hit her head!" Tulip yelled in a panic. "Get someone!" I hit my head? I didn't feel it. That must have been why the room moved. "You'll be okay," Tulip said soothingly. I saw her loom above me, her face framed by her hair. My jerking body began to slow and I was able to breathe a little easier. By the time the seizure had ended, I was lying flat on my back, spread eagle and panting like I had just sprinted a mile. The girl who Tulip had attracted with her screams had returned with a math teacher, who also doubled as the school nurse.

"What happened?" he asked, crouching beside us.

"I, I, I had a..." I tried to wheeze an answer, but I could not talk with my racking breaths and gave up. I glanced over at Tulip.

"We were talking and she started to have a seizure," she told Mr. Davies. "Her head was in my lap, but she fell off. I'm sorry, I really am! It was just so violent!"

"Don't apologize," I exhaled, wanting to comfort her. "You did everything right."

"Beth, does your head hurt?" Mr. Davies asked me. I knew he would not question me about the seizure, all the teachers knew about my epilepsy. To be honest, my whole body was aching but the back of my head did throb a bit. "Yeah," I answered. "Is it... is it bleeding?"

"No," Tulip replied. "No, you're not bleeding." She probably would have freaked out even more if I had had blood coming from my head.

"Are you dizzy, Beth?" Mr. Davies asked.

"No."

"How many fingers?" he continued, holding his left hand up in a peace sign.

"Two," I answered.

"Can you sit up?"

"No," I said straight away. "Not without help. I can never move well after a seizure."

He took a deep breath through his nose. "Would you like to call your dad? Have him pick you up?"

"No," I declined. "It's just a little bump. Give me half an hour and I'll be fine."

"You're sure?" Mr. Davies said, taking my forearms and pulling me into a sitting position, leaning me against the wall.

"Yeah," I grunted, adjusting myself into a more comfortable position. I was still very weak and ended up sliding back toward the floor. Mr. Davies caught me and slid me upright again.

"All right," he sighed. "There's about"—he looked down at his watch—"fifteen more minutes until third period starts. You're sure you'll be all right?"

"I'll need some help to get up the stairs, but I should be fine," I assured him.

"I'll help her," Tulip offered, sitting next to me and stretching her legs out in front of her.

"Okay." Mr. Davies stood up again. "If you feel dizzy or anything, have someone come and get me," he instructed. "All right. Thank you, Belle."

Who was Belle?

"Don't worry about it," Tulip chirped. "Happy to help."

Mr. Davies gave me one last look that read, *I should just make her go home*, before leaving the girl's bathroom.

So Tulip had a name. From our last meeting, I knew that she had already known mine.

"Thank you," I mumbled. I knew that having seizures was nothing to be ashamed about, but I always felt bad and embarrassed after I had one in public. "I'm sorry you had to see that."

"It's all right," Belle said, staring at her feet. "I've seen Mr. Davies take care of someone before."

"No, not that." I almost laughed. "The seizure. I'm sorry. I know I look like I'm being possessed or something. They're not fun to witness... or have."

"It's okay." Belle shook her head. "It's not like you meant to freak me out."

A silence fell between us and I closed my heavy eyelids. I was always exhausted after having a fit. Concentrating with everything I had, I willed my right arm to lift off the cold linoleum floor.

Nothing.

Just a finger twitch? Please? Please, move?

"Damn it," I hissed, opening my eyes. I grasped my numb, immobile hand and dropped it on my lap.

"You really can't move it?" Belle asked in a near whisper, as if she was afraid I might take offence at the question.

"Well, the tumours that cause my epilepsy are in the left side of my brain, so the seizures mainly affect the right side of my body. Then, afterwards, I have this thing called Todd's Paralysis, where I can't move certain parts of my body. Mostly my right arm. I mean, watch this." I stared down at my legs, and with a huge amount of mental effort, bent them both at the knees. They were still wobbly though and crumpled back to the floor in about ten seconds. "Now, watch this." I glared down at my right hand, still resting in my lap. *Come on, come on, come on! Move!* Finally I was able to flex my fingers open and into a fist. My muscles were still burning, but it was better than a dead arm. "That's all I can do."

"Wow." Belle shook her head again. "That really sucks balls."

I laughed. "Yeah, it really does."

"Is there any treatment? Medication or something?"

"Yeah. I'm on three different medications and I had unsuccessful brain surgery when I was thirteen. The doctors originally thought that I only had one tumour in my brain, but when they opened me up, they found six more. They were all too close to the motor strip, a part of the brain that can turn you into a vegetable if damaged, to safely remove."

Belle gawked at me. "Really?"

"Yeah." I nodded. "Had to shave part of my head for nothing."

We were silent and I tried to move again. I grunted when I was able to get my thousand-pound legs to bend and stay bent, and sighed when I got my right hand to flex without pain following the movement.

I reached into my bag for my phone and sent Fuzzy a quick text (using only my left hand, of course).

```
-I had a seizure in the girls' bathroom. Can you
   help me 2 class? -B

-which bathroom?? -F

-beside the cafeteria -B

-be right there -F
```

"Is someone coming to get you?" asked Belle, who had been watching me text.

"Yeah," I said, putting my phone back in my bag. "We have the next two classes together and it won't be the first time he's carried me to them—granted the others were piggyback rides that I mooched…" I turned at the waist and looked her straight in the eye. "Listen, thank you so much for helping me. I could have really hurt myself if you hadn't been here."

"Don't worry about it," Belle shrugged, smiling. "Besides, I owed you for those flowers. Worked like a charm, by the way. My ex was demanding to know who they were from."

"Glad I could help."

"Beth?" Fuzzy's voice filled the bathroom. He hovered in the doorway.

"I'm right here, come in," I called, waving him in.

"Hey." He came over to me and crouched next to me, much like Mr. Davies had. "Are you okay?"

"She bonked her head a bit, but she seems fine," Belle informed him.

"Can you move?"

"Some." I flexed my hand, looking up at him. "Not a hundred percent yet, though."

"Yeah, I bet. Does your head hurt?"

"A bit. I'm fine, really," I said. "I just need your help to get to class."

Fuzzy looked confused. "What? Hell no. I'm taking you home."

"But you said you would," I said indignantly.

"No, I texted that I'd be right there." Fuzzy grabbed my bag, wrapped his arm underneath my shoulders, and helped me to slowly stand. "Look, you went to the two important classes you have this semester and I have my mom's car. I'm taking you home."

"I already told Mr. Davies that—"

"What classes do you have next?" Belle talked over me, getting to her feet.

"Resource centre and Thomas for last class," Fuzzy told her.

"I'll tell them you're not coming."

I made a huffing noise in protest, but we all knew Fuzzy had won.

When Fuzzy pulled the car into my driveway, he got out and opened my door for me. I gripped his arm to steady myself, because my legs were still very wobbly. He helped me into my house, up the stairs, and into my bedroom.

I flopped down face first onto my bed, completely drained.

"Will you be okay here?" my best friend asked, putting my bag at the end of my bed.

"Yeah," I muttered into my pillow. "You should get back to school."

"Although this is a very valid excuse to skip, you're probably right," he sighed, sitting on the edge of the bed. "I could use this time to read the rest of *Hamlet*."

"But you won't," I laughed, "You're gonna read *Lord of the Flies* again or something."

"At least it's not *Catcher in the Rye*," he joked.

"Don't even start, Fuzzy." I kicked at him and he laughed.

"You're probably right, though, I should go." He sighed heavily. I rolled onto my back and sat up. "Thanks for driving me home," I said, wrapping my arms around his neck and squeezing him. Fuzzy hugged me back and held on after I let go. "You should go," I whispered, my arms hovering at my sides.

"Right." He almost flew off my bed. "I'll, uh... I'll see you tomorrow."

"Uh-huh," I nodded, looking at my hands. I listened to him leave my bedroom and exit the house, before laying back down and falling into a deep sleep.

When I woke up, I rolled onto my side to face my desk, noting the time on my alarm clock.

"Four thirty?!" I nearly shouted. I had been asleep for four hours?!

I stretched my arms out and flexed my fingers a few times. They were back to normal, so I trusted my body enough to get in the shower without falling.

Taking a clean towel from the linen closet, I stepped into the bathroom and stripped down to my birthday suit. I turned the water on so hot that the room was steamed up within a minute.

After washing and rinsing my bleach-fried hair, I wrapped myself in the towel and headed back to my room, nearly running right into my dad.

"Oh my God!" I cried out, startled. "You're home early!"

My dad looked at his watch. "No I'm not. It's five." He looked over my head at the steam-filled washroom. "How long were you in the shower?"

"I'm not sure," I lied. *About half an hour.* I stepped around him to get to my room, but he stopped me.

"Beth, I got a message from the school today."

"Oh?"

"Yeah," he confirmed, crossing his arms over his chest. "Said you missed two classes?"

"I had a seizure at lunch and Fuzzy gave me a ride home," I explained.

"Are you okay?" my dad asked, shifting from suspicious to worried in less than a second.

"I'm fine," I assured him. "I only missed RC and drama and I have my English homework here, so I didn't miss anything." I shivered in the hallway. "Look, I'm soaked and in a towel; can I go get dressed?"

"Go do your homework. I'll call you when dinner is ready."

I turned away and went into my bedroom, closing the door behind me.

About an hour later, sitting on my bed and re-reading a part of *Hamlet*, I heard a knock on my door.

"Come in," I said, just loud enough to be heard. Amy stepped in and smiled. "What's up?" I asked.

"Dad's using the computer; can I use your laptop to check my email?"

I gestured at it and she took a seat at my desk, turned on my computer, logging out of my account, and into hers. We did not say anything while I read and she typed out a reply.

"Girls! Dinner!" our dad hollered after a while.

"Coming!" we called in unison.

"Thanks." Amy smiled, closing my laptop and standing up. I crawled off my bed.

"Anytime."

Dinner was pasta with garlic bread and rather quiet. When my dad asked what was wrong, I lied and told him I was thinking about my *Hamlet* essay. Really I was thinking about D-Day. The next day.

"Are you worried about it?" my dad questioned, swirling his spaghetti around the prongs of his fork.

"No, not at all. It's not due until Monday." I waved his question off.

"Well, don't leave it to the very last second." He looked pointedly at Amy, who averted her eyes and blushed.

"I won't." I laughed at my procrastination-prone sister. "Actually, I have some ideas so I should go and write them down before I forget." I made as if to stand up, but my dad pointed at my dinner plate.

"You didn't finish," he said disapprovingly.

"I'm really not all that hungry," I said in all honesty. "I'll wrap it up and eat it later."

Dad made a grumbling sound that Amy and I knew translated to '*I don't like it, but I know I have no argument, so fine.*'

I left the table, put my dinner in the fridge, and went back to my room.

I lifted my laptop off my desk and settled back down on my bed, leaning against the wall. I opened the screen and was about to open a word document when I noticed that the current open window was Amy's email and there were five messages from 'Secret Admirer'.

Unable to contain my curiosity, I clicked on one from Monday:

Amy,

I can't stop thinking about your blue eyes and the way that they seem to see right into my soul. You are far too beautiful for the likes of me but—

I closed the email and opened another, sent on the weekend:

Amy,

I wish I had the heart and bravery that you have. The only thing I can take credit for is being smart.

I skimmed over the other three but could not read them all completely. I found them all rather creepy. I would have talked to Amy about them, but she had not come to me, and I did not want to confess to her that I had gone through her private messages, so I closed the window and told myself to put the creeper out of my mind.

I did actually complete my *Hamlet* paper, and at around ten, my dad poked his head in to say goodnight.

"Don't stay up too late." He eyed my laptop, which I had perched on my legs.

"Don't worry, I won't," I fibbed.

"NIIIGHT, BETH!" Amy yelled from her room.

I took in a deep breath and shouted back. "NIIIGHT, AMY!"

"Will you two keep it down? Honestly, you're two doors away from each other." My dad sighed, closing my door.

I fished my headphones out of my bag, still at the end of my bed, and plugged them in. Opening my video files, I clicked on my *CSI* collection and watched one of my mom's old favourites.

I remembered watching this one with her and figuring out who the killer was before she did, which was a first. I smiled at the memory and pulled a teddy bear into my lap.

When the episode was over, it was nearing eleven and I was not the slightest bit tired. That probably had something to do with the four-hour nap I'd had.

"One more episode won't hurt," I mumbled, then paused before selecting it. Instead, I doubled clicked on a movie that I had not watched in over a year.

The Blair Witch Project.

While I watched the fictional idiots psych themselves out in the woods, I thought about the actual good times I'd had with Connor. They were limited, but it still kind of ached that I would be saying goodbye to such a huge part of my life. And Lynn. My lip trembled and I buried my face in the teddy bear, crying into the soft fur.

When the movie ended, it was nearly one, and although the movie was stupid, I was even more awake. It was a little scarier to watch it all by myself... at night. So, being the masochist I was turning into, I started to watch *I Am Sam*. I had watched that movie exactly four times. Once with my mom, once with my dad, once with Jane, and once with Connor, and had cried every time. Already this movie was incredibly sad, so I ended up bawling into my (now soaked with my tears) teddy bear. The first time I had watched it, my mom had held me and we had sobbed together. Hell, even Connor had cried during it. When *I am Sam* wrapped up in its heartwarming ending, it was four in the morning and I had to get up in three hours. I closed my laptop, put it next to my bag at the bottom of my bed, and lay down. Of course, it was when I was nearly asleep that it hit me. It was officially D-Day.

A new kind of tears started to form. What was I going to do? What was he going to do? How was I going to break Connor's heart? I mean, he had told me just the day before that he was planning on *marrying* me. What if he tried to hurt me?

Curling into a ball, holding my teddy tight, I cried into my pillow until I finally drifted off into a restless sleep.

CHAPTER 32
D-DAY

What felt like five minutes later, my dad was loudly knocking on my door and shouting for me to get up. When I did not reply, he came in.

"Bethy, get up!" he said, clearly irritated. "You're going to miss your—What's wrong?"

I could tell I looked worse than shit. I knew my eyes were puffy from crying and my nose was probably all pink. Not to mention the guaranteed bags under my eyes from lack of sleep.

"Can I stay home?" I croaked, my throat raw from sobbing.

Dad noticed that I was cradling a teddy bear in my arms, something I had not done in ages, and even then only when I was very upset. Considering that this was the first time I had asked to stay home since Connor had cheated on me with Jane, my dad must have known this was very important to his first born.

"Yeah, Beth, you can stay home." He walked over to me, sat on the edge of my bed, and put a calloused hand on my forehead. "You're not warm."

"I'm not well." I rolled onto my back and looked up at him. "I'll text Fuzzy and ask him to email me any homework that might get assigned."

"I still have to work late," my dad said apologetically.

"I can take care of myself."

"All right, I'll call the school and say that you won't be in today. Go back to sleep."

"Mm-hmm."

With that, my dad left me alone, closing my door with a *click*. I picked my phone up off my desk and sent a quick text to Connor before I passed out.

```
-wont be in today. Got no sleep -B

-can I still come over after field trip?? -C

-course -B

-get some rest. Youll need it ;) -C
```

"Ugh," I moaned, before texting Fuzzy and Rudy as well.

```
-no sleep. Wont be in today.
```

They both sent the same text back: `still D-day?`

```
-yup
```

Both sent: `-sleep well`

I put my phone back and fell asleep in seconds.

I woke up around noon. I stretched and checked my phone. Two new texts, from Rudy and Fuzzy, saying they hoped I was feeling better. None from the guy who was supposed to be my boyfriend... whom I was dumping today. Tears sprang to my eyes again and I sat up.

"You're doing this for both of you," I told myself. "It's not fair to you and it's not fair to Connor." I repeated this as a mantra. "It's not fair to you and it's not fair to Connor; it's not fair to you and it's not fair to Connor..." I took deep breaths until I felt myself calm down. Feeling miserable, I reached down to the end of my bed and pulled my laptop onto my thighs. I opened it and watched a ton of re-runs to cheer myself up and get my mind off what I was going to have to do later that day.

After about two hours of watching Steve Carell make the most awesome ass out of himself on *The Office*, I finally got out of bed and ran to the bathroom. I had denied my bladder release for far too long.

In three and a half hours, Connor and I would meet up at the diner so I could break up with him. I still needed a distraction, but I was getting way too restless to stay in bed watching re-runs I had seen so many times I could mouth all the words along with the actors. So I changed out of my pj's and pulled on my running gear, strapped my iPod to my arm, and went down to the nearby trail where I had run from Connor not long ago.

I turned on my running playlist, and with Imagine Dragons singing in my ears, I started jogging at a nice rhythmic pace. I passed the post with a sign that read '3K mark' and sped up, trying to convince myself that if I ran a little faster, my past couldn't catch up with me. When I reached the '4K mark' sign, I thought, *One more K and everything will go back to normal.* I pushed myself into an all-out sprint, past the 5K mark, and finally slowed when I saw the 6K sign a few yards away. I halted beside it and put my hands on my knees, my chest heaving.

What was I running from? Why was I trying to kid myself? My past would never go away and nothing would ever be normal again. Why would I think running would change that? And what was I thinking, running 6K? I still had to run back, damn it!

"Way to go, Beth," I grumbled, turning back the way I came and taking my time getting back home. As I jogged, I thought of ways to tell Connor it was over.

Connor, this isn't working.

Connor, I don't love you.

Connor, there's only so much asshole I can take.

It took me almost an hour to get home and I was slick with sweat, my clothes sticking to my chest and back. I went into the washroom and peeled off the gear one piece at a time, dropping them beside the sink (except for the iPod, which I put in the bathroom drawer). Then I turned on the shower to a nice cool temperature and stepped inside the tub, closing the transparent shower curtain. I remained under the strong stream for some time, turning the heat up eventually and letting the current run down my back, the hot water relaxing my muscles. When the water starting going cold of its own accord, I got out, and knowing that my dad and sister would be home late, streaked to my room.

Putting on a very un-sexy pair of underwear, lounge pants, and a tank top, I curled up under my blankets, watching *House M.D.* on Netflix. Eventually, I heard a knock at the front door. Heaving a very dramatic sigh, I paused the episode just as House was saying that it was never lupus. I put my laptop on my desk beside my cell phone and left my room.

Huffing down the stairs to the front door, I opened it just as Connor was about to knock again. One hand was raised in a fist, mid-knock, and the other clutching a cheap bouquet of roses. Again, my favourite are daisies. He grinned and handed me the flowers. It was pouring down rain, harder than the shower I'd just had. I guessed Connor had read the forecast, because there was an umbrella under his arm and he seemed to be completely dry. What was he doing here? He was supposed to meet me at the diner in, like... an hour.

"See?" he said, stepping past me and into the foyer, "I can be romantic."

"Yeah." I nodded, smelling the roses and leading the way to the kitchen to find a vase. "Thanks, Connor. This is sweet."

"I know."

"Makes it less sweet when you acknowledge the sweetness."

"Then I didn't know."

I rolled my eyes as I filled one of the many vases we had gotten from Marmee's funeral and carefully set the flowers inside it.

"Look, Connor," I began, placing one hand on my hip and turning to face him, "I wanted to meet you at the diner. I really don't feel like doing *that* right–"

"No," Connor cut me off in a voice so low and rough that it could not have belonged to him. "No," he repeated, this time pointing a finger at me. "You said okay. You told me you *did*."

When did I go that? I sighed and marched past him, trying to feign indifference to his frightening tone. "Uh, no I didn't. And even if I did, I'd have changed my mind." I started down the hall. "People do that."

"No, *you* do that!" Connor corrected, grabbing my elbow and pulling me in to the front of his body. "Now change it back."

"No," I snapped, trying to yank out of his grasp. He snaked his arms around my waist and held me closer. I could feel him against my lower back. "No, I won't." My heart was hammering and I tried to fight against his grip, but he lifted me off the floor.

"You know what, Beth?" he snarled, as I squirmed against him. "I don't care either way."

I started kicking my legs and screamed at him to put me down, but I may as well have been a rag doll in his arms as he strode down the rest of the hall to my room. I reached over my shoulder trying to claw at his face and neck, angering him further and making him kick the door closed harder than was warranted. He shoved me onto my bed. I tried to crawl off of it, but he was on top of me in less than a second, pressing me down on my stomach and holding my right arm behind my back so that my hand was between my shoulder blades.

Connor straddled me, holding my free arm down above my head so tightly that it hurt. "You're always such a tease, Beth," he said. I felt the tiny hairs on my neck rise.

"Connor, please don't do this."

"I'm your boyfriend, Beth," Connor continued, as if he had not heard me. He ground his crotch against my ass and I tried in vain to squirm away from him.

"Please—"

"And since I'm your *boyfriend*, you should be doing *girlfriend* duties," Connor spat.

"Connor, please, you don't have to do this!"

"But!" he shouted, twisting the arm he had behind my back to an even more unnatural and painful angle. "You keep failing to do that! Don't get me wrong, when you do do it is amazing." He ground his groin against me again, harder this time. Hot tears fell from my eyes and onto the pillow my face was pressed into. "But lately you say you will and then you flake. I *could* go get it from someone else—"

"More like buy it from someone else!"

Mistake.

"Damn it, Beth!" Connor yelled and let go of the hand he had pinned against my back. I thought for a moment I was free, but then his weight dropped onto me and I cried out in pain. He started pulling down my lounge pants with one hand.

"No!" I screamed, kicking my legs, the only part of my body that I was able to move. When my pants were only hanging off one ankle, I tried to clamp my thighs shut but wasn't able to before Connor wedged his knee in between mine. "No, Connor, no please!"

There was sharp tug and a ripping noise. Connor dropped my torn underwear beside my face.

His breath was hot on my neck.

My back and right arm ached.

My heart pounded.

My throat was raw from screaming.

Connor let go of my left wrist, which was still above my head, and I felt him adjust himself.

There was pressure, and then in my mind, I heard the voice of Coach Foster (of all people) say, '*It's simple physics.*'

"NO!" I shrieked.

I pulled my left arm to my side and bent that leg so my knee could touch my elbow. Connor's leg was bent, so I couldn't hook his ankle, but I was able to shove hard off the mattress with my left limbs. Connor rolled onto his back from the force and I took advantage of his surprise by elbowing him hard in the nose.

"Argh!" he cried, covering his face to protect himself from further blows. I sat up and hammer-fisted him in the balls, then jumped off the bed, grabbed my phone off my desk, and bolted into the bathroom.

I slammed the door shut, opened the drawer next to it so that it couldn't open all the way (because my dad still hadn't installed a new lock), and slid down it to the floor.

I unlocked my phone and called the first person I could think of.

It wasn't until Rudy answered on the third ring, and demanded to know what was wrong, that I realized that I was sobbing.

"What's going on? Where are you?" His voice was laced with worry and perhaps some anger.

"My bathroom," I blubbered. "I'm in my bathroom."

There was a slam on the door I was leaning against and I was jolted forward a bit.

"Beth! Beth, open the door!" Connor yelled from the other side of it.

I whimpered and buried my face in my knees, the phone still pressed against my ear.

"Beth, what's happening? Is that Connor?" Rudy asked in a far gentler voice.

"Yeah, is it," I said, my voice shaking. I screamed when Connor hit the door, demanding to know who I was talking to. "Rudy, he's scaring me," I whispered.

"I'm coming over; give me ten minutes." Through the phone, I heard him grab a set of keys and then the sound of a door closing. "Leave the door unlocked."

"Okay," I said, knowing that I couldn't get to the front door, but hoping Connor didn't think to lock it, and hung up just as Connor pounded on the bathroom door again.

"Beth! I mean it, open up! It was a misunderstanding, I'm sorry!"

I cleared my throat and called out in as calm a voice as I could manage, "You better leave now, Connor. Somebody is coming over."

There was silence for a moment... and then, "Are we okay?"

"Just leave, Connor."

"Beth, please, I'm sorry. I didn't mean it. Any of it." I didn't reply. He sounded genuinely upset and disappointed in himself. "Please don't leave me. Don't stop loving me. Please."

"Connor, you need to leave. Now." I said these words as slowly and clearly as possible, sitting half naked on a cold linoleum floor. "I will never, *ever* speak to you again." This was not how I was planning this break up to go, but since when did my life go according to plan? "We. Are. Done. I am not yours in any way. Not your girlfriend, not your significant other, not the girl you're going to marry. Not even your friend. You are just a bad, *bad* person and the next time I see you, will be too soon."

I heard an audible sniffle coming from the other side of the door. "This isn't how tonight was supposed to go, Beth," Connor said. "I love you, Beth. You can't leave someone you love."

I spun around so that I was on my knees facing the bathroom door. "I DON'T FUCKING LOVE YOU!" I screamed at the top of my lungs, slamming my fists against the door and making it shift in its frame. "I AM IN LOVE WITH SOMEONE ELSE! AND BEFORE YOU EVEN ASK, IT IS NOT FUZZY! LEAVE, YOU WORTHLESS PIECE OF SHIT! YOU ARE NOTHING! YOU ARE A COWARD AND A WASTE OF SPACE! GET"—I hit the door—"THE"—I hit the door again—"FUCK"—I punched the door with both of my fists—"OUT OF MY LIFE!"

My chest heaving, I listened for a response. I heard a muffled sob, and then, to my surprise and relief, footsteps going down the hall and descending the stairs, the front door opening, and finally, the front door closing again.

I remained propped up on my knees, my palms resting on the door, my head bowed, and panting.

It was done. It had only taken months, an attempted rape, and a bathroom door as a barrier for me to finally have courage to break up with someone Fuzzy and Rudy had both labelled as the 'world's biggest asshole'.

A rumbling car engine being turned off outside reminded me that Rudy was coming over. "Shit," I hissed, getting to my feet. *If Rudy sees me like this, he'll know what happened. Or what almost happened.* I could not tell anyone what Connor had done without it somehow coming back to hurt Lynn. How could someone so evil be related to someone so kind? If he wound up in jail, it would taint her reputation as a fantastic teacher and warm-hearted mentor. If Connor ended up in juvie, it would be a manner of minutes before everyone knew... and wondered where Lynn had gone wrong as a mother. I had just broken Connor's minuscule heart; I could not break her significant one. I heard three loud knocks on the front door, followed by the sound of it swinging open.

"Beth? Beth? Where are you?" Rudy called from the foyer, closing the door behind him.

"Damn it," I breathed. I looked around frantically, trying to figure out how I could get out of this situation without having to ask Rudy to pass me a pair of panties and jeans through a mostly closed door. I pulled off my tank top, unclasped my bra and slid it off. Then I grabbed a clean towel off one of the hangers and wrapped it around me, knotting it closed just below my collarbones. I heard Rudy climb the stairs and call my name again, and I exited the bathroom, my hand around the knot to be sure the towel wouldn't drop to the floor.

"Beth, where are—Whoa." His jaw dropped. He was drenched from the downpour outside. His shirt was clinging to his chest, his hair was plastered to his forehead and face, and his staring eyes were taking me in. I couldn't blame him; I was practically naked. That didn't stop the blush that started to heat my face. It's not like he had not seen my body before, but this was a very different circumstance. After about five silent seconds, Rudy closed his mouth and averted his eyes, staring up at a light fixture. "I, uh, are you okay?" he stammered, his hands clenching and unclenching at his sides, as if he were resisting the urge to touch me. Sudden relief and the feeling of safety swept over me, and with three long strides, I threw my arms around his shoulders and began to cry into his chest. Without hesitation, Rudy wrapped his arms around me, pulled me closer to him, and whispered sweet nothings in my ear. "It's okay. You're okay. I'm here. I'll take care of you, Beth." When my sobs subsided and my knees started to give way, Rudy bent slightly and scooped me into his arms. "Which room is yours, Beth?" he whispered.

"On the right," I whispered back, reaching up and touching his shadowed jaw. There was nothing sexual about the caress or the way he was holding me; it was tender and careful. Exactly what I needed—what I had needed for a long time. I'm not saying that my heart wasn't hammering faster that Usain Bolt could run, but my mind was not racing. I just knew that I was safe now. I knew that now that I was in Rudy's arms, nothing could hurt me.

Rudy carried me to my room and carefully laid me down on my bed on top of the sheets. I grabbed the ripped panties lying beside my pillow and shoved them between the wall and the mattress, before Rudy could see. Rudy joined me on the bed, sharing my pillow. His hands hovered above my side for a few moments, as if he could not decide on a safe place to touch me. He decided on my elbow, running his hand up to my shoulder and back down in a gentle caress.

"Did he hurt you, Beth?" he asked quietly, his voice comforting and controlled. I hated lying to him but did not have a choice.

"No," I whispered.

"Did he try?"

"Kind of."

"How do you mean?"

"I dumped him. I told him what I really thought of him. That I don't love him, that he's a waste of space. He... didn't like that at all. I ran away from him; he chased me. I locked myself in the bathroom where I had left my phone earlier and called you. He left and I got in the shower. Wanted to wash him off me, you know?"

"You told me on the phone that you were scared?"

"I was. I dumped him and he was really angry about it. Said 'you don't leave someone you love' and I told him that I didn't love him and to get out of my life. I'm kind of surprised he left, actually."

"You did dump him then?" Rudy questioned, his fingers pausing midway up my arm. I nodded. Rudy's light blue eyes lit up so much that they were almost grey. He was silent for nearly a minute before finally asking, "Will you be mine? You're not his anymore, right? Will you be mine?"

"I've been yours for a long time, Rudy."

We were silent for a few minutes, staring at each other as if we might not ever get to see one another again. A black curl was resting just beside the corner of his eye. His stubble was a little lighter than the hair on his head, which I found interesting. He had a small scar just above his right eyebrow and another on the edge of his chin. Or was that a hair?

"I'm going to kiss you now," Rudy whispered, tracing a finger down my nose. "Is that all right?"

"Of course, it is." I smiled. "I'm yours. You can kiss what's yours."

Slowly, Rudy lowered his mouth to mine and kissed me so gently that I might not have known it was happening if I hadn't been able to feel his breath against my cheek. It was brief and full of longing, tenderness, and even desire. When he pulled away, Rudy rolled onto his back and pulled me onto his chest, where I lay my head and listened to his heartbeat and rhythmic breathing.

We fell asleep like that: me completely naked, except for a towel, and him still fully dressed, including his sneakers.

We woke up to the sound of my dad coming in the front door, talking to someone on his cell phone. "I already told them that those counter-tops are pricey, but did they listen? No."

"Oh shit!" I yelled in a whisper, sitting up and clutching my towel to my body. "Shit, shit, shit, shit, shit, shit!"

Rudy nearly leapt off the bed, and was looking around as if hoping to find the portal to Narnia somewhere in my small room. "What do I do?" he hissed, his eyes unable to focus on one thing for more than two seconds. I pointed to the window. His shoulders slumped. "Are you serious?" I nodded. "We're on the second floor." I nodded again.

"Beth? Whose truck is that outside?" My dad's voice called from the foyer.

"Damn it." I pointed at Rudy. "Turn around." I did not want him to see me naked in a situation that was not intimate. Rudy spun in a circle. Wow, he was really panicked. "Go face that corner." I nodded at the far wall. He did as I said, and not bothering with underwear or a bra, I pulled a pair of jeans on under my towel and a shirt over my head. Then I pulled the towel loose, throwing it at the back of Rudy's head teasingly. "Okay, sit on the bed." Rudy walked backward until his knees touched the bed and he sat down, still not looking at me. I could not help but laugh at how stupid it looked.

"Beth? I asked you a question," my dad called from down the hall. "Beth?" I grabbed my script from beside my bed and opened the bedroom door.

"Yeah, Dad?" I said, stepping into the hall, pretending to be engrossed in a song that I don't even take a part in.

"Whose truck—Wait, who's that?" He pointed into my room and narrowed his eyes. "There's a boy on your bed." His eyes went wide with surprise, and what looked like hope, "and it's not Connor. Did you dump Connor? And who is that?"

"Dad, calm down," I sighed, shaking my head. "This is Rudy. He plays Roger in RENT. We're running lines." I held up the prop of my lie, fanning the pages for emphasis. "And yeah, I broke up with Connor."

My dads' eyes went wide and then he strode to me and picked me up in a bear hug. "Oh, thank God," he said, rocking me back and forth, clearly pleased with this news. "So glad I don't have to put up with that ass-hat anymore."

"Good use of the word 'ass-hat', Dad, but I currently have a guest, so…"

My dad put me back down and grinned at Rudy, who was smiling in amusement. "Oh, well… nice to meet you then." Rudy gave a little wave from my bed. "Leave the door open."

"Do you really want to hear a song about AIDS?" I asked, raising an eyebrow.

"When you have a boy in your room? Yes." Dad nodded and headed to the kitchen.

As per his instructions, I left the door open (like, three inches), sat in the middle of my bed, and began to sing "Seasons of Love". Rudy joined in, an impressed smile on his face.

That day might have sucked, that evening might have been a nightmare, but that night… that night was wonderful.

CHAPTER 33
THE SECRET ADMIRER

The next day, I felt lighter than I had in ages. There was a hundred and sixty pound weight off my mind. To celebrate the fact that I no longer had the ball and chain from hell attached to me, Rudy had asked if I would have breakfast with him.

"That sounds nice," I smiled "It's a date."

"Okay, so I'll meet you there in about forty-five minutes?" Rudy said. I agreed and hung up. We were going to eat at a small diner not far from my house, so I had insisted that I could walk instead of having him pick me up.

The morning was perfect, from the blue skies above me to the wonderful person I was going to see. A small part of me thought that Connor might be hiding in some bushes, waiting to jump out and grab me, but I pushed the thought to the back of my mind. Nothing could put a damper on today. At least that's what I thought until I got a text, right after Rudy had paid for my omelet and his pancakes.

With a loud *vvvttt* sound, my cell vibrated beside my empty coffee mug. I picked it up and looked at the screen. A text from Connor.

> -thought u should know that im amy's secret admirer. Please don't b mad. C u at school. -C

"What the fuck?" I breathed, reading it again to make sure that it said what I thought it did. No, this could not be right. Amy had had this creeper since February. There is no way that guy had been, of all people, my boyfriend. Connor had been cyber-stalking my little sister?

"Beth, are you okay? You don't look so good," Rudy asked, reaching across the small table and touching my arm. "What's wrong?"

"It's Connor," I said, still staring at my phone.

Rudy made a face. "Just ignore it. He's not in your life anymore." He took a sip of his mocha, licking whipped cream off his upper lip.

"No, no, he's admitting it." I finally looked up at Rudy, who looked confused. "He's just admitted to cyber-stalking my little sister. My thirteen-year-old little sister."

When I said it out loud, I could feel my shock turn into anger and hate. Rudy's jaw dropped and he looked as though he was waiting for me to yell "Psych!" and start laughing.

When I did not, he shook his head a little and asked, "What do you want to do?"

I looked down at the text again. I noticed that it was an IM, not a text, meaning that it had been sent from his computer.

"Take me to his house," I said, standing up and picking up my purse. "He's there and I'm going to have a few words with him."

Rudy followed me out of the diner and walked me to where he had parked his truck. He unlocked it, got in, and started it as soon as I closed my door.

"My little sister, Rudy," I said, as he pulled out of his spot and started driving to Connor's house. I had told him the area he lived in once before, so he more or less knew the way there. "My little sister!"

"I know, I know." Rudy reached over and put a hand on my knee. Usually that action would make me feel tingly, but at the moment I barely noticed it.

I repeated the phrase, "my little sister" the whole drive to Connor's house, while Rudy answered with "I know, I know."

Rudy turned off the truck across the street from my ex-boyfriend's house. There were no cars in the driveway, so I knew that no one else was going to be home. Good.

"Stay here," I demanded, undoing my seatbelt and opening the door (with difficulty).

"But Beth—" Rudy began.

"No." I pointed at him sternly. "Stay." I got out, slammed the door, and stormed over to Connor's house. Stomping up the front steps, I threw open the door without knocking, just as Connor was coming out of the kitchen.

"Oh, Beth, hey," he said, walking down the hall toward me. The sight of him made my heart race and fists clench. "I was just—"

"MY LITTLE SISTER!!" I screamed, and without a second thought, I clenched a hand into a fist and punched him hard in the jaw. Connor's head snapped back and he stumbled, slamming into a wall.

"Are you insane?!" he yelled, rage flaming in his eyes. I stepped into him and threw an uppercut into his gut.

"I am sick of your *shit!*" I cried, over the sound of the wind being knocked out of my ex-boyfriend. He bent forward from the force of my punch. "You're disgusting and pathetic! I *hate* you!" He stood up straight and reached a hand out toward me. I was not sure what he planned to do with it, but whatever it was, I was not going to let him. I threw a roundhouse kick that slammed into his ribs. Connor hit the wall beside him and tried to grab onto something in the hopes of staying on his feet. His fingers grasped a coat rack and he ended up bringing it down on top of him. It looked so stupid that, had I not been panting with rage, I would have laughed. "Stay the hell away from me, away from my sister, and if you even so much as look at her again I'll fuck you up so bad that you'll be shitting your own teeth." *Where did that come from?*

"Crazy bitch," he wheezed. He rolled onto his side, clutching his injured ribs.

"Sadistic asshole," I spat back at him.

With that, I turned on my heel and left the house, leaving Connor curled up on the floor. By the time I was crossing the road to Rudy, who had gotten out of his truck and was leaning against the cab, I was grinning from ear to ear. I could not remember the last time I had felt so liberated. My knuckles hurt like a son of a bitch, but it was worth it!

"I heard everything," Rudy said when I was a few feet away. "Is he all right?" I jumped up and wrapped my legs around his waist and my arms around his shoulders.

"I don't care," I replied honestly "And that felt *so good!*"

A few hours later, I was in the bathroom dabbing at my skinned knuckles when Amy walked in. Had it been anyone else, I probably would have freaked, but when Amy and I were in the washroom together we usually needed to tell each other something important. Our dad could walk into our bedrooms whenever he wanted, but he could not walk into a bathroom while we were in it without the risk of seeing one of his daughters on the toilet. So the bathroom was our safe place.

"Hey," Amy said, taking a seat on the edge of the tub. She looked kind of nervous.

"Hey, what's up?" I asked, biting back a hiss as I tugged a bit of dead skin that stung like a hangnail. Oh well, it was worth it.

"I know who my secret admirer is," Amy announced, staring down at her hands, which were folded in her lap.

I froze and looked at her in the mirror. "Yeah?"

"Yeah." She paused and swallowed before looking up at me. "It's Connor."

"I know," I said, turning off the taps and turning to face her, shaking my hands dry. "He texted me today telling me that it was him."

Amy's jaw dropped, much like Rudy's had. "Did you dump him?"

"No, I beat the shit out of him," I said. "I dumped him yesterday."

"You *what?!*" Amy exclaimed, shooting to her feet. "And you *what?*! Why didn't you tell me?"

"I wasn't feeling very talkative," I shrugged. More like my mouth had been attached to Rudy's. Then I explained how I had gone to Connor's house after I got the text.

"And you beat him up?" she said excitedly.

I held up my hands to show her the skinned parts. "I gave him hell," I said proudly.

Amy grinned, pride filling her features. "Awesome." She beamed. She paused for a moment, like she was trying to decide whether or not to say something, and then caved. "So are you with that guy you like now? Rudy, was it?" I smiled and she raised her eyebrows. "Really? That was fast."

"You know what?" I said, leaning against the counter behind me and crossing my arms. "I really don't care what people are going to say. I haven't loved Connor for a long time and I'm not going to let anyone get in the way of the tiny bit of happiness I've got in my life now—happiness I deserve."

Amy nodded and gave me a hug. "Good for you." I squeezed her back and heard her mumble, "What the crap?" She pulled back and looked down. "What's that?"

She poked my belly button ring.

"Ouch!" I cried, swatting her hand away. "Stop that."

"What is it?" she said, pointing at my navel. I lifted my shirt up a bit and she gasped. "Dad is going to kill you."

"If he finds out," I said in an almost warning tone.

Amy smiled. "I guess I owe you for beating up my stalker."

I dropped my shirt. "We'll call it even."

CHAPTER 34
FREEDOM

Two days after Connor opened my can of whoop-ass was the first Monday I had not dreaded since I first started high school. I was still beaming with pride at what I had done on Saturday. When I reached the locker, I thought of Rudy, and making out with him in the truck, listening to Coldplay after dropping by Connor's house.

I must have been staring at my combination lock, because next thing I knew, Fuzzy was behind me, asking if I had forgotten the code.

"Huh?" I snapped out of my flashback and turned to face him, tucking a lock of hair behind my ear.

"What happened?" Fuzzy gaped at my knuckles. A grin spread across my face again. I was doing that so often my face was beginning to hurt.

I stepped away from the lockers and grabbed his elbow. "Come with me," I said, pulling him to a classroom I knew would be empty. I locked it behind me and turned to face my best friend.

"Okay, you look like you won the lottery, Beth. What's going on?"

I bounced on the balls of my feet, feeling giddy, and took a deep breath. "I broke up with Connor on Friday and found out he had been stalking Amy."

"And you're *smiling?*"

"Shut up and let me finish." I held up a finger. "I went to his house and beat the shit out of him. So no I'm not with Connor and *he's* all bruised up instead of me."

Fuzzy stared at me for a moment. He seemed to be debating something in his mind. "Screw it," he finally said.

Before I could do anything to prevent it, Fuzzy reached out, wove his fingers through my hair and kissed me like it was his last breath. I will admit it: He was a good kisser. I took a small step back, but ended up bumping into a desk behind me. Fuzzy reached down and gently grasped my leg, pulling it up and around his thigh. He leaned farther into me until our chests were firmly pressed together and one of his hands skimmed my ribcage. Caught up in the moment, I let him continue. It was not until he moaned my name into my mouth that my brain shouted, *What are you doing?! This is Fuzzy!!!* I snaked my hands between us and pushed gently against his chest, leaning away from him slightly and breaking the kiss. We were both panting.

"What's wrong?" he asked, staring into my eyes as if searching for answers.

"Fuzzy, no." I shook my head a little from side to side.

Fuzzy closed his eyes and pursed his lips, as if forcing himself not to say something he would regret. He gently let go of me and rested his hands on either side of desk I was still propped on, caging me in. He did not do this to frighten me; he just knew that my first instinct would be to run from a situation like this. Fuzzy hung his head, as though he were ashamed of his impulsive action.

"I don't understand," he croaked. "I thought that you..." He swallowed hard and I saw his arms flex in frustration.

I bit my lip and shook my head again. "No, Fuzzy." There was a screaming silence between us.

Finally, he looked up and made eye contact. "Why don't you love me?" I preferred the silence.

"Fuzzy... you can't control who you fall in love with," I pointed out. "Take me for example," I sighed. "I *do* love you, but I'm not *in* love with you. You're my best friend."

"Beth, I don't—" He froze suddenly and realization seemed to dawn on him. He dropped his arms and took a step away from me. "It's that guy. Rudy." It was not a question. I did not reply and that confirmed his suspicion. "Fuck!" he swore loudly, making me jump. "It's been three days and you've already moved on?"

"Fuzzy!" I yelled in a whisper, not liking where this was going. People were going to hear him. "Fuzzy, it's been more than three days."

"It—Wait, what?"

I sat down on the desktop and sighed. "Rudy and I have been fooling around for a few weeks now." I glanced up at him. He was watching me intently. "Rudy kissed me once and even though I *swore* it would never happen again, it did. It happened a lot actually." I omitted that a lot more had happened not twenty-four hours ago. "I'm sorry; I wanted to tell you, but if Connor had found out there's no telling what he might have done."

"I'm pretty sure you knew what he'd have done," Fuzzy snarled.

"Fuzzy, stop," I whispered, not even wanting to think about it. "He'll never touch me again."

Fuzzy walked over to me and sat down next to me, rubbing his face with his hands. "I'm so embarrassed. I shouldn't have kissed you," he groaned.

"It's okay." I shrugged. "I did lead you on."

"I'm not going to lie," he admitted, glancing over at me. "I'm glad I did it, even if it was just that one time."

Unsure of what to say, I nervously tugged at my hair. "We're still friends, right?" I choked out. "I don't know what I would do without you."

"Yeah, Beth," Fuzzy nodded, putting an arm around my shoulders. "We'll always be friends." He did not look happy when he said this. He looked as though he had just nailed his own coffin shut.

I smiled at him consolingly and slowly slipped off the desk. "We should get our stuff. Classes will start soon," I said, starting for the door.

"Yeah," Fuzzy agreed, meeting me at the exit as I unlocked it. "By the way, I think your hair looks good up *or* down."

I laughed quietly and opened the door, stepping into the hall and heading back to our lockers. I grinned when I saw Rudy leaning against mine, his legs crossed at the ankles.

"Hey, Rudy," I beamed. He straightened up and kissed me.

"Hey, man." Fuzzy nodded at Rudy, who nodded back. This might be awkward for a while. He looked away from the two of us, as if my new boyfriend and I were a very unappealing sight.

"What the *hell*, Beth!" We heard the shrill cry from down the hall, followed by pounding footsteps. Candice. "Connor dumps you and you don't even text me? Call me? Facebook me? Are you kidding me?" she accused, pointing a finger at me.

"Hang on, wait," I said, as Candice got right in my face, looking furious for being kept out of the loop. I shook my head, trying to clear it so that I could take in what she had just said. "Did you just say that *Connor* dumped *me*?" I held up a hand in front of me and took a step back.

She crossed her arms and tilted her head to the side. "Well, yeah," she said, "that's what Connor told me, anyway. Said you weren't good enough for him."

"And you believed that crap?" Fuzzy gaped at Candice. "Why?"

She shrugged. "I have my reasons." She glanced at Rudy. "Your *promiscuity* for one."

Urge to slap rising...

"What did you just say?" Rudy took a step toward her, but I reached out to stop him.

"You know what, Candice?" I sighed, stepping up to our locker and opening it. I handed a couple books over to Fuzzy, took a sweater of mine from the top shelf, and then turned back to her. "Fuck you."

"*Excuse* me?" she gasped, stepping away from me as if I had actually slapped her.

"You heard me." I snatched up a late library book and shoved it in my bag. "Fuck you. Fuck this. Fuck our 'friendship'. You and me?" I pointed at myself and then at her. "Done."

"But, but," she stammered, staring at me with her big blue eyes. "Why?"

"Because you're a cunt." It was the first time I had used that word. I think I saved it for the right person. Her eyes went wide and her cheeks flushed. I continued before she could get a word in or make me feel bad for saying it. "Because you and Connor deserve each other," I spat, kicking the locker closed and leading the way down the corridor, a grinning Fuzzy and a confused Rudy right behind me.

When we had gotten to the first floor, where I was going to move my stuff into Rudy's locker, we saw Connor walk in the building from a side entrance. He was wearing aviator sunglasses and had a large bruise on his swollen jaw. I heard Fuzzy breathe the word "awesome."

"You know, only famous people and douche bags wear sunglasses indoors, right?" Fuzzy joked.

Connor slowly removed them and both Rudy and Fuzzy burst into laughter when they saw the black eye I had given him. I smiled proudly at it.

"You're an infamous douche, so I guess you can get away with it," I proposed.

"Psycho bitch," Connor insulted, putting his glasses back on and hurrying away from us.

"Oh, and no one is going to believe that *you* dumped *her*, dude!" Fuzzy called after him.

"And Candice needs a new locker-mate!" I added, laughing as Connor picked up his pace and almost ran up the staircase we had just come down.

"That was fantastic," Rudy grinned, kissing my cheek.

Out of the corner of my eye, I saw Fuzzy smile sadly. I know he wanted to be with me, but I think he was happy that I was with someone who was going to treat me the way I deserved to be treated.

I decided not to tell Rudy that Fuzzy had kissed me. In retrospect, I should have, but I did not want the moment to cause more grief than it already had for my best friend. It was already tainted by my denial, so I decided that I should let him have that one moment between us stay between us.

CHAPTER 35
OPENING NIGHT

Rudy and I were standing just off stage and the curtains were going to go up in about five minutes.

"You nervous?" he asked, wrapping his arms around my waist from behind.

"A little," I nodded, leaning in to him.

Rudy chuckled in my ear. "A little?"

I smiled and held up my hand in front of us with my thumb and index finger about an inch apart. "Little bit."

He kissed my neck lightly, sending shivers down my back. Rudy absentmindedly began to twirl a lock of my hair, which had been curled for the play, around his finger. The red dye had by now washed out completely, leaving me with long blonde hair that was so bright it was basically yellow. My dad would not let me dye it back to its natural brown, so I was stuck with fluffy yellow hair. In an attempt to switch parts with me, Lindsey had tried to point out to Mr. Thomas that Mimi was supposed to have curly dark hair and be Latina.

"Do you know Mimi's lines?" Mr. T had asked her, an eyebrow raised.

Lindsey's face had fallen. She clearly had not thought that far ahead. Nor did she have dark curly hair or Latin heritage.

"Do you think *he'll* come?" Rudy asked, breaking me out of my hair-related trance.

I did not have to ask who he was talking about by the way his entire body had tensed when he asked the question. "No," I replied flatly.

Since our confrontation in the hallway, Connor had made sure to stay away from me. He switched desks with whoever sat the farthest away from me in classes and steered clear of any route I might take to my classes.

Fuzzy, Rudy, and I claimed the windowsill in the cafeteria and Candice had tried to join us once. When the three of us just stared at her, expressionless, she gathered her things up, glaring at me and mumbling "promiscuous" before marching away.

"One minute! Positions, everyone!" Mr. Thomas called out behind us. Rudy squeezed me once and let his arms slowly drop to his sides. I turned to face him and brushed a gentle kiss on his cheek.

"Break a leg," I whispered, before giving him a little push onto the stage.

Rudy strode over to his place and threw me one last grin before the spotlights turned on and the curtains began to open.

The audience hushed and Brett, sitting on a metal chair centre stage, said the first line of the play: "We begin on Christmas Eve..."

While I waited for my queue, I peeked through a hole in the curtains to take a look at the audience. The only seats I could see were in the first row. I felt my brow furrow when I noticed one of the seats was empty.

Who doesn't sit in a front and centre seat in a packed auditorium?

Then I saw a sheet of paper on it and squinted to make out what it read:

Reserved for Marmee

I gasped and bit my lip. Beside the empty seat sat Amy, Dad, Auntie, Uncle Mitch, and Fuzzy. I blinked back tears, because my queue was coming up.

"I can do this, I can do this..." I whispered, gathering myself together and getting into character. The rest of the cast walked on stage, singing about how they were not going to pay last year's, this year's, or next year's rent.

Sure enough, besides a couple of hiccoughs with Lindsey's lines, the opening night went perfectly. We even got a standing ovation. After we took our bows and watched the curtains close, we all grinned at each other like idiots on our darkened stage, feeling like we ruled the world.

"Come on," Rudy smiled, tugging on my hand for us to exit, but I caught sight of Mr. T.

"No, no, you go ahead," I told him. "I'll meet you in the drama room."

"You sure?"

"Yeah, go ahead."

Rudy hesitated but did as I asked.

I made my way over to the director, who was looking down at the clipboard he always seemed to carry while in the auditorium.

"Mr. Thomas?" I said, tapping his shoulder. "Mr. Thomas?"

He turned and beamed down at me. "Beth! You were fantastic!"

I smiled sheepishly up at him. "Thank you. I had a great director," I replied. "Listen, Mr. T, I saw the reserved seat."

He looked worried for a moment. "Should I not have?"

"No, no, that's not it." My voice cracked and I ran my fingers through my hair. I could not think of how to explain how much it meant to me.

"Beth, you okay?" Mr. Thomas asked, putting a hand on my shoulder.

I found that words could not express how much that simple gesture had meant to me, so instead of forcing out a mere "thank you", I wrapped my arms around my favourite teacher, who hugged me back, hearing everything I did not say.

I let go before it got awkward and gave him a little wave before going to rejoin my cast-mates and Rudy.

"Hey," he said, when I entered the drama room.

He and Fuzzy were sitting on the fainting couch, waiting for me. There were a couple of co-stars in the room as well, packing up their things.

"Great job, Bethy!" Fuzzy grinned, standing up and pulling me into a tight embrace. "That really was awesome, you guys," he addressed everyone in the room as I pulled away.

There were a few 'thank you's and 'cool's as the cast members made their way out of the room.

"Well, I'm off," he said, pulling on his jacket. "It really was a great play."

"Thanks, man." Rudy smiled appreciatively.

Rudy still had not completely warmed to Fuzzy, and vice versa. Despite my efforts to convince him that there was nothing between us, Rudy continued to see Fuzzy as a minor threat.

Once everyone had left, I sat down next to Rudy, swinging my legs onto his lap. "Bravo," I said, as he leaned in to kiss me.

"Encore," he said, when I kissed him back.

I grasped the front of his shirt and pulled him in to me as I lay back on the couch. Rudy's fingers wove through my limp curls. I pushed my hands up the back of his shirt and wished I could bring him closer to me. I felt the hard muscles of Rudy's back while he traced his fingertips over my exposed midriff. I sighed into our kiss and felt him smile. Pulling my hands out from under his shirt, I held his biceps in my small hands. Rudy slowly began to kiss my neck and I relaxed beneath him, pulling off his leather jacket.

"I love you, Beth," he whispered, before returning his mouth to mine.

My eyes snapped open. Did he just say that?

He continued kissing me as if the world's most important sentence had not just escaped his lips. Maybe he did not realize that he had said it? Maybe he was pretending that he hadn't? Maybe he's waiting for me to return the sentiment?

I mean, I did love him... but it was such a huge thing to say after only two post-Connor weeks.

"Hey," Rudy said, interrupting my train of thought. "Where are you?"

I blinked and looked into Rudy's beautiful blue eyes. He had his weight on his forearms on either side of my head and was looking down at me with concern. "Are you all right? It's like you zoned out for a minute. Not crazy romantic, seeing as we're making out."

"Yeah, I'm right here." I smiled and touched his face. "I'm just tired. It was a big night."

"Do you want to go home?" Rudy asked, bending down and kissing the tip of my nose.

"I want to stay with you." I sighed, running my palms up his chest. "But it *is* getting late and my dad will be expecting me home soon."

"Well, I don't want to get on his bad side," Rudy decided, sitting up. "I should get you home."

I propped myself up on my elbows. "You don't want to keep kissing me?" I pouted.

"Trust me, I do." Rudy laughed. "But I also want your dad to trust me with his daughter." He gathered my coat and bag and led the way out of the classroom, where we bumped right into Mr. Thomas.

"You two are still here?" he said, surprise written all over his face. "The show ended forty-five minutes ago. It's almost eleven."

"We were, uh... tidying up," I lied quickly. "The drama room was a mess?" I noted that my voice raised at the end of the sentence, as if I were asking our director to believe me.

Mr. T gave me a look that summed up his disbelief, but merely nodded. "Mm-hmm." He smiled and walked around us into his classroom.

Rudy grasped my hand and pulled me the rest of the way outside before bursting into laughter.

"What?" I asked, starting to laugh myself.

Rudy gasped. "Tidying up? Really? That's... that's the best you could do?"

"Better than just standing there," I chuckled, pretending to be offended as we made our way through the parking lot.

"But still, tidying up?" He snorted. "I mean, I've seen your room, Beth."

"Oh, shut up." I smacked his arm as we reached his ancient truck.

Still laughing slightly, Rudy unlocked the passenger door and climbed in. I watched him almost trip over the gear shift and settle into the driver's seat before clambering in after him. I slammed the door closed and went to buckle myself in, but Rudy said, "You're gonna need to do that again."

"Do what again?"

"The door. The latch is—never mind, I'll do it." He leaned over me, smirking when his hand brushed against my chest as he reached over me to open the door again.

"Hey!" I gasped in mock horror, covering myself. "Cop a feel much?"

"Oh, you liked it," Rudy laughed, slamming the door again and seeming to flick the handle in an odd way. "You really need to, like... heave the damn thing and then... look, never mind. Just let me do it from now on, otherwise it'll swing open if I make a semi-sharp turn."

"You're kidding." I gaped at him as he settled back in his seat. "Now *both* of the doors are broken?"

"Yep." He nodded, putting his keys in the ignition and looking in the rear-view mirror to check the surroundings behind us. "It's a hunk of junk, but I love it."

I turned to face the dashboard, smiling out the window. It was endearing how attached Rudy was to his—

"You piece of crap!" Rudy yelled beside me. I whipped around to face him. With one hand he was turning the key over and over again, while with the other he was slamming a fist against the steering wheel. "You son of a—Start! Goddamn it!"

"What? What's happening?"

"The stupid thing won't start!"

"Well, what do we do?" I asked. I had never experienced car trouble before.

He sighed loudly, and seemed to deflate. "Not the first time this has happened." Somehow this did not surprise me. "So I know what to do. Okay, we need to get out," he said. I grabbed the door handle and it opened with no pressure from me. I decided to keep that to myself. I hopped out and Rudy crawled out after me. "I'm going to pop the hood," he told me. "Can you grab the crowbar from under the seat?"

I blinked at him. "Uh, yeah, sure."

"Thanks."

He passed me and I looked under the seat for the crowbar. It was not hard to find. I handed it to him while he glared down at the uncooperative engine.

I jumped back when Rudy raised the crowbar above his head and brought it down hard on an engine part.

"Rudy!" I cried out when he did it again. "Rudy, what are you doing?"

He stopped, the crowbar raised again, and glanced at me. At the startled look on my face, he must have realized that I had no freaking idea what the crap he was doing.

"Oh, babe, this is the starter," he explained, pointing at the part he had been assaulting. "You have to whack it a few times then—What? Why are you looking at me like that?"

"Babe," I said flatly.

"Huh?"

"You called me babe," I explained.

"I did?" Rudy said, hitting the starter thingy again. "Must have slipped out."

"Like how 'I love you' did in the drama room?" I asked. I knew there was probably a better way to approach that, but the opportunity presented itself.

Rudy slowly lowered the crowbar and looked at his feet. "You heard that?"

"You said it in my ear."

"Beth, look—"

"Did you mean it?"

"Did I—Well, yeah." Rudy put crowbar on top of the cab of the truck and stepped over to me. "I did mean it. I just wanted to say it at the perfect time."

I bit my lip. "What's wrong with right now?" I asked quietly, looking into his eyes.

His breath caught in his chest and he took my hands in his. "Beth?"

"Yeah?"

"I love you." When he said it, his entire body seemed to relax, as if he had been holding this information on his shoulders for a long time.

"Rudy?"

"Yeah?"

"I love you too."

A big grin spread across both of our faces while we took in these words. Standing together in our school parking lot, we stared at each other for a moment before Rudy's arms snaked around my waist and he pulled me in for a long, lingering kiss, which I returned. I wrapped my arms around his shoulders and held him tight, never wanting this moment to end.

Eventually, he did pull away, grinning. "I love you."

"I love you too," I replied again, smiling right back at him.

"This is awesome," Rudy said, his mouth an inch from mine. "I've wanted to tell you that for so long. So awesome."

"I awesome y—I mean, I love you." I giggled. "I *love* you."

Rudy laughed at my slip up. "No, no, I like it. *I awesome you*, Beth."

I beamed up at him. "I awesome you, too, Rudy."

CHAPTER 36

FAREWELL FUZZY

"Are you coming over later?" I asked into my cell. Since RENT wrapped up, Amy was trying to get Rudy to come over so she could get to know him better, instead of us stowing away in my bedroom to 'practise our lines'. She was thrilled when I brought him home and introduced him as my boyfriend.

"Yeah, of course. Do you want me to pick you up at school?" Rudy replied. He had the last half of school out today for a grad trip to the breakwater. "I can pick you up in the parking lot?"

I looked over at the soccer field and a grin broke across my face. "How about under the bleachers?" Rudy chuckled on the other line and agreed to meet me, in forty-five minutes or so, where we had shared our first real kiss. We said our 'see you soon's and hung up.

Cutting across the student parking lot, I stopped in my tracks when I saw a very familiar silver Nissan Versa parked by the tech building. What was Fuzzy doing here? I had gone to the library after drama to see if they had the new Colleen Hoover novel (they did not), and wandered around the fiction section for over half an hour before leaving with five novels in my book bag. Usually Fuzzy was out the door the second the bell rang on Friday afternoons—sometimes even before that, now that our final exams only included resource centre.

I started walking to my friend's car and saw that he was sitting behind the steering wheel, with one hand covering his eyes and the other closed into a fist and pressed against his chest. He looked... morose. When I reached the car, I bent down and rapped on the passenger-side window with my fingertips. Fuzzy jumped and quickly turned to see what had made the noise. I saw that, for only the second time since I had met him, he was crying. Horrified, I yanked open the door, threw my bag into the back seat, and sat down beside him, closing the door behind me.

"Fuzzy, what's wrong?" I demanded, worry pulsing through my veins. I touched his arm gently. "Are you okay?" Stupid question. Of course, he wasn't okay.

"Beth," Fuzzy sighed, reaching out and running his long-fingered hand down my hair to my arm, and then to my elbow and resting it there. He closed his eyes as if pained. "I can't do this anymore."

I blinked, confused. "What do you mean?" I asked, my brows furrowing. "What have you been doing?"

"Watching you," Fuzzy said, taking his hand off my elbow and placing it on his knee. "I've been watching you be happy. Happy and in love."

"I don't understand."

"I can't watch you be with someone else anymore." He said bluntly.

My breath caught in my throat and I leaned away from him. "I, I... what?"

"You heard me, Beth, and I can't do it anymore. I'm so glad you're not with that bitch-squealer anymore, but I want you to be happy and in love with *me*."

"Fuzzy, you said—We talked about this. You said that you were all right if we just stayed friends." I protested, "In the computer lab, we talked—"

"I can't just turn off my feelings, Beth!" Fuzzy yelled. It was the first time he had ever raised his voice to me. "Have you ever been in love with someone you couldn't have?"

"Fuzzy, *please* don't use that word," I pleaded.

"Love, Beth! *Love!*" Fuzzy shouted, slamming his hands on the steering wheel for emphasis, and then gripping so hard that his knuckles turned white. "And of course you haven't! You could have whoever you wanted, but is it ever me?! NO! It never *has* been and it never *will* be! And in case—*in case*—you were wondering, it HURTS! That's how it feels, Beth! It physically freaking pains me!" The tears I had seen in his eyes earlier had surfaced again. "I came to school every day and saw you used as arm candy by Connor, when you deserved someone who wanted you for something other than your looks, which he constantly put down, and that *sucked!* And now I see you every day with Rudy, and every day it breaks my heart! It never gets easier, Beth. I go home after classes, try not to think about you with him, and then come to school the next day and am reminded again and again that I'm not enough for you! That you don't—" his voice cracked, "that you don't want me." My eyes stinging, I looked down at my lap, my fingers entwined together, fidgeting anxiously. I was a beat away from saying that I did love him, just not the way he wanted me to, when Fuzzy added, "I'm switching schools, Beth."

"What?!" I gaped, looking up at him again. He was staring at something vacantly over my shoulder. "No, no, you can't! This is high school; it's evil! I need you! You're my best friend—"

"Stop," he said flatly, holding up a hand as if directing traffic. "I don't want to hear how I'm your best friend and how you love me like a brother. I want more than that. I just can't do this anymore, so next September, I'm starting at the high school where my dad teaches: Crest High."

"Fuzzy—"

"The paperwork is already done, Beth. It's just... too hard to be around you." He dropped his hand and looked at me, distress visible in his eyes. "Please don't make me feel worse than I already do. I know that I'm important to you, but I need to do this. You must understand that."

Tears were streaming out of my eyes and I nodded. I felt like an asshole. Because of me, my best friend was switching schools—to our nearest rugby rivals no less. "I'm sorry," I whispered.

Fuzzy sighed, his shoulders slumped in what seemed like defeat. I guess it kind of was. Rudy had won. "Don't apologize, Beth," he said, putting an arm around my shoulders in a comforting way. Because that's what he was and always had been to me: comfortable. "You didn't do anything wrong. You can't help who you fall in love with... or who you don't."

I turned in to him and wrapped my arms around his broad shoulders. "I'm still sorry." I wept. I felt as though my heart was breaking. Not as badly as his had been, time and time again, but I swear my chest was aching. Fuzzy kept his arms at his sides for a moment, while my tears dampened his neck. Eventually he embraced me in return and rocked me back and forth, as though comforting a small child. We remained like that for several minutes. I only broke our connection when he pressed a lingering kiss on my temple. We slowly let go of each other, the first awkward silence between us filling the car. I averted my eyes, grabbed my bag from the back seat, and opened my door. When one foot was on the concrete of the parking lot, I faced my oldest friend, and said, "I do love you, you know."

He reached forward and wiped the tears off my cheeks. "I love you so much more," Fuzzy moaned in a whisper.

I fully exited the car and closed the door behind me. It started almost instantly and I watched Fuzzy drive away. I took a shuddering breath and turned back to the soccer field to meet my boyfriend. When I was hidden under the bleachers, I sat down cross-legged and tossed my book bag aside carelessly. I brought my hands to my face, and once again, began to cry.

Sooner than I had thought, Rudy joined me. "Babe?" he said, concern filling his tone. "Oh my God, what happened? Is it Connor? That mother—"

I shook my head, dropping my hands. "No, no, I wish," I gushed, wiping my eyes. "No, it's, it's Fuzzy."

"Wait, what?" Rudy said, appalled and placing himself in front of me. "I don't understand."

Sniffling, I explained what had happened only moments ago in Fuzzy's car. The crying, the confession, the hug, the words exchanged. I omitted the kiss. By the end of my rant, Rudy was rubbing my arms soothingly with a frown tugging at his mouth.

"It's okay, Beth. It makes sense. It sucks, but it's what's best for him." He leaned forward and kissed my cheek. I wrapped my arms around his neck and kissed him passionately. I used the small amount of strength I had to push myself in to him until he was flat on his back, his big hands on my waistline. I straddled him, my chest against his, running my hand up under his shirt. When I ground myself against him, Rudy groaned and grabbed the hand that was now playing at his belt buckle. "Wait," he mumbled into my mouth. I continued to kiss him fervently. "No, Beth, wait," he said, a little more sternly. I ground against him again. "No... *no!*" Rudy grabbed my hips and lifted me, placing me on the grass beside him.

"Rudy, please, I need—" I protested, reaching for him again.

He propped himself up on his elbows and shook his head, "No, you don't *need;* you *want.* I know what you're doing."

"What am I doing?" I said, a little snottily.

"You're trying to use me to forget about the pain you're in. I understand, but it's not right for me to take advantage of the situation. You're sad. *Feel it.*"

I heaved a sigh and sat back. "I know, I know. I kind of got into the habit of doing... *that* after my mom died. It's a good distraction from reality. From feelings."

"It's okay, Beth," Rudy said, rubbing my knee soothingly. He got to his feet and took my hand to help me to my own. "Come on, let's get you home."

I did not see Fuzzy the next Monday. Or Tuesday. For the rest of that week, or the next.

Turns out he neglected to mention that he had gotten notes from his parents to excuse him from the last two weeks of school, since his exams had been completed.

He really was completely out of my life.

Fuzzy had broken my heart.

CHAPTER 37
MEET THE NELSONS

"Don't worry, they'll love you," Rudy said, reaching over to my nervously fidgeting hands and stilling my tell of anxiety.

"All of them?" I asked, lacing my fingers through his. Rudy had a large immediate family (at least, large compared to mine) with three siblings and both parents.

"Yes," Rudy chuckled, "all of them." It was the evening of Rudy's graduation ceremony. Instead of going to a party like a normal eighteen year old, he had insisted that I come over to his house for a celebratory dinner and to meet his (gulp) entire freaking family. "Oh, just one thing… sorry babe, but I'm gonna have to ask you to try and hold in the swears. Get them all out now if you have to, but try not to cuss around my parents."

"I'll try my fucking best," I said, glancing at my phone before putting it in my purse. Still no word from Fuzzy. I had reached out a couple of times with no reply. Rudy had told me that I should let him be, and that he would come to me when he was ready.

Rudy turned into his driveway and parked next to a Mazda 3 in front of the house. I took one last deep breath, opened the door, and stepped out onto the well-kept, lush lawn. Rudy got out clumsily after me, grabbing my shoulders to keep from falling over.

"Sorry," he muttered, standing up straight and fixing his shirt, "got caught on the seatbelt."

"Great. Now that's broken."

"Ha ha." Rudy grunted. "Well, shall we?" He gestured to the front door, and as if by magic, it flew open and a blonde, glasses-clad girl around twelve years old bounded outside. She hurried across the porch and down the steps, clapping gleefully.

"She's here!" she cried, beaming and pulling me into a hug, which I returned, confused. "She's here!"

"We know," a middle-aged man who was climbing down the steps said. "We heard the damned truck from a mile away." He had to be Rudy's dad—same hair, same eyes, same brow, same height even.

"Beth, this my youngest sister, Bella, and my dad, Mac," Rudy said, as soon as his sister let go of me.

"I am so excited to meet you!" Bella squealed, beginning to clap again. "Rudy has never brought a girl home before!" Mac reached out and I shook his hand. His grip was firm and he smiled at me, then nodded at Rudy, as if to say *So far, so good.* "You guys, she's here!" Bella called out again.

"Yeah, the neighbours know," said a boy who seemed to be a ten-year-old version of Rudy.

"This is my twin, Landon," Bella said, rolling her eyes at Landon's sarcastic remark.

"I'm the good one," Landon joked, giving me a small wave.

"Martha and Amber are in the kitchen," Mac told Rudy and me, leading the way to the front door. Rudy offered his arm to me and I looped mine through it.

"How are they twins?" I whispered to him as we left the other two to bicker, albeit good-naturedly, about who was the good twin. "She's so much taller."

"Tallest in her grade." Rudy nodded. "She used to get teased about it, but she just teased right back. 'Go pick on someone your own size' sort of thing." He looked me up and down. "She's your height."

"I stopped growing at twelve. I was also the tallest in my grade until then," I said, shaking my head in embarrassment.

When we stepped inside the house, Landon and Bella behind us, I recognized *Abby Road* playing on the stereo. "Oh, I love this album!" I exclaimed, before I could help myself.

"I know," Mac said, smiling. "Rudy told us. Well, he told us *Rubber Soul* was your favourite, but I don't have that one, so next best thing."

I looked up at Rudy, my eyebrows raised. "He told you what my favourite album is?" Rudy's cheeks turned pink.

"One of the many things he told us, actually," Mac said, leading the way into the kitchen.

At the oven, a tall slender woman, whom I could only assume was Rudy's mom, grinned over at me and strode over to us. "Hi, Beth," she said, giving me a quick hug. "I'm Martha, it's so nice to meet you at last." I hugged her back.

"You as well," I smiled.

"And this is Amber," Martha gestured to a curly haired girl around Rudy's age, standing at the far counter. She grinned at me and held up both of her hands, as if surrendering.

"I'd give you a hug too, but I'm cutting up cod and I've heard you're a vegetarian. Don't know how strict you are about it..." she said, wriggling her fingers in an odd sort of wave.

Once again, I looked up at Rudy. "I'm surprised you even remembered that."

His cheeks turned red now. I could tell Mac was getting amusement out of his son's discomfort.

"And, uh... that's By." Rudy nodded at a dark haired boy, around nineteen, sitting at the counter. "He's Amber's boyfriend."

"Nice to meet you," By said, coming around the counter to greet me. I found out then that he had not been sitting on an island stool, but in a wheelchair. I hoped I hid my surprise.

"You too." I smiled, shaking his outstretched hand.

"Well, that's everyone." Rudy shrugged, gesturing toward the sitting room. "Do you want—"

"A tour?" Mac suggested before Rudy could finish *his* offer: hanging out on the couch.

"Yes, I'd love that," I agreed and began to follow Rudy's dad around the house, as though I had not just been there the previous weekend while everyone was out.

"Rudy says you built this place yourself?" I questioned, looking around his bedroom as if for the first time. I saw Rudy behind his dad, eyeing his bed and glancing at me with an inappropriate smile on his face.

"I did, indeed." Mac nodded. "Used my own lumber too."

I blinked. "How did you manage that?"

"I used my own trees. Come, I'll show you."

I followed Mac down the hallway from Rudy's room and back down the steep staircase to the sitting room. Martha was on the couch and seemed to be helping Bella with some homework. "Done with the tour?" she asked, looking up at us.

"I'm just going to show Beth the backyard," Mac answered, nodding to the den, which had a back door I hadn't noticed.

"Well, it's a beautiful evening; I'll come with you," Martha said, standing and leading the way through the kitchen, where Amber was now peeling carrots and By was searching through the fridge.

"Now, Beth, we don't have many rules in our house," Mac said, as he made his way through the den, "but I do have one that I stand by." I glanced at Rudy nervously. Exactly how much had he talked about me? "Make yourself at home here," he said. I relaxed. "If you're hungry, get some food. If you're tired, lay down. Oh, and for Christ's sake, don't ask to use the bathroom. Just go."

"I suppose I should wait until I'm actually in the bathroom to go, though, right?" I said, before I could stop myself. *I just made a poop joke in front of my new boyfriend's dad.*

Thankfully, Mac laughed and said, "If it's not too much to ask."

When we reached the glass back door, and I could see the acres of land Mac and Martha had made their own, I stopped in my tracks, stunned at the beauty of the fields in front of me. Stepping into the yard, I took in the beautiful grassy field surrounded by trees.

"So this is why you didn't need to buy lumber," I said, gazing around at the cedar and fir trees that seemed to be in a competition to see who could touch the clouds first.

"Got that right." Mac nodded "This whole field used to be nothing but forest. You'd never have thought that there was a place like this so close to the city." He crossed his arms and looked around fondly. Down the centre of the field was a shoulder-height wooden fence that Rudy was now leaning against.

"Look," he said, pointing. I followed his gaze to see that, in the left side of the field, five alpacas were grazing in the somewhat overgrown grass, with their short tails and long ears flicking back and forth.

"Note how they stare at you if they feel you looking at them," Mac said, nodding at one that was standing beside a small barn. Sure enough, it was standing stock still and challenging me to a staring contest. I quickly lost. In the field opposite, a vegetable garden was circled with wire netting and flowers. About five feet behind it, I saw what I thought looked like a small tool shed, with more wire netting surrounding the perimeter and roof. I was proven wrong when a bright yellow bird flew out of it and perched itself on a pear tree within the wire. It was an aviary. Two more birds joined their friend on the branch and I started walking closer to them for a better look. Rudy followed me, his parents hanging back by the garden.

"I've always pictured getting married in front of this," he said, looking back and forth between the birds and me. "At least, I have for the past couple months." He then smiled down at me and I glanced over my shoulder at Mac and Martha. They were watching us with knowing looks and talking quietly with each other. I did not say anything but beamed up at him in response to his not-so-veiled hint at what he saw in our future.

By the time everyone was sitting around the large wooden dinner table (which was probably the only thing in the house Mac did not make), I felt like I had known these people for years. When Martha saw how little I had put on my plate, she handed Rudy a bowl full of mashed potatoes and peas. "Rudy, put some more on her dish," she said. Rudy took the bowl started to fill a spoon, but I held up a hand.

"No, no," I shook my head, "I'm fine, really."

"Nonsense," Mac said, placing a fair amount of broccoli beside my small pile of garden salad. "You'll waste away."

"Listen to the old man." Rudy smiled, adding the potatoes to my plate as his mom had requested.

Before the night was over, I had learned that the Nelson family were very big fans of board and card games, Mac was teaching at Crest High, Martha was a rather gifted painter, Landon played the bagpipes, Bella was hugely into horseback riding, and Amber was taking three different dance classes. Part of me was aching to know how By had ended up in a wheelchair, but I decided that I should wait until I knew him a little better before asking.

Framed pictures of generations of Rudy's family were hanging from nearly every wall of the house. The Nelson men all seemed to look very similar and I found myself wishing I had been able to meet Rudy's granddad, who had died the previous May.

"It was so nice to meet you," Amber said, when Rudy was getting ready to drive me home. She hugged me tight, as if making up for the hug she had not been able to give me when we first met. "We'll see you soon, right?"

"Yeah, if you'll have me." I nodded.

"I thought I told you to make yourself at home," Mac said, wrapping an arm around my shoulders. "Come over anytime."

I received hugs from Martha and Bella on the porch, and exchanged waves with Landon and By, before Rudy took my hand and started to pull me away from them to the driveway. "See you soon!" Martha called after us. I waved one last time before climbing into the truck after Rudy.

"So?" Rudy asked once we were on the road again. "What did you think?"

"You're really lucky," I replied. I could not help but feel somewhat envious of what he had.

He smiled and I saw sympathy in his eyes. "I know," he said.

"Good."

Rudy glanced over at me. "Good?"

"Yeah. Not a lot of people have what you do and some that do take it for granted. I'm pretty sure Amy and I would commit murder to have the family you do."

"I'm sorry, Beth—" Rudy began, his expression changing to one of regret.

"No, no, don't be sorry, Rudy," I said quickly. "I'm so happy you have them! And... and honestly, I hope to be around for a while. I'd like to spend more time with them."

"Just them?" Rudy glanced at me, an eyebrow raised.

"Well, you're not bad company either."

"Good, because I'm not going anywhere."

CHAPTER 38

GRADE 12

Needless to say, the following year went a *hell* of a lot smoother than the previous one. I am not saying that it was by any means easy (I was, after all, still in high school), but no parent died and the boyfriend I had was not in the least bit abusive.

At the beginning of the year, I found myself rather depressed though. I was constantly expecting to see Fuzzy beside my locker or waiting for me in the drama room on our fainting couch, but the hopes were for naught.

I also discovered that, for years, I had been so wrapped up in my relationship with Connor, Candice, and Fuzzy, I seemed to have failed to make any friends outside of that small group. Luckily, Rudy had introduced me to his friends over the summer, two of whom were in my year. Melody and Caleb, who had adorably been together since winter break of freshman year, had no problem with me third-wheeling with them in the halls. I became friends with Melody slowly, and then all at once—practically overnight. I'm not kidding. I found out what it was like to have a true girlfriend. A girl who doesn't judge by hidden jewelry or the number of guys you've been with. Who is honest about prom dresses (brutally honest). Who is great to laugh with at fart jokes or to cry with about past injuries, whether physical or emotional.

Although Melody was not my sister by blood, I still thought of her as one. Soon Rudy began to joke that we would make a cuter couple that she and Caleb. Caleb did not really like that, which I took great pleasure in, talking about how beautiful our babies would be. She was stunning, so I was not wrong. Soon after our first meeting, we began hanging out every Friday night, without fail. Sometimes we would double date with our boyfriends, but we would end up having our own conversation about who we thought was better looking in random pairings of celebrities—Alex Skarsgard or Ian Somerhalder?—while the guys chattered on about rowing or the Vancouver Canucks' slow demise. When their conversations would start, Melody and I would look at each other and off we would go. *Well, they're in their own little world now, so… Paul Wesley or Theo James?* We rarely went a day without at *least* texting each other. On days that were a little too hectic to actually be able to have a cyber conversation, we would text each other three blue hearts. It was our way of saying 'I love and appreciate you. I'm thinking about you, I just don't really have time to talk!' The reply was always three blue hearts back.

 I literally never spoke to Candice after I told her off at our locker. It seemed that she also had never bothered to make friends outside of our little group, because I never saw her with anyone between classes, at lunch, or after school. I would spot her hiding out in the library once in a while, or in the cafeteria trying to figure out how Fuzzy had prepared his coffee in the mornings, because she had always taken his. What surprised me the most is that Connor seemed to avoid her too. I was certain that he was going to try and sleep with her (if he had not already) when we had ended… but she was always alone. I can't say that I felt bad for her, because I would (unfortunately) be lying. Candice had been a transparent and addictive airborne poison; without realizing it, you would breathe her in, unhappiness and anger would fill your lungs, and somehow, she would make you feel guilty for wanting to get away from her. No one should have to suffer from a person like that, so if I saw her in the halls alone, I would feel relief that she was not currently making anyone suffer from her guilt-inspiring toxicity.

Connor avoided me like the plague for the most part, and Caleb seemed to be under strict orders from Rudy to stand close to me if he ever saw Connor coming my way. The first time this happened, Connor had been walking in our direction from the biology lab and Caleb had stepped close to me and stared him down, even though Connor had been texting someone at the time. This quickly became a theme. About three months after our grade twelve year started, I was surprised to see Connor hand in hand with none other than tulip girl. So much of me wanted to grab her shoulders and shake her, telling her to get out before the Stockholm syndrome sunk in, but for all I knew, Connor had grown up or at least changed some after everything that went down the year before. As much as I hated that motherfucker, I did not want to ruin his chances at happiness.

In early December, Connor surprised me again. I was at my new locker, taping a picture of Melody and me over the grates of the door, when I felt someone tap me on the shoulder. I turned around and saw my ex-boyfriend standing about four feet from me. It had been a long time since we had stood so close together and I could not help but take a small step back and take him in. Connor's hair was washed and growing out; he was wearing a shirt that I had bought him over a year ago, faded jeans that were a little too big, and of course, his sandals strapped on his feet—in December.

"I'm not going to hurt you." This was the first thing he said to me since the previous May.

"I can't promise the same thing."

"I just wanted to ask you something, Beth," he sighed, rubbing his eyes with his thumb and index finger.

"Yeah?"

"Yeah." Connor paused, staring at my locker door. It was covered in photos of Rudy and me, along with a few of Melody and Amy. "You never put a picture of me in your locker."

"Candice wouldn't let me," I said, glancing at a photo of Melody and me laughing on the breakwater the week before. We had been freezing, with scarves wrapped around our necks and lower faces, but there was obvious laughter in our eyes despite the biting wind that was sending our hair in every direction. "She said it made me a hussy."

"Jesus."

"Yeah." I nodded, crossing my arms over my chest. "You said you had a question?"

"I just... I just wanted to know if you've been happy?" Connor mumbled, shoving his hands in his pockets. "Since we broke up, I mean."

Surprised, it took me a moment to reply. "Well, yeah. Now that I'm around people who like me for who I am and aren't trying to change me, I'm really happy. There are other things that you did that made me unhappy, too, but I don't think I need to mention those." Connor looked around, worried that someone might overhear me.

"Yeah, I know. I *know* what I did was wrong. There are things I did and said that I shouldn't have. And I wanted to say thank you for not telling anyone about them," he said quickly.

I lifted my chin. "You mean the police." He nodded, but just barely. "I didn't do that for you."

His eyebrows drew together, "Then who—"

"Hey! No! *No!*" Caleb's voice rang down the hall. I looked and saw him and Melody walking toward us.

"You sleeping with this guy, too?" Connor mumbled, just before they reached us. I did not retort.

"No! *Get the hell away from her, asshole!*" Caleb said loudly, as if scolding a dog that just took a piss on a carpet. "Go on! Go! Leave her alone!" Melody stood beside me, her arms crossed and a perfected, beautiful-yet-menacing glare firmly in place. I don't know how she did that; when I glared it just looked scary... depending on who you asked.

Melody looked at me and her gaze softened. "He bothering you? You know I'm more than happy to help you beat him up again. That's what besties are for." Her dark eyes flashed back to my ex with a clear warning in them. *Get lost.*

Connor scowled at them, then at me, and stalked off.

That was the last time I spoke to him.

As the one year anniversary of my mom's death came ever nearer, my chest was getting heavier and heavier—as if her ghost were sitting on me but would not put her whole weight on me until the exact day.

When that day came, her ghost tore right through me. It was not just a weight but actually a brand new gaping hole in the centre of me. I was empty again. It had been a year since my mom decidedly left everyone she cared about and who cared about her. It had been a year since she abandoned me and Amy and her twin sister. It had been a year since she decided that no one in her life was worth enough to actually stay on this earth. It had been a year since, after not drinking for three years, she had bought a bottle of cheap wine and downed it along with every single pill in her house.

Every. Last. One.

I spent the day with Aunt Melanie and Amy. We went shopping for a good three hours, buying shirts in bright colours and scarves with intricate designs—things you would not wear at (or associate with) a funeral. Afterwards, we went out to lunch. Mac would have been disappointed in the amount I ate, although (something told me) he would have understood. After Auntie dropped us off at home mid-afternoon, Amy went out to meet some friends and I went into my room, where I planned to stay for the foreseeable future. Just as I had collapsed face-first onto my bed, my back pocket began to vibrate, alerting me to an incoming call. Expecting it to either be Rudy or Melody (I had received over a dozen three blue hearts so far today), I reached behind me and pulled my phone out, answering it without looking at the screen.

"Hello?" I said, my voice muffled somewhat by the pillow.

"Beth?" said a very familiar female voice.

No fucking way.

"Lynn?" I whispered, hardly daring to believe it. Even though she taught at my school, I had not spoken to her since before I broke up with her son. Granted, I did not take an art class so there was not really a reason for her to speak to me, but she used to stop in the halls to say hello before Connor, um... went too far.

"I'm sorry it's taken me this long to talk to you, Beth," she said now. "Connor was very upset about what happened between the two of you and, well, he *is* my son..."

"You don't have to explain," I said, sitting up. "I knew that breaking up with Connor would put a damper on our relationship... that's why it took me so long to do it."

She was silent for a moment. "I remembered that today is the anniversary of what your mom did." No one ever had the nerve to actually say what it was that she did. I could get away with saying 'fuck' as often as I wanted, but if I said the word 'suicide' people sometimes visibly winced.

"Yeah, it is," I confirmed.

"How are you holding up?" she asked gently.

"I-I'm holding. But I'm not up."

"I can understand that," Lynn said in her motherly tone. "Beth, I want you to know that, even though you and Connor ended a long time ago, I've still been thinking of you and you're still very important to me."

"I am?" I choked, rubbing at the ache in my chest.

"Of course! I grew to love you like a daughter and that love does not go away!" she insisted, and my vision blurred. "I just want you to know that, if you need to talk about anything, just let me know, okay? I'm here for you, Beth. That hasn't changed... but I wish I had told you sooner and I apologize for that."

I swallowed the stinging knot in my throat and nodded, although she could not see me. "Thank you," I whispered. We were both silent for a good minute before I thanked her for calling and told her that I should probably go.

"Okay, you take care of yourself, all right?" I heard her voice crack.

"I will," I said, and hung up the phone.

As much as I appreciated her phone call, I knew it was not going to happen. I couldn't go to Lynn for help when seeing her would remind me of Connor, and that *she* was the reason he wasn't in jail. She was far too closely associated with one of the worst nights of my entire life.

Although after that day Lynn did greet me in the hallways and I said hello back, I did not call her when I needed advice or someone to talk to. I had Amy, Aunt Melanie, and Rudy to vent to or laugh with. I had Melody to talk to about Rudy, and of course, I had Rudy's entire family, who had adopted me into the Nelson clan. Having kin does not always mean you have family. If you have friends, if you have people you can count on and talk to, you have family.

EPILOGUE

SEVEN YEARS LATER...

"Hey, babe?" I called from the living room of our small apartment. I was sitting cross-legged on the floor, ten wedding magazines circling me, a planner in my lap, and a pen in my hand, nervously tapping the invite list in front of me.

"Yeah?" Rudy said, entering the room, a bag of chips in his hands.

"I was wondering, um..." I did not know how to word this. Fuzzy and I had not seen each other in years.

"Are you okay?" Rudy asked, putting his snack down on the coffee table and sitting down next to me, looking down at the planner in my lap. I nudged it closer to him and tapped my side of the invite list with my pen. At the very bottom of the page, I had just added the name "Fuzzy" with a question mark beside it.

"Oh," Rudy said, and took a deep breath, the corners of his lips producing a frown. "Are you sure, Beth? I mean, it's been what... six, maybe seven, years since he last spoke to you?"

"I just..." I sighed. It may have been ages, but I still thought of my old friend frequently. "I would feel awful if I didn't at least send a 'save the date'." I knew Rudy was still uncomfortable when it came to even talking about Fuzzy. Years after my friend had dumped me, Rudy had confided that he'd felt threatened by my friendship with Fuzzy. It made sense, but it did not stop me from missing my ginger-haired friend. Last I had heard, he was a bouncer at a local club.

"Honestly, babe, I don't think he'll come. And it would be weird if he did. Think about it, the guy confessed his love to you! If he watches you marry the guy you denied him for... I would sympathize with him," Rudy pointed out, rubbing my back gently in a consoling manner.

I heaved a dramatic sigh and buried my face in my hands. "Well, if you think he won't even come, it won't hurt to at least send him an invite, right?" I dropped my hands to my lap and looked into my fiancés beautiful eyes. "Please, Rudy? For me?"

Rudy let out a small laugh and picked up my left hand, brushing his lips against the giant ring he had placed on my finger during a vacation in California three months earlier. "Okay. For you. But you can't pull that card for another week."

I kissed him and scratched out the question mark beside Fuzzy's name in the planner.

Two weeks later, after returning home from my job as a graphic designer, I opened our mailbox to find an impressive number of envelopes in it. I pulled them out and headed up the eight-flight staircase to our apartment. I flipped through the mail, uninterested in the junk mail, the Visa bill, and the postcard from the dentist reminding Rudy of the teeth cleaning he was due for. I stopped mid-step when I recognized a messy scrawl I had not seen since high school, written on a small envelope I had sent out ten days before.

Unable to wait until I reached the apartment, I sat down on the step I had been standing on, tore open the RSVP envelope, and pulled the small card out of the folds. My heart pounding, I turned the cream coloured card-stock over and read the five words written over the dinner options in black sharpie:

I'm sorry, I just can't.

Disappointment flooded me and I pressed the card to my heart. Rudy had called it. To speak my truth, I was not surprised, but I could not help but feel a little guilty and a small bit hurt.

I took a deep breath, closed my stinging eyes for a moment, and then got back to my feet. I continued up the steps, putting the rejected RSVP back in its envelope, and shoving it to the bottom of my purse and Fuzzy to the back of my mind.

I was sitting in a lounge seat that Rudy's parents had placed in his old room after he moved out, wishing that Fuzzy could have swallowed his pride and come today, when Amy bustled into the room.

"Okay, Bethy, it's time," Amy announced, entering the room where we had been getting ready for the last two hours.

I felt an excited grin spread across my face and I looked over at our cousin, Ellie, then at Melody, and then back to Amy. They were all beaming at me.

"You guys look so beautiful," I said, standing and giving them each a hug. "Thank you, so much."

"Stop it, you're going to make us cry," Ellie demanded, waving her hands in front of her face.

"We got eighty people outside waiting, let's go," Amy said, fixing my veil so that it was centred down my back, the beads tickling my shoulder blades.

My now twenty-year-old little sister took my hand in hers and pulled me down the hallway to the top of the staircase, which ended in the foyer of Rudy's parents' house. Before we made our way down to our dad, Amy leaned over and gave me a quick kiss on the cheek. I heard Ellie, now a professional photographer, take a photo of the moment.

"I love you, Bethy," my little sister said, her voice full of emotion. "Marmee would be so happy."

"I love you too, Amy."

Giving Ellie and Melody one last hug, I reached down and bundled up the front of my wedding gown, so the chance of falling and breaking my neck was less likely. I had always found that this steep and semi-spiral staircase made me a little nervous.

Ellie and Melody held the train up behind me, while Amy helped guide me down the narrow steps. I saw my dad standing at the foot of the stairs, grinning up at me with unshed tears in his eyes. When I reached the foyer, and it was safe to release my grip on my beautifully beaded, fitted ball gown, I embraced my dad lovingly.

"You look beautiful, sweetie-pie," he whispered in my ear, kissing my temple.

"You look quite dapper yourself," I admired, tapping his gold bow-tie, which was just barely visible beneath his bushy beard.

"The music's gonna start soon!" Amy exclaimed, shoving a bouquet of yellow daisies, red zinnias, and baby's breath into my hands and straightening my veil once more.

My heart sped up and I glanced out a side window into Rudy's childhood backyard. I found my mind wandering to the first time Rudy had brought me over to introduce me to his parents and what Rudy had said to me in front of the aviary. Now our friends and family were seated in front of it. I could see Rudy, standing beneath an archway my dad had made just for us, speaking to our marriage commissioner. I felt tears start to fill my eyes again.

"Help," I pleaded to no one in particular, blinking rapidly, willing the tears away.

"What?" Amy said, looping my arm through my dad's and joining the best man, Rudy's younger brother, Landon.

"I'm gonna cry!" I panicked. "Make me laugh!"

"I think Melody farted," Amy blurted, linking her arm through the one Landon had offered her.

"I did not!" Melody said, sounding offended from her spot beside Caleb, who was also a groomsman.

"Well, it worked," I laughed.

Then, just as the clock chimed to tell us that it was three o'clock, an acoustic version of *All You Need Is Love* began to play through speakers that had been set up outside.

Ellie began to walk arm in arm with Rudy's dad, followed by Melody and Caleb and then Amy and Landon.

Then everyone stood as my dad and I made our way down the red-carpeted aisle toward the love of my life, so we could finally say 'I do'.

"Look at him," Rudy whispered into my neck.

"I am," I said, continuing to stare.

We had celebrated our two-year anniversary not four months ago, and now it was January and we lay on a hospital bed, looking fixedly down at our son who was asleep in my arms.

"Can you move over a bit?" Rudy requested, "I really can't fit on this bed. Private rooms should come with twins beds at *least*."

Chuckling at the effort that was needed on Rudy's part to not fall off my hospital bed, I gently moved closer to the bed railing to my left. The last thing I wanted to do was wake my six-hour-old baby.

I had been in labour for ten hours before I let Rudy take me to the hospital. All I had wanted to do was sit on the couch with Mr. Darcy (yes, my mom's cat was still alive and well) and watch *The Office* while Rudy got some sleep. I must have been in some kind of shock or denial that Logan was coming early. I had been able to hear my husband pacing in the room above me as I clenched the sofa cushions in my fingers and cried silently through each contraction, with Mr. Darcy staring at me as if I had gone insane. By the time Rudy had called the on-call doctor at the hospital, who had insisted that he get me to a hospital by any means necessary, I was in so much pain that I could not sit down, lie down, or stand without biting my lip or repeating the words, "I'm okay, I'm okay,

I'm okay," as if it were a mantra I had adopted. Six hours after we arrived at the hospital, I had a baby boy in my arms.

"I am going to love you so much," I had gushed, ignoring my husband's tear-streaked and beaming face and my aunt Melanie, taking picture after picture of her great nephew. I had asked her to be in the delivery room with me. "I am never, *ever* going to leave you. I promise."

Now Rudy lay on his side, an arm around my waist and his head resting on my shoulder, gazing down at the little person we had decided to try and make on his twenty-sixth birthday. It had taken a day to conceive. "Thank you, Beth," he said now, his breath tickling my neck. "Thank you for making me a dad."

I turned my head momentarily to give his dark-haired head a chaste kiss. "I would say 'anytime', but I'm not doing that again for a while," I mumbled.

"Fair enough," Rudy said, tracing a calloused finger down Logan's tiny arm and holding his miniature hand with two fingers.

My eyelids began to droop after a few minutes of silence between the three of us, and my head began to loll sideways until it was resting on my shoulder. Rudy took our son from my arms, and as much as I wanted to, I did not have the energy to protest. "So tired..."

"So, are you nearby?" Rudy's voice woke me the next morning, as the light from the window was warming my face. "Yeah, parking here is a total bitch... No, no, Logan is asleep. I'm sure you can hold him." I turned my head to face him, slowly opening my eyes, "Oh, she's waking up. I'll see you soon." My vision had just become clear enough to make out Rudy, putting his phone into his pocket, picking up Logan, and grabbing a to-go coffee cup from a table by the door. "Morning, babe," he smiled, walking over to me and handing me the coffee. I pressed the button on the side of the bed so that I was sitting in an upright position and gave both of my boys a quick kiss before taking a longing swig from the coffee cup.

I watched as Rudy took a few steps back; he seemed to be craning his neck to see out the door of my room. "You sleep well?" I asked, taking another sip of coffee. Rudy did not seem to hear me, still peering into the hospital corridor.

"Sorry, what was that?" he asked, folding his arms more securely around Logan.

"Your sleep? Was it all right?" I nodded to the fold-able cot still laid out beside my bed. "I know those things aren't comfortable."

"Seeing as I hadn't slept in about twenty-four hours, I didn't really notice the springs digging into my ass," he told me, momentarily flicking his eyes away from the door to smile jokingly at me.

"What are you looking at?" I asked, placing my coffee cup, now half empty, on my bedside table. "Am I really that hard on the eyes?"

"Of course, you are!" Rudy insisted. I hoped he had not been listening again.

"What did you just—"

A huge grin split my husband's handsome face and he waved someone in the corridor over to my room. "Hey, you made it! Come in, come in!"

"Rudy, I look like ass! Don't—"

My voice got caught in my throat when a tall, handsome, strawberry blond man shuffled nervously into the room, carrying a bouquet of blue daisies in his hand. He caught my eye almost sheepishly.

"Hi, Beth," he said in a familiar low voice, putting the flowers beside the bassinet Logan had slept in.

"Hi, Fuzzy."

AFTERWORD FROM THE AUTHOR

I know that some of the things that I've written about are tiptoed around or considered taboo, but the fact is that these things really happen. They happened to me, and chances are, they've happened to someone you know in person: a friend, a family member, or a classmate. Every person who I wrote about is, or was, a person in my life. I had to re-arrange the time-line some, so that the book didn't span more than four years, but it happened. I'll admit that I did exaggerate some parts and make some things up, but nothing was unrealistic.

I did have an abusive boyfriend, but it never actually went as far it did with Beth. Although, had I stayed with him any longer, I am *certain* that it would have happened. He had *that* violent bedroom manner. The reason I stayed with him as long as I did was because of his mom; that was true. I was also worried that he might hurt me if I left him. To be honest, the night I finally broke up with him, he didn't try to rape me. Let's just say that what he did had something to do with an ad on Craigslist he had posted. I found it and dumped him in a rage. Finally.

I never did speak to Candice or Connor again. I honestly don't know what happened to them. Frankly, I don't care. Unfortunately, I did have a falling out with Fuzzy (although not like the one in the book), and I haven't spoken to him since. I still think of him often and hope that he is happy and well.

My mom did commit suicide when I was sixteen. Chapters three and four are word for word *exactly* what happened the day I found out. I found out, years later, that my sister doesn't remember a thing that happened that day, but she did remember that our mom was dead and how she came to be that way. When I finished the first draft of this book five years ago, I gave her a copy and she couldn't read it, afraid to learn what had happened that day. Boo, if you did read this, I'm so proud of you and can't wait to call you "Doctor".

The way I handled the news of my mom, and the emotions that came with it, was not healthy at all. Instead of dealing with what I was feeling, I just had sex. Really bad, really clumsy, really gross, and increasingly violent sex. But think about it... how was I supposed to know that it was an unhealthy way to cope with a death in the family, when I had never lost anyone before? Like Rudy said, *"You're sad. Feel it."* It hurts, but it needs to be done so that you can heal. Unfortunately, my tendency to have sex when I was upset didn't end until years later, when my husband said those exact words.

The thing is, when someone so close to you dies, there *is* no moving on. Especially if it's suicide. I know my mom was in pain, that her default mood was sad, but that was no excuse for what she did. There were two hundred people at her funeral. She had friends, she had family, and she left all of them feeling hurt and betrayed. She's was hurting, I know, and I am sorry for the hidden pain she was in. I just wish she had gone for help.

Killing yourself is the most selfish thing you can do, and saying it's brave is a *damned lie*. My sister, not to mention my aunt, needed her in our lives and still do. I'd even settle to be able to call her and ask what she thought of the series finale of *CSI*. But because of what she did, I can't.

Now, at twenty-six, with a son of my own—and how much joy I get just by looking into his beautiful eyes—I can't even *imagine* leaving him. She should have been here to see me get married, to see my sister get into med school, to meet her first grandchild... and every day it hurts that she chose death over seeing the unexpectedly beautiful futures her two daughters had. My sister and I are not victims of suicide, we are survivors. We are broken, yes, but we know how to fight.

ACKNOWLEDGEMENTS

I would like to cheesily thank some people for the creation of this book:

First off, my husband, who continued to urge me on when it came to writing it to begin with. I probably wouldn't have gotten past the first re-write had it not been for you and your insistence on the truth being told.

Second, to my sister. Boo, you are an inspiration to so many people. With our past, people would be expecting us to work the streets... not be a writer or in med school.

To my dad. Papa, even with the little we had, you gave us so much. We are forever grateful.

To Auntie. Without blinking, you stepped in when Marmee died. I was able to come to you when I had boy problems, when I had pregnancy problems, and even when I was having the baby. Thank you for everything.

To Melissa. <3 <3 <3 Pretend those are blue. Oh.

To Judy, for reading the first manuscript and catching all of the grammatical and spelling errors, yet still reading the story.

To John, for being outraged that his wife got to read it before him. Thank you for your notes.

To Mr. Penty, for calling me your hero and still directing *The Laramie Project*, even though both of our moms died within three months of each other. *You* were *my* hero in high school.

To Ally, for insisting Fuzzy have the ending he deserved.

To Fuzzy (who will remain nameless), for everything he did for me that year.

To Ony, for keeping my manuscript warm by sitting on it when I wasn't looking.

To Lynn (again nameless), for everything she did.

To readers, for reading the story and hopefully enjoying it. Don't stop reading!

And lastly, to Harrison, for... well, little boy, you haven't done much yet but eat, poop, sleep, and cry a little. But when you're old enough to read this book and see the dedication, I hope it embarrasses you.

Love to all of you,

Liv

CPSIA information can be obtained at www.ICGtesting.com
Printed in the USA
LVOW11s1424130816

500059LV00006B/41/P